GATEWALKER

A FARSEEKER NOVEL

JOANNA STARR

StarFire

Gatewalker
Published by Starfire Enterprise

Cover art by Deranged Doctor Design

www.joannastarr.com

ISBN-13: 978-99957-917-6-6 (Paperback edition)

ACKNOWLEDGEMENTS

Thank you to Jon for his unending support and patience. Thanks to Jill and Kathy for their excellent editorial work, and to the Deranged Doctor Design team for their wonderful cover art.

A special thank you to Ian, my precious Beta Team, my ARC Team, and to all the great people on my FaceBook group who never fail to make my day. Thanks to the Cosmos for making this work possible.

I would also like to thank you, the reader, for joining us on this epic adventure.

A FARSEEKER NOVEL

GATEWALKER

JOANNA STARR

For our birthright

1

DREAMWALKER

Silence spread through the streets in a leaden wave. Merchants ceased trading, their hands pausing mid-air and the tinkling coins they held becoming still. Men straightened their shoulders, hunting the shadows for the threat. Women hugged their arms. Children stopped playing, their laughter fading into echoes as they ran back to their parents' sides. Sleeping dogs stood up, their ears pointed, noses twitching.

A gust of wind lifted the magenta and saffron canopies stretching between the coral-stone houses and shielding the market from the baking sun. In the sudden gaps between the billowing fabrics, a rich blue sky peeked through, and sunlight spilled down onto the quartz flagstones, making them gleam.

The gentle breeze vanished. Sandalled feet paused. Smiles left peoples' lips. The silence deepened. Nothing was heard. Nothing was seen.

All was felt.

The feeling screamed within those gathered: a feeling, a

knowing, shared telepathically—it spread through every one of them like wildfire.

Something is wrong!

But the people knew nothing could be done.

Thaya alone moved, stepping past mannequins that were people frozen in fear, as if time itself stood still, until she reached the edge of the market where the canopies ended and sunlight blazed unhindered upon the street. Her eyes travelled up the smooth walls of the houses to the clear sky above. Her hand lifted to shield her eyes from the sun, her golden painted nails and jangling silver bracelets catching the light prettily.

Five sky ships appeared there, blatant, predatory and menacing in a peaceful world. They sped silently above in a perfect chevron alignment and moving so fast, she would have missed them had she blinked. Long, tubular, and the size of three Lonohassan galleons lashed bow to stern, the sky ships were mostly black in the sunlight. An unnatural, painful static prickled the skin between her shoulder blades, and Thaya shuddered in sudden revulsion.

She came to steps leading up the side of a house. In a daze, she gripped the handrail and hauled herself up them, past a potted plant with draping evergreen leaves, and up to a neatly swept patio on the flat rooftop surrounded by a low wall marking the boundary of the house.

Other people already stood on neighbouring rooftops and patios, their dresses and robes in shades of dandelion and marigold billowing in the wind, their hands shielding eyes that were glued to the skies.

Thaya's throat constricted.

Another craft, this one enormous, surely the size of an island, hung silently in the sky. It was low, not more than half a mile from the ground, black and thick and disc-shaped. There were many parts to the ship; protrusions and depressions and antennae-like objects covering its top and underside. A behemoth, an ugly monstrosity, a hungry predator. It did not belong here in this peaceful place, their beautiful home.

A thick, blood-red beam burst from beneath it towards the ground, but where it hit, she couldn't see. It had to be striking the sea in the centre of their circular city, she thought, and she'd always had an innate ability at finding the truth. Birds darted into the air from where the beam struck, squawking and crying until hundreds of white specks circled over the gold-gilded rooftops. The birds turned in a wave and fled towards the safety of the green mountains in the distance.

It was the silence that frightened Thaya the most, not the Invaders' ships...the silence of her own people, the utter helplessness. It caused a physical reaction in her stomach that made her feel sick.

Beyond the beast, several leagues away and hazy with distance, she glimpsed another round, predatory shape. She closed her eyes and cast her mind further than her eyes could see. There were more crafts. Many more. Her beloved planet Urtha was encircled.

The ground trembled as if the planet herself shivered, and then there came a terrible roaring sound. She imagined it was Urtha screaming.

The red beam stopped, the enormous crafts lifted slowly higher into the sky, and then moved so fast they virtually vanished.

Gone.

Yet something terrible remained.

The trembling didn't diminish now that the ships had left; it increased, shaking as if a great monster beneath the earth was awakening. The patio trembled, and then the entire house she stood upon jerked violently, throwing her against the boundary wall. An enormous crack snaked across the roof and beneath her feet. She forced a breath in, trying to inhale past the fear that clawed up her throat, and felt the cloying overpowering panic building in the people of the city. The wind grew, whipping her dark hair around her face, and the strange roaring intensified.

She squinted at the horizon. It was moving oddly, like a mirage above a road in the hot sunshine, all wavy and indistinct. In the distance, it looked like nothing was solid anymore and she could no longer distinguish the sky from the sea. The mirage moved rapidly closer, and the whole world appeared to be turning to liquid.

The sea! It was rising!

Water swelled higher and higher, closer and closer. As it neared the land, it became a great wall of rushing muddy blue, easily higher than the temple sanctuary towering over them gracefully a mile away. Their sacred temple was dwarfed by it.

Thaya looked at the yellow flags marking the administerial buildings in the square a few streets over. They flapped serenely in the breeze, unaware of the impending doom. Could they not see the watery terror speeding towards them?

She couldn't move. There was nowhere to go. Death was coming for her.

A low moaning made itself heard through the din of the blood rushing through her veins, and it crescendoed until her ears thrummed with it. It came from the people, the combined sound of thousands of men howling, women screaming and children crying—a sound she had never heard before, never wanted to hear again.

How high was that wall of water raging towards her? Fifty yards? A mile?

There was nowhere to go. Death was coming for her.

The house upon which she stood was on a low hill. She had an elevated view of the city, could see even to the harbour and the white boats within it. She watched in horror as the muddy blue maw of the sea simply swallowed them. The wall of water touched the edge of the city, shattering warehouses, roads and bridges, turning them all to rubble, adding their quantum to its gigantic muddy mass. It rushed to engulf the crystal sanctuary but could not break it. Defiantly, gracefully, the temple sank into the wave, silently refusing to shatter, refusing to become part of the monster.

Thaya realised she was crying.

The wall of death slammed into her.

The screaming people, howling wind, and roaring destruction fell to silence once more. There was only the rush of water.

Thaya's world became bubbles, mud and debris, and the sting of salt water as it forced its way into her eyes, her nose and her mouth. Her ribs cracked with the force, the breath exploding from her lips, her suddenly tiny body swept up by the monster.

Her back slammed into something hard. The wall of a house? The quartz flagstones? Terrible, crushing pain. Her hands clawed for a surface that was miles away.

God, help me!

The desperate need to breathe. Water filling her lungs.

"Awaken, young Ena-shani..."

A voice spoke. Quiet, yet coming from beyond the din and terror, from somewhere else entirely.

"Help me!" she screamed, but how could she be speaking when her mouth was full of water?

"*Awaken, young Gatewalker...*"

Her heart beat dully—the roar of water, the excruciating pain, the torrential chaos, bubbles and dirt—faded with each beat.

Reality flashed between the maelstrom and cold darkness.

"*Ena-shani, awaken...*"

Silence. Darkness.

Thaya felt herself slowly rising, the pain leaving her body as well as the heaviness that filled her limbs. She wanted to hear that voice again. It was soothing; it meant she wasn't dying alone.

"Do not let your past haunt you."

The voice spoke clearly and calmly, soothing her terror —a man's deep voice filled with wisdom and a pleasing accent she had never heard before. She felt as if the owner of the voice knew her in some way.

"My past?" Did he mean the tsunami and her city?

"Yes," the voice replied.

But I don't live in a city, and I've never seen a tsunami... It's a dream, a nightmare, a very real one.

Her world began to brighten, and she felt physically, mentally and spiritually lighter, relieved.

"It wasn't a dream...and yet it was not my memory. It can't have been, can it?" she asked, as the voice seemed to know things.

"Not a dream, no, but a memory..." the soothing voice said.

Trees took shape around her, their leaves orange in the

light of a setting sun. The whole world became painted in hues of gold, auburn and bronze. Peace and safety—such feelings were blessedly abundant in this place. *Thank the Creator.* She was no longer in that place; she could breathe deeply again.

A neat path led through swaying grasses speckled with indigo flowers to an ornately carved fountain. It consisted of a wide bowl, about waist height, that continually filled with water—from where it came, she could not decipher—which then overflowed to spill into the large, shallow, stone basin at its base where white water lilies bloomed. Thaya noted the exquisitely carved stone flowers and ivy that wove up its sides, and that the water flowing through it was extremely clear and fizzing with effervescence as if a Saphira-elaysa had purified it.

Her gaze left the fountain and settled upon a very tall, regal man who was leaning against the upper bowl.

He was dressed in flowing clothes that shimmered. His perfectly straight hair was pale, not grey, not white, not mauve, but somewhere in between, and it flowed over his shoulders and down his back. His tunic and wide, loose trousers were the same colour as his hair, and equally regal and flowing. She stared at his ears; they were long and ended in a point. He wasn't human—his aquiline features were more akin to a dryad's.

His elegant fingers, like a musician might have, swirled lightly in the water. But his fingers caused no ripples and she stepped closer, wondering if it wasn't liquid at all but a mirror of some sort. The liquid mirror trembled and clouds rushed over it. The wall of muddy blue water appeared again and the anguish of the people filled her ears, the roar of destruction, the shattering of her city...

"Lonohassa," she gasped, pain clenching her stomach.

She tore her eyes away. "You saw my...dream? You can see what I see? The water must be magical."

He looked up at her, and she caught her breath involuntarily. His eyes were large and almond-shaped, and were also the most amazing shade of deep violet. He was beautiful.

He smiled and she blushed, dropping her gaze to the now still and clear water mirror.

"I do." He inclined his head. "For I am an *Ephlendry,* a Dreamwalker, an *oneiromancer* as you might say in your language."

Thaya rubbed her eyes; was this all real? "I must be dreaming. Why am I here? Where *is* here?"

"You were tormented, so I came." The man spread his hands.

"You helped me in that nightmare?"

"I assisted you in disentangling yourself from the memories of the past. I have been meaning to approach you, and now seemed like a good opportunity."

Thaya raised her eyebrows. "You can enter dreams?"

"Yes, though that was no dream, and so I could not enter fully."

She shook her head. "But it's not my memory... Look, my hair is wavy and mid-brown, not straight and dark, and, okay, my nails can be painted, but my hands are different, wider and calloused, and I saw them as slender and well-kept..." She felt these minor things she'd noticed were silly as if this man would have even noticed them anyway. "...Um, never mind. More importantly, I'm alive, and you say that was the past."

"Not a memory from this lifetime, no."

She closed her mouth; his words had stilled her next question and she stared at him.

I had a previous lifetime there, in that city? I know that was Lonohassa; that wondrous civilisation destroyed thousands upon thousands of years ago in the Cataclysms. The land from where the powerful ones came and from whom the blood flows in my veins. A great flood destroyed all, so the myths and holy books say, but they do not mention the crafts from the stars that caused it...

She shook her head, trying to work everything out. "Who are you?"

The man smiled at her, a smile that made her blush. "You might think of me as a representative of my people. I am the one to whom you will give the gift."

Thaya frowned. "Gift? I have no gift to give. I am sorry."

"Not yet. But soon you will. My people have been waiting for it for a long time."

"Is this a dream?"

"Look at your hand."

Thaya looked down. Her left palm bore a faint white swirl, all that remained of the Nuakki slave brand the Invaders from Rubini had forced upon her. She remembered that time clearly. She closed her hands. *Not a dream.*

"You are *Ena-shani,* are you not?" The man raised an eyebrow. "A Gatewalker?"

Thaya tilted her head. "I can use the ancient portal-stones that lead to other places, but I have no name for me."

The man nodded satisfactorily as if that answered his question. "And you are also the gift-bringer, the *Ellasheem,* for whom we have awaited."

Thaya did not know what he meant. She rubbed her forehead, trying to piece everything together. "Khy—my friend—and I, we rested by the portal stone last night. Is that how you reached me? Or did I sleepwalk through it?"

Had she accidentally entered a portal and gone somewhere strange?

He must have seen her worried frown, for he said, "Worry not, *Ena-shani,* I reached for you and came to you when I felt you struggle. You rested in a place where the veils between our worlds are most thin, and this thinning is aided by the *Unna,* the portal stone, as you call it."

A flicker of concern suddenly passed across his face, out of place in this setting. "It is time you returned, Gatewalker; your Saphira-elaysa Shining One has need of you. This was but an initial greeting, a friendly first contact between us to prepare for our inevitable meeting."

Flames suddenly boiled across the surface of the water in the bowl, making her jump. The water rippled and bubbled, and screams echoed all around them. Everything around her became hazy, including the man; only the fire in the bowl remained vivid. Before she could speak, the world exploded into fire, and Thaya was blasted backwards.

Thaya lay on the grass. The man and the fountain had gone, and instead, she blinked up at the underside of an enormous beast gliding above her. It was covered in green scales, paler on the belly, and its great membranous wings spread wide on either side of it. Giant talons, as thick as her arms, clipped the tops of trees that were ablaze with fire, and a long tail with a barbed end trailed behind it. Its reptilian head angled down. It opened its mouth, and a huge bout of flames spewed out.

The world above filled with fire, just like she had seen in the mirror waters only seconds ago. Thaya lifted her arms to shield against the ferocious heat. There, darting through the trees, she glimpsed the shining creature the dragon chased.

"Khy!" she screamed.

The Saphira-elaysa—'unicorn' in dryad-speak—leapt through ferns and boughs. Dragon fire rolled towards him, but shimmering white magic flowed from his horn, extinguishing it. His silvery-white mane gleamed, and he moved with astonishing speed through the forest, faster than the dragon could fly.

The unicorn was her friend, and his name was Khy-Ellu-menah-Ahrieon Saphira-elaysa—so, Khy for short. He was more than her friend; he was her soul twin—a joining that had occurred when they were mere babes, pure innocence, when she had touched his horn and he had placed it in her hand. It was a holy union. The divine presence was there, but it had never been seen before, and so some believed it a curse, something that should not have happened.

After a lifetime of emptiness, of searching, and of slavery to beings from far distant planets, Thaya had found that to which her soul had been bound and reunited with her soul twin. Now they were together once more, they were free, and nothing could separate them, not while either lived. And at this moment her friend needed her.

Thaya lifted her hands, felt the soulfire build in her solar plexus, and let it flow down her arms, out of her palms, and over the flaming foliage. The dragon fire hissed under her golden fire and dissipated.

The dragon struck down with its jaws. Khy reared to meet it with his horn. A great clang, as of metal hitting a bell, rang out, and a crack of magic flared between the two creatures. The dragon snorted and shivered and jerked up suddenly. It beat its wings and wheeled away.

A roar came from behind Thaya, and she whirled

around. The foliage trembled, and huge, upright lizard-men burst through the leaves, running straight towards her. They were seven-feet tall, maybe more, with hard scales covering thick muscles, and armed with blades and weapons she hadn't seen before. She didn't have time to count them, for the two nearest suddenly spread thick, stumpy wings and glided fast over the ground towards her. She turned and ran.

Sensing her plight, her soul twin raced towards her.

Keen instinct, or Khy's silent warning, made Thaya dodge to the right. A thick, arrow-like projectile constructed of pure metal shot past her in the space where she had just been. She grabbed hold of her fireshot—a firearm given to her by the non-human Aragoths—turned, aimed, and fired in barely a heartbeat.

Fire bolted from the short, fluted barrel faster than an arrow. The ball of hissing fire hit one of the flying draconids and flared brightly. It consumed the lizard-man; his howls and flailing body ceasing abruptly as he was turned almost instantly to ash. Her accuracy had improved tremendously since the Agaroths had given her the gun-like weapon.

Another upright lizard leapt to take its fallen comrade's place and flew too fast for her to evade. Clawed fingers grabbed her where they could: her hair and the arm that was holding the fireshot. She cried out in its crushing grip.

The reptilian opened its mouth, rows of yellow fangs gleaming sharply and ready to rip her throat out. Her free hand found her knife, and she plunged it into its open jaw, the only place she could reach. The blade passed easily through the soft flesh at the back of its throat. The beast jerked and choked red blood over her. They fell together, writhing. She wrenched her knife free before it could clamp its teeth on her arm, but the draconid was already lying still.

Another reptilian screeched, and two more came on to

attack. Khy shoved past her and ploughed into them, rearing, trampling and spearing one straight through the chest with his horn. The Saphira-elaysa tossed his head, his powerful neck lifting the reptilian clean off the ground, and hurled it against a tree with such force the trunk cracked.

The other reptilians forgot about Thaya and turned upon their new foe.

A deafening roar shook the trees and sent her to her knees. She glanced up at the sky to see a strange sight. A ship moved in the sky, not one she had seen before, for it was constructed of smooth metal all over but irregularly shaped and three times the size of the Vormae's small, round disc crafts. Behind it, the same size as it, a dragon pursued and attacked.

Beams of orange rays burst from the craft, striking the beast and searing a blistering wound along the dragon's side. The dragon roared, bucked then howled fire from its mouth. The fire engulfed the ship until it burned red and so hot, the craft's metal began to pucker. The damaged ship lurched dangerously in the sky, made a strange groaning noise, and then sped off too fast for the eye to follow.

The dragon beat its wings hard, trying to chase it and roaring ferociously.

As if Khy and Thaya no longer mattered, the reptilians turned and bounded after the dragon and the ship. Thaya found herself in the way of one trying to get past, but rather than pause to attack her, he—at least she thought it was a 'he'—knocked her to the ground and leapt over her.

She got to her feet and stared after it. Khy came to her side, and they started to follow them, but the lizard-men bent over onto all fours and ran like hounds, leaping over fallen trees and bushes so fast Thaya quickly fell behind. Suddenly they shimmered and became indistinguishable from the dense foliage. The only sign of their passing was the crack of twigs and the swish and bending of branches.

Magic. It had to be, thought Thaya.

"Wait, there are more," Khy said, pulling up hard, his long ears swivelling back and forth, detecting sounds she couldn't hear.

He was right, she could *feel* unrest in the forest. It came from behind them and was moving closer. If she closed her eyes and became still, she would see more reptilians out there, but she couldn't pause; they had to get out of here.

2

DRAGONS AND SPACESHIPS

"Wait! My pack! I left it at the portal stone." Thaya looked back the way they had come, at the smoke-filled and smouldering forest. It didn't look inviting.

"I can hide us for a short time," said Khy. "But no magic can conceal us from a dragon for long."

He circled his shimmering horn in the air, and a fine mist fell about them. They stood silently for a moment as the spell took effect, and the shimmer from his horn began to fade as his power receded. His usually immaculate white mane and tail were matted, and his beautiful mauve coat was muddy, singed and clotted with dragon saliva.

He always looked so pristine, she chuckled at his dishevelled look and laid a hand on his neck. "Well, that was a surprise."

Khy snorted and nodded in agreement, his indigo eyes opening wide. He sniffed her and checked her over for injuries. She was a mess as well: grazes covered any bare patches of flesh, and mud and grass stains covered her clothes. Thankfully, the reptilian hadn't ripped out half her hair; she'd only just managed to grow it back past her shoulders since her head had been forcibly shaved by Nuakki slavers.

Her arms and ribs were bruised and painful, but there was nothing more serious. She smoothed his mane, pulled out a twig, then checked his other side where she paused and gasped. "You're injured! So I *did* feel something back then."

A deep, blackened and bloody gash about a foot long tore down his left rump, and he wasn't putting his full weight on that leg. The gash was hot when she placed her hand near it.

"I've stopped the bleeding," said Khy. "The dragon-fire could not harm me, but dragon teeth...I let it get too close. Too many Ordacs got in my way..."

"Ordacs... So that's what they are." Thaya knew very little about Urtha's reptilian invaders, but myths of dragons and aggressive humanoid reptilians abounded in their myths and legends. She sighed. Her life this past year was determined to have her running into every evil alien race currently plaguing the planet.

She came from a village where nothing happened, where people didn't even believe in magic or dragons or people from the stars, but when the Vormae came and sent their Shades after her, she fled to save her town. A deep sleep was cast upon them, and since that day, they no longer remembered who she was.

No, it happened before the Vormae came; it happened when I went into the Old Temple, a long-forgotten place of ancient megaliths built by my ancestors from Lonohassa. There I found two alien skeletons: one of a cat-person and the other a human-like man. I also found an ancient scroll and a relic. The scroll had a message from temple-builders, and the ancient Looking Stone showed me things I needed to see. It forged a link

*between me and the unsuspecting Vormae, and I saw Khy
whom they had captured. It was THEN that the Vormae came
for me...*

Thaya touched the area close to Khy's bloody injury and
his sides spasmed. She held up her hands and pooled her
soulfire inner power into her palms until they glowed white
and golden. Carefully she moved her hands just above the
injury, feeling cool, healing energy leaving her. Her left
rump spasmed and tingled as she worked as if she felt a
little of what he felt. The injury shivered, and tiny black
specks began to fall out of it. She worked as fast as she could
but couldn't get the wound to close completely.

"You won't be able to do more than that," said Khy. His
voice was strained, and he breathed heavily; the process was
clearly painful. "We should get moving to somewhere safe."

She lowered her hands. "Maybe we can try again later."
The injury worried her. Khy had been injured before, but
he'd always been able to fix himself.

"Dragons are magical creatures," said Khy. "When two
magical beings injure each other, the injury remains. She
will also be suffering."

"It's a *she*-dragon? You managed to injure it?"

"Yes. To both. It's often the way when two magical creatures fight; if the fight is to the death, then both will probably die, not just one. There is no victor. We are immortal.
The she-dragon carries a wound across her side to her
thigh. It will not mend itself."

"Good." Thaya hoped it hurt too.

Under the shimmering cover of concealment cast by
Khy, they pushed back through the forest, stepping lightly
over the smoking ground, and clambering over the
destroyed trunks of fallen trees as quietly as they could.
Dawn light grew slowly in the overcast skies, but there was

no dawn chorus. The silence of the birds let them know the enemy was near.

They came to where they had rested for the night until the dragon had rudely awakened them. The portal stone was a huge, single monolith, as thick as a hay bale and rising five feet from the ground. It was smoothed and rounded from millennia of weather, and whatever inscriptions had once been on it—and she knew that there had been—had long since worn away. Thaya had the Truth Sight, the ability to see or know the truth of things—one of her few skills, as she saw it. It wasn't a particularly rare skill nor one that ever secured her employment more easily than someone who didn't have the skill, but it had its place. It was a shame more people weren't interested in the truth of things, she thought.

She grabbed her pack and Khy became still, his gaze seeing far away. "They're moving to the north of here but not coming closer."

"Well, that's a relief," she said. "Still, I don't want to stay here."

Tentatively, she placed her hand upon the stone, for this was her other gift, an incredibly rare ability to access the power of the portal stones, an ability only the ancient and advanced civilisations of myths and legends had been able to do. It was a skill she had no idea how to use, and it was why she currently journeyed to the learned and esteemed magi living in their remote and hidden temples far away from anywhere.

The latent, earthly energy within the stone responded to her touch, and her hand tingled with warmth. These ancient stones had been erected by advanced people from long ago, people from incredible civilisations destroyed and fallen to ruin. The people of those times were expert magi, they could use the powers of the elements according to their will. They had placed the stones here to mark where the natural energy flows of the planet intersected: ley lines, meridians, pathways, gateways, vortexes and portals—they had many names.

This was only a singular stone, so it marked where only a few lines of energy intersected. Not all intersections were marked, and not all intersections were static. Many portals were roving as the natural energies of the planet flowed around the globe, according to the sun and the moon, the seasons and the planetary cycles. The ancients had understood all these things.

But intersection markers were not all that they were; this was a portal stone, and the energies here could be used by those who had the power to do so. That power was carried in the blood of the descendants of the ancients, the pure humans of Urtha from long ago before the Invaders came and corrupted and changed them. Within Thaya ran the blood of the ancient peoples of Lonohassa, or so dear old Maggy had told her. The old woman had saved her from a Vormae attack when she was no more than a baby. How fared Maggy now, she wondered?

Thaya placed her other hand on the stone, and the stone pulled upon her eagerly but she resisted. Had it been a star portal, a whole star map would have opened up in her mind, and in the blue-black of that space, millions of stars would have pulsed before her with an enormous latticework of light connecting each point to the other like silver thread.

Now, only a faint portal map opened up, and she looked upon a few faint dots and lines leading out from her to other faint points. The other points would be places upon Urtha, but she didn't know where they were and it didn't mean she could reach them. Often, she found a portal stone didn't work or it was out of alignment. Maybe the points led to a ravine and she'd tumble to her death, or perhaps it led deep underwater and she'd drown; she hadn't the skills or experience to tell.

Wherever it might lead, she didn't fancy any more danger right now. Her skills and her knowledge were rudimentary at best—there were no teachers or trainers for her on the subject of portal travel and portal mechanics. As far as she had found, she alone had the skill to access them.

"Better not even try to use it with that dragon near," said Khy. "She'll feel it, and dragons can easily travel through dimensions and worlds following you."

"It would be easy to just leave here fast, saying it worked, of course, but you're right, it would be unwise to use it now," Thaya agreed. Not that she knew anything about dragons or that they could travel inter-dimensionally. "I can't tell where it leads or even if it works. Guess we'd better go the long and slow way on foot."

"I smell humans," said Khy. "It's faint but maybe there's a settlement close by."

"Mhmm, I could do with a hot meal." Thinking about people reminded Thaya of the man in her dream. In the chaos with the Ordacs, she'd forgotten about him.

He looked so strange, stranger in memory than at the time. He wasn't pale-skinned and black-haired like the Agaroths.

"Gatewalker," she murmured. Slowly she lifted her palms off the stone, and the forest around her came back into view.

Khy pricked his ears forwards and waited for her to explain.

"While we slept, I had these dreams, only they weren't dreams but—"

"Memories," Khy finished for her. "I saw them, parts of

them. The city, the alien crafts, then the rising sea and quaking earth."

"You can see into my dreams?" Thaya looked at her soul twin. They had only been reunited a short time, knowing each other only when they were babes and then torn apart ever since. There was a lot they were learning about each other and their peculiar connection.

Khy angled his head. "I can, and you can see mine, but oddly you do not always remember them. I'll be dreaming my own dream, and then I will feel-see yours beside it."

"Did you see the man?" Thaya asked.

"No, only the flood, the destruction."

"He said he could read my dreams, too, and that he was a Dreamwalker, only he wasn't human."

"Describe him."

Thaya did so, recalling every detail as she slung her pack over her shoulder. They headed into the forest away from the path.

"The Elvaphim," said Khy. "Elves, humankind call them."

"We do? I've never heard either name before," said Thaya with a frown.

Khy continued, "Once, a long time ago, humankind and Elvaphim were friends, visitors to each other's worlds. But now the veil draws thick between you as Urtha descends into darkness."

"How can you know this?" Thaya asked, working her way less than quietly between two blackthorn bushes and popping the fat, juicy berries into her mouth on the way.

"We remember," Khy said simply.

Thaya sighed. "It's going to take me a long time to understand you Saphira-elaysa, and everything, really. At least the Elvaphim are friendly. He said the veil between our worlds was thin in this place. I think he's got the wrong person, though, for I don't have a gift to give him."

A dragon roar broke the silence and shook the ground. They froze, breaths held, hearts pounding, and stared at the sky. A strange mechanical noise followed, like the sound of a blazing fire becoming an inferno. It was so loud, they couldn't be sure how close it was—and then an explosion rocked the earth.

———

They could see nothing but shaking trees and bushes from where they were.

"Half a mile. In that direction." Khy indicated with his horn ahead and to the right.

Without considering whether they *should* investigate, they both headed that way, their shared curiosity stronger than fear. It quickly became hard work trudging through the undergrowth that no human feet had ever stepped through. Thaya found a swathe of ferns and pushed through them faster.

Licks of orange fire appeared through the trees ahead. She slowed and kept close to the trunks for cover, then stopped behind some bushes.

Goodness, a fallen craft!

An inferno blazed, and the heat scorched her cheeks even though she was well back from it. The sky ship lay smashed against a ridge of brown rock, a trail of scorched trees and blackened stone marking its passage to its final resting point. The metal was twisted and bent from the crash and buckling in the heat. Figures swarmed before it.

Ordacs!

The reptilians ran around the blazing ship, shouting.

Out of the sky, the enormous dragon descended. She landed heavily on the ridge beside the ship, making the ground shake. Thaya squeaked and hunkered, the sudden wash of dragon fear making her body quiver. She closed her eyes and breathed deeply until Ordacs barking orders made her open them again.

The dragon was inspecting the downed craft, nudging it with its nose and claws, appearing impervious to the flames. Thaya felt magic moving, a strange feeling that was hard to describe, like wind blowing, or the pressure of a force field, or the charge of electricity in a thunderstorm. An Ordac wearing a red cloak held up a golden staff. Power emanated from him in waves combining with the dragon's own magic.

Wind howled from nowhere, tearing across the land, bending the treetops and sending leaves and debris flying. The flames hissed and roared, battling the tornado, and then they were extinguished.

They wield powerful magic, thought Thaya dismally. *Better try to avoid them at all costs.*

Smoke billowed thickly, sending clouds their way and choking them. She and Khy crouched lower, trying to stifle coughs. She muffled herself with her sleeve, and Khy stuck his nose into a bush.

When the smoke cleared, Ordacs entered the shell of the craft. Thaya kept low as the dragon swept her eyes in their direction. Surely the beast could smell or sense them? Hopefully the smoke concealed their scent.

Thaya strained to see more. The Ordacs who had entered the ship soon emerged carrying a bundle. The dragon lowered a wing, and they scrambled up it onto her back. With two great beats of her wings, the dragon lifted into the air and circled the air currents to climb higher.

Thaya saw the deep, bloody gash on her side, Khy's recip-rocal injury. She hoped it hindered her.

They watched the dragon and her minions fly east. Thick, grey clouds hung low above the dragon, but every now and then, a shard of sunlight broke through and gleamed off her green scales. Only when she was a speck that finally disappeared did Thaya take a deep breath and move. A bird dared to tweet somewhere in the trees.

Khy looked at her. Slowly, together, they emerged from the trees and padded towards the broken craft.

The ship was still hot, almost too hot to get close, and it looked like it had been torn into two pieces, maybe by the dragon, maybe by the crash. One half was virtually flattened.

"What did they take?" she wondered aloud.

Khy shrugged. He flipped over a piece of debris with his horn and looked at his distorted face in the tarnished, bent underside.

Thaya peered inside the broken hull, careful not to touch the hot metal. Could anything have survived that? Probably not the inferno even if they survived the crash. Blackened mounds lay crushed beneath twisted metal and fallen debris. Human? Nuakki? Alien? She suspected the latter but whether friend or foe remained a mystery. Cautiously, she drew back, not wanting to venture farther in. Besides, the reptilians could return at any time.

"Let's be gone from here," said Khy, wrinkling his nose distastefully. "They were already fighting each other before they attacked us."

"They were? I guess I was asleep. What were they fighting about?" she asked.

"No idea. Maybe for what the Ordacs took from the ship? I couldn't tell what it was."

They moved swiftly away from the smouldering ruin and back into the forest. Pine trees were more numerous than oaks up here in the mountains, and a chill hung in the air. Autumn was well under way, but at least they had made it through the Narrow Passes before the snow came.

She pulled her coat closer around her, grateful to Khy for finding the village from where she'd bought it. Why people lived up in these cold climes when the valleys offered warmth and sustenance, she couldn't fathom. How far was it to the magi from here? She didn't dare try and guess. Hundreds of miles, probably more. It might even take her a year to get there.

No, it can't take that long!

But as she pushed through the undergrowth, the reality of her life settled upon her. *I have no home, not anymore. Not since the Vormae attacked us and caused my family to forget me. I survived several Vormae attacks, the Nuakki Slave Mines, and now I've fought off an Ordac... How many more Invaders are there?*

Not for the first time she wondered what it would take to free Urtha from them.

We have other-worldly friends, though: the Leonites, the Agaroths, and there are more...but if the people are ignorant, asleep, what hope is there? We can't look to people from the stars to save us. I have to get to the magi; there lies our hope.

The wisest and most learned people in all of Urtha would surely be doing something about it. She was going there for tutelage, for them to teach her magic and how to hone her blooming skills. *The soulfire that burns within me.* She flexed her hands and felt the tingle of it in her palms.

I'll join their ranks, their army of resistance fighters, and help fight the off-worlders in whatever way I can.

The sound of water rushing over rocks piqued her thirst. "Listen, hear that? There's a stream nearby—let's drink. That smoke has parched my throat."

The river was narrow, fast-flowing, and deep, and bordered on either side by great boulders. Khy found a wider, flatter section beside a bank of small, dark pebbles. He stepped his front hooves into the river and lowered his horn to purify it.

Thaya watched spellbound as the water ran clearer and began to sparkle. A dragonfly hovered nearby, and birds hopped on overhanging branches to observe the Saphira-elaysa at work. Silver fish darted closer, and it seemed as if the grass turned greener around them. Sunlight broke through the clouds, and for a moment, the world was lush, vibrant and at peace.

Khy had this effect on nature. All the Saphira-elaysa did. They were not of Urtha but visitors who brought healing and tranquillity, and all things in the natural world welcomed them.

Thaya crouched down beside him, refilled her canister, and drank the pure, cool liquid. Health and vitality flowed into her with each sip, cleansing her parched throat and quenching her thirst. She cleaned the dirt off her clothes as best she could, and washed her face and hands, the energised water tingling over every scrape and scratch.

Holding her fireshot, she inspected the weapon Arothia-Ra had given her—a truly life-saving gift from the leader of the Agaroths. It was, for all intents and purposes, a gun, but unlike her father's shotgun, it consisted of a short, thick, singular fluted barrel made of a bright metal like polished silver but tougher than steel. Etched upon it were symbols or runes that held power, but she had no understanding of what power or how they worked. The handle was smooth, dark wood that fitted her grip perfectly. It fired no normal shot but a ball of special fire that engulfed, then disintegrated anything it struck. She swallowed, remembering the woman she had killed in that city far into the future.

It was called London, and the woman...it was self-defence. Besides, that was no ordinary woman, that was a Fallen One, a vampire, probably an off-worlder.

Still, the memory disturbed her deeply. She had never killed anyone before, had never been forced to.

The Agaroth, her good friend Arendor, had taught her how to use the fireshot. She missed him keenly right now and twiddled the silver ring on her finger that he had given her. A ring of protection, of power in some manner, and of connection to the Agaroths. Was he still watching over her? Hopefully she would see him again in the future. She turned back to her fireshot.

'When it runs dry, soak it in pure water and then fire to refuel it,' Arothia-Ra had said. But how could she tell if it needed refuelling? Over time, she would understand how the weapon worked, and it would understand her, Arothia-Ra had explained. Well, here was water made pure by a Saphira-elaysa, so she dipped the weapon into the shallows and laid it in the sparkling liquid. It fizzled faintly but it could be the effervescent water rather than the fireshot itself. She lifted it out and noticed it gleamed brighter. Pulling on the centre of her being, she drew Soulfire into her palms and watched the white-golden light spread from them and circle the gun until the weapon began to glow. Okay, it wasn't real fire, but it might work.

She inspected the weapon, holding it inches from her face. Was it charged? She couldn't say. "Maybe I should drop it into some real flames just to be sure," she muttered. No time to make a campfire now, though; it would have to wait until later.

A noise that wasn't the wind in the trees or a bird tweeting caught her attention.

She became still and motioned to Khy. His ears twitched back and forth.

It came again, a faint sniffle or whimper, not too far away. Were the reptilians back? Were they being watched? But the hairs on her neck didn't stand up, and she could sense no danger.

Quietly, she stood and hunted in the undergrowth. It came again, making her pause—someone sniffing, over there by the rocky crevice and broken tree stump. Fireshot in hand, she stalked towards it.

The whimpering came sporadically, muffled. She peeled back the ivy and foliage concealing a gap between a rotting tree stump and a crack in the rocks. There, in the hollow, covered in tear-stained dirt, a small boy crouched. He shivered and hugged his knees, his fear-filled eyes wide and owlish.

3

FORSAKEN

Khy peered over Thaya's shoulder. The boy shrunk deeper into the hole, then opened his eyes wider at the Saphira-elaysa.

"What's a little boy doing out here all alone?" said Thaya. "Where's Ma and Pa? The lizard-men didn't hurt them, did they?"

The boy forced his gaze to the ground and shook his head. After a moment, he stared up at Khy again. Could he see the Saphira-elaysa for what he really was or did he see only an ageing warhorse, Khy's clever disguise when amongst humans? Thaya pursed her lips and let out a long sigh. *Great, what am I supposed to do with a child?*

"Well, we can't just leave him here," she said to Khy.

"He can't have come too far from his home," said the Saphira-elaysa.

"Come on then, let's get you back there." She reached into the hole, but the boy drew back.

"I can't, they'll kill me." He snivelled and looked about to cry again.

Thaya smarted. "What? Who could want to kill a little boy?"

Memories of the Nuakki slave mines washed over her: the children forced to work as hard as the adults for a small bread roll; everyone dressed in rags and kept in the darkness... Then there were the Vormae who just vaporised everyone, even little children... *And now there are the Ordacs marauding the countryside.*

The boy shook his head. "No, it's none of them, although that's why I'm hiding right now."

Thaya dropped her hand and stared at him. "You can hear my thoughts?" If he could, then he had special abilities, much like she had, and like Maggy had. One did not *just* have the gift of telepathy; usually it came with other powers, too.

The boy nodded slowly. "Yes, but only when I focus really really hard." His gaze fell to the ground. "That's why they threw me out. That, and...other things. I'm banished. Cursed. They say I am 'forsaken.'"

Thaya stared at him for a long moment, the word 'forsaken' sounding a lot like the word 'Discard' which was the Nuakki order to terminally remove any slave no longer fit to work. And yet, none of the Invaders had done anything to the boy—only his own people for his abilities that they did not possess or did not like.

Banishing 'special' children was unfortunately common, even in Havendell where she was from. Shunning those who did not fit in was the norm because people were afraid. It made her angry.

Thaya smiled warmly at the boy. "Let me guess, you're a Truth Seer, and you *know* I mean you no harm? Perhaps you can tell I'm a Truth Seer, too?"

The boy nodded.

She glanced up at the clouds. "Well, look at it this way, kid: you can't stay here, and neither can we. That dragon might be back along with those reptiles, and whatever they were attacking in the sky, probably isn't friendly either. If you come with us, you'll have a better chance of surviving. Alone, there's not much."

"Where are you going?" For the first time, he looked hopeful.

"We're travelling to the magi, the ones of the highest order called The Loji. It's a long way." She indicated in a general easterly direction, though she had no idea exactly where she was going.

The boy looked into the forest, thinking about it, made up his mind, and crawled out of his bolt-hole. He stood up, dirty, skinny and ragged but otherwise no different to any other kid his age, at least not on the outside. What had he done to be banished by his people? Thrown out even by his parents?

He hung his head as he walked with them towards the river. "It's not their fault. The priest told them to do it, but those priests aren't like us, they're not...they're not human. They hate me." He scooped river water into his mouth and splashed it over his grubby hands and face. "The unicorn made the water sparkle!" He laughed and splashed it every-where, the droplets glistening like diamonds in the sunlight.

Thaya smiled as the purified water brought life and energy back into the child. But how was she going to keep him safe? She could barely protect herself and Khy. She couldn't have the burden of a child on their long journey.

Take him back to his village and give his parents and the priests what-for. Those meddling acolytes, they're worse than the fallen Invaders. It's THEY who should be cast out.

"I got angry." The boy ceased his splashing and became

serious. "And when I do that, bad things happen. The fire came."

Thaya pooled soulfire into her palms and showed him her glowing hands. "Fire like this?"

"Wow!' The boy stared in awe. "Sort of, but it's more like fire, hearth fire." He held his palms up like she had, closed his eyes and scrunched up his face.

Nothing happened.

He dropped his hands. "It doesn't work like that; it only comes when I'm angry or hurt. Sometimes when I'm glaring at something, fire starts where I look. I don't know why—no one else can do it."

Thaya closed her palms and the soulfire receded. The boy's powers were not like her own. From what little she knew, the boy had more of a magician's skills within him. Hers were not that; she didn't know what her power was.

"I don't know what it is or how to use mine either." She looked to the east over the mountain range. "That's why I seek the magi; they'll be able to tell me more."

The boy looked disappointed; perhaps he'd wanted her to explain what his powers were.

They started walking with Khy leading the way. The river revealed more of its banks farther on, so they stuck to its pebbled shores whilst it headed in their direction.

"I don't think the magi will help," said the boy, shaking his head. He stooped to pick up a small, flat pebble.

"Oh? How so?" Thaya cast him a side glance.

"There's a magi in the priesthood. He's the one who told my parents to throw me away. They did not even want me for the gods." The boy's voice broke, and he struggled to control himself.

Cold shivered down Thaya's spine. "Want you for the gods?"

"Uh-huh." He nodded and skimmed the stone. It bounced three times on the water's surface then sunk.

"I've never been able to do that." Thaya grinned at the boy and picked up a flattish stone about the size of her palm. She threw it into the river, watched it give a weak splash, flop and sink. "My brothers poked fun at me for being a girl all my childhood. Tsk."

"My little sister can," the kid said proudly. "I taught her properly. She's with aunty right now, but I wish she were here, we'd have fun."

"What about these gods?" Thaya turned back to the topic.

The boy rubbed his eyes. "It's an honour to be chosen, the greatest, but even they didn't want me. Only the second-born can go, and I am, and they always want boys. If I'd been chosen, then I wouldn't have been thrown out."

Not being 'chosen' clearly agitated him and concerned Thaya. "Where would you be if you'd been chosen?" Thaya asked.

He looked at her, squinting, as if he thought her a bit simple. He shrugged, maybe deciding she wasn't one of his people and thus ignorant of their ways, raised a finger and pointed at the sky.

The chill down Thaya's spine intensified. "Sacrifice?"

The boy nodded, his eyes taking on a strange look she'd seen worshipping acolytes' wear—one of religious fervour.

Thaya took hold of his arms and crouched, bringing her eyes level to his. She felt power in the child simply by touching him. What surprised her even more was that she could feel things through her hands as if her palms could somehow 'read' things. Had it always been there or were her powers growing? She focused on the boy. "Now, you listen to me. I've seen these gods whom we're forced to worship, and they are not gods at all, but Invaders from fallen places. What's more, I've felt the pure light of the true god, the pure source of all that is, if you can even call it that, and it requires no sacrifice, human or other. It loves life, and it's the extreme opposite of death and sacrifice."

The boy drew back, afraid of the fire in her eyes. Gently, she let him go, and they continued walking without speaking.

They sacrifice the second-born, which makes them as bad as the off-worlders. Or, more likely, the off-worlders make them do it, and the ignorant people do what they say. He said they weren't 'like us', after all. They probably punish the people, too, if they don't obey. That's how it is down here. I'll return the child to his family and confront these so-called 'priests' if I have to.

Misty rain began to fall, and the river turned away from the direction Khy had set. Thankfully, he instinctively knew which way was east; Thaya didn't have a clue without the sun to show her. They pushed through thorny undergrowth for far too long, and Thaya sighed gratefully when the forest became sparser and the ground rockier. Khy limped more and more on his wounded side, and she worried. If a Saphira-elaysa could not fix his own injury, that was a problem.

"Here, let me try the soulfire again," Thaya said.

"We should keep going." Khy was reluctant to pause.

"I insist."

He didn't fight. "All right."

His wound was hot as if dragon fire still burned him. His skin quivered as she tried to cool it with her soulfire and heal it in some way that hopefully her magic knew how to do. She let her hands drop after a few attempts. Nothing had changed except that he quivered less.

"It helps the pain," he told her, though his voice was strained. "Yes, the dragon fire still burns there and will continue to do so until it is healed."

Thaya stroked his neck. His soft hair glimmered white, purple and almost black, depending on the light; he was not just one shade but many. All Saphira-elaysa were white, apart from him. He said it had happened after they had touched and become soul-bonded—two babies from vastly different races becoming joined in a deep, unbreakable manner.

His race, the Saphira-elaysa, believed it was unnatural but allowed for its existence as they allowed all things to unfold. But Thaya knew it had happened through some kind of divine will, a chance change in the cosmos helped along and fully endorsed by that benevolent source of all that was. And she did believe it to be benevolent, unlike the other gods they had all been taught to worship.

No, I KNOW it to be so. I felt its love, its purity. It was like nothing else.

"Did the dragon do it?" the boy asked, pointing at Khy's wound. Thaya realised she didn't know his name.

"Yes, but don't worry, he got her back." Thaya winked and the boy giggled. "What's your name? I can't just call you 'kid' or 'boy.'"

"Derry," he replied.

"All right, Derry, well I'm Thaya, and my friend here is Khy. We're going to take you home, but don't worry"—she held up her hands when the boy paled—"we're going to make sure everything's all right. You want to see your ma and pa again, don't you? Maybe your little sister? You see, if you stay out here, you'll die. Maybe even those lizard-men will get you."

The boy chewed his dirty fingernails, then nodded. "I don't think my parents really wanted me to go, but they're afraid of what I can do. They say it's the 'devil's work' and that I'm cursed. They think I'll kill everyone just by accident."

"Why don't you get them to take you to the magi?" Thaya suggested. "Maybe when you're older and bigger?"

"I'd like that," Derry replied, though he remained subdued.

"*He's afraid,*" Khy spoke in her mind, their telepathic link also a part of their bonding. "*And for good reason. I see within him deep fear towards his leaders. It's probably unwise for the likes of you and I to visit his people.*"

"*I can't just leave him here to die,*" Thaya replied. "*I just hope we are not returning him to his death.*"

"*I thought you would say that. So be it.*"

A wide track appeared before them, skirting the edge of a long, low ridge that stretched between two distant peaks. There was little cover here, and the wind tugged strongly on her coat. Thaya reluctantly stepped out of the trees onto the ridge.

After an hour of trekking, the boy pulled on her arm. "My family is down there."

He pointed to a track she had missed, part-hidden by a boulder. It led over the ridge and down the other side.

"Will we make it before dark?" she asked.

Derry shook his head. "Not even if you ran."

Thaya had hoped to find another village to rest and dine in—a warm barn or maybe even a bed, a seat at someone's kitchen table if she offered them some coin, but it was not to be this night. She sighed; nights spent on the mountain were hard and cold.

At the ridge's crest, she paused and took in the expanse. Endless mountains stretched out in all directions; their peaks and troughs lay without order or mercy on the eye. A long, hard journey lay before her, and this detour was only hindering them. She shifted her pack and carried on.

Thankfully, the other side of the ridge was in the lee of the wind, and the misty rain stopped, allowing the temperature to rise. Still, without tree cover, the three of them stuck out sorely, an easy meal for any passing dragon.

"Don't worry, I've shielded us," said Khy, reading her worries.

She squinted above them and could just about make out the faint shimmer of a dome around them. *Thanks for Saphira-elaysa magic.*

They reached the first hint of shrubbery dotting the craggy mountainside ahead, and Derry paused. "Look." He pointed.

Smoke rose from a distant hill swathed in forest and far down in the cradle of three mountains. The town or village from whence it came couldn't be seen from this vantage point, but it was clear they weren't going to make it before nightfall.

"How long have you been wandering around, Derry?" Looking at him, it must have been days. Thaya shook her head. *The poor kid—what's wrong with people?*

He lifted his fingers and counted them. "Four. No, five, I think. I can't remember when my bread ran out."

He must be starving, too!

At least there were rivers he could drink from.

"I had to cook bugs," he said quietly.

"Urgh." Thaya wrinkled up her nose, and he laughed.

"It's better than having them raw," he added.

"Slugs and snails and puppy dogs' tails...so little boys truly are made of them." Thaya laughed and winked.

"I guess..." He grinned and rubbed his nose. "I'd love a puppy."

Knowing the settlement was close, Thaya shared her food abundantly with the hungry kid and didn't ration. He wolfed down stone bread, hazelnuts, dried fruits and the rest of the green berries they had harvested as they walked. She made a fire as darkness closed in, and they cooked chestnuts in it.

When he offered her his pre-cooked and shrivelled black slugs, she politely declined. "How did you cook them?"

"In the beginning, for the first two days, I was really upset. The fire came easily... But then I got tired, and it went away."

"You wandered a long way on your own." Thaya tried to fathom how far.

"At first I ran—they made me."

Thaya controlled her anger as she took out her small blanket and wrapped it around him. It meant no pillow for her tonight, but the boy needed it more and she had her cloak.

Exhausted, he curled up and was fast asleep before full dark had fallen. She watched him for a time, then stood and went to tend Khy.

Laying a hand on his neck felt as if she touched warm silk. "You've said nothing for hours."

He looked at her, his indigo eyes drinking her in. Understanding passed silently between them. He was in pain, pain that would not go away and could not be healed by either of them.

"What do we do?" she asked softly.

"If I don't heal it, it will weaken and kill me. The only place where I know I can heal is returning home to my kin, to the Ellarian Fields. Either I leave now and return, or I leave later, permanently. I am no protector in this state. Besides, in the boy's village, the likes of you and I will be treated with even greater hostility and suspicion than they show upon their own kind. I, at once want to come with you, but also do not. I could watch from the trees, but should something happen, how useful would I be? I like it not. Let me suggest that you leave the boy on the outskirts and come with me. You have been welcomed to the Ellarian Fields as it is, but the boy cannot come. The journey alone might damage him."

Thaya looked back at Derry. "If I leave him alone, they'll just drive him out again or, worse, kill him."

Khy nodded. "They might."

"He has his trust in us—I cannot betray him—I can't leave him." Thaya shook her head and looked at Khy. "But the thought of you leaving...is far worse." The breath caught in her throat at the thought of being without him. How she'd love to visit the Ellarian Fields, too.

"I would not be gone long," he said softly. "Funny how I fear for you amongst your own kind. Humans have many problems to overcome."

Thaya nodded. "Has it always been so? I wonder. Something tells me once we were not so...violent. Not so fragmented."

In her mind's eye, yellow and orange sheets lifted in the

breeze, revealing deep blue skies and a warm sun...a place of peace, communion, harmony. A time long, long ago, when the people were one, when they spoke without words and shared their thoughts openly...

Then THEY came and everything changed...

Thaya blinked, the remembered dream leaving her mind. *We were one once; we were whole.*

"You are looking into the collective human memory," said Khy. "A past that has somehow been forgotten by your race. It is unnatural for any species to not remember its past."

Thaya nodded. "Perhaps one day our memory will be returned to us."

An owl hooted somewhere close, and something rustled in the bushes. The night was dark, overcast, still and close.

"When will you go?" she asked.

"Now."

"I thought you might say that." Thaya hugged her arms.

Khy lifted his head. "There are human hunters in this forest, probably from the boy's clan. I'd prefer to go now before they wonder about your...horse."

Thaya smiled. Khy hated disguising himself as a horse to the human eye, and some he could not fool, especially those who could use magic. But he was right, a lone woman with the boy would be better than the feel of magic a unicorn always brought with them.

Khy started walking into the trees, and Thaya followed. They came to a small stream, nothing more than a trickle of water. She laid a hand on his back and let it trail over him as he stepped into the rocky brook. With one look back at her, he turned and followed the water, hooves glinting as he trod. A thick, shimmering mist rose from the water and engulfed him. With a bright flash, Khy was gone, along with the mist, and the forest plunged into darkness.

Thaya swallowed the lump in her throat and stared at the place where he had been for a long moment. She turned and headed back to the campfire smouldering between the trees. Sleep did not come easy that night, and without her protector, her hand never left the fireshot tucked in her belt.

4

THE MAKING

DAWN BEGAN TO BREAK. IT WAS A GOOD ONE WITH RIBBONS OF pink blazing through the clouds.

"Where's Khy?" Derry pushed himself up and rubbed the sleep from his eyes.

"He's gone," Thaya replied.

"His wound?" asked Derry.

"Yes, he has to return home to heal it."

"Oh." The boy lowered his eyes, suddenly sad, then whipped them back up. "Wait, you just spoke to me in my head!"

Thaya gave him a mysterious smile and spoke out loud. "Yes, I can speak telepathically, too, just like you. We have similar abilities."

He looked in awe. "You can teach me how to do it better? I just sometimes hear peoples' thoughts when I concentrate hard, *sometimes*. I don't speak to them in their minds."

"I think you can teach yourself with practice, but the key is finding someone who can also telepath—and they are rare these days."

She kicked dirt and pine needles over the ashes of their

fire, then tucked the blanket into her pack and slung it over her shoulders. "There's a stream we can drink from over there—clear, fresh, mountain water, then we'll head-on."

They moved quickly now that they travelled downhill, and the clean, rich scent of pines filled their nostrils, and sunshine warmed their backs whenever it broke through the clouds. They stopped for a late, swift breakfast consisting of the last of her stone bread and raisins, then they set off again. Derry chattered on about his explorations and discoveries since his banishment, mainly all about insects.

"Worms taste best, but only when cooked," he explained. "Otherwise they're too gooey."

Thaya felt sick.

In the late afternoon, the smell of woodsmoke reached them, and the track became wide and well-worn. An anxious feeling settled in Thaya's stomach, and Derry ceased chattering. A high fence made of stakes appeared through the trees, and the boy grabbed her hand and clung tightly.

Through the open gate, she glimpsed houses made out of wooden beams, some raised fully off the ground. A man with a mop of greying-brown hair and carrying a heavy load of logs paused to stare at her as they approached, his eyes widening as they fell upon the boy. Derry lowered his gaze and stared only at the ground.

"Mister Kibbs," Derry whispered. "He's all right, but he won't say a word against Klara, and she don't like me ever since I stole an egg. I didn't know it was her egg. The chicken laid it outside its coop."

"Klara is his wife, I take it?" Thaya said from the corner of her mouth.

"Uh-huh." Derry nodded.

"You there, sir," Thaya called out.

The man tried to hurry away, but his heavy load hindered him.

A woman stepped out of the house, her long skirts a patchwork of mended tears, and her bedraggled hair breaking for freedom from the kerchief that tried to keep it in check. She looked at the boy, clasped a hand to her mouth, then hurried down the steps and ran away into the village.

The man dumped his logs in front of the house and planted his fists on his hips with a sigh as they approached him. "You, boy, bring nothing but trouble. I'll admit, I didn't think I'd see you again. It's not right, what they did, but who are we to judge the gods?"

Thaya snorted. "What gods fear a little boy?"

The man's eyes widened, and he performed a gesture in the air as if to ward off evil spirits.

Thaya's mood darkened, and she gripped the boy's hand more firmly. "Where are his parents?"

The man pointed into the village. "There, miss."

"You!" Another man shouted, capturing everyone's attention.

Thaya looked at him and went cold. This man was clothed similarly to an Illumined Acolyte, the priestly class back home in Havendell, in a long, plush, yellow robe—they wore orange in Havendell—with a loose cowl over his head. He held a short, ornately carved staff or walking stick, which he waved in the air at her.

She didn't like the acolytes, nor the gods they worshipped and forced on the people, but they carried an air of authority and a pent-up fury that made her nervous. He glowered as he stalked towards her. The hairs on her neck and arms prickled; it was as if he was scanning her with his mind or something—did he have magical powers? Was this one of the magi the boy had mentioned?

Derry shuffled behind her.

The priest spoke. "You bring a cursed child, one that is damned, back to our peaceful village. The penalty is, at minimum, imprisonment." The priest was almost shouting, and his overzealous gesticulating was unnerving. Had he not been wearing priestly attire, anyone watching would dismiss him as a madman.

I'll bet they are mad, all of the acolytes, and power-hungry.

"Some welcome," Thaya muttered to herself. She held her hand up for temperance, gritting her teeth against the anger she felt inside. "Stop, priest, I merely return to you one of your own: a starving little boy. What beasts could cast out one so young and helpless? What mighty gods fear small children unable to fend for themselves? Shame on you!"

The acolyte smarted as if he had been slapped. Had no one ever dared to speak back to him? Judging by the growing crowd of villagers cowering at her words, she guessed she was not endearing herself or improving her situation.

At the edge of the clustering people, a lone woman stood. She caught Thaya's eye because she was huge! She was easily as tall as the tallest man there and dressed as a warrior in a studded jerkin, leather bracers and grieves. Her blonde hair was braided tightly back and out of her eyes, and her well-muscled arms were folded beneath her large bosom. Unlike the withering, mud-covered villagers, she stood tall and defiant, and her hawkish eyes looked from the boy, then to Thaya, then to the priest and hardened dangerously.

"Only a witch pays sympathy to the devil!" screamed the priest. His face turned red, and he veritably jumped in the air.

Thaya would have laughed had Derry not been whimpering behind her, and the ever-impending threat of an incited mob of villagers lunging for her. The villagers whispered to each other and opened their eyes wider in fear at the acolyte's words. Thaya glimpsed the warrior-woman's hand go to the thick, short sword at her side and was grateful the woman's gaze remained on the acolyte.

Everything darkened around Thaya as if a light had gone out somewhere, and she looked about herself frowning. Was that the priest's doing? *He has magic; he's using some kind of control upon the people, faint but there.*

Thaya held up both hands and felt the faint stirrings of her own power, her soulfire. She was surprised to find the darkness lift, and the agitated crowd grew calmer as if she had somehow pushed back the darkness.

Whatever had happened was not lost on the Illumined Acolyte, and his eyes narrowed menacingly. Thaya shifted uncomfortably, sweat prickling her back.

The priest raised a finger at her and hissed. "You bring that boy back at your peril."

He whirled away, and the now rather large crowd fell back fearfully from him. Sobbing came from somewhere, and a woman dressed in an old worn and faded blue dress pushed through the people.

"Derry?" she whispered. Her eyes had dark circles under them, and she was too thin to be healthy. A man, as thin and as tired as she was, grabbed her arm to restrain her.

"Ma! Da!" Derry shouted. The boy ran to them, and the

father let her go. The woman fell to her knees and embraced her child, sobbing.

Thaya smiled. Derry was safe with his parents and her job here was done—better get the hell out before anything bad happened.

"He's not going to forget that, or you," a woman said behind her, her voice robust though she spoke softly.

Thaya turned. The warrior woman had come up silently and now stood, adjusting the buckles of her bracers.

Thaya shrugged. "It's okay. I'm just leaving."

"It might be too late for that." The woman nodded ahead.

Beyond the dissipating crowd, three Illumined Acolytes now stalked towards them, including the one she'd had the pleasure of speaking to. He raised a finger and pointed at her. The parents of the boy and two other villagers intercepted the acolytes, and shouting began.

"You make enemies easily, I like that." The woman laid a particularly heavy hand on Thaya's shoulder and squeezed, making her wince. "Especially when those enemies are evil people. Come, let's go elsewhere while they're indisposed. Be good for them to cool off, though they'll not let this go. I know a quiet place where a meal can be offered in the hospitable manner we used to give visiting guests."

The woman walked off quickly. Could Thaya trust her? She couldn't trust the acolytes, that was for sure. After a moment's hesitation, she thought about a meal and hurried after her.

———

Thaya had to run to keep up with the woman as she took a winding route south through the village. The ground was slippery and muddy given the recent rain, and Thaya noticed many of the houses were raised off the ground on thick poles, suggesting damp and flooding were common.

The warrior woman walked up the stairs of one of the houses and disappeared inside without closing the front door. Before Thaya could reach the top of the stairs, the woman stalked back out, her face hard, a knapsack slung over one shoulder and a new longsword in her hands. Thaya fell back against the bannisters, but the warrior woman swept past her and buckled the second sword around her waist.

"Expecting trouble?" Thaya asked, swallowing.

"Always," the woman replied without pausing her stride.

Thaya ran after her, thankful the sword wasn't to be used on her...*yet*.

Taking a route away from the path through a gaggle of geese and across the grass, they came to the perimeter of the settlement marked by a wall of stakes rising about twelve feet high and encircling and protecting those within.

The warrior woman touched them as she passed, counting silently, then paused and pushed on a stake hard. With a creak, the stake swung outwards, and the woman squeezed through the gap.

I love secret doors! Thaya grinned and followed after her.

When she was through, the woman pushed the stake back until it was flush with the others, and hurried towards the thick darkness of the forest.

"Come." She motioned Thaya to follow. "It's not actually far."

They made their way along a very rough track gently sloping upward through ferns and trees. Past a cluster of huge boulders, the ground levelled out and the path widened. Beyond the rocks on their right, a cliff ran down into a deep ravine. Thaya peered over the edge and down at the sheer drop where trees clung precariously to narrow ledges. The warrior woman stuck close to the wall on the left, and they had to inch along the cliff's edge when it narrowed dangerously. Thaya kept her eyes up and away from the drop plummeting to the forest floor a hundred yards below. She breathed easier as the rock path widened and found herself suddenly in the mouth of a cave.

The cave entrance was circular and about fifteen feet high. It was unremarkable, receding straight back into the rock about twenty yards, the end of which lay in a neat stack of logs. A few paces back from the entrance, a ring of fist-sized stones circled a pile of ashes, above which hung a spit and an iron pot; it was clearly a well-used campfire.

The warrior woman dropped her pack down beside it. "Help me make the hearth."

Thaya assisted her in carrying logs and kindling, and the woman got to sparking them alight with flint and tinder.

"I'm Thaya," said Thaya as the woman blew upon tiny flames.

"Engara," the warrior replied.

Thaya nodded. "What about the boy?"

"He'll be all right, for now. But the priests, they'll be planning. They never rest."

The flames soon crackled high, and Engara reached into her pack and poured a canister of water into the pot. Next, she added chopped vegetables: a leek, carrots, and mountain potatoes. She poured a powdered substance in from a small sack and tore off handfuls of a plant Thaya wasn't too familiar with. It smelled pungent and herby as she sprinkled it in.

Finally, she sat back on her haunches. "Sit, please. Let me offer you a meal. The hospitality of our people has vanished over the years. Hard winters and hard toil, especially when we must now appease the gods like never before."

"I'd prefer to stand," said Thaya. She was restless and didn't want to hang around in this place too long, waiting for the acolytes to catch up with her. But after a moment and a grumble from her stomach, she sat down next to the woman.

"Where are you from?" asked Engara, her blue eyes like the sky on a clear day, filled with interest.

"Brightwater. A small village south and west of here in a valley near the sea."

Engara nodded. "I'd like to see the sea at least once in my life."

Thaya tried to imagine never having seen the ocean and couldn't. "It goes on and on for miles. When you're in the middle of it, there's nothing but flat blue, no land to be seen anywhere."

Engara shivered. It was odd to see the tough woman afraid. "That must be frightening."

Thaya smiled. "You get used to it. It's actually quite liberating. You feel free, *really* free."

Engara grinned, her teeth a perfect row of white. "I love that. You've come a long way, traveller, and with no sword, or at least none I can see. Is that safe for a woman?"

"I have hidden weapons, and a friend whom I'll rejoin soon," Thaya said.

"That's good to know. And you found this boy? I doubt you wanted to visit this place..."

Thaya agreed. "I'm travelling east, to the Magi of Loji. Then the dragon came, and many Ordacs. We were in their path, and they attacked us. Did you see the sky ship?"

Engara frowned and rested her chin on her interlaced

fingers. "Dragons? They are a myth! Ordacs, however, I've seen them marauding the land. Big, aren't they? They don't come too close very often, nothing for 'em here."

Thaya paused. How could she not have seen the dragon? It would have been visible for miles around flying over the mountains. "The dragon was huge and noisy, south of here and above the mountains. You didn't see or hear it?"

Engara shook her head and eyed her as if she were making it up.

Thaya sighed. "Well, perhaps it was out of view on the other side of the ridge." It wasn't true, but Thaya decided to protect her integrity. "The boy saw it, too; we were both hiding from it."

"You have a fresh Ordac wound, so I believe most of what you say." Engara pointed to the three shallow claw marks on her arm. "You were lucky, their claws can disembowel in a heartbeat."

There is the crashed ship, Thaya thought. *I'll show her the wreckage when I leave. A day's walk shouldn't be too much for a warrior.*

"Are you from this place? You seem different to the others." Thaya hoped it wasn't too bold, but she'd spoken enough about herself for now.

"Half of me is. The other half is from the north where my mother came from. I am a Shield Sister, as my mother was before me, and part of the Shield who protect this village from bears, wolves and raiders from the north and east. There are only four of us now when once there were eight—eight before the priests came and downgraded our positions. But anyway, no one ever comes to us from the south and west."

Engara pulled out wooden bowls and spoons from her

pack and dished out the boiling soup. "There's no bread, I'm afraid. I didn't have time to stop by Jenna's."

Thaya took the bowl gratefully, the first hot meal in days. It was too hot to eat so she held it in her hands, enjoying the warmth and the delicious smell.

The sun was trying to break through the heavy clouds, and every now and then, a beam of light struck the trees stretching out below them. Beyond the ravine swept a bowl of evergreens and a line of cliffs in the distance.

"The boy, Derry, he said he was cast out because of his *abilities*," said Thaya.

"That boy is trouble." Engara rolled her eyes and blew on her soup. "Perhaps the devil lives in him, but he didn't deserve *that* for his crimes. His parents are weak; the boy needs a strong hand. Our people have become weak. It's happened since *they* came when I was but a child. Once I would have believed casting children out was right. Once I believed everything they taught us—I even enforced the laws they gave to us—until they came for my own son…" Engara swallowed audibly. "Ah, I don't want to talk about that, not to a stranger who doesn't need to hear it.

"However, that boy, in his childish rage, burned down Levin's house. Near killed his wife, too, but that, and a whole string of lesser happenings, wasn't what got him cast out. It was when he one day pointed at the priests, all trance-like and weird he was, and said, 'Your days are numbered, and one day soon, what you are will be revealed, and the cloak you have cast upon the people will be lifted.'

"I've never seen the priests look so frightened; it was weird. And then they flew into a rage. The poor kid was stripped naked, beaten, locked in a cell, and then cast out. I thought they would have done the Making there and then, but they did not."

"The Making?" asked Thaya. The poor kid had been through a lot.

"You don't know the Making? What gods do your people worship?" Engara looked at her as if she were simple.

"Useless ones." Thaya blew on her soup.

Engara barked a laugh, almost spilling hers. "Quite. Well, the Making is the greatest blessing whereby a soul is chosen by the gods, given special favour, and then sent straight to them with no punishment for previous sins, not in this lifetime or others. Heavenly bliss awaits those chosen for the Making."

Engara's voice took on a hint of awe, although there was an uncertain look in her eyes, and her hands gripped her bowl and spoon tightly.

Thaya let out a long, silent sigh, trying to let her anger out with it. "They took your son," she stated sourly.

"It was a great honour." Engara's hands became white with her grip, and her jaw clenched.

"So why are you angry?" Thaya trod lightly. She was in no mood to have another argument with these people; she just wanted to leave and get back on her own journey.

"I miss him." Engara's gaze drifted from the middle distance down into her soup bowl.

"Of course. He's your son." Thaya sipped the soup. For such a quick and simple meal, it was full of flavour and surprisingly filling.

"I stopped believing in the gods that day." The warrior woman's voice was barely a whisper. "But that does not bring my son back."

"Is that why you helped me? Because I brought the boy back?"

Engara nodded. "Yes, but also because you stood up to them. You weren't afraid."

Thaya frowned. "I was afraid but I hid it. I don't like those acolyte bastards."

Engara blanched as if Thaya had blasphemed, then laughed nervously. "They are in charge; they control all of us, for a hundred miles."

Thaya grimaced. It wasn't what she wanted to hear. *A hundred miles of trekking through acolyte territory... Perhaps I'd better return to the portal stone. Perhaps it would be safer to try and navigate through it, if I can even get it to work.*

Engara spoke quietly, cupping her bowl of half-eaten soup and staring into the flames, forgetting Thaya was there. "I believed it all, every word they uttered, words of the gods from the mouths of the most holy. When I became a Shield Sister, I even helped them take people's second-born... I can see their parents' tear-stained faces so clearly... Then one day they came for mine. If it's such a great honour and gift from the gods, why didn't it feel like it? I felt as if my guts were being torn out of me. My first died a babe; why did they take my second? I should have been allowed to keep him...The rules are rules, and they cannot be broken, or the black fire we will face."

"No." Thaya shook her head. "We owe bloodthirsty gods nothing!"

If Engara had heard her, she didn't show it and continued to stare far away. "By rights, I should have been Shield Mother of this tribe. Maybe, if I hadn't been a half-caste... The people liked and respected me but they didn't dare go against the dictates of the acolytes. I was so young when my mother—the previous Shield Mother of this tribe —died mysteriously, and my father was left broken. The acolytes decided he should go on a journey, a long pilgrimage to a far distant place to heal his black grief. And he went and has been gone twenty years. This tribe is bereft of leaders; well, the acolytes took his place as king and my mother's place of Shield Mother. Then our ways ended. And now we're poor, pathetic and weak."

Engara's shoulders slumped. Mechanically, she lifted her spoon to her lips and ate her soup.

Thaya watched the warrior woman, trying to imagine how bad it must be to lose both sons. What could she say? "Why don't you leave? Come with me a little way. I'd be glad of the company until my friend returns. There seems little for you here."

Engara shook her head. "I cannot leave the people I have sworn to protect. Besides, my daughter lives with her husband in the neighbouring tribe. I've thought of joining her there, but I would no longer be a Shield Sister and would begin again as a Shield Daughter for the next ten years—then I'll never become the Shield Mother I was trained to be. A Shield Mother rules the tribe, a warrior, not some weakling priest!" She rapped her chest.

"Then why don't you fight them? Rally the clan to your side and drive them out!" Thaya didn't like to utter such revolutionary words—this was not her land, her ways, or her clan—but what was it that kept the people down and afraid? Surely the woman had thought of this already.

Engara looked at her, her eyes wide. "We tried, a decade ago, and the gods came down and cursed us. Our crops failed, a pestilence fell upon us and a third of our people died. Some of the women remained childless, and are now too old to bear. That is how I know the gods exist."

Thaya scowled. "I don't mean to put you down, but why would the Almighty care to strike down a poor and pitiful clan? It makes no sense..."

Engara didn't have an answer; she just shrugged as if such things were beyond her and not meant to be known by a mere human. "Did your people throw you out, too?" There was a tentative look on the warrior woman's face.

"What, because I blaspheme against the gods?" Thaya chuckled.

Engara coloured in embarrassment. "Well, I've not heard one speak as brazenly as you."

Thaya set her empty bowl down, a sudden pang in her heart at the memory of the people she'd left behind. "No, a curse fell upon *them*, if anything. Shades came, from the Vormae. You may or may not have seen them in their small, round, flying ships, like a disc." Engara shook her head but listened curiously.

"Well, it's a long story, but my people simply forgot who I was." Thaya shrugged and left it there. She didn't want to tell the woman any more of her long story, not yet, not when she barely knew the woman, and superstition and ritual hung heavily upon these people. "I met a close friend who was also adrift, as it were, and now we seek the wisdom of the Loji Magi."

"Wizards are powerful"—Engara nodded—"but I distrust them. Not all that they do is holy. I can see you're on an important mission, one where I hope you'll find your answers and peace. When night falls, I'll trek with you to the border, make sure you get away safely."

"Thank you." Thaya sighed in relief at the thought of moving on. Had the warrior woman not offered, she would have gone alone anyway. She stretched her legs out and leaned back against a rock.

5

REVEALING THE UNSEEN

A HAND SQUEEZED THAYA'S SHOULDER GENTLY, WAKING HER. She blinked open her eyes and looked from the glowing embers up at Engara. It was dark beyond the mouth of the cave, and her back was sore and stiff from the hard ground.

Thaya rubbed her eyes. "Oops, I didn't mean to fall asleep."

The warrior woman's face danced with shadows in the dim light. "We should go now. It's dark and we won't be seen."

Thaya nodded, yawned and stretched. She sorely missed Khy, but at least Engara would be her companion for a short time. She'd feel less anxious with her at her side instead of little Derry; worrying about protecting a kid wasn't much fun.

They drank water from their flasks, then left the cave. Engara allowed no light, and inching along the edge of the cliff, knowing there was a deadly drop, made Thaya's teeth chatter. She took deep, steadying breaths until she reached the trees, then wiped her sweaty brow.

"We'll stay off the path for now until we've put a good

few hours between us and the town," said Engara. "Let's stay silent and move as quietly as possible."

Thaya nodded.

After about half an hour, Thaya whispered, "Won't you be missed? They'll know we've gone together."

"Not necessarily—it's my scout tonight anyway," Engara replied softly. "Usually I go with Tennar, but he's twisted his ankle. It certainly wouldn't seem odd to anyone if you just left after that incident anyway."

Thaya nodded. "Makes sense."

It wasn't easy pushing through the undergrowth in the dark, but a half-moon cast its light between clouds often enough and the trees opened up a little when they started moving up hill. With relish, Thaya imagined being on the road again with Khy and far away from this place.

"I'm grateful for your help—you didn't have to," said Thaya.

"You don't need to thank me. How my clan treated you is disgusting. Guests are honoured in my mother's clans, and they used to be honoured here. Guests might be messengers from the gods; they must be treated as such."

"There is much fear and suspicion in the people," said Thaya.

"The acolytes put it there. We were proud and confident once. Rich, too. Now look at us." Engara sighed.

"Why did you let them in?" Thaya asked.

Engara let out a long breath. "It's complicated. I was only a girl at the time. There's an old temple, you see, and the acolytes lay claim to all the old temples. I think they try to harness the latent powers there or something, I don't know. But strange things were happening: people going missing; disturbing noises in the night; people seeing strange non-human figures in the forest who then vanished before their eyes. People began to think they were being haunted or cursed in some manner.

"So, deals were done between the acolytes and my mother and father—the clan leaders—to provide spiritual and divine protection for the people of Taomar. You see, the first priests were more humble—some were even kind—but others came, more powerful and high-ranking, and their demand for more...payment, as it were, increased. Bit by bit, they took power from the people and had it for themselves. By the time I became an adult, the acolytes were fully in charge of everything."

"Sounds like the acolytes brought the problems with them, to begin with," said Thaya.

Engara stepped over a fallen bough. "I've often thought that. Some of us whisper about it to each other in our mead cups, but none dare speak openly about it because it's blasphemous to slander the people of the gods."

Thaya snorted but decided to say nothing.

Engara looked up at the sky. "Dawn is an hour away. We'll rest at the Dug Out about two hours from here."

The Dug Out was simply a very shallow cave. They rested as the sun warmed the valley, and ate dark bread and dried foods from Engara's pack.

"There's more to the dragon story," said Thaya.

The warrior woman raised an eyebrow. If she didn't believe in dragons, would she believe in ships that could fly in the sky? Thaya decided to try and to air her suspicions as to why the priests might have treated her so—something which she'd been thinking about the entire journey. "It attacked a ship, one that flies in the sky. Have you seen sky ships? It would have been visible above the mountain even in Taomar. Then the dragon landed by the wreckage, and Ordacs swarmed it; I saw it all. I think that's why the acolytes reacted so strongly toward me. I think they're somehow involved, or at least in communication with the Ordacs. I'm not a witch, but I am a Truth Seer."

Engara snorted. "That's enough to have them label you as a witch. We saw or heard no flying ship and no *dragon*—I have to say, I'm having a hard time believing that. The acolytes send us out to fight Ordacs; why would they be in league with them?"

Thaya sighed. "I don't know. I was hoping you might be able to shed light on it. My feelings are rarely wrong, and I feel strongly about this. They don't like the kid because he has power, and it's clear they don't want any of the normal people having any power that might threaten them."

Engara cocked her head. "Now that I can believe. I'm certain that's why they advised my father to go on a pilgrimage to heal his broken heart after my mother died. They wanted to be rid of him and to stop the people loyal to him from rising up. I guess I'm weak—it should be me who leads the people now—but how can I lead people afraid of the gods? I'm no priest..." The warrior woman stood and held out her hand.

"The people have to want to be free." Thaya took Engara's outstretched hand and let herself be pulled to her feet. "But anyway, let me show you the sky ship, then you'll see what I've been talking about."

It was a hard slog back up the hill she and Derry had trotted down, and Engara set a fast pace, but with each step, Thaya's spirits lifted. It meant they were farther from the village.

They finally crested the mountain ridge in the late afternoon, sweaty and thirsty.

"I should leave you now and return, but I must admit, stranger, you have my curiosity regarding this dragon and flying ship." Engara drank from her canister and wiped the sweat from her brow.

Thaya shrugged. "We've come this far; it wouldn't take too long to get to it, and the terrain is flat and easy."

How would Engara react when she saw the ship, the blackened scorch marks, and the giant claw marks made by the dragon? Would she believe there was something going on between the presence of Ordacs and the acolytes? What was more worrying was that the people hadn't seen either in the sky, when surely someone from the clan would have?

The journey along the ridge took longer than expected; it was further than she'd thought, but eventually the sharp, acrid smell of soot and smoke still hanging in the air hit them.

They came to the ridge of brown rock, and Thaya gasped; there was nothing there. Where was the sky ship? The dragon claw marks in the dirt? The black marks scouring the rocks?

Thaya whirled around, hunting for a sign of something, *anything,* but all that remained was that old smell of soot and burning. "It was right here!"

Engara hunted the ground, too, side-glancing at her curiously as if to check if she were mad or not. "Are you sure this is the place?"

"Absolutely!"

The warrior woman shrugged, and there was a moment of awkward silence.

Thaya stood still, hands on hips, and hung her head, thinking. *How could everything be gone? Did they scrub the rocks with soap to get rid of the marks? No. Did I imagine it all?*

Possibly, but then Derry and Khy saw it too... But more importantly, WHY would they go to the efforts of covering it up?

"Somebody doesn't want people to see something," Thaya said it under her breath, lost in her thoughts.

"Who?" Engara asked, thinking she had spoken to her.

Thaya lifted her gaze and stared at the sky. "Who? Why?"

She walked to where the ship should have been, and had she not been looking, silent and thoughtful, she would have missed it. The barest tingle brushed her skin like warmth or wind or static. She lifted her hands, palms outwards, and closed her eyes. There, a definite tingle felt stronger in her hands. It was like pressing against the sheerest fabric or the gentlest breeze.

"There's something here." She frowned, concentrating hard on the subtle feelings.

"You can feel something? Are you a witch?" Engara sounded worried. Thaya could hear the woman shifting nervously.

"No, I'm just a country girl, but I *can* sense things. That's why I'm going to the magi." She could feel the warrior woman's gaze on her, clearly spooked she might be a witch. The acolytes had surely put the fear of the gods into these people.

Thaya focused again and ever so gently pooled her power, her 'soulfire' as Khy had described it, into her palms. The tingling feelings grew stronger, and she felt a definite pressure right there in the air, this time like pushing her hands through the surface of water. Could it be a force field that hid something, perhaps similar to Khy's wards and shields he created to conceal them?

Her hands warmed as she pooled more soulfire into them, and she heard Engara gasp. So what if she saw her hands glow? What was more important was who had hidden what had happened here and why.

"Reveal it to me," Thaya whispered. At once, power surged through her fingers. She stepped back in shock. Before her, the air shimmered as if a blanket was being pulled back, and beyond the fake reality of smooth stones and empty ground, a different reality revealed itself.

Engara inhaled sharply. "Oh my."

Thick, black scorch marks scarred the rocks for several yards. Engara's eyes were wide as they fell upon the twisted and destroyed remains of the sky ship and the giant claw marks in the earth. The warrior woman rushed to inspect them.

Thaya simply stared at her hands. *I asked, and the power responded to me. How did I reveal the unseen?*

She looked at the destroyed ship. It was different; more parts had been removed. "The craft was larger than this, but parts of it are missing now, and look, it's severely crushed." Thaya inspected the ship, feeling deeply unsettled. Who had been the crew? Were they good people deserving of some kind of burial ceremony or were they like the Ordacs themselves; invaders bent on plundering their planet and slaughtering the people? She wished she knew. And where had the parts gone? Here, a section of hull was missing, and there, one of its antennae was gone. There were no other people near here, so it could only have been the Ordacs removing bits. *Or the acolytes.* The last thought seemed ridiculous.

Engara crouched and inspected the twisted, bent metal. "Okay, so now I believe you, but what the Ordacs do, that's up to them. And to be quite honest, we only ever see them from a distance; they don't seem to be interested in what we're doing."

Thaya didn't believe it. From her experience, no invading off-worlder ever let the people be, but she didn't say anything. Something weird was going on. She peered into the mangled opening, but it was too crushed to get inside, and too dim and burnt to make anything out.

Engara rubbed the tip of her scabbard into the deep grooves in the rock made by the dragon's talons. "Reckon it'll come back?"

"Well, *someone* came back to cover it all up," said Thaya.

"Someone with magic." Engara nodded.

Thaya rolled her shoulders back. "But you're right, I'd rather not be here if something does return. You'll look after Derry for me? Good. Talk to him; he saw what happened, too. He'll be all right as long as he keeps calm. If I were you, I'd look at sending him to one of your sister clans. He certainly doesn't deserve to be thrown out and left to die."

Engara smiled. "I will do all I can. Looks like I've got something interesting to tell my people now, and I'll probably get myself into a whole lot of trouble with the acolytes, too. The magi you seek are east, a long way east." She pointed to the distant mountains where dark clouds gathered. "Five miles past the road to Taomar, there's a dry shelter we created, high on the rocks, that provides good respite from the elements. Ah, unless you know the area, you'll miss it. I'll come with you; I've just about enough provisions left for two, and if I return home now, it will be too soon for my standard scout. Besides, you're the most interesting thing to happen in years. It's been good to get out and hear about the rest of the world out there."

Thaya smiled. "You're welcome to join me. I'd be glad of the company. Maybe even my companion will catch up with us. He's fleet of foot, shall we say."

Engara rolled her eyes. "You might have convinced me

about the dragon, but this mystery friend of yours, you sure he's not imaginary?"

Thaya chuckled, and they turned and headed towards the mountains lumbering under the moody sky in the east.

"You see that ridge?"

Thaya followed where Engara pointed and picked out a craggy ledge partially concealed by trees. "Uh-huh."

"Follow it a little ways, and see where it seems to disappear? Well, it's a trick of the eye, for it actually just recesses more. You can't see it from here, but there are bushes up there and a small shelter we've built for protection, hunting, and spying—although there's not much to spy on; no one comes here."

Thaya embarked on her first taste of rock climbing and hauled herself up the narrowest of climbing holds. Engara was unbelievably fast for such a large woman. Thaya just thanked the Creator that they weren't going that high.

The bolt hole was a flat plateau surrounded by bushes and concealed from the ground. Engara's team had erected a low, wooden shelter just large enough to lie and squat under. They settled down and made the place home for the night.

Looking up at the stars, Thaya undid her collar, thankful for a fairly warm evening given the clear night. "So, what would you really like to do? It doesn't sound like you're too happy in Taomar. Shouldn't you have a husband somewhere looking out for you?"

Engara smiled. "Shield brethren don't take spouses."

"Oh," said Thaya, wondering about the woman's children.

"But we may have as many lovers as we wish. Our children will always be Shield Children. The settled life? It was never for me. And what I want to do? I love my people and could never leave them, but I long for my mother's way of life: the nomad, travelling wherever our will and the seasons and migrations take us. Staying in one place in houses that don't move...I don't like it." Engara pulled a face that showed her distaste.

Thaya could relate to that. "I know what you mean. Once I hated the thought of leaving home; now the very thought of staying makes me feel trapped."

Engara nodded. "Exactly that. Trapped. I also long to find my father. I believe he's out there somewhere, maybe so far away he can't return by himself. And I want to lead my people to prosperity, like our golden days of old, but I often wonder if *they* even want that; they seem to spend any spare thoughts on the gods."

"Pah, that's the acolytes' doing," said Thaya.

"I think you're right."

They talked long into the starlit night, longer than they should have for an early start, and when the conversation fell quiet, Thaya pulled her blanket close around her and wished Khy was with them. Her sleep was restless...

Derry appeared before her, and great licks of flame surrounded him. He opened his hands, and they flared with fire. He pointed at a group of acolytes who huddled together and he started screaming hysterically.

"Liars! Liars!" he shouted again and again. The acolytes' faces filled with rage, and they clawed at the air, trying to reach Derry, but the boy's flaming hands drove them back.

Thaya turned away. In the darkness behind her sat the elf she had met in a different dream, glimmering with his own diffuse light, his face serene and beautiful as he spoke. "Did you find the gift yet, Ellasheem? It is close."

"No, I don't know where it is," Thaya said.

A beautiful, golden-white light began to grow a few yards away, and the elf looked at it with a smile. "Ah look, your friend has nearly healed."

In the bright light, Thaya saw a Saphira-elaysa form: a single, golden horn, an elegant horse-like head, eyes of deep indigo.

"Khy!"

She started towards him, but the dream faded to darkness, and the echo of her word rolled around her.

Thaya opened her eyes.

The sky was pink with the dawn, and Engara snored softly a few feet away. No birds sang their morning chorus, and no wind blew, the forest was absolutely silent, so what had awoken her? Trusting her instincts, Thaya sat up, alert.

She squinted over the terrain and into the forest beyond. There, right at the edge of the ledge by the bushes, the air shimmered. Thaya peered closer, and then three acolytes appeared out of thin air, dressed in their orange robes. The one with the strange conical hat, and the same one Thaya had had the misfortune of dealing with earlier, clenched his fists and narrowed his eyes. The other two acolytes wore no hats, just cowls that cast their faces in half-shadows and made their expressions unreadable. They must be lesser acolytes, Thaya thought, and the head priest was the scary one glaring at her.

"Harbouring witches, Shield Sister?" he hissed dangerously.

Engara jerked awake, then leapt to her feet. How she managed to grab and unsheathe her sword in the same motion was beyond Thaya.

The warrior woman stared at the acolytes and, with some effort, reluctantly sheathed her sword. "Father Inkesty, ahem. Having provided our guest hospitality in the form of a simple meal, I have now escorted her safely during my usual scout. As you know, Taomar always delivers a good welcome to our esteemed guests and visitors."

Father Inkesty smirked. "No, I don't think so, Shield Sister. We're *all* returning to Taomar. Devil worshippers must be put on trial to prove that they are not so. What are you afraid of? If they're not harbingers of evil, then they are free to go. You wouldn't want to jeopardise the good people of Taomar again with curses, diseases, and pestilence brought about by witchcraft, would you, Shield Sister?"

For all Engara's fierce looks and attire, she became meek and withdrawn in the presence of the acolytes. That alone made Thaya angry. She tried to control it even though the air was swiftly charging with aggression. She could fight; the acolytes stood between her and freedom and a painful drop off the ledge if she messed up.

Thaya cleared her throat and spoke. "I think it's clear to see for anybody who's not a halfwit that I'm not a witch, and neither am I going to stand trial for simply bringing an abandoned child back to his parents. Casting out a defence-less boy is where the true evil's at."

"Hold your tongue, witch!" the acolyte priest snapped.

Thaya licked her lips. *I could do with you right here, right now, Khy!* Her hand went to her belt, but her fireshot wasn't there; she'd put it in her pack like an idiot! She looked around. Where was it?

A half-smile twisted the head priest's face as he held up her pack. How had he got a hold of that? *Magic is at work!*

"We can't take any chances and let a witch have her tricks and potions, can we?" Father Inkesty sneered.

"I'm not a witch!" Thaya scowled, and her palms began to tingle with energy.

The head priest lifted his staff. "Come on now, we can do this our way, peacefully and without a struggle."

The air shimmered around them as power came from the staff. Thaya gasped as something wrapped around her and began to lift her bodily.

"No!" Golden light flared from her palms—not the flaring fire she was used to, but a shimmering mist that cancelled out the power flooding from the staff. Engara's eyes opened wide in horror—she clearly didn't like anything to do with magic.

Father Inkesty hissed at her like a snake. "So you see, we *do* have a witch!"

Thaya raised her hands in warning, but in barely a blink, one of the other acolytes was beside her. He hadn't moved, at least not that she had seen, and he had somehow translocated the ten or so feet between them.

He clapped cold iron around her wrist, yanked her forwards and clamped her other wrist, and the energy in her palms vanished. She struggled against the acolyte and the iron manacles, which felt blisteringly cold.

Magic again. Something's not right!

Thaya began to panic. She fought to release the pent-up power inside her through her palms, but the iron prevented it!

"I'm not a witch—"

The last thing she saw was the short staff connecting with her temple, and the world shuddered and disappeared.

6

THE GODS HAVE SPOKEN

SHOUTING ROUSED THAYA, AND PAIN SHOT IMMEDIATELY through her body.

"Let her go!" a woman yelled.

"Stop dragging her!" growled a man.

Several women's voices shouted over the top of each other, so she couldn't hear what they said.

"Get off me, peasant!" said another man, followed by the sound of a scuffle.

"Leave it or you'll follow her. I'm warning you!" a third man shouted.

"Thaya!" a kid wailed from further away. It sounded like Derry.

Through the immense pain throbbing in her temples, Thaya opened her eyes. Mud, puddles, and filthy, sackcloth-covered feet appeared, shuffling forward on either side of her. Her head was bent down by something hard and heavy, and her hands were tied painfully tight to the back of it.

Wood—a stake or something wedged on my shoulders.

Her feet were also tied, and she was being dragged head first through the dirt, which was just as well since there was no way she was strong enough to stand right now. She tried to look forward, which was impossible given the lump of wood behind her head.

"Is she a witch?" a hushed female voice asked.

"No, she's our guest! Is this how we treat visitors?" replied a familiar voice.

Engara! Thank God you're here.

"But she saved the cursed one and brought him back to damn us. The gods won't be happy," replied the first woman.

"What do the gods care about a little boy? Fool!" Engara growled.

That's right, Engara, you're beginning to understand.

Thaya smiled despite her pain. She tried to muster the soulfire within. If she could burn away her bindings, she could run. But the cold iron that pressed into her wrists was doing something to prevent her power from rising.

"You can't cast your evil spells here, witch!" An acolyte grabbed her by the hair and bent her head painfully so he could look into her eyes. His gaze was wild, bordering on mad. "It's to the dungeons with you for defying the will of the gods!"

Thaya was about to retort, but a stave appeared and smacked against her temple. She fell sideways into the mud and flopped onto her back. Villagers surrounded her, bleary in her vision, but she could still read their expressions: some clasped hands to their faces in worry or fear; others scowled and shouted angry words at her. *They believe the priests,* she thought.

Acolytes shoved the people back, and the one Engara called Father Inkesty loomed over her. Thaya stared at him. There was something strange happening to his eyes; they shifted from brown to golden, and his pupils lengthened into slits, like an animal's. His head wobbled, too, becoming hazy and indistinct as it shifted form, lengthening from the nose into a blunt snout that she was certain had scales on it.

She blinked hard and stared again. Now his face was normal, and his eyes plain brown as before. What on Urtha had happened?

He blinked, too, as if he had seen or felt something, and then a wave of fury consumed him. He slapped her hard across the face, making stars dance in her vision. His other hand raised that infernal stave, and she braced for the blow that just might kill her.

Nothing happened.

She squinted open one eye.

Engara was at her side, her hand gripping the acolyte's wrist, her muscles like iron cords restraining the man.

"This is out of control!" Engara shouted.

Inkesty snarled. "You overstep yourself, Shield Sister!"

The warrior woman pulled him up and away from Thaya. Three large men dressed in leathers and armed with thick swords matching Engara's, came to stand beside her. They were quiet, watchful, but shifted from foot to foot nervously. No one stood against the acolytes, not ever. Thaya wished she was far away from this place.

Inkesty was virtually spitting rage, his chest rising and falling fast as he struggled to contain himself, but contain himself he did, which surprised Thaya.

So Engara still holds some clout, some authority here. I'll bet they hate that.

"Be careful, Engara," Inkesty said quietly. "Be careful that the gods don't strike you down where you stand. We will not have this clan fall back into savagery and godlessness."

Engara's face became pinched as something battled within her.

With a nod from Inkesty, she released his wrist, and he yanked it back. Rubbing it, he glared at the warrior woman. Beyond them, Thaya glimpsed Derry struggling against the hands of his father. The boy's dirty face was scrunched up and tear-stained.

"I've had enough of this place," Thaya growled. "Get this thing off me, and I'll be on my merry way." Thaya wanted to sound annoyed, but her voice was weak and wavering.

"I don't think so. We're not done with you yet, or the boy." Inkesty turned his damning glare onto her. "The gods have spoken, and they will purge the land of desecrators and evil."

Thaya closed her eyes and sighed.

I've landed in the snake pit. Khy was right, I should have never come here.

It began to rain. From her position of being dragged over the ground by the stake across her shoulders, she couldn't see where they were taking her. People wearing yellow and orange robes surrounded her, more than the three she had seen, and no one said a word. Mud became dark grey cobbles that quickly turned slippery and wet in the drizzle.

They turned uphill along a winding path. After a while, they slowed, and the sound of a heavy door being unlocked and then creaking open could be heard.

They dragged her inside and dark, cold dankness enveloped her as the door swung shut. The hairs on her arms stood up, and a brazier flamed alight. *Lit by magic—I can feel it.* But she didn't get to see anymore. There came a loud crack, pain in her head, and the brazier dimmed.

It was completely dark when she next opened her eyes, and exceedingly cold. She was curled up on the floor in a puddle. She pulled herself to the right where the floor was drier, and her shoulder pressed against a cold, hard wall. Dripping water echoed. She was in a small, enclosed space, and her hands were still encircled by the cold iron.

Warmth, I need warmth!

She shivered and tried to pool soulfire into her palms. Nothing happened. Something blocked her efforts.

It's this damn iron!

How the hell did it do that? A vague memory of a myth about fairies hating iron floated into her mind. It blocked their powers or made them feel ill or something. It had to be more than just iron; the material was very dark, almost black.

These acolytes have knowledge, sacred knowledge they keep from the rest of the people. So, what happens now? I rot in prison? Trapped again...the story of my life.

Light came from above, and a breeze. She stood up, surprised to find her feet weren't bound, and on tiptoes, she peered through a tiny, barred window to see a grassy space and then forest beyond. Darkness descended as the moon disappeared behind heavy clouds. She breathed deeply of the damp forest air, suddenly finding it clean and fresh and full of freedom.

She sighed and drew away from the window and began feeling along the walls until she came back to the barred window. It was a square cell, probably five feet by five feet and just enough to lie down if she did so diagonally. One of the walls was a door, a thick, wooden door enforced with metal. She slid down it, hugging her knees against the cold. Something didn't add up. The acolytes' reaction to her was too much—they knew something, or sensed something about her, and they were afraid.

They always overreact, though; they are known for their obsessive overzealousness. But still, she felt something more was going on.

The people didn't see the dragon, or the ship for that matter, but could the acolytes, with their magic abilities, have witnessed it? She'd been there, she had fought the Ordacs, but there had been no acolytes, so how could they know? She leaned her head back against the door and went over the events again and again.

Thaya awoke to a sound and sat still. The rustle came again from somewhere just outside.

"Thaya?"

Engara suddenly appeared at the barred window, making her jump. The warrior woman's eyes darted left and right fearfully, then she stuffed bread and dried food through the bars.

"Thank the gods, there you are," Engara said. "Look, I can't stay long; they're on alert. We're trying to get them to release you. This is madness! We'll be back, don't you worry."

"Wait!" Thaya called, her voice hoarse. But the warrior woman was already backing away, looking left and right, and then she disappeared into the bushes. Thaya sighed and drew away from the window. She wasn't hungry at this moment, but rather than have the acolytes burst into her cell and take her food away, she quickly ate it, wishing she had some water to wash it down.

The food brought comfort and some warmth, and she curled up in the least wet corner of her cell.

· · ·

The cell brightened with the grey dawn, rousing her from sleep, and the prison walls closed in around her.

I've got to get out of here!

She stood up and frantically searched the walls, the door, the wet and muddy floor for any hint of an escape route. A loose rock, a crack in the wood, a way to bend the bars—but there was nothing.

After an hour and with her body aching from the cold and the ordeal, she sunk onto her knees and leant back against the wall. As she did so, the sound of stone rubbing against stone caught her attention. She wriggled her back uncomfortably, and the noise of the loose grinding stone came again. She turned around and inspected the wall, finally able to see through the gloom with the brightening day.

One of the dark grey bricks was split diagonally, probably by frost and time. Maybe if she wiggled it out, she could use it to dig her way out of here. She smirked at the ridiculous thought but set about pulling it free anyway. It came away as a long shard of dark rock, too blunt to be anything other than a bludgeoning weapon.

I can't fight with that! But perhaps she could break her iron bonds with it.

She tried to strike one with it but couldn't even get the angle to hit it.

"Useless." She sighed, then froze at the sound of a voice. She pricked her ears. It was muffled, barely audible, but there—a man's voice, too indistinct to recognise, and it was coming from the other side of the wall.

She set the rock down and inspected the hole from which it had come. It was deep, and at the other end there was a tiny hole where light came through, either from many candles or sconces, for it was very bright. Movement came again from the other side, and she squinted through.

The floor was shiny, polished wood, and acolytes walked across it several yards away, their silk-slippered feet just visible under orange and yellow robes. She could only see them from the waist down and counted four. She felt that the room beyond the wall of her cell was large, and she strained to hear what they were saying, but they were too far away.

The acolytes paused their stride and spoke amongst themselves. Other footsteps approached, heavy, too heavy for slippered feet. Two more acolytes joined the four, and another walked amongst them that made her cry out. She clasped her hands over her mouth for this one was not human.

Beneath orange, silken robes tied by a golden sash—the mark of the highest rank an acolyte could attain—walked large, clawed feet covered in dark green scales, a thick tail trailing behind.

Thaya fell back from the hole, smothering her mouth to control her gasping.

An Ordac! It's a god-damn alien wearing acolyte clothes!

Thaya struggled for control, then forced herself back to the hole.

There was another Ordac! Its scales were paler, and it wore a lower-ranking silver sash, but still ranked higher than all the humans there.

Oh my, what is going on here? The acolytes are in league with the Ordacs, and the people have no idea!

Voices became raised. Ordacs hissed and growled words in Familiar, the local tongue, but she struggled with the accent to be sure what they said. Two human acolytes raised their voices and gesticulated angrily as the other humans pressed closer.

"I will not do it! We're pushing the people too hard, too fast. They will suspect!"

The Ordacs growled, their tails swishing, as the other humans shouted. Suddenly, they were fighting. The two gesticulating humans struggling against the other humans as the Ordacs watched on.

"Get off me!"

"You're making the gods angry!"

"It is *you* who'll bring down their wrath!"

"Listen to the voice of reason—"

The shouting intensified.

One fell. She saw his face clearly between the jostling, slippered feet. He was shaven-headed, in his late forties, with blue eyes and a round nose. His expression twisted into pain and then shock. He held his hands out in front of him. There was blood on them and a patch on his robe by his stomach that swiftly darkened and spread. All the acolytes, apart from one and the Ordacs, fell upon him, small blades glinting in their clenched hands.

Thaya watched, transfixed in horror. Blades flashed; blood dripped. A clenched hand passed across the fallen acolyte's throat, and then red gushed from it, soaking the polished floor. The other acolyte who had stood back tried to turn away. He slipped and fell over his fallen colleague, his robes ripped and bloody, his screams gargles.

"Be gone!" shouted an Ordac at the braying acolytes, and stepped forwards.

Magic light flared, momentarily blinding Thaya and breaking her transfixion. The other humans whimpered and fell back in fear, blood soaking into their slippers, and then they ran away from the fallen men.

The Ordacs fell onto all fours, reminding Thaya of the predators that they were, and lunged for the bleeding men that were no longer moving. Beneath golden cowls, she saw green and mottled brown snouts filled with rows of inch-long fangs. With unrestrained savagery, they tore into the men's bodies, ripping off chunks of flesh, bone and glistening viscera and swallowing it whole.

Thaya forced herself back from the spyhole, hands covering first her mouth and then her ears as she tried to shut out the sound of their gluttony. With trembling hands and sweat rolling down her temples, she shakily shoved the shard of rock back into its hole. Hugging her knees to her chest, she rocked back and forth on her haunches. A new kind of terror settled in her stomach and chilled her to her marrow.

The hours passed. The light falling in through the tiny, barred window moved across the wall. It wasn't sunny, but it was enough to keep her connected to the outside world, enough to keep her a little bit sane. She thought of a hundred stupid ways to break out of her cell, but it all came down to one: her friends on the other side of the wall were her only hope.

They're ruling the show! The off-worlders are running the whole thing, and the people have no idea! But I knew that; somehow, I've always known something dark and not-human sits at the top of those temples. Our supposed spiritual leaders, our religious guides are pawns! And now here I am, trapped in their clutches, and Khy is far away...

. . .

When the door to her cell screeched open, and yellow candlelight fell into her cell, her heart began to pound.

A lantern was shoved in her face, the light blinding compared to the gloom of her cell.

"It's time for your trial," a man said. She blinked against the light, trying to determine his face under his cowl. "Put this on."

He threw a robe at her, a dirty and worn, unbleached, woollen thing.

"No."

She threw the robe down, never intending to dress up as one of them or be a part of their rituals.

She didn't quite see what hit her—perhaps nothing did, and it was pure magic—but pain flared across her face, and stars danced in her vision. She found herself prone atop the discarded robe and gasping. Several pairs of hands dragged her to her knees, undid her manacles, and the robe was yanked over her head and arms, and tied at the waist with rope. Still in a daze, her wrists were clapped back into the manacles, and she was forced onto her feet and staggering between them as they hustled her out of the cell.

The corridor was dark. She couldn't make much out beyond the glare of the lantern, other than that she was surrounded by three or four acolytes. Another door screeched as it opened ahead, and light fell upon the steps leading up to it. They emerged into another corridor brightly lit with lanterns along the wall and the same polished floor she had seen the men die upon earlier. If their colleagues felt any remorse or loss, they failed to show it.

Thaya longed to feel the soulfire in her palms once more, but the iron cuffs prevented it from coming.

They paused before a huge, arched door twice her

height and with intricate scrolls and strange lettering carved into it and painted in gold. The rest of the door was painted an orange-honey colour, the same hue as the robes most acolytes wore.

An acolyte rapped on the door once with his short staff, and it was opened silently by two acolytes on the other side, their faces sombre and dark in the shadow of their cowls. Their eyes were hard as they looked upon her, and she kept her face expressionless, her head still pounding from the earlier blow.

They walked inside, and by her reckoning on the route they'd taken, this had to be the room the men had fought and died in earlier. She swallowed and did all she could to not glance in the direction of her cell. Was the loose stone visible? Had other prisoners before her found the same spy hole? If they had, and for anyone who had the misfortune of being locked in there, she didn't want to give the game away. The gushing blood, the man's horrified face—she couldn't rid them from her mind. She realised she was staring at the spot where the blood had spread, bright red on golden floors. She tore her gaze away and looked around the room.

Well, it wasn't a room but a huge hall or ceremonial chamber. A large dais, a single step high, rose in front of her, and upon it, an impressive, gilded altar stretched the entire width, covered in red velvet. The altar didn't look painted; could it be made of solid gold? Her mind boggled at the worth of it, should it be so.

Despite its impressive craftsmanship, something about the altar made her shiver. She looked instead at the enormous obelisk rising behind it and towering over everything and everyone, a single, round column inscribed with pictures, symbols and letters which weren't Familiar. It reached almost to the high-arched ceiling above, was thick and cylindrical at the sides, and phallic like—it must be more symbolic than anything else, she thought, for it wasn't attractive. At its top, flared a star, an unusual nine-pointed star.

I've seen that somewhere before, a long time ago, but where?

She tried to remember. It was probably in one of the books in the library she'd spent so much time in during her youth, trying to find anything she could about Lonohassa.

They paused before the altar and, apart from the two acolytes gripping her arms, the other acolytes stepped up behind the altar and turned to face her. There were eight in total, and moving in front of the others with a smirk on his face was the acolyte High Priest Father Inkesty.

"Let the trial of the witch begin," said her nemesis the other side of the altar, and he picked up and unrolled a scroll.

Thaya swallowed.

7

TRIAL OF THE WITCH

THAYA HUNTED THE SHADOWED FACES OF HER JAILERS, looking for any sign of reptilian features but finding none. Where were they? Were they watching from some hidden place? She noticed none of them were women either. She had seen some female acolytes in the past, but never many. They preferred men and it was well known that they considered women weak. She tried to ignore the dull thumping of her heart as the acolyte read aloud from the scroll.

"Neom mutharis. Esatum del belitum, eratin day cumna."

Thaya had no idea what language he was speaking, she had never heard it before. It may as well be Ordacian for all she cared. As soon as she thought it, her inner sensing told her it was true. She frowned. Was the whole order worshipping some Ordacian god under the guise of another? The people would never know. Acolyte temples were highly secretive and elitist; no common man would ever have stepped inside these halls...unless they were condemned.

Condemned!

A shiver went down her spine. She no longer needed to

understand what the priest was droning on about in his monotone voice; something bad *was* going to happen to her.

"This is all nonsense!" Thaya said aloud, causing the speaker to pause and glare at her. The acolytes gripped her arms tighter and shook her. She persisted. "You're making all this up, whatever it is, these charges are in a language I neither know nor care to."

The High Priest continued, but she spoke over him.

"What I want to know is what your deal with that dragon is, and the invading Ordacs with her."

The speaker did pause then, his knuckles turning white as he gripped the ends of the scroll. The acolytes behind him shifted and murmured to each other under their breaths.

Thaya ground her teeth. "You're all liars, and you lie to the people here, enslaving them for your own ends." She scrutinised each of the acolytes, and did a double-take on the one to the farthest left when his face shimmered oddly. The acolyte turned and spoke to the man beside him, his eyes becoming large and golden, the pupil split down the middle. His nose became long, thick and snout-like as his skin mottled green and brown.

Thaya closed her eyes and swallowed, trying to control her suddenly weak legs. But closing her eyes didn't help, for she saw more behind her lids: a row of human figures, indistinct in her mind's eye, but the two on the end were overshadowed by tall, hulking figures with tails.

She gasped and sagged between her jailers, who responded by shaking her roughly as she struggled to keep on her feet. A strange whispering began in her mind—it first sounded like a simple hiss—but if she concentrated, she could hear words being spoken. It appeared to be coming from the hulking figures. Magic moved, or a power of some sort seeped all around, cloying, suffocating and making her feel giddier. She had to get out of here; she needed the fresh air of the woods.

She heard screaming coming from somewhere, echoing and strange as if it came from within her own head. She saw blood splatter over the phallic-like obelisk behind the altar and blood soaking the golden altar top, but when she opened her eyes, nothing had changed. The altar and obelisk stood unsullied, and nobody screamed. She began to take deep breaths.

Great, so I'm seeing things now in this creepy temple...

She didn't know whether to close her eyes or keep them open, but she needed to get away from this place. Bad things had happened here... But how could she fight eight acolytes, two of whom appeared to be non-human?

"Get on with it, br-brother," one of the acolytes holding her arm commanded. He stumbled over his words, and he looked uncertain. Had he felt the strangeness she had?

"There are no dragons, only in the minds of witches!" The High Priest glared at her. "We shall have no evil here, nor let it live in the world to destroy and corrupt others. We have also studied your relics, which no normal human carries. The evidence for witchery is irrefutable. The punishment is either a whipping and a casting out, or death. But first, explain to us the devilry in these items so they may be appropriately destroyed. Mark my words, acolytes, these dark objects have been crafted from elements not found on Urtha, and no human hand has made them."

The acolytes nodded solemnly, and she swore she saw a long, red tongue dart out of one of their mouths.

The speaker held up his hands. In one hand, dangling between finger and thumb, was her fireshot, and in his other palm, the silver ring with circles on it that Arendor had given her.

So, they can't work out what they are or where they came from? Rather than destroy them, they want to know how they work for themselves. But the gun is obvious—it fires like any other shotgun, unless it doesn't work for them? The Agaroths said the fireshot would be linked to me and would get to know me in a similar way that a pet might, and I would learn its powers over time. Hmm, it must be that. They tried to use it, but it didn't fire, did it? And they want to use it for themselves...

Thaya shrugged. "The ring was given to me by a friend and is quite clearly made of silver." She played dumb. The ring never scratched or tarnished and when placed next to silver appeared whiter and shinier. The symbols on it were Agarothian and powerful though she knew not how they worked or what they did. For her, it was sentimental and maintained a connection to her off-worlder friend whom she was not about to expose to these idiots.

She decided to lie about the fireshot and test the acolytes. "I found the gun in the crashed spaceship up there in the mountains. Incidentally, it was the same sky ship the Ordacs and dragon raided after attacking it and killing its inhabitants. I don't suppose you've seen any of them round here, have you?"

The acolytes shifted, and she imagined the two on the left having lizard tails that swayed. She was afraid, yes, but her situation, given their condemnation, could not get any worse. This was a setup; she had seen something they did not want her to see, and now they were trying to find ways to get rid of her.

One of the acolytes to her left walked to the speaker and whispered in his ear. Thaya watched intently, but there was no hint that the acolyte was anything other than a man.

How then did I see him shift? Maybe it only becomes apparent when there is power or magic in the air...

The speaker sniggered. "Only a witch sees dragons when there are none. Let us be done with this evil business and quickly. Take her outside. Ten lashings for insolence and lying, and exposure to the elements should loosen the truth from her tongue."

———

Outside, the rain had stopped, and a cold wind blew under overcast skies. It was dark although dusk was only just beginning. The temple from which they emerged nestled against a tall cliff face that hid it from the town. Tall ever-greens surrounded it, further hiding it from view. It was well made from huge blocks of dark grey granite. The upper sections were of paler stone and looked to have been constructed recently, but the lower sections were well worn and old, ancient probably.

So, they built their temples on ancient places.

Now that she thought about it, the enormous temple in Havendell Harbour near her home also had a ring of massive old stones forming the base and foundations.

They jerked her forwards along the path, and she could no longer inspect the temple behind her. Ahead, smoke rose from hearths, and the smell of suppers cooking made her stomach rumble. Thaya thought about running, but they maintained quite a grip on her arms. They had magic, too.

The path widened and straightened as it led towards the eastern gate. There, to Thaya's surprise, a small crowd of people had gathered and started walking towards them. Leading them, with a sword sheathed against each hip, was Engara. Her face was hard, her blonde hair tied firmly back, the spiky ends of which splayed around her head like a halo of flax. At her sides, her Shield Brothers walked, all armed and armoured as was their fashion. Behind them hustled a ragtag gaggle of villagers dressed poorly in aprons, shirts and woollen cloaks. Some leaned on pitchforks and hoes, hardly menacing weapons.

The acolytes slowed their pace, their expressions becoming uncertain.

"Release our honoured guest. I command you as the leading Shield Sister of Taomar."

Taomar. She hadn't even been here long enough to get to know the place, Thaya thought. It mattered not the name of the village; trouble seemed to find her wherever she went.

Father Inkesty hissed. "Shield *Sister* Engara," he sneered her title, "you really have overstepped the mark this time."

Engara tossed her head. "It's *you* who have gone too far, Inkesty! Too long have the people of Taomar suffered your encroachments, our freedoms taken one by one in the name of your greedy god. You stole our freedoms as you stole our children, sacrificed, screaming to the Great Lords who never required this of us, not until *you* came."

Yes, Engara, yes! Thaya cheered in her mind at her bravery.

Engara's face had swiftly turned bright crimson with rage and emotion. Thaya started to worry the warrior woman was about to burst. *She's angry and upset about losing her son.* The situation was about to turn ugly, fast.

Though her warriors stood firm, the peasants behind them spoke fearfully. Beyond them, Thaya glimpsed the other villagers hovering on their doorsteps. Two women cried on their balconies...had their sons been taken, too? Thaya licked her lips; now was a chance to get free, but with her hands bound what could she do? Did Inkesty still have her fireshot?

Stupid me, I should have kept my eyes on them as we left the temple!

"Thaya," a child screamed her name.

"Derry?" Thaya looked around.

"Shut it, witch!" Inkesty turned, and quick as a whip, struck her across the face. Thaya fell as stars flickered in her vision, but the other acolytes yanked her back up. "It's you who has caused all this unrest!" His face was red and livid to the point of madness.

Father Inkesty addressed the crowd, his voice confident and commanding. "People of Taomar, this witch is causing the unrest you see unfolding before you. Will you suffer a witch in your midst? If you do, the Lords will strike you all down where you stand!"

The peasants behind Engara looked at each other and then at Thaya, uncertainty in their eyes.

"Thaya!" Derry cried out again.

There he is! She glimpsed the grubby child beside a house, struggling in the grip of his parents.

"Let me help her! Help my friend," he wailed.

Something was brewing in the air; it was filling with erratic energy. The entire town was like an unlit bonfire, ripe and ready to explode. Sweat trickled down Thaya's back.

"People of Taomar, I can assure you I'm not a witch but simply a traveller passing through. Please—"

Inkesty struck her across the other cheek, and Thaya tasted blood in her mouth, her own fury rising.

Damn these iron cuffs!

"Enough!" Engara shouted, her voice booming loud. The warrior stepped forwards.

"Arrest her, as well!" Inkesty ordered.

The acolytes did hesitate before they, too, stepped forwards. Their movements instigated the actions of Engara's warriors who leapt to her side.

Inkesty raised his staff.

Quick as lightning, Engara drew her sword, followed a heartbeat later by her warriors. "It's my sworn duty to protect the people of Taomar with my life, as my mother did before me and my father who was king. How dare you arrest me." Engara's eyes gleamed, and she watched everything like a lioness stalking its prey.

"Then protect your people and all of us from the dark art of witches!" Inkesty spat, but he did not make a movement.

Derry screamed, and Thaya wasn't quite sure what happened first: the streak of flames that suddenly crashed through everyone from the front or the separate blast that sent everyone to their knees from behind.

Reeling on the ground, Thaya glimpsed two acolytes rising in her side vision, the same acolytes who had shifted briefly into reptilians.

Fire and wind born of magic, flared and gusted, once again throwing her flat against the ground, and in that instant, she saw not two humans in her side vision, but two huge Ordacs dressed in orange acolyte robes and holding before them two identical short staves. She blinked, and they were men once more. She lifted her face from the ground and spat out dirt as she struggled onto her knees.

Ahead, the only person standing was Derry, his parents dazed and groaning on the floor behind him. Derry was screaming in a fit, his face upturned to the sky and his hands held claw-like at his sides. From his hands flared licks of orange flames and a blackened scorch mark led from him to where the people had stood.

"Derry!" shouted Thaya, gasping as she got to her knees, struggling against the iron manacles. "Release me, I can help him!"

No one listened to her, and the energy built again. The warriors were on their feet, but so were the acolytes, and now all held up their staves, their faces oddly calm. From everything that Thaya had seen in her life, magic was going to destroy everything faster than swords. Engara and her warriors did not stand a chance...unless Thaya acted fast.

Curse these shackles! Where's my weapon?

She glared at Inkesty's back, and something peculiar happened: an item glowed within his robes—the unmistakable shape of her fireshot outlined in red—then it faded. She stared at it, and it glowed red again and then was gone.

My fireshot is reaching for me; it wants me to find it! Does it know I want to find it? How can it be? Arothia Ra said it would mould to me over time, that I would come to understand its powers and uses as it would come to understand me and mine. It can reveal itself to me even through cloth!

Thaya jerked forward, managing to tear off her captors' grasps whilst their attention was on the recovering mob ahead of them. She grabbed Inkesty's robes just as he leapt towards Engara. The warrior woman howled and ran forwards, unrestrained rage vivid in her eyes. The robe tore in Thaya's hands, and they fell as fire burst from Inkesty's stave towards the Shield Sister. Engara leapt aside expertly, and Thaya entangled herself in Inkesty's robes, hunting for her fireshot and dragging the priest to the ground.

Her hand touched the fireshot, and she grabbed it. The weapon grew hot, flared, and burned away the material ensnaring it, leaving it free in her grasp. Some of the swirling symbols etched on the metal glowed with yellow light. She stared at them in wonder. Another symbol flared at the tip of the fluted barrel, and then the one beside it, then the next, and so on in a straight motion, moving faster and faster along the barrel to the hilt. Her hand throbbed first with heat and then a cold so freezing she opened her hand to drop it, but the fireshot remained welded to her grip.

"Aaaah!" she shouted as light flared around her hand, burning heat and cold. The iron around her wrist glowed, burned, froze into solid ice, then shattered.

She wanted to stare at it, but the fist of an acolyte connected with her temple, knocking the sense from her. She floundered as he dragged her off Inkesty and tried to disarm her, but the fireshot refused to leave her grip; they'd have to cut her hand off to release it! A sickle-shaped knife appeared in an acolyte's hand—they intended to do just that.

Behind her, Engara screamed along with her other warriors, and the acolytes turned their attention back to them. Heat and magic scorched the air, and in the corner of her vision, Thaya saw a house on stilts blazing in flames.

Derry!

In the mayhem, only two acolytes remained calm. Together, they stood facing the battle unfolding behind Thaya, palms raised, one with a stave, one without.

So, they didn't actually need devices to command magic... Their faces were blank, so blank they almost didn't look human. *Because they aren't.*

Inkesty's attention was on Engara. The warrior woman was on her knees, hand clasping a bloody stream running from her head and down over her face. Another warrior lay prone, face down in the mud, his body smoking. The other villagers beside them dropped their hoes and pitch-forks and turned and ran. A younger acolyte grabbed

Thaya's weapon and tried desperately to yank it behind her back.

Thaya jerked her hands free and smacked him hard with the weapon. He fell back in shock, grasping his bloodied temple. Inkesty brandished a knife and lunged at Engara.

Thaya raised her fireshot at her enemy, but a terrible foreboding came from behind her, a solid thing settling in her stomach. With all her desire, she wanted to shoot the High Priest who had beaten her and thrown her in prison, and who was about to hurt her friend, but her gut instinct told her who held the real power, who was really in charge. She had a chance; she held the element of surprise. She turned from Inkesty, in slow motion, so it felt, and aimed and fired at the nearest of the two calm acolytes.

Golden fire flared from her fireshot, and in those flames she saw the huge shape of the Ordac standing there in acolyte robes. The Ordac turned to face her. His green eyes blinked and narrowed, a red tongue flickered out of his snout. There was no time for him to counteract the firebolt careening towards him. He dipped his head gracefully—was he acknowledging his defeat? Was he acknowledging her victory? The fire engulfed him. He raised up his hands and looked to the sky like some majestic statue, and then disintegrated into dust.

His comrade was not so calm.

The pretence that this was a human before her suddenly vanished. No longer was there a man but a hulking Ordac towering two feet over her. Her bravery vanished, and she stepped back, her blood running cold, her stomach clenching. She side-glanced the chaos of burning houses, roaring warriors, and screaming villagers. Could they see what stood before her? Could they see what these acolytes condoned and who they really served?

An older man, menacing his pitchfork at the acolytes from a safe distance, suddenly paused, his toothless mouth opening in horror at the beast before her.

Yes, they can see.

"Deceiver!" Thaya screamed.

The Ordac bared his fangs and held his clawed hands in front of his chest, like in prayer but with the palms cupped. Dark light like shadows swirled between them.

Thaya stood fast and raised her left palm. Soulfire, so long held back by the iron manacles, roared within her and rushed into her hand.

The reptilian's dark light burst forth, flowing over and surrounding her in a bubble of strange gel-like darkness. She could still see the outside world, but it was as if she looked at it from within a swirling globe of black-stained glass. She released her soulfire and golden-white flames shattered the bubble.

The Ordac snapped his jaws and glared dangerously. Lights danced in his eyes, and power built around him.

Thaya was painfully aware that Engara and Derry needed her help; the kid was still screaming uncontrollably, but she could do nothing. Her own death stared her in the face.

8

WITCH OF TAOMAR

FIRE BURST OVER THAYA'S HEAD TOWARDS THE ORDAC, forcing his attention away from her. She couldn't see where it came from but suspected Derry was the cause. She wanted to attack the reptilian, but the split section she'd gained was now for her friends.

She raised her fireshot at Inkesty. He was looming over Engara who was prone on the ground. The woman's bloodied hand was reaching for her sword, but it was a foot too far away. Instead, she grabbed Inkesty's leg and pulled to stagger him. Thaya lost her shot and luckily hadn't fired. She took aim again, but now the warrior woman had rolled on top of the High Priest. A dagger appeared in her hand, and Inkesty fought madly as Engara pressed it towards his throat. Thaya couldn't shoot without risking Engara's life.

Thaya felt something behind her and dropped to one knee. A staff thrummed in the air above her head. She rolled and jumped back on her feet to face the Ordac who hissed and bared his fangs.

She didn't have time to find Derry. She glanced to her

right and glimpsed a bundle of rags smoking on the ground where he had been.

Derry!

It cost her.

The ground moved below her before she felt the pain of the blow to her face. She hit the dirt hard.

The Ordac gripped her arms with thick, scaled fingers, his claws raking her flesh as he spun her over. She raised her palm, filling it with flaming soulfire, but instead of striking her hand away, the Ordac slammed his palm against hers. His other palm he pressed against her forehead.

Frigid cold bolted through her, and she screamed.

"What are you?" The Ordac's low, growling voice echoed in her head. It could speak telepathically?

Her soulfire was somehow caught flaring in her palm, trapped by the Ordac's hand.

Thaya felt a pulling sensation, a strange feeling in her mind which she tried and failed to resist. Images came to her: Engara's face lit by the campfire as they ate their soup; her arrival into the village and Inkesty confronting her; saying goodbye to Khy and watching him leave; then an image of when they stood beside the trashed aircraft.

They're my memories; he's reading my memories!

"Who are you?" the Ordac demanded, gripping her painfully.

"Curse you!" Thaya growled back telepathically.

The Ordac blinked, his greenish-yellow eyes opening wide and his long pupils narrowing to slits.

"Yes, I can mind-speak, you stupid lizard! The question really is, who the hell are YOU, Invader?"

Rather than resist his peculiar mental hold on her, she pushed forwards and fought to enter his mind. There was resistance, and then something gave. She found herself in front of a set of moving images. It was such a surprise, she flopped in the Ordac's grip, her sudden weight overbalancing him and pulling them both to the ground.

There were many images, a chaotic tumbling of them that flashed by without any order or according to any timeline.

In one, she saw blue skies filled with dragons, hundreds of them moving in the same direction. In the distance, another group of dragons flew towards them. Their roars made her legs tremble, and danger cloyed the air. The next image was of an embryo inside an egg with a see-through shell. The embryo was curled up and hugging its own tail, its visible pink heart pumping with life. Another image appeared: a procession of Ordacs walking along a red carpet, bordered on either side by more Ordacs who all had their heads bowed in ceremony. The Ordac walking at the front of the procession wore blood-red robes that swished above her clawed feet. Thaya didn't know how she knew she was female; she just did.

The flashing images made her dizzy and nauseous. She couldn't control them like he could control *her* thoughts and memories.

These Ordacs are masters of the mind.

Her invasion into his mind could only have lasted seconds, for the Ordac screeched and pulled physically away from her. She struggled to hold onto the mental connection, realising she held some power over him this way. He fought her but could not release her palm; a powerful energy magnetised them. She understood that to release the connection, both parties had to will it, and she did not.

More images came and faster, a blur she could not focus on or control. His muscles bunched, and he roared. Exhaus-

tion hit Thaya like a brick, forcing her to release her grip
and pull back. The Ordac tore away from her both physically and mentally, and she cried out, the pain of their
sudden separation leaving her mind and body reeling.

Panting, the Ordac spread short and stubby wings that
had been hidden under his robes and leapt into the air.
With an ear-grating roar, he lifted up and away.

Coming to her senses, Thaya hunted for her dropped
fireshot. There it was, half-hidden by dirt and leaves. She
grabbed and raised it. The Ordac turned and was fast
moving away but might still be in range. She was about to
fire when he simply vanished.

What the hell?

Thaya sucked in a breath and hunted for him, but he
was gone. She slowly lowered her fireshot. She tried to walk
but stumbled, her left leg sore and bruised and pulsing with
pain when she put weight on it. The Ordac had fallen on it
with his full weight. In a daze, Thaya turned to the village
and saw a chaotic scene.

Many houses were on fire. Those closest to her were
almost burnt through, just blackened, smoking ruins.
People ran this way and that, trying to salvage their goods,
their families, and carrying buckets of water that they threw
upon the relentless inferno, the pitiful contents vanishing
instantly in a splash and a hiss.

Thaya's eyes travelled over the strewn bodies, mostly
villagers and some fallen acolytes. Her heart became heavy.
*This place was a tinderbox waiting to explode, and I just
happened to be the spark.* She wiped her eyes, a terrible
sinking feeling settling in her stomach. These people hadn't
deserved death.

The smoke cleared, and she saw Engara on the edge of
the village, swaying.

"Engara?" Thaya called out.

The warrior woman arched her back and tilted her head to the sky, but her eyes were closed. Blood dripped off her sword, off her muddied and bruised arms, and down her temples. Her lip was split and swollen, and her corn-coloured hair matted with blood and dirt. She was a fearful sight that faltered Thaya's limping steps.

At Engara's feet lay a body dressed in acolyte robes, and a few paces beyond, a muddied and bloodied round thing the size of a kid's football. Blood congealed beneath it.

Thaya inhaled sharply and looked away from the decapitation scene. She grasped the warrior woman's arm. Engara looked at her, the whites of her eyes starkly white in her bloody and muddied face, her corneas as clear and blue as the summer skies. Her gaze took a while to focus, and then recognition formed in them.

"Thaya?" She sighed, hunched over, then sunk onto her haunches. Thaya sank down with her.

Engara shook her head. "He did something to me. I couldn't...I couldn't breathe, see, or hear. I was fighting in darkness."

"Magic. These acolytes have powerful magic," Thaya said. "We have to help the people. The village will be lost."

Thaya stood and made to go, but Engara grasped her arm. She looked down at the warrior woman.

"No," Engara shook her head. "Let it burn. For all that I've seen...this place is damned."

"You don't believe that, do you?" Thaya wanted to scoff, but the look in the woman's eyes made her uncertain, and besides, she was a newcomer here; who knew what horrors these people had endured? Had they witnessed the sacrificing of their own children? Thaya didn't want to think about it. "But we must help the people."

"Yes." Engara nodded and took Thaya's outstretched hand.

They started walking into the village, and Engara paused beside a body, one of her Shield Brothers. His face was grey, blood soaked his beard, and his brown eyes were vacant.

"Iyed," Engara whispered. She crouched beside the fallen man and with one hand, closed his eyes forever. She whispered words that Thaya couldn't decipher, then kissed a pendant before concealing it back under her tunic. "I saw him fall. The acolytes you fought, they did something to him from afar. I can't explain it."

"Magic," Thaya said simply.

Engara nodded and with some effort, stood. "Others have fallen."

Coughing through the smoke, they pressed forwards into the heart of the village. A heavy rain began to fall, eliciting a few feeble cheers. Villagers were frantically lifting smoking beams from a collapsed section of housing, and muffled cries came from somewhere below. Thaya and Engara joined them and helped pull out debris, but all the while Thaya's eyes hunted for Derry. Was the kid all right? Had he run away? How much of the fire was his doing?

A voice yelled clearer from beneath the rubble. It took all of them to lift a wooden wall panel, and beneath it a frightened, half-buried, old man looked up at them. Two villagers grabbed his arms and pulled him out to safety. People smiled and hugged each other; Thaya and Engara slapped hands.

It was hard work, looking for survivors, putting out the fires resistant to the rain, and helping the wounded. Though the rain helped dampen the flames, it hampered everything else, and the already slippery ground quickly turned to mud.

It was at the western end of the village that Thaya saw three bodies, two large and one small, just dark mounds from this angle, lying in the mud and rain. She ran to them, her heart thudding in her throat.

The smaller bundle of smoking clothes groaned, and she fell beside it.

"Derry!"

The little boy's face was miraculously free from injury and washed clean from the rain, but the rest of his body smoked, and his clothes appeared melted upon him.

"Thaya? It hurts!" he cried, between sobs.

She wanted to hug him close, but that would hurt him more. "I'm so sorry, Derry." She blinked back tears and gently stroked his face. Slowly, she lifted her hands and called upon the Soulfire. Her whole exhausted body and mind ached while trying to bring it forth, but after a moment her hands began to glow. She moved them over his body until his sobbing quietened and his face scrunched a little less.

"I killed Ma and Da. I didn't mean to." Derry's voice was a scratchy whisper.

"No Derry, you didn't. It was the acolytes."

"They would have killed you like they did my brother and everyone else."

"You saved my life, Derry," she soothed. "Now the village is free. I thank you with all my heart."

Derry shook his head and scrunched up his face with the pain. "No, because the dragon will come."

Thaya shivered and looked up at the sky but could see only smoke and rain clouds. "The people will know that evil came to them; they'll have seen the Ordacs disguised as acolytes."

Derry shook his head again and spoke in a gasping voice. "They cannot see the evil ones; it's like they have been tricked. Some might but most can't. I tried to tell them the truth, then they threw me out."

"Shh, Derry, try not to speak. We must get you to a healer." She tried to scoop her arms under him, but he began to groan and shake, so she stopped.

"Try to rest, Derry."

He nodded but his lip trembled. "Where's Khy? He's returning soon; I dreamt it."

Thaya blinked and tears fell. Dear Urtha, how she needed her soul twin here right now. "I wish he was here, too."

Derry swallowed with some difficulty. "Why am I so cold when I'm on fire?"

He suddenly went limp in her arms, and his head flopped to one side. Thaya held him against her gently as if he were made of the finest glass.

Time passed. There was only silence beyond the sound of rain dripping into puddles.

Thaya jumped when a hand squeezed her shoulder, and she looked up into Engara's haunted face. The rain had stopped. The bodies of Derry's parents had been removed, she hadn't even noticed them take them. "How long have I been here?"

"An hour, and you haven't moved," said the warrior woman.

Slowly, on creaking legs, Thaya stood, the small form of

Derry still in her arms. The boy's face was grey, but he looked utterly serene.

"Did you see them? The Ordacs I fought?" asked Thaya.

"Ordacs?" Engara frowned. "I saw you fight like a lioness against fire and magic. Those priests..." She shook her head, her eyes wide. "No men of god should fight like that.

Thaya pursed her lips. What was wrong with the people here? They were under a spell; they couldn't see what was in front of their eyes. "Derry saw them. You're being tricked. Those whom I fought were no men but...but off-worlders. I'm going to get to the bottom of this." Despite her fiery words, grief and fatigue inflected her voice.

With Engara guiding her, they made their way back to the remains of the village where people had hastily erected a low pyre. There, she placed Derry alongside his parents. Her tears fell silently as Engara led her away.

In the remains of a smoking house whose lower floor miraculously still stood, Thaya glimpsed the flash of an orange robe through a gap in the door. She stopped up short, and Engara followed her gaze. In the next moment, the warrior woman was running forward, her sword in her hand.

"Engara!" Thaya ran after her.

The priest emerged from the charred house. He was one of the younger ones, and his eyes were wide in fear, his bald head muddy and bloody, and his orange robes torn and burnt. He reached a hand forwards, gripped the air and pulled his fist back in a strange motion. He vanished and, in a blink, reappeared several yards away, running as fast as he could.

"Stop!" Thaya shouted, throwing her palm forwards. To her surprise, her soulfire responded, and the acolyte was caught in an invisible grip. She stared at her glowing hand.

He struggled frantically but couldn't break free, and Engara closed the gap between them.

The warrior woman grabbed hold of the priest and viciously swung him to the floor. She was easily a foot taller than the skinny man. Thaya ran to them as Engara slammed her fist into the man's face, knocking him senseless.

"You see this?" The warrior woman gripped his collar and jerked his head to face the devastation of the village. "All this death and destruction is your doing! I hope your gods curse you for it in the afterlife, for I'm about to send you to meet them!"

The warrior woman had exchanged her sword for a dagger, and the acolyte was choking from the throttling grip Engara had on him.

Something within Thaya turned. Despite all the sorrow and fury she felt, despite seeing in the corner of her eye the pyre with Derry's body burning on it, to kill the acolyte now, after so much death, would be wrong. And who was to say how much of a hand he had in this anyway? He wasn't Inkesty, and she barely recognised his face. He was young, just a novice.

"No, Engara." Thaya gripped her wrist.

The warrior woman turned and glared at her. "What?" she shouted.

"I can't let this happen." Thaya felt unnerved but knew it was the right thing to do. "He might be innocent."

"Bullshit! He's mine to kill; I have no such qualms!"

Engara tried to tear away, but for some reason, Thaya was able to hold the powerful woman back. It had to be her will and her Soulfire at work; she could feel it tingling in her solar plexus and her hands.

"How dare you use your witchery powers on me!" Engara roared.

Thaya shook her head. "You know I'm no witch. This man must be given a second chance. To kill him now would be cold-blooded. It would be murder. He's not fighting you, he's trying to run away."

Engara's stare was livid. "If you let him live, he'll take his poison elsewhere and spread it. Who knows how many innocents he has killed?"

"It could be none," Thaya said quietly, not quite believing it. "But we can't kill him like this, it would make us like them."

It took a long moment and extreme control, but the warrior woman stopped resisting her. In a quick motion, she let go of the acolyte and threw down her dagger and then her sword. She pulled in close to Thaya's face. "He does not deserve your mercy."

Engara whipped her wrist away, and Thaya released her grasp. She swallowed against the hard lump in her throat watching the warrior woman stalk away, then turned to the acolyte who was on his hands and knees, coughing. She grabbed hold of him by the forearm, feeling the soulfire fill her palms. He felt it, too, for he winced and clenched his jaw.

"You've been given a second chance, by ill or by good remains to be seen. But if you cross either of our paths again, by the Creator it will be your end." She threw him down, swallowing again and watched him struggle onto his feet, then run into the forest. Had she done the right thing? Engara would probably track him and hunt him down anyway. The warrior woman was right on all counts—he didn't deserve her mercy, nor did he deserve to live—but Thaya couldn't kill him. To do so at this moment felt very wrong. She stared into the forest where he had gone.

Sometimes things go bad, we mess up, perhaps we all deserve a second chance. What if it had been me? I would never have joined the acolytes in the first place, but perhaps I would like a second chance. Will he only do bad again? He still deserves the opportunity; we all deserve the opportunity to make amends. Or perhaps I'm just being weak...

She picked up Engara's sword and dagger and walked back to the smoking village deep in thought, her emotions and her body feeling like they were in tatters. It didn't really matter what anyone's else actions were, it only mattered what her actions were, and she had chosen mercy over revenge. It felt, even now, like it had been the right thing to do. There was something in that, and she wanted to sit in a quiet place and think about it for a long while.

Instead, she hunted for Engara, but she was nowhere to be seen, although she found one of her Shield Brothers salvaging items from the debris. He stood as she approached, a metal spoon and crockpot in his hands, his face barely visible under layers of soot, dirt and dried blood.

"These are Engara's," she said, passing him the sword and dagger. He took them from her with a nod. "I'm going to check the temple," she added.

The man wiped his forehead. "Be careful, that place is...cursed."

Thaya shrugged. "It can't be any worse than what just happened here."

He pursed his lips and nodded but said no more.

With some trepidation, she left the village, entered the quiet of the forest and approached the looming, grey-bricked building. She hadn't had the pleasure of viewing it properly before; either she'd been locked inside one of its cells or was being dragged face down in the mud before it.

Her eyes travelled down the building, from the smaller stones at the top to the larger ones lower down, and settled on the enormous, pale foundation stones at its base. Her eyes widened, and she paused. The base stones were veritable boulders, far too large and heavy for even a hundred men to lift.

They look like the stones in the Old Temple ruin back home, only pale pink rather than yellow. They're ancient, truly, this whole structure has been built on something far, far older. Maybe there was an ancient civilisation here, too, like back home. Maybe they came from Lonohassa, or somewhere else where evil and cataclysms had befallen them and driven them out.

For Thaya, the ancient megaliths were a sign of an extremely ancient and advanced race of humans, long forgotten by time and complacent peoples. Holiness and magic thrived in the distant past, and she wished she could reach out to it.

She placed her hands on her hips and looked up the temple's towering, ominous spire with a shiver. Strange statues of creatures with long tongues and fangs surrounded its base; they looked like a mix between a dog and a lizard with snouts, pointy ears, long tails and scales. At its tip, reaching high into the sky, was an iron pole with a round ball at the top, extending the height of the spire by another yard. Thaya looked again. On second thought, the pole was too black to be iron.

Some kind of black metal I've not seen before. Hmm, or maybe I HAVE seen it before.

The manacles they'd bound her with, which somehow stopped her soulfire, had been of a similar dark metal, possibly the same type.

Maybe it's reptilian metal and not from Urtha at all, she thought. As she stared, a faint ripple flowed out from the round ball. She squinted at it harder, and it happened again, a ripple, as if she was looking at the sky reflected in a lake and someone had dropped a pebble into it.

An ear-breaking scream made her jump. Moments later, a book the size of a paving slab crashed through one of the heavily decorated, stained-glass windows. The book bounced once leaving a crater in the sodden grass, and landed with a thud in the mud. Thaya glimpsed Engara's blonde locks inside as she stalked past the broken window.

On the warpath for more evil acolyte things, Thaya thought with a smile. At least the warrior woman was venting her rage usefully.

Thaya was about to make her way inside when a strange whispering filled the air, and a dull ache began in her head. She looked around. There was no one there—were the whispers coming from inside her head?

She found herself staring at the book. It had a symbol on it: a nine-pointed star with two snakes, maybe more, entwined around it and eating each other's tails.

There was a nine-pointed star at the top of the statue behind the altar in their temple; it looks to be in the same style.

Slowly, she walked towards it, and the whispers intensified.

It's just a book. One of their stupid holy books, or an evil spell book or something.

But now she thought about it, there was something more about that symbol. She'd seen it a long time ago, someplace else. Nothing surprising there, not when she *had* spent her childhood lost in the library.

She squatted on her knees and touched the symbol. Suddenly, images and information appeared in her mind, as if she were seeing through her hand and her hand was receiving or detecting information about the book. It was exactly the same sensation she felt when she touched Portal

Stones, only now she looked upon a sea of images and not a map of the stars. A cacophony of voices suddenly murmured in her head. She tried to focus on the words, but they spoke a language she did not recognise, and their voices were strange, deeper, more rasping.

Not human voices! Her dull headache intensified. *What am I seeing?*

Simply asking the question caused the images and information to become more ordered in her mind. She saw again where she had first seen the symbol: high shelves reaching to the ceiling and filled with row upon row of books, and between the shelves were benches, and on those benches, people sat reading.

Yes, it was in the library, I remember now.

In front of her were stacks of books waiting to be shelved, and on top of one of the stacks was a book with many symbols upon it, including the nine-pointed star and snakes. She whispered aloud the title: "Of the Mystic and Grand Races of Yore."

She traced the star and sought the Truth. "The star is a sun...or a planet...and the snakes? They mean a clan. Of people? No, it's the symbol of an Order, and the people are Ordacs."

In her mind, she saw a vast hall filled with Ordacs, and before them rose a beast of black scales and smoke. It was a black dragon, the largest she'd ever seen.

Ordacs...is this their symbol? Could it be the name of the black dragon? Do other reptilians from their planet call themselves something else?

As soon as she asked the question, a bright image flashed in her mind: a blue reptile surrounded in light and with brilliant eyes that shone gold like the sun. The reptile was serene, meditative, the opposite of the hulking black dragon.

Even just thinking it, the black dragon reappeared before her. She tried to look away from its glowing amber eyes, but they stared right through her. She tore her hand away from the symbol on the book, and the black dragon vanished. Her hand throbbed with heat, and the images flickering in her mind faded with every heartbeat.

The strange whispering suddenly ceased, leaving her in a deafening silence that made her giddy. She looked up at the overcast sky. How much time had passed? She should go and find Engara.

A creeping sensation stole over her, and she shivered. Suddenly the book twitched, jerked, then flew open, its crisp, ecru pages leafing forwards and backwards as if unseen hands flicked through them. The pages revealed the same vivid images she had glimpsed in her mind, and symbols and text she didn't understand.

9

SECRET CHAMBERS

THE WHISPERING VOICES GREW LOUDER, AND PECULIAR GREY wisps formed and swirled around the book.

Ghosts, evil spirits! Thaya's breathing became fast and shallow. She started to back away.

Above the book, a ghostly, skeletal hand reached out of the air and pointed down at a page. The pages ceased flicking back and forth and stayed open, revealing lines of text written in blood-red ink. She squinted at the scrawling writing, but the language was foreign. The voices spoke louder, no longer whispering but chanting as if reciting a prayer or even the words on the page.

The wisps dancing around the book took form, becoming ghostly, half-dog, half-lizard beings like those decorating the temples' rooftops. They yipped and yelped and snapped at each other as they ran around the book.

Someone screamed. Thaya jumped and whirled around. A huge, wooden candlestick smashed through another stained-glass window, and a red-faced Engara stood the other side, fuming.

"Engara? The book!" Thaya shouted and pointed at it.

Engara squinted and paled. "I'll be right there." She disappeared from the window.

Thaya silently stepped back from the ghostly creatures, hoping to get away quietly.

Thunder rumbled.

She glanced up. Storm clouds built above the spire and circled its tip. The pressure grew, and her heart began to pound. More ghostly shapes formed, this time of people—the tall forms of adults and smaller forms of children. There were lots of children. None of them moved liked the lizard dogs; they simply stood in a semicircle, several yards from the book.

The Ordac voices grew louder, becoming threatening.

"The dead have risen—those whom they sacrificed!" Engara gasped, making her jump. The warrior woman had come up behind her silently, her sweaty, red face turning deathly pale.

"How can you be sure?" Thaya was sceptical.

"Who else would they be? One of them could be my son! Look! The evil hounds are growling at them!"

Engara was right. The hounds stopped bounding around the book and turned to face the semicircle of humans. The human ghosts stepped forwards slowly, one foot at a time, and the hounds growled louder. More dogs bounded out of the ether to join the others until there were over a dozen reptilian canines.

A spectre's face appeared half a yard from Thaya's cheek.

"Release us!" it cried, making her leap out of her skin and raise her fireshot. She stood there shaking, but the ghostly face was already fading.

"Maybe we should get out of here," Thaya rasped.

"We can't, look, we're surrounded!" Engara raised her sword and crouched into a fighting stance. Many ghostly humans now stepped forwards towards Thaya and Engara and the book, and more lizard dogs appeared. One ran at them, snarling and baring its teeth. Engara swiped at it with her sword, the blade passing through its ghostly flesh, and it yelped and ran back to its pack.

"Release us," a ghost wailed.

The others picked up the chant, and their pain-filled moaning became an unbearable cacophony.

"Release us!"

"Thaya, do something! They're asking *you* for help!" Engara hissed.

"What? How can I help? I'm not a magi or a priest!" And she certainly had no powers to exorcise the dead. And yet she knew, she felt, Engara was right, these ghosts were asking for her help.

"Release us!"

"How?" Thaya cried.

She let her hands fill and glow with golden soulfire, but what was she supposed to do with it? The baying of the reptilian hounds and the wailing of the people were driving her mad. She held her hands out in front of her and let the soulfire burst from them of its own accord. It arced straight into the book, sending the ghost hounds scattering.

The book burst into golden fire, and the pages began flickering back and forth frantically again. The images on the pages moved and contorted, and the whispering voices screamed and chanted louder. The human ghosts ceased stepping forwards and stood still, murmurs of awe and expectation emanating from them. The hounds ran back to the book, howling wildly and snapping at the golden flames licking it. The book shivered and then exploded; a bright bubble of light flared out and the force field knocked everything, both living and dead, to the ground.

Thaya's ears rang with the explosion, and she tried to shake the haze from her head. The book had gone, disintegrated. The hounds sat on their hind legs, lifted their snouts, and howled mournfully. They began to fade, and a strange silence descended. The human ghosts turned to Thaya as if they expected her to do something more. She raised her eyebrows.

"You are released now?" Her voice shook as she posed the question.

A great releasing sigh came from the ghosts, and then they began to fade like the dogs. The ominous pressure pushing down on her abated, and she felt faint from the sudden release. She sat down heavily on the grass, and Engara leant on her sword, breathing hard. As her Shield Brother had her primary sword, Thaya was beginning to realise the warrior woman was never unarmed. Both women took deep breaths.

"They were the ghosts of the dead, the missing and the sacrificed. I recognised some of their faces." Engara shivered and muttered to herself. "They are released now, rest in peace."

"I'm glad we could help in some way," said Thaya, still trying to understand what had happened. "What were those *things?*"

"Gargoyles. Demons. Protectors of those acolyte filth and their decrepit texts." Engara scowled and spat onto the grass.

Thaya shivered. "Have you finished in there?" She nodded to the temple and its smashed windows, hoping Engara's rage had subsided somewhat.

"Hardly. That foul, desecrated place needs to be torched to the ground. Come, there's something I want to show you. I think it could be magical."

The last thing Thaya wanted to do was to go into that building again, but she couldn't let Engara go alone, and neither did she fancy standing out here on her own. There could be more ghosts...

With a shiver, she walked back into the place that had been her prison. People had entered here and never left. Where had they been killed? Her gift for knowing the truth didn't fail her, and her mind replied with images.

On the altar...near where they murdered those two other acolytes. Blood Magic.

Blood Magic? She'd never heard of that term before. Add that to the list of questions she wanted to place before the magi. This prison really *did* need obliterating and all evil purged.

Thaya shivered as they stood before the altar in the enormous hall. Engara had done a good job of breaking most of the windows, pushing over all the pews, and toppling all the statues that her strength allowed, along with anything else that could be tipped over, thrown, or dislodged.

Engara gripped her sword tightly. "Derry had a dream he told me about once. He didn't trust anybody in the village other than the Shield. We only half listened to his stories of course, he's just a kid, but he was never one for lying. Derry said he saw a dark chamber beyond the altar that even most acolytes weren't aware of. He was weird like that, seeing things in his dreams that no one could possibly know, or indeed live to tell about." The warrior woman visibly shivered.

"I wasn't here when they cast him out but was with my Shield Brothers hunting. The rage I felt when I learned what they'd done...Then I saw you return the boy, and I knew it should have been me standing next to him. The people of Taomar are *my* responsibility. Imagine all the guilt I felt inside for it not being me who saved him. I respected you from that moment forward, and I knew you were a good person. You taught me something that day: bravery of a different kind. Even if you were a witch, like they told everyone you were, I knew I couldn't let them harm you, our guest, like I had failed Derry."

"The hardest thing is to stand up to your peers," said Thaya. "Had it been my village watching me, judging me, and with all the power of the acolytes, would I have gone against them all? I doubt it. I know what the acolytes can do, they twist the truth, distort people's minds. You can't blame yourself for what happened to Derry."

Engara looked unconvinced as she turned her gaze back to the altar. She then strode behind it and touched the wall as if looking for something.

"Where's this magical thing you mentioned?" Thaya came up beside her.

"Well, I couldn't find the hidden chamber Derry mentioned, so I reckoned it was magically hidden or something. Like maybe this is a magical wall or there's a magical level or...I dunno, you're the one with the special powers!" Engara sighed and ran a hand through her hair that was now resembling a small haystack with strands breaking loose and sticking out of her braids and clasps.

Thaya approached the wall, hunting every nook and cranny for anything peculiar. "Let's see what we can find." She lifted a hand and touched the smooth, pale yellow, painted section to the right of the rounded obelisk statue.

Warmth grew in her hands and pressure in her mind. Images, a feeling, a knowing. She pulled her hands an inch off the wall, and the images vanished along with the warmth and pressure.

"So strange," muttered Thaya.

"What is it?" asked Engara.

"Huh?" She hadn't realised she'd spoken aloud. "It's... hmm, I don't know how to explain it, but more and more I'm able to *see* things through my hands. I don't know how or why; it's not magic but something else... It's like I can read things with my palms."

Engara frowned, but Thaya couldn't offer her any more explanation. "It's for this reason, and other similar things, I'm going to the magi. Maybe they can help me understand these strange powers. Maybe they can help me use them better, for good, of course."

Engara arched one eyebrow. "I've seen too much evil done with magic to ever believe it's a good thing. Look at Derry; his own powers killed him."

Thaya remembered the Nuakki with their magic, enslaving humans to work in the mines, wiping their memories and all that they were from their minds. She shrugged. "I agree. I've also seen many evil beings do evil things with great power they should not have, but to better understand my powers will give me greater control over them. I've yet to know whether magi can be trusted. I've met only one, and she was good."

Thaya raised her hands and placed them on the wall again. Immediately the warmth, the pressure, and the images returned. She tried to order them, to understand them, but they were hard to grasp, slippery like eels, and obscure as if she were in a dark room with only a dim glow to light everything. She wasn't entirely sure if she saw things or felt them; it was more of a see-feel sensing.

She tried to navigate around the area she was sensing. "I see a room, somewhere beyond this wall, or maybe beneath it. I sense it behind and below, but how to access it? The walls are smooth, not made of brick, like a room carved out of a cave. There are tunnels leading off from it, but I sense these are sealed, and not even the acolytes know of their existence."

Thaya wondered what the room was used for and heard her pulse throb in her head.

Darkness. Terror. Pain. Blood dripping. Feeding.

She sensed Engara wanting to know what she saw and reluctantly repeated what she had seen and felt. She heard Ordacs barking orders at each other in their hissing language. She felt magic, dark and heavy—was it Blood Magic? If she pressed for more, she'd see it, but she didn't want to, she felt sick from the feeling as it was.

There's more to the chamber, though, what is it?

The image grew lighter as if a candle had been lit, and she welcomed the warmth and light that forced away the darkness. She squinted at the light and realised it wasn't a candle but a light that stayed still, powered by some source she couldn't determine. It didn't feel like magic, was warm, not hot like a flame, and it was contained in a round, glass, jar-like apparatus.

Faces appeared, smiling children, laughing adults. Some of the women had their hair held up in elaborate braids while others simply wore it long and straight. The men, too, had hair and beards that were neatly trimmed, and everyone was dressed simply in smart, clean tunics. Their faces were tanned and rounded, not as hard and angular as the people of Taomar. They were dignified, but she *knew* they weren't royalty; they were ordinary people.

When? she wondered. A sense of great time passing came to her, possibly even eons. She held her breath and realised she was looking at something that had taken place a very, very long time ago, but how long, she couldn't know.

She spoke what she had determined. "In the beginning, the chamber beyond wasn't intended for darkness or magic, it was a temporary dwelling place for ordinary people. Once this was deep underground, but humans don't like living in caves. Why would they be here?"

Engara's voice came from far away. Thaya wondered if the woman was far away or if she was just so deep into the image it simply sounded like she was. "There's a myth, an ancient legend, before even when the sea became salty, that the world was attacked, and great changes happened. The people were led underground by beings of light, and for thousands of years they lived there until it was safe to return to the surface. In more recent myths, it is said this whole area used to be under the ocean, so maybe great changes have occurred."

Thaya swallowed, suddenly afraid of what she had seen, the weight of eons pressing down upon her as the Old Temple near her home used to make her feel. "I, too, have vague memories of those myths. If we don't know our own history, how can we ever know ourselves?"

"A wise question, I feel, but not one we can ever answer," Engara replied. "The Priesthood like to build their temples on ancient places. Maybe those places were originally built on places of power? Maybe the acolytes can feel this power and want to use it for their own purposes."

"Yes, I think that might be true," Thaya agreed, feeling the image fade as she no longer pressed it.

"Did you find a way in?"

"Oh, I shall search for one." Thaya resumed her concentration, no longer querying but probing with her mind for a way to get into the room, for something that moved or opened, like a door or a handle.

An increasing sense of urgency pushed her on, and she suddenly felt a presence, a faint, gentle presence brushing the corners of her awareness, barely there. She found an archway. It was blocked by stone when once it wouldn't have been blocked at all. *Does the stone move?* She imagined it rolling—not like a ball would roll, top over bottom, but more like a planet would rotate on its horizontal axis. No human strength could move such a stone; only those with magic or similar power.

"Talk to me, Thaya," said the warrior woman.

Thaya blinked, her eyes adjusting to the light of the chamber. "We have to hurry—I don't know why—but we have to be quick. There's a stone that moves—a big one. I might be able to move it if I have the right kind of power."

The warrior woman set about feeling the wall, too. "If you can read stones, I think you can move them. This should be destroyed too," she said, touching the phallic-like obelisk. "Hey look, there's a faint line here."

Thaya had to stand on tiptoes to inspect the line that was at Engara's eye height.

"Want me to lift you up?" Engara asked sweetly.

"Yeah, right." Thaya snorted. "Hmm, the line runs all the way round, but it's barely a hair-breadth. And look at the base, and there by the wall, there's no dust. It's like they swept this bit but not that. Hmm, this could be it but how to—"

As she pushed upon the base of the column, it moved, easily, without a sound and as if it weighed nothing. An enormous disk, cut out of the obelisk and taller than she, slowly swung out under her tingling hands, revealing an arched doorway in the wall behind it.

She hadn't used magic, not that she was aware of, or any strength, and yet when Engara had pressed upon it moments before, it hadn't budged. Thaya looked at her hands. Would she have been able to open it had the iron manacles been on her wrists? She doubted it.

There's clearly more to power than just magic... What exactly is soulfire—the power of my soul?

A foul draft exuded as the base of the disc finished opening. Thaya and Engara stood still and stared into the darkness, the silence palpable as each expected wraiths to appear before them.

10

EIR'ANDEHARI

POOLING SOULFIRE INTO HER HANDS FOR LIGHT AND INCITING A wary look from Engara, Thaya stepped into the darkness. She didn't need the light for long, for as she walked down the ancient steps moulded out of solid stone, a white light grew ahead.

The gentle presence Thaya had felt earlier became stronger, and she remembered the handsome elf-man by the fountain she had met in her dream. His presence was so strong, she was sure he was right beside her.

"This is it," he whispered, making her jump. His excitement was palpable.

Is he really here? Thaya wondered, looking around but seeing only Engara. *Does he mean the 'gift'?*

"Yes," his whisper echoed back.

Thaya frowned. What was this strange gift?

The light ahead grew brighter as they neared, somehow activated by their presence. It came from a crystal or glass lamp about two palms wide, set in the middle of a stone table. The table itself was carved out of the solid ground with spaces underneath for seated people to put their legs.

"The room is small," said Engara behind her. "Large for a family to prepare and eat dinner maybe, but it's not a function room or temple; it's a living space, you're right. But look at two fake doorways yonder, they're filled with solid stone and don't go anywhere, strange."

"Once they were through-ways into passages," said Thaya. "That's what I saw at least. Someone must have blocked them up."

She turned her attention back to the glowing object. The thick glass looked broken, for one side was smooth and round and the other was sharp and jagged. "Like a crystal ball broken in two."

"Eir'andehari!" The elf-man whispered in her mind in awe. Thaya heard his whisper echo around the chamber, but Engara didn't respond so the warrior woman couldn't have heard it.

"Eir'an-de-ha-ri," Thaya slowly repeated aloud the name she heard in her head. "The Eye of Ahro."

"What did you say?" Engara turned to her, frowning. "It sounded Elvish." The warrior woman surprised her with her insight.

"Eir'andehari? Yes, it does. I heard it in my head. Do you know Elvish?"

Engara laughed like a little girl. It sounded loud in the cave, and the light twinkled prettily as if affected by the sound. "My favourite myths and fairy stories as a child were always of the elves. I named all my toys with Elvish names."

Thaya smiled. It was funny to see the girlish side of this imposing warrior. "I had a dream, and in it an elf-man came to me. I feel his presence close... I think he's looking for this."

"Then take it and let's be gone from here," Engara said with a shiver. "Don't worry, I won't destroy it. There's nothing else in this room to waste our time on unless we can blow out the stone blocking the tunnels."

The thought of wandering through dark tunnels for days gave Thaya the shivers. "No, let's go."

"Hurry, Thaya, something comes!" the elf-man suddenly said loudly, urgently.

She ceased her inspection and grabbed the object. Suddenly, its light went out, plunging them into darkness. Through her hands, images flooded from the object into her mind. The elven relic wanted her to know something, and she scrunched her eyes shut.

A terrible screech.

The ground shaking.

Masonry falling.

Fire. Fire everywhere, burning everything and igniting even stone.

She remembered the book Engara had thrown through the window and again saw its pages flickering back and forth to Ordacian chanting.

It's a spell; they were chanting a spell! A spell to do what?

Again, a terrible screech echoed through her mind.

A summoning spell? The thought made her go cold.

"Come on, Thaya!" Engara grabbed her arm, snapping her out of it. They ran and plunged into the light spilling through the doorway.

That terrible screech came again, but this time it wasn't in her head. It sounded like a hundred eagles screaming at once. Engara yelped and cowered. The ground trembled so violently, Thaya fell against the golden altar clutching the broken, crystal relic to her chest.

"What in hell is going on?" shouted Engara, drawing her sword.

Another terrifying screech was drowned out by the sound of cracking stone as the entire roof beyond the obelisk collapsed. Bricks, mortar and tiles cascaded and shattered on the polished floor just as the relic had shown Thaya only moments before. Any remaining windows shattered, and great gusts of wind billowed dust and debris into the air.

Fire, as she had never seen before, spewed along hallways and through broken doorways. It fell as an orange torrent, smothering everything. Thaya and Engara fell back against the wall, shielding their faces from the debris and the heat. The fire engulfed everything—even the stone burned.

An enormous, scaled talon, with claws half a yard long, smashed down upon a still-standing section of temple wall, flattening it.

Thaya gulped in air and stared up into the enormous face of a dragon.

"Oh shit!"

Thaya couldn't move. Her legs simply wouldn't respond. Everything within her screamed at her to run. She even thought she heard the elf-man scream it, too, but she couldn't. Neither could Engara. The warrior woman was hunched over and leaning against the wall, trembling. She was only just managing to hold her sword in a flaccid grip. The crystal relic pulsed with light in Thaya's grasp and then darkened again.

"That belongs to me." The dragon's voice was deep and rumbling yet distinctly female. It breathed a bout of choking sulphuric gas over them, its green eyes narrowed into dangerous slits and its upper lip peeled back into a snarl to reveal hideous yellow fangs. It was the same dragon she and Khy had faced before, and only narrowly escaped

Thaya was so surprised to hear the dragon speak, it broke through the terror that had rooted her to the spot.

"Apparently, it doesn't," she retorted, then did what her senses were screaming at her to do: she ran.

Clutching the relic, she leapt over fallen masonry towards a collapsed section of a wall, hoping to draw the dragon away from Engara. The dragon followed with terrible speed.

Thaya jumped, tripped and slid down the other side of the rubble.

I'm mad! Truly mad! No one can outrun a dragon!

Her hands glowed with soulfire, but what the hell could that do for her? The dragon roared, and Thaya whimpered. She dared to look back and saw the enormous flying lizard spread its wings high in the ruin of the temple. Its tail smashed through the obelisk, the spiked end acting as a wrecking ball as it slammed through stone and turned it to powder.

Great God, I hope Engara is still alive!

The dragon whirled around again and smashed its tail through the turret, sending the entire structure crumbling to the floor. The black-iron rod at its peak fell, pulsing strangely, and the sky trembled. Suddenly, lines of molten red snaked above as if a great dome of glass was fracturing and melting in the heat. It vanished, and Thaya suddenly felt a release, as if a constant noise had finally stopped or a pressure headache had abated.

Light flared from the relic in her hands. It glowed, but

darkly, and inside it moved black clouds mixed with midnight blue and indigo, like stormy skies at night.

"The dragon and her kin used the Eye and the black metal to keep the people of Taomar asleep, to keep them from seeing the truth," the elf-man whispered in her head reminding her he was there. But he was worryingly faint and far away.

Thaya had a hundred questions. How did the dragon get the elven relic? Had the Ordacs stolen it from the alien ship? Were elves driving the ship? But there was only time to run, to run and try to not look back.

There came a moment of silence. The forest was just ahead, if she could just reach the trees...

The behemoth landed just yards in front of her, shaking the ground and flattening pine trees as if they were mere matchsticks. Thaya skidded and fell onto her knees. The dragon whipped her tail, and Thaya, unable to move out of the way fast enough, flattened herself on the ground. It wasn't enough. The tail slammed into her, knocking the wind and sense out of her, and she watched the ground fall away below. The elven artefact flew out of her hands. She screamed and grappled for it, then crashed into a tree. Bark and pine needles tore at her skin, boughs crunched her ribs, and she thudded heavily to the ground.

"No," the elf-man whispered faintly in her ear, and then she couldn't feel him anymore.

The dragon lunged after the tumbling relic and with a victorious roar, caught the tiny thing in its huge talons. Every muscle in Thaya's body groaned and trembled as she pushed herself onto her knees.

The dragon began hunting for her through the forest.

"Where are you, little elf-friend? You shall not live; none of them here shall live."

Thaya stood up, letting the soulfire fill her. "You stole

that from them! You enslaved the people here! How many have your spawn murdered and sacrificed?"

"They all belong to me!" The dragon roared, and with one swipe of her tail, felled the trees standing between them, flattening Thaya's cover.

Thaya cowered under the falling debris of bark boughs and leaves.

She stood, clenched her fists, and glared at the beast. The dragon breathed in, its nostrils glowing red, and Thaya raised her hands. The dragon roared, sending a rolling inferno towards her. Thaya released her soulfire.

What happened next was not what she expected. A flaming tornado didn't engulf her; instead, everything turned cold and grey as if she had plunged into a dense fog. It was so thick she couldn't even see her feet, and so heavy she couldn't hear anything but a faint wind in the trees.

A sound came from behind her. Footsteps. She turned.

No, not footsteps, hoof-beats.

She knew that gait! Her heart jumped with joy, and she squinted into the fog, hesitantly making her way forwards.

"Khy?"

His horn was the first thing to appear out of the fog, shining silver and gold, and humming with magic. Indigo eyes bright with uncanny, other-worldly intelligence beheld her. At first he appeared white, but when the fog faded around him, his coat became shimmering lilac.

She ran and flung her arms around his neck. He pressed his chin against her back. Her twin soul had returned to her; now they were whole, now they were strong. There were no words, just a moment of being, a moment to reconnect.

Thaya pulled away. "The dragon! She has the elven crystal. You cast this fog and not she?"

He nodded. "You cannot fight a dragon, so it looks like I returned at the perfect time."

"Perfect timing? How about returning before they threw me in prison?" Thaya's voice was shrill.

Khy flicked his tail. "Prison? Hmm. I returned as soon as I could. The wound was worse than it looked. It might never fully heal."

Thaya bit back a retort and looked at where his wound had been. His hair now covered it perfectly.

Khy looked around him. "If we leave the safety of the mist, we'll have to face a raging dragon."

"We have to! What about the people?"

"I'll not let you go out there. The risk is too great."

Thaya shook her head. Khy's injury must have been bad, he was always up for a fight. "We can't just leave them to their deaths, they could be burning alive right now!"

"And what, exactly, do you think you can do?" Khy's eyes were wide with intrigue.

"Fight with me. Help me get back the elven crystal."

"I know nothing about fighting dragons. And it's a big one."

"Neither do I, but..." Thaya swallowed, suddenly uncertain. "But they killed Derry."

Khy flared his nostrils, his gaze turning back to searching the mist. After a moment he said, "Then we should do something."

Thaya squealed and clung to Khy's back as they exited the mist at full speed. The plan was simple: lead the dragon away from the people and hopefully get away themselves.

The mist became fire. Trees cracked and hissed in the

flames while boughs fell in their path, forcing Khy to leap over them. His horn flared brightly like a beacon, and somewhere close, the dragon roared. That terrifying noise made her tremble. Sweat prickled her skin, and her hands tingled with soulfire. Her fireshot was safely tucked in her belt, but what good was that against a dragon? She dared to glance back and wished she hadn't.

Through the smoke and flames, the dragon's enormous head emerged. Huge fangs protruded over its lip, and it appeared to be grinning. Its eyes narrowed at her and then widened as it focussed on her mount, its wings faltering. Instead of closing the gap between them, the dragon kept its distance.

She's afraid of Khy!

The realisation surprised Thaya. She had to still be suffering from the wound Khy had given her.

"Fire!" she screamed as dragon flames rolled towards them.

Khy banked right, and the flames rolled over his protective shield. His horn glowed, and lightning arced from it like a whip over their heads and smacked into the dragon's snout. The dragon roared and twisted in the air, falling behind. Thaya looked down. They moved so fast, the ground was a blur beneath Khy's hooves, as if he no longer touched it at all.

She looked ahead. It was growing dark beyond the smoke. Dusk had fallen. She couldn't see the people of Taomar through the trees, smoke and fire, but she did catch glimpses of the destroyed temple. It was completely flattened, just blocks of rubble and mortar. And where was Engara? Thaya's mouth dried.

A steep wall of mountain loomed above the trees before

them—an unscalable sheer cliff. Thaya gritted her teeth, hoping Khy had a plan.

"Call your power to you—combine it with mine," Khy spoke in her mind.

She wanted to ask 'how' and 'why' but did as he asked. She filled her solar plexus with energy, let it rise within her, and then pushed it down her arms and out of her hands that gripped Khy's mane. She felt him draw upon it and their energies mingling, doubling, then trebling as they became more than the sum of their parts.

The wall of rock appeared through the trees. Golden light flared from Khy's horn into the cliff face. A thick line of light appeared on the rock as if invisible hands drew upon it. The line moved up, across, then down, drawing a rectangle of light in stone. The stone melted away and the rectangle became a doorway of light. Thaya shut her eyes and screamed as they galloped through it.

They didn't slam into hard rock crushing every bone in their bodies; they ran, quite simply, into a field of light. An ear-piercing screech came from behind them, followed by a great boom that shook the world. The light faded to dark and a sudden silence. A sense of a deep enclosed space engulfed her, and a heartbeat later, they exited into the overcast gloominess of dusk.

Thaya gasped. They were several hundred feet higher up the mountain than where they had entered it, running on the narrowest, most precarious ledge even a goat would stumble on. She clung to Khy as they reached a wider plateau.

He skidded on shale as he tried to slow, his flanks quivering, his muscles bunching as they came to a sudden stop.

Her blood pounded in her ears, and she swallowed. Was Khy as afraid as she was? She'd never really seen him afraid, and she didn't detect it now. *Uncertain, perhaps, but not afraid.* His ears were pricked forward as he looked down at the dragon floundering on the mountainside below them.

Blood smeared the dragon's left wing. It hung lower than the right as she struggled into the air. The dragon roared and lifted higher, coming closer. Thaya held her breath, and Khy's horn pulsed. The shimmer of a concealing shield descended, and the dragon's gaze passed over them, seeing only rock. The dragon roared and circled once more before turning away. The forest fires cast its underside in orange as it flew low over them. Thaya watched the beast silently as it tilted its wings and lifted into the clouds, heading towards a distant mountain range.

It's gone, thank the light, and along with it the elven relic...

Thaya slowly let her breath go. "How did you do that, open a doorway through the rock?"

"I didn't, you did," Khy replied. "You created an opening, and I facilitated it. It was a good idea." He nodded.

Thaya blinked. "How did I do that?" she murmured, going back over the events. "I did imagine us going through the rock as if into a tunnel, like going through portals, but I didn't create the thing."

"Imagination and magic *are* power. Together, they are creation," Khy explained. "You imagined it, I directed it, with willpower."

"We can do that? Together?"

"Of course. Especially so with our connection."

Thaya began to think of the possibilities; a whole world of power and magic opening up to her. *But then I'd need to understand how Khy directed his willpower...actually, there's a lot I need to understand!*

She thought about Engara. "We'd better get back to Taomar, or what's left of it. Pray there are people still alive."

Even with Khy carrying her, it took a long time in the drizzle to carefully descend and control-slide down the mountainside. She constantly scanned the skies for the dragon, her ears listening for any sound of Ordacs. There were none. The drizzle also quickly dampened any remaining fires.

They didn't make it all the way back to Taomar, for along the road a line of weary people walked, heads hidden in hoods, gazes cast down at the ground in front of them. They didn't even carry lanterns to light the way. Thaya dismounted and ran to the tall figure leading them.

"Engara?"

The warrior woman looked up, and beneath the soot and blood, her blue eyes shone, and she smiled. "Thaya! I thought you were—"

The two women embraced, and Thaya gasped in the other woman's bear hug.

They drew apart and Thaya said, "Is this all there is? There are only a hundred or so people from a town of thousands."

Engara looked down the bedraggled line of homeless people. "These aren't all. There are some who wouldn't leave and some too sick to leave. These are the ones who want to go or want to follow me. I'll protect them until I can no longer. I will lead the people, *my* people, in the way my mother did before me, and her mother before that."

"You're now Shield Mother, as was your birthright." Thaya smiled at her friend.

Engara blinked back tears and stood tall. She squinted through the drizzle at Khy who stood some way away. "I see you've found a horse."

"This is my companion, the one I told you about."

"You waited for a horse?" Engara raised her eyebrows.

"Not just any horse." Thaya winked.

Engara gave her one of her peculiar looks again as if she thought her mad or telling a crazy truth.

"Look again." Thaya smiled.

For a moment, Khy caused himself to shimmer, and Engara's eyes widened and lit up with wonder. "Oh my! Can it be?"

Thaya nodded. "Yes, but it's a very long story. One for when we're seated before a fire in your town's tavern and cupping hot soup and wine."

Engara laughed and gripped Thaya's shoulder, but her eyes kept darting back to Khy.

"Indeed, Thaya of Havendell, you are without a doubt the most peculiar and interesting person I have ever met. You'll always have a place in our homes and at our table wherever our paths may meet. But for now, you are right: that dragon might return, and Ordacs might already be swarming the land. We must go. We make the long journey to my sister's clan for food and shelter, then we will begin our life anew."

The warrior woman pointed to the northeast, but Thaya's destination lay a long way east. As much as she wanted to travel with her new friend, she could not. And what of the relic the dragon had stolen? Thaya sighed. The elf couldn't expect her to fight a dragon, could he?

"Here, take this." Engara unslung a sack from her shoulder and passed it to Thaya. "Provisions. It's not much, and it's not good, but our stores were burned. Don't worry about me, there's another on the cart there."

Thaya took the sack. "Thank you, for everything. We would come with you, but..."

Engara smiled and shook her head. "We don't need another Derry just yet; the gods bless him and rest his soul. I hope you find the magi and learn all that they can teach you."

With one last hug and no more words, Thaya stepped back and let Engara lead her people past. She had a strong feeling that she'd see her friend again.

11

LIONS' ROCK

BENEATH THE SHELTER OF AN OVERHANGING CLIFF FACE, THAYA slept soundly next to Khy, enjoying the safety of his presence, the warmth of his body, and his smell that was of earth and freedom. She was beyond exhausted, but now that she was with her soul twin, nothing in the world mattered.

Sleep came, bringing fast and vivid dreams as she processed the events of the day. Nearer dawn, they took on a different, calmer flavour, and she passed from one dream into another where a being of light walked towards her. The being was small, the size of a child, a silhouette of a boy that was familiar, and a faint face formed out of the light.

"Derry?"

"Thaya." The boy's voice was calm, wise even, and he smiled serenely.

"Derry, is it really you? Are you okay?"

"I don't hurt anymore, Thaya, and I can't hurt anyone else either."

Tears filled her eyes. "I'm so pleased, Derry. I'm sorry I couldn't save you."

"It was time, Thaya. I wanted to go because I'm needed elsewhere."

Thaya nodded but she struggled to accept he was dead; it shouldn't have happened.

Derry continued, "There's something I want you to know. I saw what they took from the sky ship; I think that's why the dragon attacked it. The people inside...they died trying to protect it. I didn't see them, but I...felt them."

"It's all right, Derry, they're gone now, too, and nothing can hurt them."

"No, Thaya, it's not that. It's they who wanted me to come to you now. What was taken must be found, otherwise many more will perish because of the intentions of the Fallen Ones."

Derry stepped forward and, before she could react, touched her forehead.

In her mind's eye, she saw Leonites: three tall, upright cat-people with fur for skin and faces more akin to lions than humans. Extreme intelligence blazed in their golden eyes, and ethereal light surrounded them. The one in the middle lifted his hands. Between his fingers and thumbs, a shard of light appeared, making it seem as if he held it. The light solidified into an object the length of her hand and as thick as her thumb. It had the qualities of both crystal and metal, being mostly white, like quartz, yet shot through with gold and silver streaks. The air around it became charged and hummed with energy, so much so that she could feel the air vibrating. The object exuded a great amount of power.

Derry removed his touch, and the image vanished. He also began to fade.

"Wait! Don't go, Derry. What is that crystal thing? Where can I find it? How can I take it from a dragon?" Were they seriously thinking she could just go get it, whatever it was? The Leonites *and* the elf-man expected her to do that?

"In the tallest mountain. Goodbye, Thaya." Derry didn't stop fading, and finally she heard his faint, disembodied voice. "You will find a way."

Thaya opened her eyes, wide awake, with Derry's words still echoing in her ears. It had been no dream.

She took a deep breath and let it out slowly. "Godspeed, beloved Derry."

She yawned and stretched. It had to be far too early to get up, given how tired she felt, but sunlight fell through the trees, and it was long past dawn. Despite the sun, she shivered in the chill air, her breath forming clouds in front of her. Khy was gone, but the ground where he had been was not yet cold.

She got up and found him standing in a stream with his eyes closed. He was facing the sun which was slowly rising between two mountains, its pale autumn light shining off his horn. This was how he rejuvenated himself. He did not eat, he absorbed sunlight—like a plant, she supposed—and he drank water only he himself had purified. It reminded her again that he was not from Urtha, that he was not like any being she had ever met or knew about. Just looking at him reminded her that the cosmos was far larger and more incredible than she had ever imagined.

She didn't want to disturb him, so she sat down cross-legged and closed her eyes, joining him in meditation.

The moments passed, but try as she might, she couldn't still her mind; the wind was cold, the ground was damp, and the urge to get going made her fidgety. *And now there's another obstacle in my path to reaching the magi: hunting dragons.*

But the dragon and the magi had to wait. Now that Derry had visited her, she had to go one last time to the destroyed ship. Maybe if she touched it, the twisted metal would tell her something. Yes, she should go back to the ship first; it could only be a couple of hours walk away, faster if Khy took them there.

"Your loud mind disturbs the peace." Khy opened his eyes. "Yes, it's cold. The sun is weak; I could never have healed my wound here. The Earth speaks to me. It tells me of a time when the world was warm and temperate wherever you went, and all life flourished. It was a long time ago, before The Chaos."

Thaya got to her feet. "The Chaos?" Could he mean the cataclysms that had destroyed her ancient ancestors and their lands?

Khy approximated a very human-like shrug. "It just calls it The Chaos. It must be very hard not knowing anything about the history of your own planet. This human forgetting happened after The Chaos, but I don't know more."

"Is it normal to know everything about your planet that occurred even before you were born?" Thaya wondered what it was like on other planets. If she could understand what was 'normal', then perhaps she could get a grasp on the problems of her own world.

"From what I've seen and feel and know, yes. A being is born with the knowledge of the history of its home because a planet and its species, particularly its guardian species, are intimately united. More than that, not only would you know the history of your planet, but also the history of your species. Before The Chaos came, this was how your people would have been: enlightened and informed. It's clear that those who brought The Chaos wanted you to forget this knowledge, to divide and separate you from the planet and from each other. It's hard to witness how things are here when you know how things should be."

"It's hard to be here even without knowing these things," Thaya grumbled. Khy's words didn't help to soothe the hatred she felt towards the Invaders. Hatred wasn't helpful, it only drained her. "Can we be healed?"

He looked at her with his deep indigo eyes. "All things are possible, but I wonder, do humans want to remember? It's like your species is asleep, wilfully asleep, so they do not have to remember the pain of what happened to them and their planet. If the people do not want to awaken, then they cannot be healed. Nothing can be done without the consent of a being, and if a being is asleep, how can they choose what they want?"

Thaya thought about that. "Hmm, but I don't remember choosing to be asleep, or choosing for the Fallen Ones to destroy us."

"No, but your spirit chose to enter creation at this time in a human body, and thus it would have agreed to take on the conditions of the human species at this time. You do not remember your time before you were here—no human does —but Saphira-elaysa remember all, even from the time when we first left the Pure Essence to become singular, to explore what is and what can be."

Thaya smiled, imagining being part of that Pure Essence, a radiant light that filled all that was. Simply hearing Khy talk about it unlocked ideas and images— perhaps they were even memories. "I would like to awaken and heal, regardless of what the human species is choosing."

"That is my wish also," said Khy. "It's my knowledge that

free will is always respected in the action of the Pure Essence and the cosmos from whence it springs."

Thaya felt a little hope blossom within her. The thought of being doomed by the actions, or lack of action, of her 'sleeping' race was not appealing.

"Many have come here, at this time, and at other times in the far distant past and the far distant future, to help humanity awaken," Khy continued. "I've considered these things often and I'm certain you are one such being. What your role is, only you can know and decide. My race comes here to bring the light, but the darker it gets, the harder it is for us to even reach here."

Thaya shook her head, marvelling at her friend. Khy's quiet wisdom was a source of wonder. "I know that by your race's standards, you're still young, and yet you know so much more than me."

Khy cocked his head. "It's natural and comes from being whole in spirit and in being. You'll know these truths when you awaken fully and remember what has been forgotten. Deep within you, you already know. Perhaps I can assist you with this. Perhaps that is why we were...joined?"

"I'd like to think that." Thaya nodded.

"Yet, I feel there's more to it than that." Khy frowned and swished his tail, thinking. "It's hard to reach, but a part of me feels the fate of Saphira-elaysa depends on humans as if we're linked in some way for our own survival. More than that, I cannot say."

After a moment of deep thought, Thaya remembered her dream that was not a dream. "Derry came to me last night to say goodbye. He said the crashed ship from the skies had Leonites within it." The sudden sorrow made her pause, and Khy lowered his gaze.

"Should we return to it?" Khy asked.

"I think so," Thaya replied. She felt the need for closure, to perform some ceremony for the Leonites who had died there, or simply just to say goodbye. "I also think we should return to that portal stone, the broken one."

Khy pricked his ears curiously.

"Maybe I can do something or see where it's broken. Lately I...I've been feeling things via my hands more and more, like seeing what the stones have seen, what they know. It sounds ridiculous but...it's such a long way to the magi." *And to the dragon,* she thought, but didn't say. She certainly didn't want to even think about it. "It might be worth another try."

———

A calm and windless dusk was falling by the time they approached the blackened and crumpled ship now visible since she had removed the concealing shield. At least sailing ships had the dignity of sinking beneath the waves. Up here on this exposed mountain ridge, there was no dignity in death, and the sad remains of the vehicle were laid bare for all to see. The sky turned pink and orange as the sun touched the top of the pine forest stretching far into the distance. All was serene.

She saw the fallen Leonites' faces in her mind and blinked back tears. Raising her hands, she leant upon the hull, closed her eyes and filled her palms with soulfire.

Fire flared across her vision, followed by screams of agony. Beyond the flames, hazy forms of Leonites moved, desperately trying to put out the fire. Fear and desperation flooded through Thaya, the same fear they'd felt, the same desperate need to protect what was in their custody. A terrible sense of failure overwhelmed her, and the burning heat of the flames scoured her face and arms.

She became aware of Khy pushing and moving her, and then the warm coarseness of solid rock pressed against her cheek and palms. All the pain, fear, and desperation flooded out of her palms in a rush, and the pandemonium vanished. In her mind's eye, the three faces of the Leonites who had perished in the sky ship looked back at her, only now their golden eyes were serene, their fur smooth and clean, and they glowed with ethereal light, like angels.

Thaya slowly let go of her breath as the normal world returned. Her hair was plastered to her face with sweat, and she shivered in the aftermath of emotions.

"Look," Khy said softly. He was pressing her gently against the wall of rock to keep her from falling.

Thaya blinked as the world came into focus, and she pushed herself back. Beneath her palms, which were still pressing against the rock, was the perfect image of the three serene faces of the Leonites—the ones she had just witnessed being burned alive in dragon fire. It looked as if an expert stone-mason had carved their faces into solid rock. Every whisker, every patch of fur had been meticulously imprinted there.

"My goodness, look at that!" She found her strength and stepped away from the wall to get a better look at the three lion-folk faces: the one who had shown her the crystal shard was staring straight at her; the other two were in profile with one looking west to the setting sun and one looking east to where the sun rose. She stared at the one looking back at her. His likeness and realism were so uncanny, it was as if he truly stood before her now. She heard—or felt within her soul—a soft sigh upon the wind as of something or someone departing, and peace settled over them.

"You did that, somehow," said Khy.

Thaya stared at her hands. They still faintly tingled. "Not exactly. They did that...through me." *Was that how they 'carved' images into rocks millennia ago? You wouldn't need tools to do it, just a certain power within.* "I don't, for the life of me, know how that happened."

"Well, I guess this place shall forever be called 'Lions' Rock.'" Khy flicked his tail and looked at her innocently. She gave a short laugh.

"Well, let's go do some more 'stone work' then." Thaya rubbed her hands together and set off towards the broken portal stone.

They reached it as the light faded, and Thaya tentatively placed her hands on the towering stone. All thoughts of a hot dinner and warm bed left her mind as she felt the static power grow in her palms. Its cool, coarse surface responded, and she resisted the inevitable pull on her body. As before, the pull was weak, and the portal map consisting of a few intersecting lines of light, appeared ever so faintly, faded away, and then reappeared again.

So strange and weak, but it's still there.

"Shall we try? The dragon isn't near," said Thaya.

Khy shuffled close but said nothing.

Thaya focused on the nearest points of intersecting light. There were two: one on the left and one on the right. She focussed on the one on the right, felt it respond to her attention by glowing faintly, and then she ceased resisting.

A tunnel of circulating light and dark appeared before her, and then she was sucked in and flying through it, screaming. She flung her arms and legs out, star-shaped, in a futile attempt to control herself, but it only served to make her spin faster in a clockwise fashion. She prayed Khy was behind her but couldn't look back. Instead, she closed her eyes.

The landing, if you could call it that, was hard. A bank of grass and mud knocked the wind and screams out of her. She lay stunned for a moment, then flopped onto her back, gasping. Khy looked down at her. Not even his mane was ruffled.

"Why?" Thaya gasped. "Why does it always have to be like that for me? I'm the god-damn portal navigator!"

"Who's there?" A woman's sharp voice came from somewhere and then the sound of dogs barking in the distance.

Thaya got onto her knees, her stomach beginning to churn violently as it always did after travelling through portals. Where the hell were they?

It was night, cool and damp, but a couple of braziers cast their fiery light not too far away. Between her and the braziers nestled a still pond surrounded by reeds and with a short jetty. To the left, a slender spear of a stone struck out of the earth about twelve feet high, and a line of stones half its height stretched into the trees.

Perhaps it was because of her recent journey through the portal, but she could see the line of stones glowing in her inner vision, and they were precisely following the ley line of the land she could feel disappearing into the trees. Torches appeared in those trees, about five that she could count, and they moved closer fast.

"Show yourselves!" a man barked, in perfect timing with the barking of dogs.

A woman, dressed all in black with a cowl framing her face, appeared from the other side of the line of stones. Blood smeared her cheeks like war paint, and the poor creature whose blood it was, hung limp and dripping in her hand. The rabbit still twitched. The woman's face was twisted in a snarl, making her look feral. A man appeared beside her, his face also bloodied, his expression also hate-filled. A thick knife, dripping blood, flashed in his hands as he stalked towards Thaya.

12

DRAGON'S ROCK

Without a word, Thaya spun away from the blood-smeared humans, slammed her hands against the stone, and let it pull her in.

For the first time, she was thankful to be spinning head over heels in a portal. She glimpsed Khy racing along behind her. Light and then dark flashed, and she slammed hard onto the ground beside the portal stone they had just left, the wind knocked out of her lungs.

"Gnuh!" She spat out dirt.

"Correct decision to leave." Khy nodded his head and flared his nostrils.

"Who were those godawful people?" Thaya clawed onto her knees, the rising vomit threatening her every move. She had to try reaching another portal gate before she started throwing up.

Again, she focussed on the nearest two points of light, but this time she chose the one on the left. She closed her eyes and let it suck her into the maelstrom. The sickening swirling whirlpool grabbed hold of her, and just as she abandoned herself to it, her feet hit the ground. Had she been ready for such a short journey, she could have landed standing up, but instead, she fell onto her backside with a jolt. Her stomach refused to wait any longer and took control. She lurched onto her hands and knees and vomited.

"Hmm, this looks more like it, forests and mountains again but not where we were before." Khy's voice came to her through the retching. Was he trying to make her feel better by focussing on everything else? Well, it wasn't working!

He carried on, "There's a stream just over there; I'll go purify it for us."

Thaya clung to the earth, gasping as the waves of hell rolled through her.

Only when they receded could she stand on unsteady legs, her vision blurred, and stagger towards Khy. His horn glowed like a beacon in the darkness as he dipped it into the stream of white water. Thaya fell on her knees beside it and splashed the blessedly effervescent liquid on her face, gulping it down from between cupped hands. She instantly felt better and invigorated.

"Wow, I think that's the cure!" she said. "Saphira-elaysa water—the perfect remedy for portal travel sickness."

Khy chuckled softly.

Thaya stood up and stretched her back. Her eyes travelled over the treetops and then up the mountainside to where a light had suddenly appeared. It looked like fire in a cave that illuminated the side of the mountain. It flickered and went out, and the mountain became dark and hulking once more. Khy and Thaya stayed still, ears hunting for sounds. A fox barked once but far away. The only sounds were the wind and the quiet cracking of the ground freezing over as the night-time temperature dropped. It was frigid in this place, wherever they were now.

"At least there are no people *or* predators. People predators." Thaya wrapped her cloak tighter around her.

Khy continued to stare up at the mountain. "You say that, but the fire up there? That was dragon fire."

Khy's words made her feel even colder. The clouds parted briefly, and starlight illuminated the landscape. They were at the very edge of the treeline, and a sparse forest of defiant evergreens stretched down the slope on the other side of the stream. The mountain that loomed over them was huge. Could it be the mountain she sought, the highest mountain?

"It is the highest mountain for leagues in all directions," Khy replied to her thoughts.

"How do you know?"

"Can you not feel it? Its power is greater because of its size." Khy looked up as if trying to see its tip. "I'm not surprised a portal stone was placed here; it could harness the power of the mountain."

In the dim starlight, Thaya looked back at the portal stone. It was quite small, no taller or wider than herself, and unremarkable except for the unusual four smaller stones standing erect around it. Had there not been the extra stones, she would have missed the portal stone entirely if she'd been passing by.

"I'm too tired to scale a mountain and face a dragon," Thaya said, stamping her feet, partly from the cold, partly from grumpiness. This whole journey and mission to find relics was becoming tiresome.

"I'll hide us somewhere protected by trees but near the portal," said Khy. He continued to look up the mountain at the place where the fire had been. Thaya sensed he was nervous. Perhaps his wound, now hidden beneath his regrown fur, made itself known, reminding him of the dangers of dragons. She was also nervous just being this close to the enemy.

Between a thick clump of trees and beneath a layer of magical mist created by Khy's wards, they made a small fire out of leaves and twigs which Khy lit easily with his horn. It gave off only a little heat, but thankfully his shield protected them from the wind and created the feeling that they were in an inside space. It also gave them light as it glowed a pale grey.

From the pack Engara had given her, Thaya pulled out a variety of dried foods, some salty, some sweet, and though all tasty, she wished she could be fully nourished with just sunlight and water like Khy. Lying down on ground that was cold and hard, sleep stole over her quickly.

"There's a miner's track cut out of the mountain, maybe a hundred years old, maybe five hundred; the mountain does not tell me," said Khy.

Thaya yawned and gave up pretending to still be asleep. She sat up and scowled, still grumpy. Khy had his eyes closed, and she felt his mind searching far away. He continued, "Rocks see time in thousands of years; a year passes in a heartbeat for them; a hundred years is but an hour."

Thaya found it fascinating, but other more pressing thoughts crowded into her mind. "That's good to know, but how long will it take to reach the cave? Are we just going to saunter in there and take what we want from the claws of a dragon?"

"I know not; I'm simply finding a route to our destination. It's your job to work out what we need to do next."

Thaya huffed and stood, and stamped her feet irritably for warmth.

A silent dawn slowly revealed an overcast sky; a single sheet of grey clinging above them with only a slight breeze to lift the dour monotony.

Thaya and Khy trod carefully along the narrow trail that had been hacked out of the mountainside by miners, keeping their voices low and checking the skies frequently. Khy continued to shield them with a shimmering layer over their heads, but any dragon could detect it if it knew where to look. They were both on edge, from the threat of the dragon and, literally, from the sheer drop to their left.

"Why do *I* have to go and find these items? What's actually in it for me?" Thaya grumbled.

"You could have declined," Khy offered.

"And offend an elf? He asked so sweetly, and he did help me out of that nightmare..."

"And he was nice to look at?" Khy glanced at her.

Thaya felt warmth in her cheeks but decided to ignore his comment. "But the Leonites...that's a different story. They lost their lives trying to protect this...thing, and that can't be forgotten."

"Well, you've answered your own question."

Thaya looked at Khy and rolled her eyes.

The ledge they walked along suddenly fell away ahead and then continued a few yards further on.

"A landslide or avalanche destroyed it," suggested Khy.

"Great," said Thaya. She placed her hands on her hips, looking tentatively over the edge of the missing section. "What do we do now?"

"We climb." And nimbly as a mountain goat, Khy skipped up and over three ridges barely two inches wide.

"Just wonderful. How am I supposed to follow?"

"It's easy, just wedge your feet *there* and cling with your hands *there*." Khy pointed with his horn at the ledges and an ominous overhang.

The blood drained from her head. *Holy hell.* Swallowing her fear to save face, she took several long breaths, then several more. *I can do this!*

Thaya flattened herself against the frigid rock and began to inch herself up. It was all good as long as she didn't look down. When her eyes strayed from the stone in front of her, the sheer size of the mountain, the expanse of sky beyond and the sliding drop into the valley below sent her reeling. Whatever useless words of encouragement Khy was currently giving her faded into the background. All she could hear were her gasps for air and her heart pounding in her ears.

Time passed, hours by her reckoning, when finally, the narrow pathway appeared below her once more. With an immense sigh, she let herself slide down towards it. Without even looking at Khy, she rubbed her freezing hands together and set off at pace.

The path took them gradually up and around the roughly conical shape of the mountain. She took stock of their position and fathomed they had climbed about three-fifths of the way. A few yards further and they came to the first mining cave.

The entrance was roughly hewn and the ceiling low, about the height of an average man, and the inside was wide enough to be able to fit four humans standing side by side. She peered into the darkness, then stepped into the entrance.

"It goes back a long way," she said, as her eyes adjusted

and she saw the fallen rubble and wooden beams to her right and two darker patches to the left marking entrances to other tunnels. "The tunnel on the right is blocked by a rock fall. This wider section makes for a good shelter though."

She made her way further in and inspected the two other tunnels gingerly, fearing they, too, might collapse at any moment. One only went back a little way, the ancient marks of pickaxes clearly visible on the walls. She touched their deep grooves, hearing again the 'clang' 'clang' 'clang' sound of helpless futility as human slaves toiled deep in the Nuakki mines where she had been held captive. She shivered, feeling the crushing darkness of miles of rock above her, the threat of the Nuakki Pain Stick stalking behind her, and sunlight a distant memory...

Only these miners weren't slaves. I wonder what they were digging for.

"Gold and silver ore," Khy replied.

"Oh, really? How can you tell?" Thaya inspected the walls for a shimmering vein.

"It's logical, really," said Khy. "There's only one reason that dragon is here. Funny, humans and dragons hunting for the same thing."

"Hmph," grunted Thaya. "Humans can't eat gold; it's the Nuakki who desire it."

Khy shrugged as if such matters were not for him.

The final tunnel went back a long way. She couldn't see the end and decided not to go any deeper.

Khy inspected the walls. "It goes deep into the mountain. Humans must have been digging here for centuries."

They left the tunnels and continued on the path. A misty rain began to fall, making the rocks even more treacherous and slippery. *At least it isn't snow*, Thaya thought, though that also looked likely given their altitude and the darkening clouds clustering above them. Each step took them closer to the dragon's lair, and each step deepened the dread she felt inside.

The path led steeply upwards. She had to clamber in parts, pressing herself against the mountain and trying not to look at anything other than the grey rock in front of her face. No terrain appeared to bother Khy-the-nimble-goat as he skipped happily along ridges and ledges that were barely there.

I'll have to get him in deep water, see how he likes swimming. Thaya grinned wickedly to herself.

They walked quietly and in silence for a long time, an unspoken mutual agreement between them that they should make no noise as they drew closer to their goal.

When the rain paused, the ground rumbled, and a terrifying screech cut through the air. A green monster suddenly flew out of the mountain a hundred yards ahead, enormous even at this distance. Thaya yelped and flung herself back against the rock, cold sweat bursting from her skin and terror squeezing her innards. The fear froze her there.

Khy remained still as a statue. Not even a hair in his mane moved.

The dragon lazily flapped its wings, turned in the air and roared again. Its gaze passed over them and Thaya's heart missed a beat. Then the dragon turned away and headed east.

Thaya couldn't move until it was a speck in the distance. "Let's go back," she squeaked.

"Now's our opportunity," said Khy.

He was right, but why did she feel so apprehensive? Something felt wrong. *The whole thing is wrong!* "I don't like this one bit." She shook her head and forced her feet forwards.

"Let's move quickly. The dragon's wound still hinders it, it's not healing." Khy's voice was thoughtful.

The news was encouraging. "Okay, let's get in, get out, and run far away," said Thaya, digging deep for some courage.

They moved as fast as they could, the cavern's entrance appearing in front of them beyond a vertical ridge of rock. Its opening was wide, like a beast's maw, ready to swallow them whole.

Thaya picked up a rock and paused just before the entrance. Tongue between her teeth, she began scraping into the wall outside the cavern.

"What are you doing?" Khy hissed.

"I'm leaving a message," Thaya growled.

"We don't have time."

"Nearly done, look, finished." She dropped her scratching stone and stood back to inspect her work.

DRAGONS GO HOME!

Khy looked at the scrawled writing then back at her. "Well, you sure told it."

Thaya nodded satisfactorily. He swished his tail and hurried inside.

She hesitated in the doorway. "If it comes back, we're trapped."

"What other options are there?" he said over his shoulder.

Khy was right, again.

Thaya stepped inside, finding immediate relief from the wind, the cold and the drizzle. The cave was surprisingly warm, *probably from the dragon's great mass and breathing smoke and flames,* she thought.

The cave was huge and…

"Wow, would you just look at that?" Thaya stared at the ceiling in awe. Yards above, and carved out of the rock, were enormous arches, broken at their base as if enormous pillars had once held them up. *Like those temples built hundreds of years ago but without walls, just rows of pillars and arches.*

What perplexed her were the sconces along the walls, for these were lit and illuminating the place. *Strange that a dragon would take time to light them,* she thought.

Between the sconces stretched stone panels carved into the walls and depicting symbols and ancient text. She trailed a hand along one, and hazy images flashed in her mind of people inscribing in stone and speaking words of power. These people were short and squat, yet powerfully built; a hardened people, not completely human and from a time so far in the past, even the images she witnessed were hazy and surreal. She felt no threat from these beings, and if they were off-worlders, they were not Invaders.

"Humans didn't create these mines," said Thaya.

"Indeed. The Merindhir were here, how interesting," said Khy.

"Merindhir?" asked Thaya.

"Yes. We call them People of the Stone, and they're from another realm. They came looking for gold and all manner of crystals when your worlds were close, but it was a long time ago. This mountain was young when they came; it does not remember them kindly."

"Neither would I with something digging and burrowing inside me." Thaya grimaced. "And what's with gold? It's just a metal."

Khy didn't have any answers, so she continued enjoying

the expert craftsmanship of the Merindhir. They were certainly masters of stonework.

"Hurry."

The voice in her mind was faint, and it wasn't Khy's. She pricked her inner ears, but it did not speak again. *It must be the elf-man,* she thought, looking around. She stopped and stared. There was something beyond Khy, something red and dripping on the floor. She realised he had positioned himself between her and it.

He shook his mane and flared his nostrils. "Don't look, Thaya."

Thaya's blood ran cold. "How can I not, especially now you've said that?"

She stepped past him and froze, staring at the mangled bodies on the floor all chewed and bloodied. "Great God!"

Hands, feet, ribs, heads...all manner of body parts—mostly human, but *here* she saw a horse's leg, and *there,* what looked like a dog or wolf—in various stages of being eaten or decaying. A cloud of flies lifted as she neared, and buzzed noisily. The smell hit her, and she reeled away, gagging and shaking.

"I guess we should not have expected much else in a dragon's lair." Khy's voice was grave. "I'll start searching."

Thaya caught her breath, "Let's get out of here." She looked down over the low wall she was leaning on. It had been carved out of solid rock and once would have curved and swept elegantly. Now it was crumbling at the edges. Beyond it lay a pile of bones, again, human and animal. How many people had the dragon brought here and devoured? The sight was not as horrific as the half-eaten corpses, but something in the macabre pit caught her eye, the dull gleam of metal beneath a skull.

She climbed over the wall and reached down, grinding

her teeth as the skull brushed her hand. She lifted the amulet, but its chain caught on a neck bone which broke, and the skull rolled across the floor sounding like a marble on floorboards.

"Eww!" She grimaced and quickly shuffled away, looking at the tarnished silver in her palm and noting the stylised, equal-sided cross with its ends flaring out to join each other and create a circle. It was familiar.

"Hey, I recognise this symbol. Hmm, but where did I see it?" A memory flashed in her mind; she was talking to one of Engara's Shield Brothers and she had given him the warrior woman's sword and knife...he had undone the neck of his hauberk, and beneath it, against his chest, swung a similar amulet, identical perhaps.

Thaya tucked it into her pocket, her eyes going back to the skull. Could they have been one of Engara's warriors? Was she looking at the remains of the people of Taomar? These bones were old—perhaps they were from tribes all across these mountains.

"Help me free them." Khy captured her attention. There was a pained expression on his face, and he remained by the pile of bodies she could not look at.

"They're dead, Khy. Nothing can bring them back. I don't want to end up as one of them, so let's just get the hell out of here." She didn't like the tremor in her voice.

"No. They are here; their spirits remain."

"What?" Thaya forced herself nearer.

"While the body remains, the soul cannot get free. They remain here, waiting."

"Waiting for what?"

"To be set free."

Thaya shivered at his words. "That's crazy. What you're saying suggests all people who have died and been buried are trapped. That would be thousands...millions of them on the planet!"

Khy shrugged. "I say only what I know. Perhaps some have 'help' from greater spirits, but these people are trapped —we must honour them."

"All right, but how? What can I do?"

"Fire releases the essence. You are human as are they, so you must provide the fire; I can provide the...exit, as it were. Join with me."

His horn glowed, and she began to understand a little of what he asked of her. Rather than take fire from a sconce, she lifted her hands and called the soulfire to her. A shard of light burst from his horn and into her palms. It felt warm and tingly, and then it flooded in a great wash from her hands down into the carnage. White fire engulfed the remains and flared brightly. A sigh of many voices echoed around the cavern and, with a flash and an explosion of sparks, the fire vanished.

Thaya stared at the pile of ash where the bodies had been, a sense of relief and closure flowing over her. "I feel a sudden emptiness as if a group of people has left the room."

"That's them." Khy's expression was serene, a soft smile turning his lips. "The tortured souls have left. Now I can see and think clearly."

Thaya felt it too, and thoughts of the dragon returning quickened her pulse. As her friend, Arendor, had taught her, she closed her eyes and stilled her mind, hunting for what she sought: any presence of the objects of power the elf-man and the Leonites had urged her to recover.

She felt nothing.

Hastily, she scoured the cavern, hunting in every nook and cranny. Towards the back, she discovered several narrow tunnels. One was blocked by stone, another had collapsed and the third appeared to be a false door whereby an outline of a doorway had been carved into the stone and recessed, but did not lead anywhere.

"I can't find them anywhere!" She huffed and turned to Khy, who was also hunting through the cave, and then screamed.

A beast landed at the cave entrance, completely filling it and blocking out the light. Huge, green eyes widened and then narrowed as they settled on her.

13

THE DRAGON AND THE UNICORN

"AND WHAT DID YOU EXPECT TO FIND IN *MY* DOMAIN?" THE dragon's voice shook the floor, and its sulphuric breath filled the cave.

Khy remained very still but Thaya's legs buckled.

"Could it be this?" In its enormous claws, the elven crystal relic looked like a pebble. It shone like polished labradorite; translucent grey shot through with rainbows.

Something pressed upon her mind and she felt the presence of the elf-man. She imagined him seated before the fountain in the serene garden where she'd met him. He was staring into the still waters and seeing the dragon there as she saw it now.

"Ah, I see in your heart that it is." The dragon scoffed gleefully and snapped her jaws. "Of course. Why else would a Saphira-elaysa and an Ena-shani rudely dare to break into great Grenshoa's house and destroy her pantry?"

"It's not your house!" Thaya rose to her feet, her voice no longer shaking. "And those people are not your food! This isn't even your realm and you're not welcome!"

Her voice echoed in the cave. Khy moved his head fractionally to glance at her. In her mind's eye, the elf-man raised an eyebrow. The echo died and a pin dropping could have been heard.

The dragon lowered her head to an inch from the floor and moved it like a snake around the side of the cavern. "Is that so? Stupid human."

Khy turned, making his horn shimmer wickedly.

The dragon paused, the unicorn's horn reflecting brightly in her enormous green eyes. "I've not forgotten our little spat, whelp." She shifted to expose the nasty red fleshy scar on her side. It glistened with puss and blood. "It never heals, it burns!"

"Good!" shouted Thaya. "Now you know what it's like. Why don't you go home and fix it and leave everyone here alone?"

Khy's clear voice rang in her mind.

"Thaya, stop taunting it."

"I'm not taunting it, I'm furious!"

"This is a very dangerous situation that's going to end badly."

"It started badly!"

The dragon lifted her snout and chortled, smoke streaming from her nostrils. "Oh, the great Grenshoa is not done here. In fact, she's only just begun. A planet belongs only to those who can keep it."

The dragon's tail lifted and uncoiled into the cavern like a giant cobra laying to rest. The entire length of the beast was now in the cave, wrapping around the stone edges and eliminating any thoughts of escape. But Thaya noticed that the lizard kept her distance from Khy.

Khy, who still hadn't spoken aloud, turned one step to face the dragon. He looked completely calm and serene, but his taut muscles, his unblinking eyes, showed Thaya he was primed to attack.

Grenshoa pressed on, the point of her wrecking-ball tail flicking dangerously. "Oh, you whelp. You think you can face me in a *real* fight? You're not even full-grown and I am five thousand, three hundred and twenty-one years old. I've destroyed entire cities with one blast of my breath. I took down my brethren's brood in the Hundred Year's War and then I took down my own mother. I can cast a sleep on you that lasts a thousand years or turn you to stone for millennia in the blink of an eye. So, answer me, whelp, you think you can fight me?"

Khy did not reply, but Thaya sensed his mind was busy, extremely busy.

"She has not fought one of our kind before," he said. *"She's nervous; the wound I gave her unnerved her."*

Thaya clenched her jaw. *"We've put our lives in danger doing stuff for other people!"*

She could see no way out. It was going to end in a fight to the death. Perhaps she could buy time to find an escape. "You stole that from the elves."

The dragon looked at her. "I took that which was trying to destroy me! I was a whelp once, too, don't you know? Some four thousand years ago the elves tried to slay me, and one of my kind long before that."

"Well, I can see why!" Thaya growled. "You set up 'home' here in a place not your own and began enslaving and eating the people."

"Only the weak!" Grenshoa shifted closer to Thaya, her eyes darting to Khy when he twitched his tail. "Removing the weak makes a race strong."

Thaya placed her hands on her hips, buying time, desperately trying to think of an exit. "And I guess they had no say in it?"

Grenshoa lifted a front talon to inspect it. "The weak

must be eliminated."

The dragon clearly had set ideas and beliefs about how things were, and Thaya decided there was no point arguing. "Who made you Queen? Who gave you the power over life and death?"

Grenshoa lowered her claw and glared at Thaya, her eyes peculiarly changing from green to a mesmerising kaleidoscope of amber shot through with blood red. "I AM life and death."

Thaya was almost lost in those reptilian eyes, entranced. Almost.

The dragon's tail lifted so fast it was a blur. Khy reared and turned. With a speed she didn't know she had, Thaya whipped out her fireshot and fired. Her shot was true. *Arendor would be proud,* she thought.

The ball of fire hurtled through the air faster than an arrow and smashed into that deadly tail. The vicious barbed tip burst into flames, but rather than disintegrate, it turned black and cracked with fissures of red blood. The dragon roared, flicking its blackened appendage and spraying blood over them.

The bloodied tail smashed into Thaya, sending her flying to the back of the cavern. Dazed, she glimpsed Khy attacking. He lunged towards the dragon's head, horn shining. The dragon fell back and swiped talons at him. They clipped his horn and gave a peculiar loud ring.

Fire exploded from the dragon's snout. Thaya threw herself down behind a wall. She dared to peak around it and saw flames roll harmlessly over Khy's shield that spread from his horn. Thaya held her breath and raised her fireshot. Against a dragon, her weapon was not nearly as deadly. She aimed for the dragon's eye, waiting for Khy to give her the shot she needed.

It never came.

A noose dropped over her head from behind. Pain flared around her neck as it tightened, and she was jerked backward against something hard. Large, cold hands gripped her neck and she managed to squeal before all breath and blood flow were cut off. Another hand ripped the fireshot from her grasp—green-scaled hands, ending in long, dark claws.

Ordacs!

Two more stepped forward on either side of her captor, growling to each other in their strange harsh tongue. Their snouts were blunt, and they wore leather and metal straps and buckles to hold weapons but were otherwise naked. Their tough scales were their armour.

Her vision wavered as she laboured to breathe, and she slumped, her consciousness waning. The noose loosened just enough to let her drag in a breath, just enough to keep her from passing out. She reached for the soulfire, but it wouldn't come; something about the noose stopped it.

Khy still battled Grenshoa with magic and fire, but the Ordacs did not intervene in the fight. Thaya wondered if they were enjoying the spectacle. Perhaps the dragon was enjoying it too.

"The battle gives us life. We live for it," a voice hissed in her head, probably the voice of the Ordac who held her. She didn't want to hear it, but she had no idea how to shut it out.

"We do not," Thaya retorted.

"We do not care about the weak," he replied, his voice low and gravelly, almost hissing at times. *"But he's not as weak as most. Neither are you, for a human. We will study you for our records."*

Thaya wondered if that was a compliment. She didn't want it, she wanted to help Khy, and she wanted to get out of here either with the relic or without it.

Khy danced and lunged in a slashing attack. The dragon whirled, her front claws scattering skulls and stones and something shiny that caught Thaya's attention. The elven relic and two human skulls rolled to a stop several feet away. She glanced at her captors. Their reptilian eyes were transfixed on the battle, red tongues darting out in delight. If only she could reach the relic!

Thaya tried struggling, tried to hurl herself backwards or forwards and unbalance her captor. He held her easily, lifted her off the ground, and turned her to face him. Noticing his thick tail and powerful legs, she saw that there was no way on earth she could have unbalanced this creature. She kicked out hard, but her feet bruised themselves against his rock-hard chest.

The amusement in his eyes infuriated her, and she kicked again but the noose holding her up soon became choking until the strength left her and she sagged. Vaguely, she was aware of the ground beneath her feet again and his chest against her back. All she could focus on was breathing.

"The Great Grenshoa grows bored, but your friend will not be so easy to capture. We will use another method."

Where was the elf-man in her head now? Thaya wondered bitterly. Where had these bastards come from? They must have been in the tunnels. Maybe the whole mountain was riddled with caves filled with Ordacs and dragons. She began to feel stupid for coming here.

Two Ordacs carried forward a box, a small, dull, grey thing only a foot long and half a foot wide. The box must be heavy, for it took two of them to carry it. It looked like a cube of solid lead. Even with the magic-dampening noose around her neck, Thaya felt power emanating from that box.

Another Ordac with a gold amulet swinging on his

chest, bent over it and spoke commands. There came the sound of sliding, then clicking, as of bolts unlocking. The lid opened to reveal a shard of light about five inches in length.

Thaya stared at the beautiful rod of glowing crystal. *It's the same thing the Leonites showed me! It's their relic.*

Holding metal tongs, an Ordac picked up the object and held it away from him. He began intoning commands, and energy moved, lots of it, whooshing forwards as light, sound and wind that made Thaya giddy.

A wall of light suddenly encircled Khy, and he staggered. Thaya cried out. The light became glowing bars, entrapping him. The Saphira-elaysa snorted and shook his head. He reared up and slashed his hooves against his prison. Light flared where he struck the bars, and Thaya screamed at the sudden pain in her hands. She felt his pain.

Grenshoa snapped her jaws shut and grinned horrifically. "So easy! My new pet. You keep the girl—humans are boring."

The Ordacs dragged her forwards. Khy looked at her through the glowing bars of his prison, his indigo eyes wide, worrying for her, not himself. He reared up again and leapt high. She thought he was trying to leap over the bars, but instead, he landed in the same space, striking his hooves powerfully down with a crack of thunder that deafened all. Light snaked through the rock beneath his prison towards them, lightning moving through stone!

It reached the Ordacs and snaked up their bodies in a flash with all the force of a lightning bolt. It threw them backwards, and they howled and thrashed. Thaya struggled on top of her writhing captor and tugged the flaccid cord from her neck. The shining crystal shard had been dropped in the scuffle and was now rolling towards her. She staggered onto her feet and ran to it.

The dragon roared and leapt after her.

The crystal shard chinked off a rock and tumbled down the steps. It had to have *some* kind of power, and Thaya had a mind to grab it to break Khy's cage. Somehow. That the Ordacs had used tongs to hold it was not forefront in her mind. Dragon fire rolled towards her, and she threw herself forwards out of the way, reaching for the shard as she did so.

A peculiar thing occurred: soulfire flashed in her palms, and the shard responded. The glowing rod stopped rolling, lifted into the air, and flew to her outstretched hands. She hit the floor as it touched her palm.

A hundred lightning bolts of power flooded through her in agonising waves. Her heart shuddered, her veins throbbed, her head pounded. Light poured through and around her, and her body felt as if it was about to explode. She might have been screaming, she couldn't tell. Something lifted her bodily from the floor, and she gripped the crystal rod between both hands and held it away and above her. Her teeth clenched so hard, she heard them crack, and all she felt was agony as if every nerve in her body was on fire. She tried to open her hands to drop the shard, but it wouldn't let her.

And then, suddenly, she could take the pain.

The agony receded, her screams died on her lips, but the power within her remained. It throbbed inside, awaiting her desire and direction.

"A true Ena-shani." The elf-man's voice was clear in her head and filled with wonder.

Through the light that surrounded her, she saw Khy as another beacon of light beyond her. She focussed her mind and imagined his cage shattering. The glowing bars that held him bent inwards, then exploded outwards.

She felt rather than heard the dragon roar. The beast appeared black in the brightness of the shard's power. Grenshoa struck at her, filling Thaya's vision with dragon fangs. The power she held struck back, a spear of light striking the dragon's forehead, and the beast recoiled with a howl.

Khy screamed, and pain shot through Thaya's leg. Something had struck him with sharp metal. Behind her, Ordacs poured into the cavern from the tunnels and even from the fake door; they were coming through solid stone. Perhaps the stone had been an illusion.

With her almost unbearably heightened senses, Thaya felt others enter the cavern from the front, not Ordacs but something else. They looked like beings of soft light, tentative yet angry, weapons raised.

Humans!

She focused through the light, and saw warriors dressed in leather and metal and armed with swords. A woman with hair the hue of straw led them. *Engara?* Her face was too hazy in the blinding light to be sure.

An Ordac grasped her ankles and tried to pull her down, only to scream and fall as the light flared over him. He grasped his smoking hands to his chest and thrashed wildly.

Khy ran towards her, trampling an Ordac and swiping another's weapon from its hands with his horn.

Ever more Ordacs filled the room. She couldn't count them now, but she was helpless in the power of the crystal rod.

"Reach for Eir'andehari. Reach for the orb; you cannot fight all," the elf-man's voice was calm but commanding. She could not disobey.

Her eyes fell upon the forgotten elven orb rocking gently

back and forth between the wall and a human skull. Thaya fought for control of her left hand and with some effort, it let go of the crystal shard. Her entire arm throbbed with pain, but the flaring light still surrounded her. She reached towards the orb.

Eir'andehari shivered, rolled, then flew to her outstretched hand. Sparks flared as it connected with her palm. Under normal circumstances, the broken relic would have been too large and heavy for her to hold with one hand, but nothing normal was presently occurring—the relic was magnetised to her grip, and she held it easily.

"Create the portal," said the elf-man in her head.

"What?" Thaya faltered. What was he asking her to do? Create a portal? How did she know how to do that? Pain instantly throbbed through her. The power of the crystal shard in her other hand could not cope with doubt.

"Create the portal," the elf-man repeated, urgency in his voice.

Not knowing what else to do, she focused on the two powerful objects in her hands and fought to bring them together. It took an age. Beyond their flaring light, a vicious battle took place, hazy in her vision from the power of the relics. Human warriors crowded beside Khy, and Ordacs pressed towards them.

On the far side of the cavern, Grenshoa snarled and bristled, staring at her and then at Khy, seemingly unsure who to attack first. Khy and the warriors fell back until they were pressed against the wall. The might of the Saphira-elaysa was the only thing preventing the dragon from smiting them all in an instant.

Focus.

Thaya closed her eyes and tuned into the relics. Serenity flowed over her and blanketed everything out, the chaotic din of fighting vanished, and the raging energy within her and the crystals she held suddenly calmed. She looked out upon waves of pastel lavender; she could physically *see* energy moving and flowing all around her.

How do I create a portal?

With the mere thought, the relics responded, the shard vibrated, and the elven crystal throbbed with light that came from deep within it. Thaya became aware of the elf-man's voice, but he was speaking to the orb, not to her, whispers in Elven she did not understand. The orb pulsed with light to each word he spoke.

Thaya focused on the crystal rod, willing it to create a portal, imagining herself touching a portal stone and the vortex pulling her in.

It all happened fast.

A doorway of light appeared in the swirling flows of purple energy. She felt something anchor solidly, a gateway, an intersection of energy whereby she understood that a bridge had been built between where she was and where the elf-man was, anchored by the will of the elven relic and the power of the crystal rod, but it was through her that the energy had combined and come to being, and she had to hold them all for them to work their power through her.

Out of that doorway of light, figures emerged, moving fast. They were tall, elegant, human-like but not human, and there were scores of them.

Elves!

She glimpsed long, leaf-shaped blades in their hands, golden shields shaped like aspen leaves, and their heads and bodies glimmered with armour. Their light, the lavender energy, and the brightness surrounding her, made them too blurry to make out, but she was very glad they were here.

She tried to see where they went, for she wanted to return to help Khy but couldn't; she was stuck holding the power of the relics and the portal, and no amount of strength or willpower allowed her to release her grip on them.

She tried to feel out with her mind and found her inner sight revealed more than her outer sight could see. A great struggle filled the entire cavern. Magic flared, blinding her further. Khy was near, his horn shining in the darkness as he drove back Grenshoa. The beast backed up against the wall and spouted flames that boiled the room. From Khy rolled a single wave of white light that smothered the flames.

Three beams of dark blue energy burst from the far corners of the cavern, struck each other somewhere above them, and burst down in a single thick beam. Khy screamed and collapsed.

Khy! Why can't I feel him?

She didn't feel anything. Usually she could feel all her soul twin's pain, but now all she felt was the power of the crystal rod.

She opened her eyes and hunted the room for the source of the blue light pouring over Khy. Purple energy still flowed around her but raging through it were many chaotic currents. At the edges of the whirlpool of magic from where the blue light spewed, stood three dark, hooded figures looking much like the hooded Illumined Acolytes.

Ordacs...Ordac Magi. I'd recognise their cloaked shapes anywhere.

Seeing that Khy was no longer able to protect her, the dragon lunged.

14

FLORIDA

THE SHARD'S LIGHT SURROUNDED AND FILLED THAYA, BUT beyond it the world fell into darkness. The clang of weapons, the shouting of warriors, and all other sound vanished.

Grenshoa's face emerged from the blackness, her green eyes turning a burning yellow that matched the sulphuric drool dripping from her fangs. Tendrils of smoke leaked from her nostrils, and potent dragon magic thickened around Thaya.

"Let's go on a journey, my little Gatewalker, just you and me." The dragon chuckled, and a grin split her face, revealing rows of teeth each longer than Thaya's arm.

An enormous claw whipped out of the shadows and grasped Thaya's hand holding the shard in a crushing grip. She screamed. The crystal throbbed and fought back, holding the dragon at bay. It pulsed brighter, angry, as if it loathed the proximity of the dragon. Grenshoa roared in its light, her foul breath billowing in great sooty bouts, her eyes glaring, but the dragon did not let go of Thaya's hand holding the crystal.

Dragon magic moved, heavy, potent, unstoppable, and the world began to spin wildly.

A tunnel of blood-red and black light spun around them, sucking them down so Thaya felt as if she was falling. It was like a portal, only larger, for it accommodated the bulk of the enormous dragon gripping her hand.

It's more like a time-rip, a wormhole that the Vormae created that time, she thought, remembering when she'd been caught in one.

There was nothing natural about this structure that bulged and trembled around her. The growing, whooshing noise and hammering, distorted energies quickly made her feel woozy. She was at the mercy of the dragon, and the only thing keeping her alive was the crystal shard that would not let her release it. As her free hand flailed, she realised she no longer held the elven relic. The dragon didn't have it either, not that she could see. It was gone.

She was jerked suddenly upwards, and her arm almost wrenched from its socket. She groaned and hung limp in the dragon's grasp as they moved ever faster, its long body snaking above Thaya, and her wings flapping lazily as she navigated the wormhole.

More like a wyrm-hole! Thaya grimaced at the ancient, Dryadic name for a dragon.

The world tumbled again, and her stomach lurched, and then they were moving downwards, the tunnel dropping into tighter and tighter spirals that made her mind spin, too. Her breath became ragged as she struggled to retain consciousness.

Frigid air and blinding light blasted her. She gasped and

came round. Cool air filled her nostrils, *real* air. White clouds surrounded her and then blue sky.

"Release it, bitch!" roared the dragon, squeezing her hands until she cried out.

"I can't!"

"Then I shall take it from your corpse!"

Grenshoa opened her talons. Thaya fell.

She screamed, her vision spinning from blue sky to white clouds and back again. Now and again, she glimpsed the dark shape of the dragon hovering above and becoming smaller as the beast watched her descent.

A deafening rumbling noise roared through her ears. She looked around expecting to see another dragon, but instead, an entirely different monster hurtled towards her, one made of metal and making a noise louder than thunder. The sound ripped through every fibre in her body and shook the whole sky.

This beast was mostly painted white, cylindrical in shape, and had long, thick, rigid wings on either side with giant, round thunder-makers beneath them. This behemoth did not change its path, nor did it seem interested in her, but it *could* carelessly crush and tear her apart.

Oh God, not one of them! Airplane. Arendor had called it an airplane. At least it won't eat me alive!

Thaya gripped the crystal rod to her chest hopelessly, asking for it to help.

Grenshoa darted into the clouds and disappeared as the craft tore past.

Small, roundish windows were dotted all along its side and there were people behind each one, people, hundreds of them, inside the craft! They looked calm even though they flew within a terrifying thunder-maker, and they had no idea that she or the dragon were there.

"Help!" Thaya screamed as she tumbled past the craft, her plaintive voice lost in the din.

There *was* someone looking her way. She stared right at him. A boy with red cheeks squashed his podgy, freckled face against the window. His eyes opened wide in shock, and his hands splayed on either side of his head.

She lost him from view as a cloud engulfed her and soaked her through. Moments later, a beautiful ocean stretched out below her, an endless deep blue, sparkling in the sunshine, and in the distance lay a beach of pure white sand with green trees beyond.

At least I'll die in something beautiful, she thought, and began to both cry and pray.

The airplane and its thunder faded, Grenshoa was hidden, and all Thaya could see was the sparkling ocean below coming fast towards her. A pulse of energy shuddered through the air, and the crystal rod flashed in response. Her heart nearly stopped, for out of the clouds above galloped Khy.

"Khy, help!" she screamed.

From his sides shone pearlescent light as if he flew on wings made of the stuff. She'd only seen him do this once before when they were escaping the Vormae, and it wasn't flying as such, but gliding. Saphira-elaysa had wings when they desperately needed them, wings made of magic. He moved fast, but it still took an age for him to reach her. The ocean was so close; would it reach her before he did? He closed his wings and dropped through the air.

He neared and opened them a little too slowly. She squealed and grabbed hold of his neck, pressing herself against it tightly. He spread his wings wide, rapidly slowing their descent with a jerk. His body quivered under the immense forces.

The water still hurtled towards them. She gasped in a breath and braced herself.

They slammed into the ocean, the sudden force knocking the breath from Thaya's lungs. They went deep, so deep the pressure crushed. Salt water stung her eyes and filled her nostrils, but she wasn't dead.

Khy kicked powerfully. Somehow she found the strength to do the same until they burst through the surface, spitting and snorting. She lay on her back, bobbing on the waves, sucking in great gasps of air. Her whole body ached and felt as if horses had stampeded over it, but at least the water was warm. Khy shook his head and flared his nostrils, grimacing. Though he looked all right, he clearly hated being up to his neck in water.

"Beats clambering on the mountainside." Thaya grinned.

"Hardly," he growled.

"That was by far the most frightening thing I've ever experienced." She rubbed her eyes.

"Let's get out of here," said Khy.

Thaya sighed and tried to swim, but her aching arms were useless. Instead, she clung to Khy's neck and let him power them both through the water.

By the time they made it to shore, a crowd of people had gathered at the water's edge, shielding their eyes from the sun as they watched the strange pair emerge.

Thaya stared at the people, then blushed crimson. They were all virtually naked.

Women wore brightly coloured but scanty material that barely covered their breasts, and certainly didn't cover their behinds. The men were all bare-chested and wore short trousers that came in all lengths above the knee. Some men stood only in their underpants. And a fair few wore hats or black glasses that concealed their eyes completely. Thaya struggled to not stare at the attire of this strange tribe clustering around her with looks of shock and awe on their faces. They wore more on their heads than their bodies and appeared completely unashamed.

Perhaps they're right, Thaya thought. *Perhaps it's silly to be wearing clothes at all, after all, animals don't...*

A little girl with mahogany skin and curly, black pigtails pointed at Khy and giggled, her dark brown eyes shining with wonder. She toddled forward, bumped against his leg, and reached a hand towards his head. Khy nuzzled her hand and snorted loudly when she squeezed his nose. She squealed with laughter, ran between his legs, then hugged and wrapped her body around his foreleg. He lifted her up and set her down, creating more squeals of joy.

"Goodness me, move aside. Let me through!" A young man pushed through the crowd, and they parted to let him pass. He was tanned with blond hair, dark glasses, and carrying a large, red, oblong thing. The ease with which he held it suggested it was remarkably light. He was also dressed all in red, a strange casual uniform consisting of shorts and a shirt but no shoes.

"Are you all right?" He dropped down beside Thaya, who was still on her knees, reeling in shock as the waves swilled around her.

"Um," she began, then nodded, too dazed to speak. She really didn't feel all right, she felt broken, both mentally and physically.

He touched her cheek and checked her over and asked her to focus. "How many fingers am I holding up?"

"Two, oh, does that include your thumb?" She found she preferred looking at his face than his hands.

"Never mind. Can you stand?"

"I don't know."

He scooped an arm around her and helped her onto her feet. She felt hard muscle bunch under his red shirt. *A healer and a trained warrior?* She blushed even harder, enjoying his attention, and the sun was very hot, making her sweat all the more.

Ah, so that's why people aren't wearing any clothes because it's sweltering!

She realised it was *she* who looked ridiculous standing in a tropical place dressed in a cloak and cold mountain gear.

"Well, you seem okay, a bit dazed maybe, but here, drink some water." He pushed a small bottle made of flexible glass into her hands.

Plastic. She remembered when Arendor had given her something similar. She unscrewed the top and drank noisily as the man continued.

"People said they saw you fall into the ocean?" The man was looking at her, but she couldn't see his eyes behind his dark glasses, leaving her feeling uncertain. His accent was strange, too, not like the people of Lonohassa or Taomar...*or London.* A cold dread settled in her stomach. She wasn't back in that godforsaken place, was she? They had airplanes there, and those dark glasses too and, and...*oh dear God! Please let this not be Earth! Please, God, oh please, no...*

"I..." she began but an incredibly loud trilling whistle cut through the air and made them both wince.

"I..." she started to speak, but it came again, sharp and loud.

People looked over their shoulders and began to

disperse, the noise causing them to swiftly lose interest in the strange girl and her horse that had come out of the ocean. The little girl hugging Khy's leg began to cry as her mother dragged her away. Children returned to building sandcastles, dogs continued their barking and digging giant holes in the sand, and adults played catch, tossing bright balls or discs to each other.

The whistling grew louder, and Thaya located its source. A man with a fat belly protruding from under his shirt, and a large, red face was running towards them, or trying to run, he didn't seem very fit. He raised one hand commandingly, and the other pressed a red whistle against his lips. He was fully clothed in a peculiar dark blue uniform with a star-shaped badge on his left lapel that gleamed brightly in the sun.

The young man tending her gave a weary sigh and turned to face him.

The fat man continued whistling until he was right next to them, which took a while because of his hampering girth. He removed his whistle and bent over, panting. The sudden cease in the noise left a ringing din in Thaya's ears that rubbing didn't improve.

He stood up, and his narrow eyes, slightly upturned nose, and round, red, and very sweaty face all made him look very much like a pig. Thaya stifled a laugh. Khy looked at her, then back at the fat man, cocked his head, and took a slight step closer to him. Thaya studied the panting man up and down while he caught his breath, and her eyes settled on the writing on one of the many badges decorating his shirt. The letters twisted and turned and then made sense to her eyes. She blinked in surprise, finding she could read the language.

On one, the words read: 'Chief Priggins.'

And on another: 'SARASOTA POLICE.'

Sa-ra-so-ta... She mouthed the words in her mind, seeing how they felt. *Po-lice. I know that word!* Again, she saw the police swarming the building she and Arendor had escaped from in London. She shivered. *Oh no, not the police again. They were working with the Fallen Ones back there.*

"Officer Priggins." The young man nodded wearily.

"Indeed, Terence. Why is it so hard to follow the rules, hmm? No horses on the goddamn beach!" the officer shouted, pointing at Khy.

Thaya looked at Khy. Khy looked at Thaya. The young man looked at Khy. They all looked back at the officer.

"It's up to you to maintain the beach according to the rules, Terence. Rules protect people." Officer Priggins waved his whistle in the young man's face.

Terence's shoulders slumped. "They were in trouble, and I..."

"How did a horse get on the beach, Terence? I'm not going to be the one clearing up the shit!"

"They came out of the water. The people..."

"I don't want to hear your nonsense, Terence."

"You just asked..."

"Now get that animal off the beach!" Officer Priggins moved towards Khy and began wafting his arms at him. Khy stood still and pricked his ears, clearly wondering what interesting thing was going to happen next. He remained still as the policeman waved his hands in his face. When he made no move, the officer paused and pointed a finger at Thaya.

"You're clearly fine, so get your horse off the beach before we...*impound* it!"

"Impound?" Khy telepathically asked her.

Thank the Creator he hadn't asked her out loud. Thaya shrugged.

"It's okay, Officer, they were just leaving." Terence looked at her pleadingly and nodded.

"Yes, um, we were just leaving." Thaya scanned the beach and the buildings beyond, wondering where the hell to go. She pointed towards a path leading off the sand and through some palm trees a few yards away.

The officer raised his eyebrow, waiting.

"Yes, um, bye." Thaya nodded and started walking on wobbly legs.

Khy nodded too, smiled at Terence and the officer, then followed Thaya. The colour drained out of Officer Priggins' face.

They were pacing silently through the white sand when a shiver rippled down her spine. Thaya glanced back at the clouds moving above the ocean. A huge, dark shadow moved in the midst of a cloud, and for an instant, a dragon's face materialised. Its eyes flared smouldering orange and then it was engulfed in the cumulus, becoming a darker patch within the billowing white.

"Why doesn't she attack?" Thaya murmured.

Khy looked at the darker cloud within a cloud. "Partly because of me, partly the humans, but also, I don't think she can; something forbids her as if she must remain hidden here in this time and realm. I feel something binds her and her race to secrecy in this place as if the magical must be kept hidden. It binds me also."

A cold realisation swept over her. "Oh no, the crystal shard!" Thaya turned back towards the beach. Her hand that had gripped the strange relic for so long was bright red and blistering. She touched a blister and smarted. "Ouch!"

"Relax, I have it," said Khy. "You dropped it when we hit the water, and it nearly sank. Grenshoa wasn't expecting me, but now I fear I've made a keen and deadly enemy."

"Thank the Creator it's safe." Thaya sighed under her breath. "Wish I knew what it was."

They fell quiet as a man carrying a bright yellow folded chair walked past. He nodded at them, curiosity in his eyes as he looked at Khy.

Thaya carried on in a whisper, "You might not be afraid of anything, but can we be sure she won't attack? There's a lot of people on that beach who have no idea about the dragon watching them."

"She would have attacked already," said Khy.

Thaya placed her hands on her hips. "I'll take your word for it. So where is the crystal shard?" She looked him over but couldn't see where he had it. "Saphira-elaysa don't come with pockets, do they?"

Khy chuckled. The air shimmered in front of them, and the crystal rod appeared, hanging in the air.

"What the...quick, hide it!" Thaya hastily grabbed it then smiled at the family of three hurrying past. Too engrossed in an argument, they didn't even notice her and Khy or the glowing crystal hovering in the air.

Thaya whispered, "If horses aren't even allowed on the beach, then I'm sure magic must be really bad!"

"Neither of us can hold it for long, it's far too powerful," said Khy. "Look what it's done to your hand."

Thaya winced at her blistered palm. It throbbed painfully. Maybe she could find a healer and some salve in this town. The rooftops of buildings and houses poked out above the trees only a short way away.

"Shall we hide it somewhere?" Thaya wondered about burying it.

Khy shook his head. "Far too dangerous. Any magical creature could find it, or any evil one, too."

"Well, we'll have to get something to put it in, something like a lead box!" She imagined a small metal box she could keep it in.

"Gold would shield its power," suggested Khy.

"Hmph. Pricey! Though it's not very big. Sheesh, why do I have to hold it? Why don't the Leonites just appear and take it?"

Khy looked around. "I think it's something to do with the place. It lacks...hmmm...a lot of energy."

The cold creeping feeling stole over her again. She glanced through the trees and glimpsed metal carts with black wheels moving fast. Just the sound and rumble of them made her shiver.

'Cars' Arendor called them, and this really is Earth but not London. It must be somewhere else but a similar time. God, I hate this place.

The same sense of being trapped descended upon her.

Khy spoke in her mind. *"It won't be like then. We have strength together, and now an object of great power. We'll find a way out. I don't think Grenshoa meant to come here, but how did she make a mistake?"*

They fell silent and watched several beachgoers pile past them, the kids shouting and carrying huge garish objects made of a thin, inflatable material and the adults carrying plastic boxes and chairs and all manner of strange items that Thaya had no idea what they were for.

"I didn't intend to come here either. I don't know why I keep coming back!" Thaya kicked a stone and watched it bounce into the bushes.

"*Perhaps it was the crystal; it did something in your hand in the wormhole. I don't know what, but it ended abruptly, I almost lost you. The whole wormhole shook and trembled... I thought it would break, and perhaps it did! And then we were here.*"

"*What about the others?*" asked Thaya. "*The elves came, I saw that, and then I think I saw Engara and the warriors.*"

"*Yes, the humans came. Without the dragon there, the Ordacs will be no match against all of them.*"

Khy's words set her at ease. Worrying about her friends as well as her own predicament was too much to deal with, and she was famished. They stepped out onto a grey concrete walkway beside a busy road. Traffic lights slowed the cars so at least they weren't careening past, and a little further on, numerous stores lined either side of the wide road.

"Horses on the sidewalk? Gee, Miss." A man tutted as he squeezed past them. Khy was filling most of the walkway.

"Sorry," Thaya mumbled.

"Sorry," said Khy, and tried to tuck himself in.

Thaya glared at him for speaking out loud, and he blew through his lips. The man was also staring at them over his shoulder, his face suddenly pale. Earth was clearly no place for horses—or, rather, unicorns—alongside magic and dragons. What on earth was she going to do with him? She couldn't lock him up in a stable. *Hah, imagine that?* And she didn't want to be alone.

"You should get something to eat." Khy nodded towards a man crossing the road, eating what looked to be a baguette filled with cheese.

Thaya's stomach rumbled painfully.

"Food means money," she said. "I have some coins, but will they work here? Back home, each country has their own coin, so I doubt mine would be accepted here. Maybe I could exchange some, there has to be a goldsmith here."

She started walking towards the stores, hunting their signs and windows for any hint of coins or gold. The high street was long, so progress was slow. Everyone looked their way, wondering why a horse was following her on the sidewalk. She tried not to meet their eyes and pretended to be absorbed in her task. Her eyes settled on a small and shady shop window where a gaudy, luminous sign flashed red and yellow.

"WE BUY GOLD!"

"That's it!" Thaya pointed.

Khy sucked in his lower lip, uninterested.

Thaya stopped outside. "All right, I'll go in, but please don't talk to anyone, it's not like Havendell Harbour this time, there aren't any witches, and no one has the ability to see through your disguise."

"I'll just wait here," said Khy.

Thaya reached into a hidden pocket and drew out a gold coin. "They buy gold; how hard can it be?"

Taking a deep breath, she stepped towards the store.

The door was stiff and took some pushing, then a loud bell jingled as she entered which made her jump. She tried to close the door, but it had stuck. After a moment of pushing and shoving, she gave up and let go. Then the door started moving of its own accord!

"What the...?" She watched and inspected the whole

thing as it shut quietly, gracefully, without any of its former stiffness.

"Ahem." A man cleared his throat, and she whirled around.

Behind a worn, wooden counter stood a short, wide, middle-aged man with a thick, black beard and eyebrows, and brown eyes which looked her up and down as if she had walked into the wrong store. He raised an expectant eyebrow above his small, round glasses.

Thaya glimpsed herself in one of the many mirrors around the room and with a sigh, smoothed her damp attire and dishevelled hair. She strode with fake confidence to the counter. At least her cloak had stopped dripping sea water.

"Please may I exchange this for money?" She placed the coin on the counter.

"Cash?" the man asked without looking at it.

"Cash?" Thaya raised her eyebrows. What the hell was cash? "Um, er, cash, er, yes? Only if I can buy food with it."

The man lowered his glasses and looked at her curiously again. "Not from around here, are you?"

Thaya forced a smile and moved her head in a circular motion, trying at the same time to say, 'yes,' she wasn't from around here, and 'no,' she wasn't from around here. She considered the airplane and falling past it. "I just landed," she said and did her best not to wince.

"It shows," replied the man. "Right, show me what you got." He set his pen down, reshuffled a stack of papers he had been working on, so they were neat, then replaced his round glasses with some strange ones that looked a bit like the thick monocle the goldsmith used back home, only with two together and each of different lengths and dimensions.

She pushed the gold coin towards him, and he bent down close to inspect it.

The bell rang as someone else walked into the store. Thaya turned to see a young man with a shock of fair hair. He began inspecting the watches in a cabinet by the mirror on the left.

"Goodness, is this an antique?" the store manager asked. He turned the coin over again excitedly. "I've not seen anything like it before. A gate and castle keep on the tail, and on the face, who on earth is that?"

Thaya decided it was better to keep quiet.

"Where did you say you were from?" the man squinted at her. "I simply can't place your accent."

"Oh, er, Brightwater, um, Havendell. It's, er, hmm, it's a long way away." Her voice faded for the last part, and she cleared her throat.

"Figures," the man muttered. "All right, well I can see it's solid gold and thick, too. I can't tell if it's an antique, mind, so I can't give you any extra for that. I take a percentage for the exchange, and you get your cash."

"Perfect!" Thaya smiled eagerly, her stomach groaning in response and causing the man to cast her another glance.

Shaking his head, he turned and disappeared through a door behind the counter. He had long, black hair tied back beneath a bald patch, and reminded her of the goldsmith back home, so she couldn't help but stare. Were there Northmen here? Dwarves? She couldn't ask him his heritage, just like she felt she couldn't ask the dwarf gold-smith back home.

He might just be short, and then I'd be embarrassed. People get offended about that sort of thing. But his fingers are wide, and his hands are enormous for his height...

He returned with a thick wad of paper leaflets. "Here you go—two thousand fresh American dollars. I've included tens and twenties for your satisfaction." He smiled genuinely, and she took the money in stunned silence.

American dollars, she said in her mind. This kingdom must be called America.

"What's this though—paper?" Thaya looked at the strange, flimsy, greenish paper that would probably melt in the rain. Words, symbols and pictures were depicted on them, some of which made a shiver go down her spine though she wasn't quite sure why.

"This is our curr-en-cy." The man leant forward over the counter. "U. S. Dollar bills. We call them notes."

"I'm not stupid," she huffed. "I know what that is, but paper?"

"They don't use paper in your land?"

"N-no. Of course not."

"Are you from the past?"

Thaya shot him a look, but the modern dwarf man looked none the wiser. The young man queueing behind her coughed and fidgeted.

"Can I help you?" The store manager turned his attention to the man, clearly wanting to be rid of Thaya.

"Yes, I want to look at this watch, but I haven't got much time," said the young man, giving Thaya an apologetic look.

The dwarf man picked up a huge ring of keys and went to the watch cabinet with the other customer. Thaya stood staring at the notes. Some were marked ten or twenty, and the rest one hundred.

This is just so strange, she thought, leafing through them. *Am I being tricked?*

The young man and dwarf man returned to the counter, and she stared as the young man riffled through his wallet and passed notes identical to hers over the counter.

"Thanks," the young man said and took the plastic bag the dwarf man passed to him.

Okay, so that IS how things are here. "Won't these get wet?"

The bell rang loudly as the young man left the store. The shopkeeper rolled his eyes and shook his head. "Keep the notes in your purse and out of sight, and they'll be fine. Now I must get on. Good day to you."

Having nowhere dry to put them, Thaya rolled them together and kept them in her hand. In a strange daze, she exited the goldsmith.

Khy and his new companion instantly shook her out of it. He was standing on the corner of the street, and there was a woman patting his nose which he was enjoying immensely. The woman wore a raggedy, purple skirt and had a shock of greying black curls. She was speaking to Khy and chuckling, whilst other people passed, giving them peculiar looks.

"Oh no, not again!" Thaya squeaked.

15

TOY SWORDS

THAYA RUSHED OVER TO KHY AND THE WOMAN.

This had happened before, Khy getting himself involved with a witch in Havendell Harbour—he just seemed to attract them. Thankfully, there were no witches now on Earth.

"He's not for sale!" Thaya blurted and laid a hand on Khy's withers.

The woman pushed her glasses up her nose and inspected Thaya. The glasses made her brown-speckled green eyes look huge and owl-like.

"Not for sale? Oh my, my dear, but I have nowhere to keep such an exquisite creature anyway. No, no, we were just sharing a mind-connection. He has such a lovely and open temperament, and animals always love me."

Khy looked at Thaya, his eyes bright and questioning, his ears pricked forward. She rolled her eyes. Why was everything so interesting to him?

Thaya cleared her throat and relaxed a little. "Right."

"You look like you've had quite a day," said the woman, looking her up and down, and nodding empathetically.

Thaya slumped. "You could say that. I need something to eat. Say, don't suppose you know of a good tavern where I can spend the night?"

The woman chuckled and pushed her numerous, jingling bangles back up her wrist. "Oh, you've got a perfect accent for that turn of phrase. There's a nice fancy hotel at the end of the high street down there, but I hope you have somewhere to keep your companion because I'm pretty sure they don't take horses."

Horses? Phew, so the woman hasn't seen through Khy's disguise. I'll bet she's suspicious though. Thank the Creator most people are disconnected with magic down here. And it really *did* feel like 'down here.' Earth was her most disliked place.

But it did raise the question: what was she going to do with Khy?

"I can make my own arrangements if you need an indoors bed," said Khy telepathically.

"Hmm, I sense telepathy about you," said the woman, making Thaya suddenly freeze. The woman laughed loudly, "Oh, don't look so surprised, I'm not called Mystic Mary for nothing! Here, take my card. Looks like you could do with a nice relaxing meditation, or a reading, or something to exercise those ghosts in your closet, or should I say, exorcise? You know, make 'em take a hike? Ha-ha!" The woman peeled with laughter, then reached into her bag and withdrew a small card painted with stars and planets.

"Mystic Mary," Thaya spoke the name and what looked like an address out loud.

Mystic Mary nodded robustly and pointed down the street. "My place is small, but perfectly formed, and my rates are reasonable." She winked and placed her hands on her hips. "But if you want a cheap night, you can stay in a cosy bed and breakfast—there are many to choose from—just look out for their signs roadside. In this little piece of paradise, you'll find no shortage of places to stay. Well, too-da-loo. You've got my number if you decide you need a spiritual makeover."

Mystic Mary majestically waved a bejewelled hand and, lifting her swathe of purple skirts, stepped off the pavement and set off across the high street.

Thaya sighed in relief. The woman wasn't a witch although she looked like one and certainly had some kind of power.

Thaya turned to Khy. "Now all we need is a box for the shard. Are you sure we can't bury it somewhere?"

Khy looked skyward. Was he hunting for Grenshoa? "I'd prefer not to have it with us, it will attract...*others*. It beams frequency and power—something to conceal or dampen that would be good. Metal like gold works well."

Thaya chewed her lip. "Well, we can't spend all our...*cash* on gold, so anything metal will have to do."

She looked up and down the high street again. Left or right looked equally as useful, so with a shrug, she went right. They passed clothes stores selling the same bright, skimpy garments the beachgoers adorned—she did notice people wore more clothes away from the sea—and other stores selling those same dark glasses everyone around here seemed to wear.

She paused before a store with an open front and a glass counter filled with delicious food. Two people stood behind it, ready to serve her.

"What'll it be?" asked the young woman dressed in a white apron and a kerchief keeping her dark hair back.

Thaya stared at the bread rolls stuffed with various fillings that made her mouth water. "The cheese one with salad." She pointed through the glass at a particularly plump, white roll with its juicy contents bursting out.

"Anything to drink?" The woman pointed behind her at a cabinet filled with different coloured plastic bottles.

"Sure. I'll have a water."

Thaya took the thin plastic bag the woman passed to her and paid with a ten-dollar note. She stared at the metal change she was given back. *Coins, real coins. But these aren't gold, silver, or anything I recognise; they look fake.*

None of the people appeared to be trying to steal from her, so rather than cause a scene, she stepped aside to let another customer order. They, too, received the same fake coins as she. It was all so strange.

Just a short block ahead, nestled a small green park only about the length of a large house and shaded by well-manicured palm trees. Thaya hurried to a bench beside a patch of yellow flowers and hungrily unwrapped her sandwich.

"Mmm, yum." She tucked in as Khy inspected the garden. A huge red and orange butterfly the span of her hand, fluttered past and landed on Khy's shoulder. He sniffed it curiously. The butterfly was joined by another, then another until the garden had eight of them fluttering around him.

Thaya watched spellbound; was the grass getting greener too? She imagined it growing even as she ate. Goodness, all the flowers were now turned in his direction as if Khy was the sunlight! A deep tranquillity settled on the place, and Thaya washed the last mouthful down with water and leant her head back.

Just a few minutes' rest...from a frozen mountain to a tropical ocean, my body is really feeling it.

.   .   .

"You can't sleep here!" The commanding voice jerked her awake.

"Wha—"

"This is a public bench, not a motel."

Thaya blinked up into the wide face of Officer Priggins. The sun was glaring through the leaves above him, and it took a while to see him clearly.

She sighed loudly. "I was just eating my sandwich and—"

"Time to move along." The officer made waving movements with his hands.

Sheesh, this guy has it in for us. Won't he just leave us alone already?

"Good to see you got rid of the horse."

Thaya stared at the officer, then turned to look at Khy who was standing by the back wall behind her. *"Couldn't you have hidden both of us?"*

"I didn't have time. I was also sleeping..."

Thaya sighed again and stood. "All right, all right."

"And put your trash in the can." The Officer indicated to a large, round box with a hole in the top a few feet away.

"What? Oh." She grabbed her scrunched-up sandwich bag and stuffed it tentatively in the hole, watching him for signs of approval. Was that what he wanted her to do? Nothing weird happened, and he made no strange faces, so she assumed she'd effected the correct behaviour.

Thaya left the tranquil garden. *"I'll go find a container for the crystal shard. You stay here."*

Khy flicked his tail and smiled.

She walked along the high street, casting one glance back at the officer who watched her go. She began to relax a little. At least Khy was safe, hidden and out of the way. He was too large to manoeuvre along the sidewalk easily anyway.

She looked in various storefronts, but nothing had what she wanted, whatever that was. She sighed and leant on the wall of a store filled with all manner of garish plastic toys for children. Outside were several baskets filled with toys to entice people inside—usually children dragging in their parents. Not all the toys were plastic; some were fabric like the teddy bears, and others were wooden or metal, like the miniature cars.

"Couldn't help but notice, miss. Cops givin' you a hard time?" A tall man with rich brown eyes, dark skin and a strange, peaked hat looked down at her and smiled. "Wanna borrow a hairbrush? I saw you get a bite to eat, so you're all set for a bit. I know where you can get some cheap clothes."

"Cops?"

"Yeah, the police."

"Oh, right. I'm fine, thank you." She smiled, the man was genuine, and there was no threat about him. He had a point: to everyone here, she looked dirty and scruffy and wore strange clothes. Maybe she even looked like the beggars back home in Havendell Harbour.

I hadn't thought of that. No one here is even dressed like a farmer; don't these people have farms?

"Okay, well, just askin'," said the man politely. "If you ever need cheap clothes, Barry's Bargains on the backroad is the way to go. We help all manner of people from all walks of life. You look after yourself now." He touched his hat respectfully and walked away, whistling a happy tune.

At least the locals are friendly, she thought.

The sun was getting lower; she'd have to hurry up before the stores started closing. She didn't want to leave Khy alone, but the thought of a warm bed really drew her.

Perhaps she'd better bury the crystal, just for a day. Her hand throbbed at the thought of it.

She started walking again, and accidentally kicked something on the ground sending it rolling into the gutter. It wasn't a stone but a hollow metal ball. She picked it up and inspected it. It was poor quality and gave a little when she squeezed. It also had a hole in it and the markings of thread as if it screwed into something else.

"Ah, there."

The pommel had fallen off a stack of toy swords in one of the baskets. She found the one missing a pommel and screwed it back on. Come to think of it, no one had swords or wore any weapon at all here, apart from the officer who had a stick and a gun.

It must be a really peaceful place, she thought.

Another thought struck her, and she pulled out the sword and unscrewed the pommel again. The hilt was made of the same flimsy metal and was completely hollow. It would never survive a man's crushing grip or any blow...but it was super light for children. She pulled off the garish red-fabric scabbard. The short, thick, fat blade was very blunt, and she doubted it could ever be sharpened. Perhaps even the blade was hollow, too.

Could the crystal rod fit inside the haft? She stuck her finger in the hole and couldn't touch the other end. It was definitely long enough, but what about the width? The sword was light, and with the scabbard, she could wear it around her waist.

I'm going to wear a kid's toy sword? Seriously?

But if she could fit the crystal into the pommel, then she wouldn't have to keep it in her pocket, slowly burning her body. Sure, the flimsy metal probably only dampened its power a bit, but it was better than nothing.

"Are you going to buy that or play with it?" A plump woman with downturned lips and greasy grey hair stared at her grumpily.

"Sure!" Thaya smiled at her.

Why the hell would someone running a toy store be so grumpy? She reminded Thaya of Mister Thren, one of her schoolteachers who also sold toys once a week in Brightwater. He was the sourest, dourest man in the land, and yet he chose to sell things that made kids happy. Weird. Her world and this one were both upside down.

The woman tutted and went inside, beckoning for her to follow.

⸻

Five minutes later, Thaya strode along the street, her toy sword swinging against her hip and a sense of hope in her heart. She went back to the little park where Khy waited.

He cocked his head as she approached, then chuckled when she explained her gaudy new attire.

"So, let's see if it fits." She shrugged.

With a swirl of his horn, the shining rod appeared before them and hung in the air, humming with power. Hesitantly, Thaya took it between her finger and thumb, bracing herself for the wave of energy. It jolted through her, making her hair feel as if it stood on end. It took all her focus to hold it, undo the pommel, and slot the shard into the cheap haft. It fitted! The fit wasn't perfect, and it rattled a lot, but with a relieved sigh, she screwed the pommel back on.

Wiping the sweat from her face, she patted Khy's shoulder. "No one will suspect, and it will do until something better comes along."

The sun was setting, and the temperature blessedly began to drop.

"I think we should rest here. Look, it's what the witch called a 'bed and breakfast.'" With his horn, Khy motioned to the building bordering one side of the park. It had painted yellow walls and cheery flowerpots adorning the window ledges, and a sign hung on the corner by the street:

BETTY'S B&B

RELAX AND ENJOY THE SUNSET!

VACANCIES

"So, you *do* think she's a witch?" asked Thaya, not liking that one bit.

Khy nodded. "Something like that though she might not call herself one. A good witch, maybe, or perhaps a Wise Woman?"

"I guess. A bit like Toothless Betty, maybe," she muttered to herself and looked at the B&B. "Well, I see nothing wrong with this place, and if I can get a room overlooking here, then we won't be too far away."

Thaya walked up the steps to the wide yellow door with its huge, silver doorknob and knocker. She knocked twice and waited.

Footsteps sounded, and moments later, the door swung open.

"Hello there!" A woman with short, auburn curls and pink lips smiled at her. She wore a yellow dress with white spots and a flared skirt.

"Hello, um, do you have a room available for tonight?"

The woman beamed. "I do. I have two left. Would you like to see them?"

"Yes please."

"I'm Betty, by the way. Come right on in."

"Thaya," said Thaya and followed her.

The house was bright and airy with painted yellow walls and yellow flowers in vases decorating every flat surface.

This woman really likes yellow, thought Thaya, finding she liked how it made everything look bright and cheery.

"Do you have any rooms facing the little park next door?" Thaya asked.

"Indeed, we do, but it's also an ocean-view room so it's more expensive than the others. It's also the smallest room; would you like to see it first?"

Thaya nodded and followed Betty up two flights of stairs. She opened a door into a small but very pretty room decorated with floral wallpaper and rose-pink sheets. There was a tiny balcony with a chair on it, and the view was of the sparkling sea. A small window on the left looked out over the park that Khy currently relaxed in.

"It's perfect," said Thaya looking at the inviting bed with pink sheets. "I'll take it."

"Wonderful." Betty clapped her hands. "The only thing is I need you to pay now. If you want another night, no problem, pay me by the day. Breakfast is between eight and nine downstairs, just follow the signs. If you need anything cleaned—" She looked Thaya up and down. "I can do that for you for a small fee. Leave your clothes in the bag on the door when you go to bed, and they'll be clean and dry for you tomorrow morning."

"Great," said Thaya.

Clean, dry clothes—although perhaps I need something lighter for here though I don't plan on staying any longer than I have to.

Thaya paid for the room and the cost of cleaning her clothes, watching her money disappear fast. By her calculations, she wouldn't be able to stay here too long *and* feed herself. As soon as she had paid, Betty passed her the room key, smiled, and left.

When the door shut, Thaya rushed over to the far window and opened it. Khy looked up at her from the park below. She relaxed, he wasn't far away at all, so she left the window and set about inspecting the room. There was another door in the small room, and her eyes widened when she opened it.

My own private washroom? Fresh towels, soap, a comb, and a toothbrush. *Pure luxury,* she thought. Taking up most of the washroom was an enclosed glass cubicle with a curious metal fountainhead hanging down from above.

She stepped inside and turned the handles, only to squeal as cold water sprayed over her. She fell out of the cubicle gasping. Wiping the water off her face, she was more shocked by her reflection in the mirror. Mud or bruises smeared her chin, her clothes were damp and grubby, and her hair was a haystack of tangles. No wonder the officer thought she was a beggar! She hated to admit it, but she smelled too. *What is that, sweat and seaweed? Dragon stink? Ew!*

She turned back to the cubicle, reached inside, and played with the levers. One turned the water on, and the other made it warmer or colder. Quickly she stripped off her damp clothes, grabbed the soap, and jumped inside.

"Mmm!" The warm water falling on her skin was heaven. On a tiny shelf were little plastic bottles filled with different gorgeous-smelling, honey-like liquids. She untied her hair and got to washing every inch of herself with all the liquids. Buckets of bubbles soon followed until the cubicle was filled with them.

She spent a good while in there until she noticed the

room was thick with steam. Reluctantly she turned off the water and dried herself with the thick, soft towel. Standards in this world were far higher than she had ever experienced.

She stared at her discarded damp clothes and wrinkled her nose at the thought of putting them back on. Betty hadn't mentioned dinner, and it didn't say 'Bed, *Dinner* & Breakfast,' so hopefully there'd be a good tavern in town.

She left her cloak, overcoat and over trousers off, and pulled on her underpants, crop top and leggings. Her shirt had dried off a bit and it was light, long and loose; if she wore her belt over it, it looked quite good, plus it wasn't as dirty as her outer clothes.

Despite feeling rather naked, she was still too hot and overdressed for the climate. She pulled her boots on and felt even hotter, but surely it had to be cooler outside now that nighttime had fallen. She filled a glass of water at the sink and drank thirstily. Smoothing her hair in the mirror one last time, she headed back to Khy.

It was still close and humid; the faint ocean breeze just wasn't enough.

Khy sniffed her all over. "Fresh skin, old clothes."

"Yeah, I'll clean them tonight. Dinner is required first though, and an early night."

"People have been going in there, hear the music?"

She looked across the street to where he pointed his horn. A brightly lit tavern with swing doors and blaring music beckoned her. Men and women in equal numbers were coming and going.

"Looks lively and friendly," said Thaya.

"I don't think they'd be so friendly as to let me inside," said Khy.

Thaya sighed. "No, I suppose not. Can't you change shape into a human?"

Khy wrinkled his nose.

"Okay, I guess not. Well, I'll go get some food for myself and come back. Shouldn't be too long." Thaya adjusted her belt and checked her hidden money pouch, her fireshot tucked under her shirt, and then her toy sword. The crystal rod hummed faintly as she adjusted the hilt.

"Right then." She nodded at Khy, then strode towards the tavern.

16

HUNTED

Thaya expected overpowering heat, smoke, rowdiness, and the smell of something good cooking.

Only one of those expectations was correct as she pushed through the saloon doors: the rich smell of food that made her instantly ravenous was accompanied by a blast of frigid, smoke-free air that made her shiver. There was no rowdiness, no drunken patrons shouting and heckling novice musicians who were too drunk or despondent to even hold their instruments correctly. Everyone was seated and there was just one musician: a man with a long, thick moustache who was singing and strumming a guitar and creating a pleasing rhythm. He wore an interesting broad-brimmed hat, sported spurs on his boots and tapped his foot in time to the beat.

Finally, a horse rider. So they DO have country folk here. Maybe he's a ranger.

People glanced at her as she walked in, but no one was that interested and all eyes quickly turned back to the man singing. Thaya began to relax into anonymity. Every table was filled with couples or families, and the only seat she could see that was empty was at an enormous bar at the back. She walked towards it, noting that there wasn't just one bar server but several, mostly young men and one woman.

She sat down on the bar stool and nearly fell off it when the round seat swivelled beneath her. She chuckled and played with the seat, wondering how it had been constructed to be able to do that. As soon as she was done swivelling, a barman with one eyebrow raised leaned over and asked, "What can I get you?"

"Er..." She looked at the other patrons seated around the bar. Every one had a different drink.

"Here's the drinks list and bar menu. Take your time. If you want a full dinner, all the tables are booked until nine-thirty, but you can always get bar snacks." The barman pushed a tall, folded card into her hands and went to serve another customer.

She looked at a long list of drinks which she had never heard of. Beer, cider or wine was usually the choice at home, and usually only beer or cider was available. Her eyes kept flicking to the drink a young woman a few seats along had. It was pinkish red, in a fancy flat and wide glass, with a tiny pink umbrella stuck in a strawberry resting across the top. Well, there was no way she wasn't getting one of those. Next, she looked at the food listed—she hadn't heard of any of these dishes either!

She looked around, hoping to see what other people had, but few were eating yet. She turned back to the menu and stared at the pictures of various dishes.

"Ready to order?" The barman appeared and wiped the bar.

"I'll have one of those..." She pointed to the woman's

drink and randomly picked some things off the menu. "...
And, er, 'Shrimps,' 'Fries', and 'Greens'."

The barman nodded. "You got it. One strawberry
margarita coming right up."

Thaya watched spellbound as he made her drink by
pouring various liquids into a metal flask which he then
began to shake and toss around as if it were a dance.

When he was done, he opened the flask and tipped
the contents into a glass which he then placed in front
of her. She stared at the piece of art for several long
moments before popping the strawberry into her
mouth. The little paper umbrella actually opened and
closed like a real one, and when she took her first sip...
Oh my! It tasted delicious—cold, tart and sweet all at
the same time! In a few moments she'd already drunk
half of it.

"Hello, trouble."

Thaya jumped at the familiar voice.

Terence smiled and rested his arms on the bar. He
looked different dressed in a flowery shirt and short, blue
trousers. His eyes—no longer hidden behind dark glasses—
were large, brown, and kindly.

"Wanna drink? My shout," he asked.

"Oh, I've just got one."

"All right, I'll buy the next then. I've got some time to kill
before I meet my girlfriend."

Thaya pursed her lips, a little disappointed. "Sure,
thanks. Please join me. I'm just getting some food, and then
I'm back home for an early night." She sipped her drink,
unable to leave it alone.

"Thanks." He nodded, pulled over a stool, then gestured
to the barman. "Hey, bud, I'll have a beer."

When he was settled, he asked, "So, you just passing

through? On vacation? Good to see you've ditched some layers. It's too hot to think out there."

"Oh, yes, um, just passing through. Me and my...horse..." Thaya wasn't ready for the casual questions; she was still getting used to their easy way of speaking.

An awkward silence followed. What was she supposed to say? She knew nothing of these people and their customs, and she wondered how funny her accent sounded to them. *He's just making conversation—relax,* she told herself.

He picked up his beer. "Listen, don't worry about Priggins, he's always giving people a hard time, locals and foreigners alike. All bark and no bite, he's not all bad."

Thaya had forgotten about the 'cop'. "I'll remember that if I have the unfortunate luck of bumping into him again. I'll have to prove I'm not some beggar or something. Let's just say today has been quite a day."

Her food arrived, and she got stuck in. It was delicious. "Mmm," she mumbled over a mouthful of chips and some sort of pink sauce.

Terence smiled and drank his beer. "Like the sword, it's a nice touch."

Thaya coloured and fiddled with the nasty plastic sword belt self-consciously. She cleared her throat. "It's a gift for my, er, nephew, and I got bored with carrying it around." She decided to keep quiet rather than dig a deeper hole.

"Say, did you get your hand looked at?" Terence squinted at it.

The blisters had calmed down, but it was still red and raw. "Not really, but it's feeling much better now. A good night's sleep, and it will be on the mend."

He nodded, unconvinced, then he finished his beer and checked his watch. "Say, you fancy another one? I got about thirty minutes. Unless I'm crashing your party."

Thaya laughed. It was a good turn of phrase. "Not at all, it's nice to have some company, especially when you're new in town."

"Uh, don't worry about that." He waved at a barman and placed their order. "Everyone here's a tourist. People come from all around to Siesta Key, America's Number One Beach, apparently. Although I've been to lots of beaches called that."

"They do?" She thanked the barman when he placed down her next umbrella-adorned drink, and Terence when he paid for it.

"Sure. Something to do with the white sand, it's unlike any beach anywhere else. They say it's not really sand at all but quartz, really fine, crushed quartz. The cool thing is the sun will bake it all day and it won't get hot like normal sand."

Thaya raised her eyebrows. A beach made of ground-up quartz? It *was* very bright, enough to make her want to wear a pair of those dark glasses. "Where's it from? How did it get there?"

"Apparently over millions of years, rivers and rainwater carried it down from the mountains and deposited it here," said Terence.

It didn't strike as true; she could feel that wasn't correct. Her hands could sometimes read stones—could they also read sand? She planned to visit the beach again tomorrow and find out.

A trill ringing came from somewhere, and Terence dug into his pocket. He pulled out an oblong device that flashed. Thaya stared at it, mesmerised. The name "Dotty" was blinking on it. She'd seen people use these small, black devices in London; everyone seemed to have one. Arendor had told her they were telephones that connected through the air, spanning across the globe to other people's devices so you could talk to them. Terence did that now by holding the phone to his ear.

Stop staring at him! Thaya scolded herself. She tore her eyes away and munched on the last of her fries as if nothing incredible or magical had just taken place. She needed to fit in, not draw attention to herself.

"Okay, I'm on my way. See you in five." He pressed a button on the phone and tucked it back in his pocket. "All right, that's me. I gotta go. See you on the beach sometime? Get that hand looked at. Take care." He patted her shoulder.

"You too, and thanks for the drink," she called after him.

The music died down as the singer took a break, and quieter music drifted from somewhere. She nonchalantly watched the other patrons, noting their attire, mannerisms and general behaviour. Apart from the fact that they were cleaner, better dressed, and clearly wealthier, given nearly everyone wore a piece of jewellery or watch, the people were just the same as back home, and that was comforting. They laughed, chatted, kissed, and enjoyed food, drink, and music, like the people of Havendell.

She stopped people-watching, settled her 'check' with the barman, and left, looking forward to returning to Khy and getting an early night.

After being so long in the strangely cold tavern, the warm, humid air hit her like a solid wall. At first it was nice to thaw out, but she was sweating by the time she reached the garden where Khy stood dozing.

"Have you been sleeping the whole time?"

Khy opened one eye. "Maybe."

He yawned and stretched his neck, then his front legs by shoving them forwards and sticking his behind in the air, much like a dog or a cat might.

Thaya tutted.

The night was young, and the streets were busier than in the daytime with people out looking for a place to eat. Muffled music from several venues drifted over to them, and the smells of various cuisines scented the breeze.

Thaya looked up at her bedroom window and yawned loudly. Thoughts of Grenshoa made her want to stay by Khy's side—could she dare to relax?

"You go to bed. I've placed a sigil on your window—can you see it?" asked Khy.

Thaya squinted up at her window. "Hmm, no."

"Close your eyes. See it now?"

Thaya closed her eyes and imagined looking at her window. There, in vivid blue, was a circle with a complex symbol, or writing, within it. The letters flowed and circled each other elegantly with no sharp edges at all.

"It's pretty; it looks kind of like angelic writing," she said, wondering what angelic writing actually looked like.

"It's our language," said Khy.

Thaya opened her eyes. "I had no idea Saphira-elaysa could write."

"All intelligent creatures can, when necessary. The spoken word is always purer, though. Writing can be distorted and twisted by those seeking to corrupt. Regarding the sigil, it acts as a deterrent to anything with evil intent trying to get in, and everything behind the sigil for several yards is protected. It will fade in the morning sun."

Thaya allowed herself to relax. "You can't stand here all night, not when you've been sleeping all day."

Khy flicked his tail. "I haven't been sleeping *all* day. Besides, I'm still healing Grenshoa's gift, and the sunlight here is far more powerful than in those mountains. I feel stronger already. But you're right, I'm not going to stay here all night. There's something new in the air—it arrived after the sun set. I'm not sure what it is, but I need to investigate. No, it's not the dragon."

He looked more intrigued than concerned so Thaya tried not to worry. "All right, but don't go far. Tomorrow we're getting the hell out of here."

She gave him a hug and headed inside. In her room, she stripped off her clothes, stuffed them all into the clothes bag, and hung it outside her door. She brushed her teeth, drank some water, and only just had enough energy to draw the curtains before crawling into bed.

Thaya stood alone on a vast expanse of white sand looking out across a royal-blue ocean. A strong, hot breeze lifted her honey-brown hair and ruffled her tunic, and above her, white clouds moved swiftly across the azure sky.

"Why am I here? Where *is* here?"

The place seemed familiar though she couldn't name it. She reached down and touched the sand, letting the cool, soft grains trail under her fingers. She scooped up a handful, and the fine particles glimmered in the sunlight like crystals. She sprinkled it into the wind and watched it carry out to sea.

On the horizon, the waves rolled, creating long lines of galloping white horses. She squinted and shielded her eyes; the sea looked strange, turbulent. Her heartbeat quickened as a white-crested wave rose higher than the rest. It moved faster than the other waves and swiftly engulfed them. Though far away, it was moving fast...what if it reached the shore? She had to get off this beach, she had to reach high ground!

She turned and started running. The beach stretched back for miles! It rose only a little, and there was no high ground in sight. She glanced back at the ocean and wished she hadn't. The wave had reached the shore, the swirling mass eating it up like a hungry beast. She tried to run faster but tripped and fell, her hands plunging into the sand.

At once, a star map filled her vision—a large one. She gasped at the mass of bright stars and the multitude of lines of light linking them all together—each point had so many connections, she couldn't count them all. Even at her location, marked by the light expanding from her, hundreds of lines reached in all directions.

A star map, not a mere portal map of Urtha's locations—this is a map of star portals.

The water!

She pulled away, drawing her hands out of the sand, and moving backwards within the map as she tried to stand up, but the world rushed away from her.

"Argh!" Thaya stumbled backwards and hit a wall.

Everything turned dark. It was nighttime in the street, and Betty's B&B loomed in front of her, the yellow sign with its pretty purple flowers swinging merrily in the breeze. The streetlamps were lit, but the place was deserted. All the taverns were closed, the roads were devoid of cars, and not a soul paced the sidewalk.

It must be very late, she thought, *or very early.* She hugged her chest despite the warmth.

Wait a minute, I put my clothes in the wash bag. What's going on? She stared down at her attire. It was dirty and grubby, like it had been before.

"Khy?"

She hurried to the garden where she'd left him, but he

wasn't there. She glanced up at her window. The sigil was gone!

Where the hell is Khy? He can't have gone far.

The wind gusted, and a can fell out of the trash onto the ground with a clang that made her jump. She stared at the word 'coke' written on it as it rolled into the gutter, then glimpsed movement on the other side of the street. She peered at the shadows in the alleyway between two buildings and saw something glint—a light or a piece of metal maybe.

Thaya moved into the shadow cast by a tree, her hand going to her fireshot, but it wasn't there! She reached for the soulfire, trying to stoke it in the core of her being, but it wouldn't spark. The hairs on her neck rose.

I should run inside where it's safe... But something in her gut told her it wasn't safe, even there.

I should run! She looked left and right along the street. *But where to?*

Footsteps echoed loudly and then stopped. Thaya sidled out of the protection of the tree and ran in the opposite direction. She glanced back. The darkness of the night was so complete, not a single star or cloud could be seen. It was as if a thick blanket clung just above and beyond the streetlights.

The darkness bulged and suddenly poured into the street as a physical thing. It rolled along the road in a gaseous wave, consuming everything so that there was nothing beyond the blackness. Enormous orange eyes appeared in the darkness, eyes that were split down the middle with a long pupil. Thaya screamed.

She hurtled around the corner into a smaller street, but the eyes in the blackness followed. The wind picked up and howled around her, sending drink cans, newspapers and trash flying. It became a tornado, trying to blow her off her feet. She grabbed hold of a signpost, noticing the sign atop it said, 'Mystic Mary' in purple on a cosmic background of stars and planets.

Is this her house? But her eyes were torn back to the approaching monstrous dark. A giant lizard's maw appeared out of the cloud, opened wide, and a wall of fire surged out from it towards her. She screamed.

Thaya gasped and threw off the covers, her heart pounding. Sweat matted her hair and made her face clammy. It was still dark outside. She forced herself out of bed and turned on the bathroom light, her previous awe with the device long forgotten. She splashed cool water on her face and gulped it down her parched throat. Though sweating, she shivered as the nightmare slowly pulled its claws out of her.

The sigil...Khy!

She strode to the window. The sigil glimmered faintly behind her closed eyes. Good, nothing had broken it, but what about Khy? She threw open the window and stared down. He wasn't there, but he'd said he wouldn't be, so no point worrying just yet. The alarm clock by her bed read 4.38 am, so when did it get light? She had no idea when dawn might arrive.

The sigil is still there, everything's okay, it was just a bad dream. A dream with Grenshoa chasing her...like hell was it just a dream!

She got back into bed and closed her eyes, trying not to worry about Khy, but there was no way she'd be able to fall back to sleep, no way in hell.

. . .

The sun was up when she next opened her eyes, filling the bedroom with light and warmth—she'd been too scared to draw the curtains shut again. The nightmare felt far away now and even ridiculous. She glanced at the clock, another intriguing device that she had yet to figure out how it worked.

Damn. 8.40 am!

She had twenty minutes to get to breakfast. She jumped in the water sprinkler, screeched at the cold, sighed at the warmth, and washed thoroughly, ridding herself of the nightmare's tendrils.

Wrapping a towel around her, she opened the door and peeked outside her room. Hanging off the handle was the wash bag, and inside were her freshly cleaned and pressed clothes.

She pulled on her linens and shirt, brushed her hair, and ran out the door. Following her nose that detected the warm, welcoming smells of toast and eggs, she entered a sunlit room where people sat at tables eating their breakfast.

Betty appeared. "Oh, good morning, Miss!" Her corn-flower-blue dress was overlaid with a frilly, yellow apron, and she held an enormous, bulbous jug of freshly squeezed orange juice. "Did you sleep well? Wonderful. Coffee? Super. Help yourself to fruit, cereals and croissants over there. How do you like your eggs? Scrambled? Wonderful. Take a seat on that table there by the window, and I'll be right back."

Thaya found herself nodding to everything Betty said. She remembered hearing the word 'coffee' spoken in London but had no idea what it was, and neither was she too sure about 'croissants' but she was certain they were going to be delicious. She took a bowl from the stack and filled it full of apple and grapefruit slices, added strawberries, and then took what she thought was a croissant.

As soon as she sat down, Betty placed a cup of something hot and black and intriguing smelling in front of her, then poured a glass of orange juice. The brightly dressed landlady smiled and whirled away. Only moments could have passed as Thaya sipped the hot, black and bitter-tasting coffee when Betty returned with a plate full of toast and scrambled eggs.

Thaya tucked into everything, all at once, and didn't stop until bowl and plate were both empty. The coffee was hard to drink, but she found she wanted more after a few sips; the eggs were divine; and the croissant was something she wished she could take back home. All memories of her evil nightmares were banished by the good food and warm morning sunlight.

I could stay here a bit longer, she mused, cupping her coffee to her lips. *That mountain was rather cold and bleak. I could live an easy life here with Khy.*

She shook her head, coming around with a start.

What am I thinking? I'm stuck here on a different planet—well, not a different planet, but certainly not in MY own time—running from a dragon who can chase me in my dreams as well as for real. I've got to get back. I've got to go now!

She stood up abruptly, her chair scraping loudly on the tiled floor and making the other people jump and look at her.

"Sorry"—she grinned sheepishly—"er, I'm late." She hurried out of the room.

17

DRAGON POSSESSION

THAYA RUSHED OUT OF THE B&B TO FIND KHY OUTSIDE IN THE garden, standing in the sun, swaying his tail lazily and looking at the butterfly that had landed on his nose.

Thank the sunlight! "Where the hell have you been?" Thaya began.

Khy lifted his nose, and the butterfly flew away. "Me?" He fluttered his eyelids. "I returned at dawn, as soon as I saw Officer Coppy's peculiar metal cart creeping along the street. We should move from here."

"They're 'cops' not 'coppys' and it's a 'car.' Don't make the same mistakes I did. Why do we have to go? Are the police on their way? I was just beginning to like it here. We've done nothing wrong, after all, and you can hide here."

Khy looked into the middle distance. "No, not the police, something else, something far darker."

"Grenshoa?"

"Yes and no. She's still about, waiting, but in the distance. No, something lesser but more numerous."

"What? Just say it!" Thaya folded her arms. *What was about to attack them, for God's sake!*

"I can only think...her minions. They have her scent or aura. I think she's rallying her...own kind. Many remain allied to dragons, even in this time. Their creed has infected many worlds and many races, so much so, they believe this planet to now be theirs. They've been here for a long time. I went for a walk, a very long one, investigating the energy around here and beyond, both in the dimensions above and a little of the dimensions below, but the lower ones are harder for us Saphira-elaysa to reach."

Thaya squeezed her earlobe, thinking about Ordacs running through Siesta Key's high street. The people wouldn't take to it too kindly. "Let's just go now then. I've got all my stuff."

Her dream flashed behind her eyes—her hand trailing through the crystal sand, the map of the star portals opening in her mind.

Khy had started walking. She followed. "Wait, I saw something in my dream."

"I saw it too: the beach, the wave, then Grenshoa. Yes, we're being hunted." Khy nodded.

"Yeah, but there's more. I saw a star map open when I touched the sand. It might happen for real. Maybe if we went to the beach—what is it?"

Khy had stopped, his long ears pricked and his indigo eyes looking far away. He didn't speak for a long moment. "Something follows or watches. We've left the safety of the sigil and my cloaking magic; to cast them again would capture even more attention. No, don't panic, just walk by my side and remain calm."

Thaya did that, her head and shoulders relaxed but her eyes darting everywhere.

"Run. Now," Khy commanded.

Thaya didn't know what Khy could sense, but the prickle down her spine made her do what he asked; she ran.

The sunlit sidewalk was suddenly engulfed in a dense mist which blanketed out the streets, the sun, the sound of their foot and hoof beats. Khy had cast a spell to hide them. Thaya looked behind her, and before the mist engulfed them completely, saw men running. She frowned. They all looked the same, wearing dark suits and glasses and carrying strangely empty expressions. They vanished in the haze, but Thaya's pulse raced.

Nedromas! She remembered Arendor's words when she'd last been chased by them across the white horse plains. *'Anything unusual or paranormal, and the Fallen Ones' hybrids come, the Nedromas—soulless beings with dead eyes, and always dressed in black suits. And no, they are not human. They are alien hybrids employed by the evil running this place and much of the world. They work for the vampires, who themselves are also alien hybrids.'*

"Keep moving," said Khy.

She picked up the pace again.

Orange light flared ahead. It looked like fire in a cloud as it bulged into Khy's mist.

Khy nodded ahead at the fire. "This is the other group I discovered, the one most closely affiliated to the Ordacs back in your time. They're not tied to this dimension."

"What? There are more?" asked Thaya. How many *things* were chasing them?

"She's using them to hunt us, so she can remain hidden. Turn left, now!" Khy veered to the left, and she staggered to make the turn. After several yards, he stopped, and everything became quiet and still. Thaya held her breath. Khy's ears swivelled back and forth.

"*What is it?*" Thaya asked him with her mind.

"Don't use telepathy; they're listening hard for that frequency. This is a safe place. Do you feel it?"

Thaya stood still and felt with her inner senses. "It's calm. I can't feel the others."

"Exactly. There's a small path ahead. It only goes a little way, but we have a chance to lose them. Move very slowly and silently."

Thaya walked along what she felt was the safe path until she pressed up against something solid. All she could see was mist; she couldn't see what was blocking her passage.

Khy twirled his horn, and the mist in front of them dissipated to reveal a purple door and a sign written on it.

SALESMEN, RELIGIOUS OR OTHERWISE, WILL BE CURSED AND
RETURNED TO THE SENDER!
GOOD PEOPLE WELCOME

Thaya frowned. Was she a good person? *Well, I'm not a salesman...*

"Hurry, knock on the door." Khy nudged her with his nose.

"All right, all right." She raised her hand, wondering who was inside since she didn't fancy speaking to anyone right now.

Her rapping echoed loudly in the mist.

A moment later, a distant voice called, "Hang on, I'm coming!" The sound of heavy bolts being drawn came from the other side, and a woman with glasses and layers of purple skirts opened the door.

Thaya blinked in surprise. "Mystic Mary?"

The woman squeezed her hands to her round cheeks. "Oh, my goodness, I knew you'd come by! You're late by about ten minutes though. And aww, isn't he a cutie?" She squeezed Khy's chin, and he giggled.

Mary peered out beyond them, narrowed her eyes dangerously, and looked left and right as if she could see beyond the mist, or perhaps she couldn't see Khy's mist at all. "Bless the light, it's frightful out there today. No, not the sweltering heat—the energy, it's all gooey and dark and... yuck! Better come inside." She grabbed Thaya's arm, then paused. "Say, you haven't seen a man with a grey tie and suit out there, have you? He's actually grey all over, even his skin and eyes, and he often carries a briefcase of doom. He might be wearing a broad-brimmed hat, also grey."

Thaya thought for a moment. "Er, no. Seen plenty dressed all in black though."

Mary looked relieved, then stiffened and moved closer, tilting her glasses and eyeing her over them with a serious look. "Believe you me, the Men in Black have got nothing on the taxman. If you see a man with the description I gave you, run. Now come inside before the psychos catch up."

Thaya was about to speak, but Mary dragged her inside.

Khy spoke quietly with his mind. *"Go. I need to wait here. They have lost us, for now. There's much protection here; the mystic has layered the place in crystal energy and wards."*

Mary waved at Khy with a big smile and closed the door.

The mystic sighed and leant her head back against the door as Thaya sighed and leant against the wall.

"You feel it too, huh?" asked Mary, and shook her head. "This energy, ugh, I simply can't stand it."

From a shelf beside the door, she picked up a wand made of wood inlaid with various coloured crystals and ending in a large amethyst point. She raised a hand and twirled it over the door, muttering words Thaya couldn't quite hear.

Thaya blinked; she could actually feel magic move and her palms tingled. It was very faint but there nonetheless.

So, this Earth does have a little magic left; it's not all gone. The thought gave her hope; perhaps what was lost could be returned. She watched Mystic Mary and got a feeling that the good witch didn't know quite what she was doing, though it was working somewhat.

"There we go, another ward on the door." The woman smiled triumphantly and put the wand down.

And how would she know what to do? thought Thaya. *It's not like I do either. Neither of us has been trained, and I'd be surprised if there were any trainers left here at all. Yet my magic, or power, is different to hers; it feels more intrinsic, from within, whereas magi and witches use the powers without, manipulating the elements, so to speak.* She wished she understood better.

Mary looked at her. "Tea? I can't tolerate coffee. Must be the English ancestry on my mother's side."

"Sure, tea is good," replied Thaya. *Tea, I know tea. Not a fan of it much, but thank goodness there are some things still around.*

"Here, sit down." Mary led her to a large room with sofas on one side and a wooden table with two chairs on the other. She pulled one back for her. "Oh, and you can leave your sword by the wall, and your belt too. We need to be light, loose and airy." Mary wafted her loose attire, shook her mass of curls and laughed.

Thaya undid her plastic sword belt and leant it against the wall beside her. She sat on the pink, cushioned chair and inspected the room whilst the mystic busied herself in the kitchen. The room was filled with all manner of plants in pots on the floor and on numerous shelves, some even reached their foliage up to the ceiling. Between the plants nestled crystals of all types and sizes, some huge and the size of rabbits, others smaller than her thumb—amethysts, tiger's eyes, moonstones, lapis lazuli, quartz, turquoise, and many others she couldn't name. The plants crowded up to the patio doors and made the room darker than she would have liked.

Mary came back carrying a tray with a steaming teapot, jug and teacups. "I see you're admiring my greenhouse. It may look excessive, but they keep the air clean and are guardians of the house." She set the tray down. "Now, I do have biscuits, but I don't like giving my clients sugar before we start. I'll bring them out after."

"After?" Thaya raised an eyebrow. Was she about to have a session of some sort? *Am I going to have to pay for this, whatever it is?* "Oh, it's not really necessary, we were just passing, and I—"

"Nonsense! Some strange things have happened lately, and you need to hear it." Mary poured the tea.

"I do?" *Maybe you should be paying me to know about everything I've just been through then,* thought Thaya.

Mary held up a little ceramic jug. "Milk? No? Sorry, no sugar yet. Indeed, you do; it's not often I have lucid dreams about dragons, crystal temples, and magical devices—and filled with a person and her horse that I've met only just the day before!"

Thaya stared in shock at the woman. *Lucid dreams?*

Mary cupped her drink and breathed in the aroma. "Mmm, organic oolong, my favourite." Her green eyes settled on Thaya's toy sword, then back to her tea that was steaming up her glasses.

Thaya sipped it, finding the smoky taste strong and

pungent but not disagreeable. She tried to work out what to ask first. "You said I was late, but how did you know I was coming? Something to do with your dreams?"

"Yes, let's get right to it." Mary set her tea down and tucked her dark, greying locks behind her ears, her gaze becoming serious.

"You are not from round here," stated Mary seriously. "You're a soul from far away, from long ago."

Thaya spluttered on her tea and quickly set the cup down.

Mary laughed and slapped her own leg. "Don't be alarmed, I could tell from the moment I set eyes on you. I would say you're not even from this world, but few of us with...abilities...are, though we wear human forms in this lifetime. That high street we met on? Full of aliens who don't even know they're not human. Don't worry, it's quite normal. I'm not the only one who can see this; other nega-tive beings and forces can, too." Mary's eyes darted to the sword and back to Thaya again.

Thaya wondered if Mary had seen the dragon for real, but she held off asking just yet—let the woman do all the talking first before she mentioned things that didn't need speaking about.

Mary took a deep breath. "You and your companion brighten the air around you, so in the evening I was shocked when a dark force appeared before me. Demonic almost, it stood right there on the rug in the middle of the room, all hazy and dark-like. It demanded, 'Give us the Light Holders! Give us the Light Holders!' over and over. I said, 'Begone, evil spirit, begone!'" Mary raised her fisted hands. "And I cast my most powerful spell, but still I had to use Bertie to help." She pointed at the foot-long, fist-thick, chunk of quartz gleaming on the windowsill.

Thaya listened as Mary spoke, chills going up and down her spine. The woman really was a mystic, she really did have powers.

"The evil spirit, demon, or whatever it was, left, and I was spent as I had never been spent before. I collapsed on the couch and fell into a deep sleep, but when I stood up, I was on Siesta Key Beach—but it wasn't like it is now. There were no buildings or people, it was just a long stretch of white sand and the deep blue ocean beyond. Then you appeared out of nowhere, and there was this shining unicorn by your side.

"A tremendous roar shook the Earth and I looked up to see a monstrous dragon flying towards you. But you weren't afraid, you just stood there, and then you held up something that burst into white light. Great power collected and swirled around you, and everything became too bright to see. Then after a moment, in that brightness, I saw a great city made of crystal, and then..."

"And then what?" Thaya gripped her cup tightly.

"Then I woke up." Mary frowned.

Thaya sighed and rubbed her eyes, trying to keep them from popping out of her head. And just when she thought Mary had finished, she started up again.

"Now you could say it was just a dream, in whole or in part, but I know the astral from the physical, and I know what is what. However, the strangeness did not end there because my watch had stopped."

She showed Thaya a petite, gold watch. "See the hands? They're stuck on one minute to nine. Now, I changed the battery only last month, and it was working until that time last night. Ah, don't look at me like I'm mad and the watch just broke, no. From the time that demon appeared to the end of my dream, no time had passed, not even a minute! I know because my favourite sitcom show's at nine, and I had just sat down to watch it. When I awoke, the program started one minute later! Now you tell me how all that happening in that time was possible? It was no dream, it was a premonition, and that demon had stopped time passing."

Thaya didn't know anything about sitcoms or programs, but she understood everything else and knew Mary wasn't lying. Could it be the Vormae's Shades? No. No Shade had the power of speech or such intellect as the demon Mary had described. She'd never thought of the Fallen Races as demons, but it was a good and fitting description.

"I don't think you're mad," Thaya said. She wasn't quite sure what to say to her and was reluctant to reveal why, or rather how, she was here—she couldn't explain easily that a dragon had dragged her through time and dumped her tens of thousands of years into the future. All she wanted was to get back home, and away from the dragon and the crystal that had caused her all this trouble.

But it is rather nice here, warm and sunny, civilised... No! This place is awful, and I have to get home.

Maybe Mary knew of a standing stone, a stone circle, or an ancient sacred place that might once have been a portal? Maybe coming here had been the perfect thing.

"Right, let's get down to business." Mary pushed the tea tray aside and put a small box on the table. "Put your fifty in here so the debt is on me to give to you. I find it easier to balance the energy that way."

Thaya blinked at her. Did the woman want payment for something Thaya didn't really want to do? Should she stand up and leave? Mary's house *had* provided her and Khy with protection though, and she couldn't find it within her to just up and out. Besides, she *was* intrigued with what was tran-spiring, and anyway, what was she going to do with all the paper money once she got home? With tight lips she pulled the money out of her pocket and leafed through the notes until she found a fifty.

"Excellent," said Mary, her eyes lighting up. She reached her silver-ringed hands over the table. "Here, give me your palms. I also sense you need protection from whatever hunts you, too, so let's see what we can do."

Thaya handed them over with a raised eyebrow. Palm-reading was not something she trusted at all.

"Hmm, yes, hmm," mumbled Mary inspecting them. "Oh my, that is odd."

"What?" asked Thaya, scowling. This was wasting time.

Mary peered over the top of her glasses. "Your lifeline does not end." She pointed at the supposed lifeline and touched Thaya's palm. Soulfire sparked like electricity. Both women jumped and Mary leapt back.

"Wowsers!" Mary squealed and chuckled. "We have a live one! Goodness, that was strong. I'm going to need a little help absorbing that energy and protecting myself." She hurried over to a bookshelf half filled with books, and the other half filled with junk and more crystals.

Thaya opened and closed her hand, wondering if Mary had seen the soulfire flare as well.

The mystic returned with a thick shard of selenite. "You know, when crystals move into different dimensions, they remain the same? Humans stay the same as well, so that is where crystals and humans are unified with shared qualities, and that's why we can use crystals to assist us to do remarkable things—good or bad. That's my little freebie for you today." She tapped her nose and giggled. "Right, now let's get straight to it."

Mary closed her eyes, held the crystal shard in one hand and reached for Thaya's hand with the other.

Thaya hesitated. "What's going to happen?"

"You're searching for something, and we're going to find it," Mary replied.

Thaya nodded. "I am—I'd like to go home. All right." She sighed and gave the mystic her hand, bracing herself for any more soulfire outbursts.

Both women took deep breaths and became still. The air drew close around them, and it became warmer, almost cloying. Mary let out a loud sigh and let go of her hand.

"What is it?" Thaya opened her eyes.

Mary glared at the toy sword leaning against the wall. "I'm sorry, I'm being distracted. Just what is it with that silly sword? It's literally humming. In the astral realm, it's positively glowing!"

Wow, she can sense the crystal rod. Thaya squeezed her chin. *Should I reveal what it is? The woman can clearly see something powerful about it.*

Thaya sighed, got up, and brought the toy sword back to the table. "To be honest, I'm pretty sure this is why we're being hunted."

Mary stared, bright-eyed, as Thaya unscrewed the pommel and tipped the crystal shard part of the way out. As soon as it touched Thaya's hand, light filled the room as every crystal large and small, flashed and glowed. Wind billowed around them, plant leaves flapped, and any paper object not weighted down went flying. Power surged into Thaya's hand, making her heart race and her skin tingle.

Wide-eyed, Mary shouted over the din. "Stop, put it away, others will feel it!"

With some effort, Thaya tipped the crystal back into the hilt and quickly screwed on the pommel. The wind vanished, the paper settled, and the crystals dimmed. Thaya wiped the sweat from her face and took a deep breath.

Mary's hair settled back on her shoulders, and she pressed her hands into her bosom, her mouth wide open. "It's okay, it's okay," she said over and over to herself. "The crystals held; the protective force remains. Phew, right, everything makes sense now, but if we don't get you to where you need to go, and that...*device*...far away from here, big trouble is coming. Far more trouble than Mystic Mary can deal with, that's for sure. Phew, mamma mia, lordy lord. Right then."

She adjusted her glasses and smoothed back her hair. "Okay, where were we? That's okay, just put the sword over there by the amethyst, yes, that big one. Right, let's get back to it. Hand—just one this time, please."

Thaya sat down and passed her hand over, palm up. Still gripping the selenite crystal in her left hand, Mary placed her right hand with her fingers splayed over Thaya's.

As Mary connected with her, a strange thing occurred. Nothing was spoken out loud, all was seen and felt internally. It was like floating on the surf as it rolled over the shore and then retreated. When the tide rolled forwards, Thaya saw images of Mary—a young woman in a long robe, her hair tied back and grinning as she received a rolled parchment, some kind of scholarship or award, from a person dressed in a long cloak and strange square hat.

The tide retreated, and she felt images of herself passing to Mary, images of her life, events that meant something important to her, and she saw again, with a pang of pain, Yenna and Fi, her adopted grandparents.

The tide rolled forwards again, and she saw images of Mary. Now she wore a white dress and was kissing a smartly dressed man.

The tide rolled back, and she was a slave in the Nuakki

mines again, the endless, soul-crushing 'chink' 'chink' of her pickaxe upon the wall.

The tide rolled forwards, and she saw a child running into her mother's arms. It had to be Mary.

The tide rolled back, and she saw herself, a child, splashing in the water, and then she resisted. Was this where she'd met Khy? She didn't want to reveal her connection to him nor his identity, she needed to keep them both safe. She could feel Mary wanting to read more, but the mystic was respectful and ceased searching.

The tide rolled forwards, a great wash of it this time, and the entire world fell away.

"What the—?" Thaya gasped. She and Mary stood together on the white sands of Siesta Key Beach. There were no buildings, people, or anything, just the sand and the sea and the wind, just as it had been in her dream.

"Oh my, this is exactly what I saw!" said Mary, holding her wild curls down with one hand. "We're in the waking dream! No, don't open your eyes or take your hand away or we'll lose the connection."

"I saw this too. Why?" asked Thaya.

Mary looked around in wonder. "I've only ever done this once before...it must be you with the power, you and that crystal maybe. I don't quite get it, but this place is a kind of connection point: both you and I are in a version of this beach. We humans *can* move forwards and backwards in time—at least with our minds—and some of us see things in other dimensions. Together, we're connected by the location, this place."

"That crystal brought me here, but why?" asked Thaya. It was the truth, the bare bones of it. She could have mentioned the dragon dragged her here too, but decided to avoid bringing that up in case Grenshoa *did* appear!

Mary shook her head at first and then stopped, her eyes opening wide. "Ahhh, the crystal was protecting you! Yes. Hmm. Perhaps it seeks something, too."

Thaya pursed her lips. She could have said as much.

"It's trying to tell you something," Mary continued.

"You don't say," Thaya muttered under her breath.

"You're trying to find a way home, aren't you? Well, this *is* the way home." Mary spread her arms.

"What?" Thaya looked around at the beach, the waves and the sky. "There's nothing here!"

Mary nodded, then frowned. "I know but, somehow, this place is what you seek, it *is* your way home."

Thaya took a deep breath. This wasn't helping. She needed to check on Khy, too. Was this place even real? She bent down and trailed her hand in the beautiful silky sand. It certainly felt real if she kept her eyes closed, of course. Mystic Mary was turning out to be no fraud.

"Yes, that's it!"

Thaya looked up to see Mary dancing happily.

"What's *it?*" Thaya asked. Could this woman actually be mad and Thaya had been too nice and accepting to think it?

Mary laughed. "It's the sand, the key is in the sand! Siesta *Key,* ha-ha! No, don't get cross. The sand, it's quartz, it's crystal. It's *talking* to us! You can feel it, I know you can!"

Thaya frowned, yet Mary was speaking the truth, she just hadn't quite caught up with her. She bent down and picked up a handful of the stuff and watched it glitter as it fell through her fingers. In the tiny sparkles she saw an image: a shining city made of crystal. She dropped the rest of the sand in shock.

"Look, you see the temple?"

Thaya looked to where Mary pointed and gasped. The exact same temple now towered behind them, some distance away. Its elegant, white pillars rose into the sky, and it shimmered so that it appeared to be carved out of a single crystal. It was the most beautiful building she had ever seen.

A deafening roar shook the earth. Thaya's knees weakened, and her insides trembled.

"Grenshoa!" she screamed.

18

SWORD AND SAND

THAYA JERKED HER HAND AWAY FROM MARY'S. THE SUDDEN loss of connection jolted through her like an electric shock; her eyes smarted and her head spun. She heard Mary yelp.

It took a moment to ground herself and focus. When the room came back into view, she found Mary slumped forwards, her hands loosely gripping the selenite crystal.

"Mary, are you okay? I shouldn't have broken the connection so fast, gosh, that was painful!" But she hadn't wanted to endanger Mary when Grenshoa appeared.

Mary moaned and rolled her head left and right, her hair covering her face. Thaya leapt up and went to her, helping the woman sit back in the chair. "Mary, speak to me. Here, have some tea. I'll get you some sugar."

Thaya started to go, but fast as a whip, Mary's hand shot out and gripped her wrist. Thaya yelped and tried to pull away but the woman's vice-like grip was far beyond her real strength.

"Mary, please let go. What's going on?" Thaya began to panic.

The woman's face twisted into a snarl, and her face

bulged and distorted impossibly. Her eyes rolled back in her skull and became glowing, orange orbs split down the middle by long, black pupils. She opened her mouth, and her teeth were fangs. Thaya twisted and turned but could not get herself free.

"Give back what you stole!" Grenshoa's roar shook the room.

Thaya cowered and tried not to look at Mary's horrific half-human, half-dragon face. "What have you done to Mary?"

"I'll kill her unless you give me the Rod."

"Let her go!" Thaya shouted, groaning from the crushing pain in her arm. Grenshoa wouldn't kill Mary, would she?

Mary thrashed and convulsed, and her distorted voice cried out, "Release me, please! Somebody, help me!"

Her voice deepened into a snarl, and Grenshoa roared. "Give it back, bitch!"

"Let her go!" Thaya screamed. Working through the pain, she pooled soulfire in her palm and focussed on the golden glow, turning it into a pale healing light. Not knowing what to do, but knowing she had to do something, she slammed her palm against Mary's bulging forehead and shouted. "Release her!"

Grenshoa screeched. Mary writhed then screamed. Her hands clenched the selenite crystal until they trembled and turned white. The selenite crystal vibrated, hummed, then exploded. The force threw Mary and her chair flying against the wall. The chair splintered, and the mystic sprawled on the floor.

Thaya ran to her side.

"Ooh," the mystic groaned. "Ooooh!"

Her face was bright red but, thank the creator, it was no longer bulging and half-dragon looking.

Shaking, Thaya helped Mary onto the sofa and fanned her face with a book. "No, don't speak. Take deep breaths and, here, have some tea." She poured another cup and the mystic clenched it in her hands, breathing raggedly.

Moments passed, then Mary spoke in rasping words between slurps of tea. "My...God...that has *never* happened before... If that *thing* is hunting you, I never want to be you. My girl, you stand in the light, but darkness swarms around you. What's for sure, you can't stay here, my home will be destroyed! I don't know where you've come from, but it's definitely not from here... I'm not sure I even want to know! Oh my, I can't handle any more truths today."

"But what do I do?" Thaya chewed the skin next to her fingernail. Was Khy okay? She wanted, needed, to check on him, but she couldn't leave Mary in this state just yet. She picked up her toy sword and tied it around her waist. "As soon as you're okay, my companion and I are off."

Mary nodded, breathing easier. "Let's get you to the beach. Hopefully all answers will be found there. We need strong sunlight to banish this evil, and no, I don't want to stay here another moment, not until I've felt the sun on my face."

Thaya nodded, but it was going to take much more than sunlight to get rid of that hellish dragon.

———————

Thaya threw open the front door and ran headlong into Khy. He was so close, his nose must have been pressed against the knocker.

"Thank the sunlight." Thaya took a deep breath and steadied herself on the door frame.

Outside, it was as if nothing had ever happened. Gone

was Khy's protective mist, along with the heavy feeling of being watched and the sound of ominous footsteps. Instead, bright, hot sunlight spilled over the houses, and a few doors down, children giggled as they played chase on the front lawn.

"*Don't be fooled,*" Khy warned telepathically. "*They're still out there, but we've lost them for now. What happened inside?*"

"*Urgh, Grenshoa made an appearance, inside Mary!*"

"*Channelling is not safe.*"

"*You're telling me. She didn't intend for it to happen. Anyway, let's get to the beach, we're all shaken.*"

If Mary thought that Khy leading the way from the house and across the street was odd, she didn't say anything. The worried frown on the mystic's face suggested she was too disturbed by everything else that had happened to notice that Thaya's 'horse' had no bridle or even a rope.

As they walked, Thaya checked every dark shadow and every alley, her eyes darting this way and that and missing nothing as they hurried along the main road. She spied a police car with flashing lights and stopped up short.

After a moment, she relaxed. *It's okay, it's just parked there, and no one's inside it.*

Thaya took a deep breath and shook her head. Now then, where had the others gone? She spotted them quite a way ahead, on the path leading through the trees to the beach. She tutted.

Great, yeah, I'm okay. Thanks for waiting, guys...

She finally caught up with them on the beach where they'd stopped a few yards from the water's edge. They were looking around as if trying to find something, and Khy appeared completely unconcerned about being a horse on a horse-restricted beach. Thankfully, Officer Priggins was otherwise engaged for now.

The beach was quiet. Only a few people jogged or walked along it, and the sea was calm with the gentlest of waves lapping the shore. For all that had already happened this morning, it was still early and before the crowds descended. They would see anybody coming long before they got here, and no one would attack them in broad daylight in the middle of a public open space, would they?

Thaya looked at Khy. His ears were forward, and he constantly scanned the scenery. *He hasn't relaxed, and neither should I.*

Mary was busy rummaging in her bag, pulling out various crystals one after the other. She held a greenish-grey rock up to the sunlight and shook her head. "Nope, no good for this. Hmmm." She pulled out a rose quartz, looked at it closely, then shook her head. "Nope, not this one either."

Thaya decided to ignore them both and focussed on herself. She closed her eyes and took several long, calming breaths, trying to find the quiet space within. What did it mean, her dreams and her shared vision with Mary? Why was this beach important? Was there a portal stone beneath it? Near it? Could the crystal sand show her things like a portal stone might?

It seemed ridiculous, but she got on to her knees and pushed her fingers into the soft, white sand. Against her side, the crystal shard in the toy sword's hilt hummed, and a faint pressure nestled behind her eyes, a building up of latent, expectant energy. But no star map showed itself to her, so what was she supposed to do? She stayed there for another minute, and a shiver ran down her spine. She kept her eyes closed and focused on it.

"*Something senses us,*" said Khy.

Mary inhaled sharply. "I've suddenly got a bad feeling about all of this."

Thaya tried to concentrate, to ignore everything but the sand between her fingers.

What do I see? What do I feel? Show me.

The pressure in her head built, and her hands tingled, but nothing happened, no image came to her.

She sighed and opened her eyes. "Urgh, nothing. Are you sure this is the place?" She asked no one in particular. *And what, exactly, am I expecting of the place anyway?* She adjusted her weight to a more comfortable position and shifted the sword to stop it from digging into her ribs. As soon as she touched the hilt, the power of the crystal within it sparked, making her jump. She gripped the hilt firmly with her right hand and placed her left on the ground. Energy flowed between the sand and the sword and then through her, making the hairs on her arms stand up. She took a deep breath, trying to control the strange feeling, closed her eyes, and in her mind's eye, suddenly saw the great crystal temple before her.

"Wow, I see it," she said. "I see the temple or palace and the city around it!"

It was enormous and entirely carved out of quartz. Incredible power hummed around her, then a roar tore through her mind. She screamed and pulled back. The image vanished as soon as she stopped touching the sword and sand. She looked around but nothing had changed: Khy still remained alert but had taken a step closer; Mary had her tongue between her teeth as she held two crystals up—

one white, one pastel blue—and was having trouble deciding between the two.

"Anyone hear that?" Thaya asked.

Khy cocked his head, and Mary shook hers, her eyes never leaving the crystals.

Maybe I heard it in my mind...

Khy spoke telepathically. *"Hurry, I don't like this...feeling of being hunted."*

"Hurry what? What am I supposed to do?"

"I'll dampen our presence as best I can, but Mary's crystals are amplifying it. If something happens, they can be filled with power and used to protect us, but I'd prefer not to be detected."

Thaya shook her head and plunged her hands into the sand. The whole ground rumbled beneath them, and sand began to rise off the floor around her. She pulled her hands out and stared wide-eyed. "Did anyone see that? Did I just do that?"

Khy flicked his tail, and Mary blinked at her and shrugged.

Thaya shook her head. *Both bloody useless! Okay, I'm not messing around now. Whatever happens, so be it.*

She plunged her left hand into the sand and decisively gripped the cheap metal sword hilt with her right. She closed her eyes as power surged through her and tried to control what she felt. Another roar cut through the air, much closer than before, as if her actions were alerting all near and far to her presence.

Ignore the noise, focus on the power, and breathe, okay, breathe.

She cautiously opened herself to the energy, letting it flow through her more powerfully and adding her own will to it.

The sand rose fast off the ground, lifting her with it at a

dizzying speed. They rose up and up, and then she shot forwards. The sand spun and condensed, and in a heartbeat, she found herself in an inside space surrounded by crystal walls, floors and ceilings—she was somehow inside the crystal temple itself!

"How did you get here?" A man's sharp and commanding voice made her leap out of her skin. Strong hands gripped her shoulders and spun her around. She stared up into the face of a man who had smoothed back, grey-white hair, a long nose, and eyes so pale, they were almost white. "Who are you?"

"Th-the crystal sh-shard, the c-crystal sand, brought me here." Thaya stammered the words out, the shock and the power still coursing through her was quickly becoming too much to bear.

"It's you!" The man's eyes opened wide in recognition. "I saw you in the Looking Field... You have the Rod, I saw it! Return it to me at once."

Grenshoa's presence—she couldn't describe it any better than that—was suddenly nearby. A wave of darkness descended over her, blacking out the man and crystal temple. She could no longer feel his hands on her shoulders. A long, scaled tail whipped out of the darkness, smacked into her chest, and sent her flying.

Thaya rolled back on the beach, winded. The crystal temple, the man, and Grenshoa were all gone, yet the pain in her chest from the dragon's blow throbbed. Khy was beside her instantly, and Mary came running over. Thaya trembled all over, the sudden jolt back into her body and the cutting from the power making her reel, and her palms stung with static as if they had been slapped.

"What happened?" Mary asked. "You just suddenly flailed backwards in a fit."

"That bloody dragon happened!" Thaya spluttered, catching her breath. "It attacked me!"

"Hmm, every time we project into the astral, it's there waiting for us," said Mary, tapping her chin. "None of my crystals are strong enough to fend that off."

"She's right. Grenshoa waits there," said Khy. *"The non-physical realm is even more dangerous than the physical."*

"Great," said Thaya. "Well, I saw the sand rise and me with it, and then I was inside the crystal temple, and there was a man there. I don't know what any of this is about, but there's something about this sand. It's not a portal, well, not a normal one that I know of, but it has portal-type properties..." Thaya trailed off, frowned, and stared along the beach that was now starting to fill with beachgoers carrying their bright, plastic floats and toys. It was like the sand and the crystal rod were trying to tell her something. She reached down and grabbed a handful of the stuff, letting the particles fall through her fingers, white and glimmering against a blue sky.

"Here stood a crystal palace, maybe a city, but a long, *long* time ago," she said quietly, looking deep into the middle distance. She imagined reaching back in time to when the city and its palace-like temples stood.

"There has been nothing here for at least fifty-thousand years," said Khy. *"That much the sand element has told me."*

"Fifty-thousand years..." echoed Thaya. It *felt* true, and yet it was so long ago, she couldn't quite imagine it.

"Well, that much we've gleaned already." Mary huffed and folded her arms, reminding them she was there and jerking Khy and Thaya out of their telepathy. "I've seen the crystal city too. Say, I have a client at 1 pm—this won't take long, will it? I mean, I'm happy to help and get rid of the bad dragon force here, but I might have to head off soon."

Did it exist during my time? Thaya wondered, ignoring Mary. *No, it was before the cataclysms...* She had no proof, only a 'knowing' that was a hallmark of those with the Truth Sight. The whole area, or rather the sand itself, appeared to be a strange kind of portal. She wished she understood such things better. And the behaviour of the crystal shard was so strange—it was like it had a will and intent all of its own.

Could the crystal be trying to get somewhere? Or perhaps it's just trying to escape Grenshoa... Does something call to it? Could it be the Leonites? Who was that man? He knew I had the crystal, he told me to return it. Maybe I need to try the sand again; maybe I need to let go completely. But to travel through the portal, I'll have to pass by the dragon...

Thaya inhaled sharply as she stared at the remaining grains of sand in her hand. "Could this be the remains of the crystal temple? It *feels* true... Oh my...yes! We're standing on all that it once was!"

The others stared at her. Khy swished his tail and chuckled, but thankfully Mary was too shocked at Thaya's words to notice.

Thaya touched the grains in her hand and smiled sadly. "It stood before the cataclysms, before it all changed," she said to herself. "It was destroyed, that much is obvious, for it doesn't stand today, but how could such a thing be obliterated into dust and sand? I don't know."

Despite the eons between her time and here, she felt a sudden connection to Mary, and to all the people on the beach, blissfully unaware of the past and the great crystal palace that had once stood here. They were the children left behind after everything that they once were had been destroyed and taken away. She looked at the modest houses and buildings that stood beyond the beach. They were as shacks compared to the awesome city she had seen. At least in Thaya's time, there was still power and magic, but now, here, there was so little left. She swallowed a lump.

"Oh no!" Mary grasped her hands to her chest and shook her head.

Striding towards them, yet still some distance away, was a man holding a black briefcase and wearing a grey tie and grey suit. Small, dark glasses shielded his eyes, and he wore a broad-brimmed, grey hat that he had to keep hold of in the breeze. Even his skin appeared slate-coloured and drained of life.

"The taxman?" Thaya asked.

"Uh-oh," said Khy looking in a different direction.

Thaya's eyes darted to where he gazed. To their right, a few hundred yards away, stood a gaggle of dark suited men glancing up and down the beach. They looked completely out of place, fully dressed in dark, formal attire whilst most people were nearly naked. Two of them pointed at her, and then, as if they were of one mind, they started hurrying towards them.

Thaya swallowed and then frowned at the screeching din. "What the hell is that infernal noise?" The shrill whistling that had been plaguing her ears for the last few moments, now made itself known to her consciousness. She rubbed her ears and tried to follow the sound. To their left, again quite a way along the beach but closing the gap fast, was Officer Priggins. His shirt was stretched tight over his round belly, and his face was redder than the whistle he puffed on. Something came at them from all directions.

"Just bloody great!" Thaya groaned at the sky.

"If we can leave here, now, perhaps it's better to face Gren-shoa," suggested Khy.

"Take me with you," said Mary, clasping her hands

together, prayer-like. "I'll face dragons, Men in Black, the plague, anything, just not that man!"

"What the...?" Thaya frowned. "I'm not a boat or carriage, I can't take anybody anywhere! Urgh, why is everything always so...*messy?*"

She took hold of the toy sword and gripped the hilt tightly in two hands. The power within the shard responded to her touch, trying to fill her. She resisted. Lifting the sword high with the blade point down, she plunged it deep into the sand, closing her eyes as the building power filled her body and erupted from her palms. In her inner vision, the sand rose and shimmered with energy. She opened her eyes and gasped. The sand was rising for real all around them as if a great wind was blowing and picking it up.

"Oh my, oh my," said Mary, stepping backwards and staring at the swirling maelstrom that whipped her hair around her face.

"I'm not going to let go this time," Thaya had to shout over the din of surging energy, and Officer Priggins' ear-numbing whistling.

The taxman raised his hand and called out, holding on to his hat even harder. The Men in Black were shouting, now running as fast as their legs could carry them. The power was still building, and the wind raged harder—she could feel it trying to lift her up. Khy stepped closer so his chest was against her back.

Mary, overcome with it all, continued to step backwards from the swirling sand, shaking her head and gripping her crystals tightly to her chest. "The energy, it's too much, I want to come but...but I can't...I—" Her eyes rolled back, and she fell onto the sand straight as a plank of wood.

"Mary!" Thaya cried.

"She's all right, she just fainted," said Khy. "This power would tear her apart. She does not have it in her blood."

Somewhere near, a dragon roared, the sound strangely distorted and echoing above them. Thaya flinched and looked at the skies, but glittering sand swirled thickly above them. She couldn't wait any longer, the forces were too much to control.

"Bye, Mary, you look after yourself!" She really hoped the mystic was all right. Unable to hold back any longer, Thaya held her breath, released her soulfire, and surrendered to the forces.

19

THEOSOS ROTOA

THE RAGING ENERGY, THE SWIRLING DARK AND LIGHT CHAOTIC forces, the churning in her stomach...this had all the hall-marks of a portal, and she was right in the middle of it. She lifted up fast with the glittering sand, her hands still grip-ping the now hot and pulsing hilt of the toy sword—the whole thing glimmered like the sand around her.

There came the barest pause in the upward motion, then the entire beach rose into the air as a giant sandstorm. The people, the sea, the sky—all were lost in a sparkling whirl-wind with just she and Khy in the centre of it. A dark patch moved beyond the sand cloud, and a great roar trembled through everything, including Thaya's innards.

The glimmering particles flew forwards with a tremen-dous sound of rushing wind and condensed rapidly.

In the blink of an eye, an entire city carved out of quartz glistened as they hung before it, and not a single grain of sand remained in the air.

Powerful energy gripped them, and with a scream, she was sucked forcefully forwards towards a balcony. A great, arched doorway on the upper floors of the temple loomed towards them. She shut her eyes and braced for impact.

Thaya landed with a thud, sprawled on the floor, and spun, star-shaped, through the arched doorway. Khy's hooves couldn't grip the polished quartz floor, and with a clatter, he smacked onto his haunches, spinning around and around like an ungainly colt on ice. Thaya lay blinking up at a smooth, quartz ceiling, trying to let the different parts of her catch up with what had just happened.

"You!" someone exclaimed in shock.

Thaya lifted her head. There was a man hurrying towards her, and his hands were glowing with golden light! *Soulfire light!* Thaya shifted onto her elbows, her jaw agape. He was dressed in sleeveless, royal blue robes trimmed with silver thread. His grey-white hair was smoothed back and his pale eyes incredibly piercing. It was the same man she'd glimpsed before, the one with the straight nose and white eyes.

"Me?" Thaya gasped, then slumped weakly as her stomach cartwheeled, letting her violently know that she'd just moved through time or dimensions faster than her body could cope with. She clasped a hand over her mouth and tried not to think about vomiting over the beautiful, freshly polished, crystal floor.

A dragon roared.

The noise shook the entire building, and frigid cold swept through every part of Thaya's body. The man froze in his tracks, his finger paused gesticulating, and the words he was about to speak died in his open mouth. He shut his mouth with a snap and whirled around, his finger still raised as he stalked away, forgetting about Thaya completely.

The dragon roared again, and a shadow paused over the grand balcony.

"Give back what was stolen!" Grenshoa screamed. Her enormous head pushed into the room, filling the entire archway. Smoke exuded from her nostrils, and yellow sulphur dripped onto the floor and steamed. The dragon inhaled, causing air to gust past Thaya.

The man fearlessly—it looked more like furiously—faced the dragon. "It does not belong to you, beast, it belongs to Urtha! Begone, foul creature, never to return!"

He whipped his hand towards Thaya. Her toy sword trembled in its sheath and then wrenched itself free and flew straight to the man's hand. He gripped the garish child's sword and thrust it towards the dragon, roaring words she didn't understand, words that commanded power.

Thaya, from her prone position on the floor, blinked and stared. It was the most peculiar thing she'd ever seen: a grown man facing down a dragon with a kid's play sword!

The man continued shouting.

Grenshoa breathed out fire.

The man did not move. He should have been incinerated, but instead, immense golden light burst from the sword to meet the torrent of orange flames spewing from Grenshoa's mouth. The flames smashed into each other, two tides of power pushing one against the other. The man roared, and the golden light burst forwards, exploding into Grenshoa with a force that made the floor shake. The light lifted the huge beast, hurled her out of the door and threw her right off the balcony.

The man ran outside.

Other people ran into the room as Thaya and Khy got onto their feet. Most looked like guards or soldiers, dressed in their highly polished, domed helmets and royal blue livery with white cuffs. They shouted orders and hefted long, thin spears that looked far too fragile to do any harm. To her surprise, they ignored her and Khy and followed the man outside.

Thaya and Khy ran out onto the sweeping balcony and stared over the side.

Grenshoa was on her feet, her talons gripping the gleaming balustrades and flowing steps below. She spread her wings, and the man lifted the toy sword again.

Thaya felt Khy's magic build, and his horn shimmered. He intended to help fight the dragon, and she goddamn would as well! She lifted her palms and felt the soulfire come readily into them. It grew swiftly, and she released it.

Three beams of golden white light—from the man, Khy's horn, and her hands—came together as one in the sword the man held. Unable to take such energy, the flimsy toy sword disintegrated into dust, leaving the crystal rod glowing brightly in the man's hand. The light burst into Grenshoa, bowling her backwards, head over tail, down the steps. She flattened the trees, rolled across the beach, and plunged into the ocean. A trail of destruction and a great churning wake marked her passage.

The man, the unicorn, and Thaya stared at the frothing waves. Other people, men, women, and children, crowded onto the crystal plateaus, rooftops, and balconies surrounding the temple.

With a roar that shook the land and made the children scream, Grenshoa burst out of the sea, nose to tail straight as an arrow. A black circle appeared in the air above her, as if a tear had been created in the sky itself, and she shot into it. The dragon and the circle vanished, and the air rippled out from where she had disappeared.

All became still, and the sky returned to blue with a smattering of soft, white clouds lazily floating past.

Thaya blinked and stared at the crystal shard. It had the power to do that? Why hadn't she used it before?

The blue-robed man nodded decisively, slowly releasing his tongue that was clenched between his teeth, and turned to her. "And that's how we deal with unwanted reptiles," he said. His eyes sparkled with intelligence and humour, and he shook the crystal rod between his finger and thumb.

"We have a ceasefire with the Order of Dac, and they are forbidden from entering these lands, and well they know it. We will *not* tolerate a breach of the peace from *any* of them."

The man turned and conversed with the guards. "Inform the council of the breach immediately. Prepare arms for defence and consider a possible counterattack. Ask Mensar what to do. He's experienced and in charge of such matters, this is not my domain."

Thaya stared at him. Not only was he holding the crystal shard easily like she had, but she also understood every word he said—not because she had exited a star portal that had given her mastery over the local tongue, but because he spoke her home language—he spoke Lonohassan.

She found her old language coming easily to her lips. "Why was the dragon after that crystal? Where is this? What happened?" For a moment she wondered if she could actually be in the future; this place was so much more incredible than the place she'd just left.

The man waggled the crystal. "More importantly, how

did *she* ever get a hold of it in the first place? This is neither a toy nor a weapon."

Thaya nodded. "I know. I...felt that. Perhaps you should give it back to me, I was tasked to deliver it to safety." She was not about to lose the thing that had caused her so much grief, and she was not one for failing in her tasks. She scrutinised him as he spoke—was this man good or evil?

He squinted his pale eyes at her. "You can hold it, how so?"

"I don't know." Thaya shrugged.

"You'd better tell me everything that's happened, including how you and a Saphira-elaysa burst out of the ethers and onto my floor." He winked at her, that same unspoken humour dancing in his eyes. He was not her enemy, she cautiously decided, but he was going to have to earn her trust.

"The crystal is under my protection. I was tasked with retrieving it, albeit unwillingly, I admit." Thaya's shoulders slumped. "But please, where are we? I can move through portals—you might have noticed—but that felt different. It felt larger, more directed..." She couldn't find the right words. She'd seen the crystal temple on Siesta Key Beach and so had Mary. Surely, that *had* to mean they were still in the same place yet in a different time?

He scrutinised her just as she had him, then spoke his thoughts aloud. "Hmm, you don't look, sound, or act like a Fallen One, and I smell no evil intent, yet you cannot read me, and you do not know the place or perhaps the time to which you have arrived. The Viewing Mirror showed me a pupil arriving mysteriously, and I would be their teacher; yet it was really they who would teach me and not the other way round, hmmm. But why now, Great One? Is our time at an end so soon?" He straightened suddenly, shook himself like a dog as if he had been in a trance, and clapped his hands together.

"Let's start at the beginning. I'm Theosos Rotoa—Theo, please, my parents were cringingly eccentric—and I'm pleased to meet you both." He reached out a hand to her and nodded respectfully at Khy. Thaya mustered some strength but couldn't match his firm grip. Heat energy flared between their palms as information passed between them. Thaya exhaled sharply.

Theo nodded as if he understood the information received from her. "You have the Truth Sight, and a whole lot more that is hidden, even from me—hidden for your protection, of course. Your connection to your companion, or should I say, soul twin, is, however, easy to read. But firstly, welcome, Thaya Farseeker and Khy-Ellumenah-Ahrieon Saphira-elaysa, welcome to my home, Elanta arn Bruah. Here it is spring, about eleven in the morning, and the year of our seeding is seven hundred and fifty-three thousand according to the First Records. Be warned, the Council will have you say it is the year eight thousand and twenty for when the, er, off-worlders brought their, er, technologies." He tapped his nose at the last bit as if urging her to be secretive.

Seven hundred and fifty-three thousand? That matched no dating system she'd ever heard of. What calendar were these people using? Back home, it was the year one thousand and sixty-eight—but that was when Havendell was apparently settled and called Havendell, though the Old Temple there proved any settlement had happened millennia before. Clearly, dating systems varied and were not reliable sources to ascertain where she was in time. She only knew she was in the past, probably a long way in the past compared to Siesta Key Beach, and even to Havendell.

"Elanta arn Bruah?" Thaya posed. "Isn't it Siesta Key or Lonohassa? I mean, you speak Lonohassan."

"Yes, Lonohassa is our great continent, and Bruah is the southernmost part," explained Theo. "Our city is Elanta, and it is in Bruah—Elanta within Bruah. But please, not here. Come, come inside. Let's settle that churning stomach of yours before it spills its contents everywhere. And you, my stunning Saphira-elaysa, come, there's space enough for everyone. What an absolute pleasure it is to have you visit us." His eyes were alight as he looked at Khy, and he bowed deeply.

Khy snorted softly. "The pleasure is mine," he replied, but it sounded more like a question.

Theo started, then smiled, clearly having not expected to hear the unicorn speak.

"Wait. The crystal, please." Thaya stood firm and held out her hand.

Theo shook his head. "No, you should not hold this until you are grounded, it has the power to tear you apart. Why do you think you are here? It was me calling for the crystal in the first place! It belongs to me—well, it belongs here, at the Grail of Urtha, and it was lost—stolen—through trickery and deceit. Let us discuss this, and more, with a crisp glass of wine and a little fine food as befits our esteemed guests."

Without waiting for a reply, the man spun flamboyantly, his robes swirling around him, and strode inside, under the arched doorway.

Thaya and Khy looked at each other, raised their eyebrows, then followed him.

"Quickly now, let's get the Rod to safety before it becomes too much for me to bear as well." Theo hurried them through a wide reception room, towards a central staircase leading up.

The Rod? He made it sound special somehow. *Surely it has a nice elven name or something,* thought Thaya.

In the wide hallway, pockets of people hustled together. Some wore worried expressions while others chatted excitedly about the dragon. All glanced at Thaya and Khy as they passed, mostly staring at Khy though he showed no self-consciousness at all.

Why would he? It's perfectly normal for a Saphira-elaysa to walk these human-built halls... She hugged her arms and tried not to show how self-conscious she felt.

A handful of people wore blue robes like Theo, and she wondered if they were magi too, for he had to be a magi, didn't he? Were they Lonohassans? Thaya tried not to stare back at them. They looked like anybody back in Havendell, for the most part, though they dressed more elegantly in pressed, pristine robes, and the faint scent of perfume hung in the air. Could they be slightly taller and fairer than the people back home? No, now she looked properly, she saw that, although a few were pale like marble statues, others were dark like polished mahogany. People from all places near and far mingled in these halls.

Not wanting to catch their gazes, Thaya instead stared at the quartz steps they ascended, the banisters, the walls and the arched ceiling. There were no lines or sections to the quartz walls, no panels on the floor; in fact, nowhere could she identify distinct building blocks or floor slabs—it looked like a solid carving, all of it. How this place had been created was beyond her.

Was this how the magi back home lived in their great halls? Magic, power, and energy moved here—it was alive in the crystal walls themselves, and she felt as if they were watching her.

"They are, sort of," Theo replied to her thoughts, making her start. "The crystals have a consciousness of their own. Forgive me for reading you, but you do think rather loudly. Do people not converse with their minds where you are from? And do not think I don't know where you're from, I've already seen the Rod returning to me from the far distant future."

"N-no, we don't speak with our minds," Thaya started. He could read her mind like the Lonohassans of old! "For my people, it's normal to only use speech, but I've been told that a long time ago, we had such skills." It wasn't time to mention she spoke telepathically with Khy, and to some other humans with the skill. Right now, she didn't trust the man enough to have his voice in her head.

Though he clearly could, he respectfully spoke verbally rather than telepathically. "Indeed. I've seen the future, and it's not good, but what's worse is that I know exactly what is coming that will make us that way. And so I, and all who care, have a different problem—we cannot make the people see or care to prepare for what will transpire."

Thaya frowned. She needed many questions answered at the same time. "How do you know where I'm from? How did you know I'd bring the crystal, which incidentally was entrusted into my keeping? You act like you've been expecting us, as if you know everything about us." She hurried her pace, trying to keep up with him whilst looking at him at the same time.

"I *have* been expecting you, I just did not know *when* you would arrive." He paused suddenly and tapped his lips.

Thaya halted abruptly, glad to catch her breath. Her control over her churning stomach was seriously being put to the test, but it hadn't taken control of her as it usually did, which was unusual.

He raised a finger, then shook his head. "No, let's not go there first. Hmm, we shall not speak of anything out here, there are other ears listening, not just the walls. Instead, let's get to my abode straight away." He eyed Khy critically up and down and nodded. "Yes you should fit."

The man whirled up another flight of stairs. The sound of people chatting dimmed until there was silence apart from the sound of their own footsteps.

Theo spoke quietly over his shoulder. "Even in these halls of light, darkness now walks. Despite being the Keeper, I feel I must be careful these days, it saddens me to say. Your coming here, that dragon, the return of the Rod...powerful people of unsavoury agendas will talk and scheme. Couldn't you have come at night? It would have been so much easier to hide."

"Wait," said Thaya. Though his pace had slowed, he still walked far too fast for her on his long legs. "How could you be expecting me? I was trying to escape that dragon! Not even I knew I would end up here, wherever here is!"

He sighed. "All right! I can see you can't wait even one minute." The man laid a proud hand on his chest. "I am a Keeper of Records, and it's my duty to know the future and the past of this domain in this lifetime."

"You are a leader but not a king," said Khy.

The man nodded and bowed. "That is correct, wise one. I am a Keeper of Records and a Keeper of Gates at my highest, and merely a humble scribe at my lowest."

"Oh, I see." Thaya thought she'd got it even though the man talked in riddles. "You write the history books."

The man looked at her as if he had not heard that term before. "In a way, you could say that. I transcribe what transpires, but it is not like writing, more like imprinting. I see with many eyes without judging so that what can be recorded is pure and not simply my version of events. I also protect the records of all that has happened on Urtha.

"So, you see, the arrival of that...*Invader*, made me rather cross. Many times, they have sought to steal the records, to change them, to destroy them and trick the people to make them believe a different history than what is so. And to cover up their ghastly attacks on us Angelic Humans. My task is not easy, but I bear it."

He paused by a seemingly blank wall. "And here we are, the back door to my rooms. Not the most opulent entrance for guests, but we live in uncertain times." He held a palm against the wall and, to her amazement, the outline of an arched door appeared in the quartz. As she stared, the outlined section of the wall simply vanished, leaving an open doorway. The solid crystal disappeared to nothing! The man strode through, fingers squeezing his chin thoughtfully.

"That's impossible!" whispered Thaya, inspecting the newly created doorway.

Khy looked at Thaya. "How can your race be more advanced in the past than in the future?"

Thaya snorted. She had no response.

"Come in, come in," beckoned Theo. "Saphira-elaysa, duck low, we don't want you scraping your beautiful horn. And in response to your question, this is *not* advanced to what we once could do in the past. You know we are *Angelic* Humans, don't you? *We* are the angels—well, we were, until the Fallen Ones came. Three seedings of humans there have been on this planet, but there will not be another, and we will not fall a third time, this much I have seen." His eyes sparkled with sudden wonder and joy. "Knowing that gives me the strength to bear witness to all the darkness that will befall us."

The man is crazy, thought Thaya. *A crazy inventor or a mad scientist like her teacher at school who'd nearly blown himself up during his latest 'experiment' with fire and something that looked like soot.*

She stepped into a round room with a domed ceiling and a very narrow but long window on the far side. Through the window swayed a rich greenery of tropical ferns and palms. In the centre of the room stood two heavy chairs and a chaise longue with deep, rich red cushions, arranged around a round, low, quartz table.

A crystal counter, seemingly carved out of the floor, curved around to her right, and beyond the counter stood a woman in a pale chiffon dress. Her hair was tied up in a silver band that created a tumbling mass of dark curls around her shoulders.

"Ayalin, my dear, please bring us my favourite post-portal stomach settler for our beleaguered guest, and some water and wine—the best red stuff. No, on seconds thoughts, make it white and cold, the day is young. And some fruit, the tropical stuff. Bring nuts too, roasted if possible.

"Oh, and on work-related matters, please inform the Council that the dragon has been dealt with, she will not return, but they must send a warning to her kind. Let them know I am indisposed with guests at the moment, but at our earliest convenience I shall call a meeting. Hopefully that will buy me some time away from the vultures that some of our members are, don't you think, my dear Ayalin? Thank you so kindly, what would I do without you?"

Ayalin nodded as he spoke, taking everything down mentally. Then she gave a warm smile and looked at Thaya and Khy. "Welcome, friends."

Thaya and Khy greeted her in return. She bowed respectfully and then left through a doorway on the far side of the room.

"Here, sit." Theo gestured for Thaya to take a seat on the chaise longue.

She sat and tried not to slump in exhaustion—the chair was remarkably comfortable. The man didn't sit, he instead went to the counter and disappeared behind it, looking for something. He returned with a large, ornate, silver box which he set down on the table. Carefully, he opened the lid and hastily placed the crystal rod onto the blue velvet cloth inside.

"Phew, one does not want to hold that for long no matter how powerful one might be." He cast Thaya a thoughtful look as he rubbed his hands together, possibly sore from holding the rod, then he shut the lid firmly.

Thaya immediately felt the power of the crystal shard vanish and sighed in relief. It was like being near something that constantly generated noise, or a draft coming from an open window—when it stopped there came that sudden relieving silence or warmth.

"I tried to find something to keep it in," she said.

"Yes, indeed," agreed the man and tapped the box. "This is the finest silver you will find, and it has also been protected with sigils. Such objects of power must be care-

fully contained and heavily guarded. That silly sword—
what were you thinking? You'll make yourself sick with radi-
ation. Hmm, never mind, you seem well enough, and I'm
more intrigued as to everything that transpired to bring you
here. I did not expect it to occur now or in this manner,
although I'm exceedingly grateful that you returned it
to me."

"Returned?" Thaya began with a frown. "I'm more
concerned about whether you can be trusted to keep it."

The man laughed loudly, genuinely. "Praise all that is
holy, I do like this one!"

In fairness, she was glad to be rid of the relic and, rightly
or wrongly, she wanted to trust this man. "It was the will of
the crystal shard that brought us here..." she started,
paused, then sunk back in the chair, rubbing her sore
temples. There was no way on Urtha she was going to be
able to explain everything that had happened. "It's all far
too complicated."

Theo smoothed the stubble on his chin as he watched
her. "Hmm, I can see that. Well, let's do it the easy way
then." He sat down on the chair opposite and pulled the
silver box towards him. He flipped open the lid again, and
the hum of power surrounded them once more. He placed a
hand over the crystal shard and closed his eyes.

Both his hand and the crystal began to glow, and his
eyes moved rapidly under his lids. "Hmm, yes, I see," he said
as if seeing images. "Whoa, now that is interesting. Hmm,
scary. Would you look at that? Well, I never saw that
coming. Ah, the toy sword, ingenious, now I understand. I
love it!"

The man opened his eyes and looked at Thaya as he
closed the box decisively. "Quite a journey you've been on.
The Rod only shows me what it has seen. I have not seen

events from your perspective, so you needn't worry about privacy."

"You were able to read the, uh, Rod? How?" Thank Urtha she didn't have to try and explain everything.

The man nodded. "It's my job as the Prime Keeper, the humble scribe, remember?"

Thaya blinked. Were his skills like hers? The man had an intense manner about him, but she felt extremely at ease in his company as if she could chat to him about absolutely anything, and not only would he not be offended, but he would also be interested in the craziest of things.

She dared to ask him, "You can read crystals? Sometimes I'm able to read stones, well, special stones, Portal Stones, when I place my hands upon them."

"Of course you can," scoffed Theo as if he already knew that. "Portal stones, crystals, star maps, ley lines, vortices, gates, dimensional blend locations and a whole host more. Fully trained and experienced, in a couple of hundred years, you'll be a Prime Keeper, too.

"Ah, wonderful, look, here's Ayalin with our sustenance."

Ayalin carried a tray laden with drinks and glasses which she placed on the table. One of the glasses was filled with a clear, fizzing liquid which Theo picked up, stirred with a thin glass stirrer, and passed to Thaya.

"Here, drink this, it will settle your stomach."

Thaya took the drink and sipped it cautiously. The drink was sour but quenching, and her churning stomach welcomed it. "Mmm, ginger and something else."

Miraculously, her stomach still hadn't emptied its contents like it usually did after portal travel, but then, perhaps it hadn't been a 'normal' portal they had passed through.

"You passed through time only, not space," said Theo, and winked as he poured wine into two glasses.

"Time only?" Was that why she hadn't been sick?

"Yes, this *is* your Siesta Key, but now it is Elanta arn Bruah, and it is fifty-thousand years or so in the past."

Thaya spluttered and spilled her drink.

20

GRAIL OF URTHA

THEO CHUCKLED, PASSED HER A TISSUE, AND CONTINUED talking as Thaya cleaned up her spilt drink.

"The Rod knew it was nearly home, at the Grail of Urtha where it is most potent, and I sensed its presence or, more accurately, something powerful in the ethers. I've been hunting for it, calling to it in the crystal caverns, for years. Then, lo and behold, you arrive with it, accompanied by exceedingly nasty unwanted baggage, and some very wanted divine baggage." He looked at Khy. "Please excuse the terminology, my esteemed friend."

Khy flicked his tail, completely unconcerned.

Thaya coughed, trying to fathom the passage of time. So, Khy had been right when he'd said nothing had existed on Siesta Key beach for fifty-thousand years. "Fifty-thousand years in the past? Is Urtha even that old? But look at this place, your knowledge...you're far more advanced here, now, in every way compared to my time. And *my* home time is closer to you than the time I *actually* came from—" Thaya became tongue-tied, lost in her own logic. "This is too much for me, after all *that*." She meant the dragon, the time travel, the portal...*everything!*

Ayalin still stood beside her, and Thaya realised she was waiting patiently, like a benevolent nurse, for her to finish her fizzy drink. She downed it quickly, swallowed a burp, and passed the empty glass to her. "Thank you."

Ayalin nodded approvingly. "You'll feel better quickly. I'll be back with the food, and some water for your friend." She smiled at Khy who smiled back.

"They see him for what he truly is?" Thaya asked, after Ayalin had left.

"Not quite," said Theo. "Some will, like me, but thanks to his potent Saphira-elaysa magic, others simply see something beautiful, a fabulous breed, and unusual to be walking these crystal halls. We have frequent visitors from far-distant stars, so people are used to seeing beings who look very different to themselves. I've seen much of the world, and nowhere is as advanced as Lonohassa, so don't be fooled by it. I know places where humans live like animals and worship people from the stars like gods. We have outreach programs to help these people, to bring them knowledge and freedom."

Ayalin returned, this time with a platter of food. Thaya recognised the oranges, bananas and grapes, but not the greenish, star-shaped fruit or the white, fleshy one with black seeds. There were hazelnuts and walnuts and something that looked like dates but longer.

Theo began peeling an orange. "So, the Rod showed me it was taken from the Leonites, and abused by Grenshoa and her minions, then retrieved by you, who, to the dragon's surprise and chagrin, was able to hold and wield it. Grenshoa thought she would wrest it from you in the dimensions between spaces, where the energy is chaotic and very unstable. She used a wormhole—an unstable construct created by unnaturally twisting, distorting, or tearing space-time— or should I say, she created a *wyrm-hole*?" He looked at Thaya, waiting for a response.

"I said that." Thaya rolled her eyes, and Khy chuckled.

Theo continued. "Little did she realise that the wyrm-hole"—he chuckled again—"ran close to the main gateway between dimensions one and three"—he spread his arms wide—"this place here, our wondrous Elanta, and star portal two in the planetary system. I can't help but wonder: had you not been holding the Rod at the time of passing through the portal, would I have felt anything at all? I can't take much credit for it though, most of what happened to cause its arrival here was its own doing, like magnets that attract."

Thaya listened intently, only just grasping what Theo was talking about. "So, she tried to use the, ahem, *wyrm-hole,* to take me and the Rod to the future? Ten thousand years into the future when Urtha is called Earth."

Theo nodded. "Yes, so it appears. These beasts are clever, cunning and extremely knowledgeable. She knew the future would have less powerful magic. I assume she was hoping your power would be less there where she could easily take the Rod from you."

"The Invaders have a greater hold on our planet there," Thaya mused. "Many came for us not long after we arrived. It appears Grenshoa rallied some of them. I really hope Mary is okay, even Officer Priggins."

"They're not interested in ordinary folk when an object of power dangles before them," Theo assured her, then he leaned close and kept his voice low as he peeled the fiddly pith off an orange. Khy stepped near to hear.

"Now listen, for we haven't much time. You can't possibly

know the turmoil and strife that's brewing within these walls: dissension, conflicting agendas, compromised persons, and talk of war—the darkness in Lonohassa grows, and even the walls have ears. We must be careful. This Star Portal Rod was stolen a long time ago, and I witnessed its return to me at some point in the near future. From what it's shown me in the brief time when I touched it, it will be again stolen at some point in the far future, which would be your time, when the blessed Leonites get involved to protect it."

He paused when Ayalin returned, and Thaya twiddled her thumbs impatiently. His servant, or maybe butler—she wasn't sure what to call her—carried a silver wine cooler filled with water which she placed at Khy's feet. Khy nodded his appreciation and sniffed the water as he waited for Theo to continue.

Thaya spoke once Ayalin had gone. "But what on all Urtha and the heavens is it? Why is it so important?"

"It powers the portals," said Theo.

Thaya blinked and closed her mouth.

He placed a hand on the silver box and continued, "It was created at the birth of our Third Seeding, along with another tool, a larger tool that powers the star portals. They are together called the Rod and the Staff, and they can utilise the power of the major energies flowing through the planet, which are also called the Rod and Staff. It is because of the Rod that you did not suffer from such severe Portal Sickness, as it is termed.

"The Rod opens up portals across Urtha, horizontal portals, you might call them, just as horizontal energies flow into and through Urtha. The Staff powers the star portals, the vertical portals, if you will, that lead upwards and down-wards to different planets and dimensions, and in the same manner, extremely powerful energies circulate through Urtha from above and below, from the different dimensions. The Staff is held upright like this"—he indicated using his arms—"and the Rod is held horizontally like this, understand? I see that you do."

Thaya raised her eyebrows. So that was why he'd held the toy sword dead straight horizontally when he faced down Grenshoa. It activated the Rod's power.

Theo drew a handkerchief from his pocket and mopped the sudden sheen on his brow. "My oh my, these tools should not be in just anyone's hand, but the universe has a strange way of working out things for the better."

"The Leonites had reclaimed the Rod," said Thaya, remembering the crashed sky ship. "I don't know how, but Grenshoa attacked and killed them; they couldn't get away. They came to me in spirit and urged me to reclaim it. Why me, I don't know."

"I know, I saw that much." Theo pushed his handkerchief back into his pocket and tapped the lid of the box. "These tools have to be kept in special containers of lead, gold and silver. This solid silver box is not enough. When they were made, a box to contain them was also created, which itself is extremely powerful. That, too, was stolen millennia ago. Countless wars have been fought for the possession of these tools but never were we able to get all three together in one place—neither us nor the Fallen Ones.

"You see, Thaya, very few people are able to hold these tools in their bare hands, much less operate them. You wonder why the Leonites chose you or, perhaps, why the Rod found its way into your hands? Well, you have the same power and possibly, abilities as do I; you can hold the Rod without it destroying you physically, and—though the two go hand in hand—you are a Gatewalker, Thaya, and the

Ordacs now know this. They will hunt you even as they fear you and try to take that power or use it in whatever way they can. I am safe here, in these walls, but if I were on the road like you appear to be, I'd certainly employ the protection of a Saphira-elaysa." He winked at Khy, and Khy nodded.

Thaya began peeling her own orange. "But why do they want the tools so much? What does it matter to them?"

"They, like all the Fallen Invaders, desire our beloved Urtha, but they cannot operate the portals as once every living, breathing Angelic Human on the planet could. They've already infected the races of Urtha; they've already infected our gene-code—that which makes up the building blocks of our bodies, that which is held in our blood."

"But if humans could access portals, why were the tools created?" asked Thaya.

Theo squeezed the bridge of his nose as if there was too much to explain. He tried anyway. "Because it was foreseen what would happen and that one day many of us would lose the ability to use the portals, and also because the portals were out of alignment. This story, our history, did not begin with the Third Seeding... There were two previous seedings of humans here before, both wiped out. This time, nothing was left to chance.

"The damage to the portals was done a long time ago when all life, including humans, was destroyed by warring Fallen Ones. Angelic Humans did not need portal tools to access the portals, their coding spoke to it directly, like yours does, like mine does. But our benevolent protectors from higher realms foresaw the future and the evil plans of the Invaders, and with the humans they created these tools to manually reopen blocked star portals.

"So, you can see why the Invaders desire them like nothing else. Other, non-Urthan races have never had the power to access her portals, they have always manipulated humans to do it, but with these tools they can access them directly. They don't need humans anymore. And if they gain control of the portals, they gain control of the planet."

Thaya stared at the silver box. To think she had held such a powerful object in her hands...to think she'd hidden it in the hilt of a toy sword...what manner of evil hunting this tool had she just managed to escape? She prayed Mary was okay.

Theo chuckled. "Do not worry, it's better that you didn't know the power of the Rod, otherwise you may have acted differently and in fear. In all truth, that dragon is not the worst thing hunting for these tools. You got off lightly."

Thaya snorted. "Not the worst thing? Uh-huh, I'll just take your word for it." She took a long, deep breath.

They were silent, for a time. Khy dipped his horn into the silver bucket, then put his nose in and drank noisily, splashing water on the floor. Thaya raised an eyebrow at him, but Khy was too engrossed.

She sighed and looked away. Her stomach had thankfully settled, and she popped an orange segment into her mouth. It was deliciously sweet and full of juice. Next, she picked up a walnut half and munched on it. It was taking a long time to organise her thoughts and find the right questions to ask. Theo gave her time to think and busied himself with a banana.

Between mouthfuls, Thaya broke the silence. "So, the Rod, as you call it, brought me backwards in time from my current location?"

Theo smiled. "Yes. And it's not a particularly attractive name, but it's what the tool has become known as."

"Right," said Thaya. "But this place is some kind of power location? A star portal?"

"Correct again. This whole area, above and below ground, is the location of what we call the Grail of Urtha. The temple is not needed, but the quartz helps to massively amplify and also harmonise the power of this place. Here, friends from the stars visit us, though visitors from other *times* are extremely rare. You appear to have come over the land in this instance, he-he." He chuckled, and his eyes twinkled at her. "This is one of the most important places on the planet, energetically speaking, because it is Star Portal Two, and thus the control lock for the first and third portals —this is advanced knowledge, by the way. There are only seven such gates to the stars on the planet, and it's the same on every planet that hasn't been tampered with."

Thaya nodded, understanding what he was saying though she had never heard any of this before. She listened with intrigue as he told her about the main energy points of Urtha and how they interfaced with each other and the higher and lower dimensions.

He paused when she rubbed her eyes. "Is this too much for you right now? Should I go on?"

Thaya shook her head; it was the most interesting and relevant information she had ever heard. "No, please don't stop. I need you to teach me because these are the very things for which I need training and understanding. I don't understand my abilities, and there's no one back home to help."

Theo smiled and reached his hands forwards, asking for hers. She tentatively placed hers in his. *What happened with Mary had better not happen here,* she thought.

His large hands took hold of her wrists and turned her palms upwards. His hands grew warm beneath hers and she found her own responding. Soon, both their hands were glowing with golden light. Khy stopped drinking to watch.

"You are a—" Theo looked at her to complete his sentence.

"Ena-shani," Thaya finished for him, the word just coming to her. She stared in wonder at the glowing soulfire in her palms which he had kindled within her.

He grinned and his corneas glowed white. "Ena-shani, yes. The Elven word sounds so much more beautiful than Gatewalker, doesn't it? Just like 'Saphira-elaysa' outdoes 'unicorn'. I have the same powers, for how else could I recognise another like me? Why else would I take you under my wing so readily? I've had many students but most I've sent to others for training as they were not Ena-shani and I could not teach them."

Thaya looked at him. "But what does it mean? How can you and I have these powers but few others have them?"

Theo let go of her hands and sat back, watching her intently. "And now you ask the questions that *really* matter, but they're actually questions only you can answer." He stood up and paced to the window, clasped his hands behind his back and took a moment to speak. "Did you play Secret Hunt as a child? The game where, on your birthday, little presents would be hidden around your house and you had to find them?"

Thaya smiled. "Yes, but we called it Gift Chase. All the kids did that." It was a fun game, one of the golden memories of childhood. She remembered squealing with delight after finding a teddy bear hidden in the awnings of their loft.

Theo continued. "Well, life is like Gift Chase with

greater and lesser secrets hidden through one lifetime. Now imagine how boring life would be if your parents had told you where they had hidden everything. You wouldn't have the joy of discovery; you would simply go and get them. And after you got them, they would have less value to you; you would appreciate them far less than if you had painstakingly searched for them."

Thaya considered this before speaking. "True, there would be no fun. But life is much harder than a Gift Chase. What if we never find these...hidden gifts?"

"Indeed," Theo agreed. "But now that's the job of the soul, is it not? Like your parents in Gift Chase, your soul wants you to find these gifts, so whilst it might not tell you where they're hidden, it's always ready to guide you or give you clues. And all you have to do is be willing to find the gifts and open yourself to your soul so you can listen for those clues it gives you."

Thaya nodded, feeling humble. "I haven't heard it explained better."

"Neither I. My great teacher told it to me that way, and I've never forgotten it. What I will say, my dear, and what I have learned, is that those of us with the power to use the portals, and the soulfire burning within us, have been entrusted by the Pure Eternal Spirit and the Cosmos to wield it, to hold it, and so we must use such powers wisely, responsibly and for the betterment of the human race and our world. We are older souls than many here, and we have been gifted such power because we cultivated it in previous lifetimes.

"We have this power because we have ascended through all the dimensions to the Creator itself...and returned to assist all others. For that is the nature of life, Thaya, to come out of the light and into the darkness, and then ascend back to the light from whence we came. All the pain we feel is ultimately caused by our separation from that light, and what all good things desire most is to return home."

The way Theo spoke, the things he spoke about, no one had ever said these things to her before. Wasn't this how the priests should speak? Wasn't this what her religions should have told her? Yes, she did want to return home to the light, it was an all-encompassing feeling that came from deep within her, but just getting back to her time on Urtha would be enough for now...or was it? Did any kind of home remain there for her at all? Or was it just familiarity that called to her? No one remembered her anymore, it wasn't like she had a nice house and a warm bed to return to. She imagined never returning home and always being a nomad. The thought was unsettling but also whispered of freedom.

"My home is with Khy." She spoke her thought aloud, surprising herself.

"Then having found your home and carrying it with you makes you far richer than a king stuck in his castle," said Theo. "I'm cursed and blessed to remain in this one place, the place which I am entrusted to protect. Sometimes I imagine being free of it all, but then I would be lost without a purpose. You are *truly* free, a wayfarer, a wandering star."

Thaya blushed, but Khy nodded as if he agreed.

"It's not me that's the star, it's Khy," she said softly.

"When I saw the Rod coming to me, I did not ever see a Saphira-elaysa in my visions." Theo's eyes were alight when he looked at Khy. "But for all I may see of the future, it is only an imprint—a timeline—of what might occur according to our current trajectory. Time is a funny, fickle thing. Nothing is truly set and sealed in stone, for there is always free will."

Thaya wanted to get back to that. "These visions told

you I was coming? Did you see it in the Viewing Mirrors?" Surely her arrival had not been anticipated? How was that possible? It was just too much to believe. Maggy, her dear friend and adopted mother from long ago, had spoken of such Viewing Mirrors—ancient, powerful relics from Lono- hassa. Like Thaya, Maggy was from Lonohassa, and together they had been imprisoned by the Nuakki. Thaya shivered at the memory and hoped Maggy had reclaimed the Viewing Mirrors from the Invaders.

"It's like them, yes, but my own more natural way of seeing into the future and the past," said Theo. "Charged and purified, the old-fashioned method of Seers in times long past. The natural element of water acts like a crystal. It has its own memories and can hold information in much the same way. Water also passes easily between dimensions; it's hard to explain with words and easier to understand through visualisation.

"But enough of the mechanics. Let's talk about what needs to be discussed. The Rod returns to me and to the Grail of Urtha where it is protected most powerfully..." His voice trailed off, the sudden gusto of his speech petering out weakly as a frown knitted his brow. When he spoke, he spoke quietly. "But when the Rod returns, so do the Fallen Ones."

"Well, there's no need to worry because we got rid of Grenshoa." Thaya picked up a handful of hazelnuts and began munching on them, wondering at the worried expres- sion on Theo's face.

He wrung his hands together and stared into the middle distance, speaking quietly as if to himself. "In that silver surface, I saw one like me, a Gatewalker, an *Ena-shani,* only young and in training, come from the future bearing that which was lost. But then come the others, and all will be changed forever, never to be the same."

A chill ran down Thaya's spine, and she saw in her mind's eye the sea rising to take them all like she had witnessed in her dream. She shook her head and focussed on what Theo was saying.

"But nothing can be done, for it must come to pass. It is a chance to be free... We have time, but not much."

A man cleared his throat, making them all jump, even Khy. "I did not know we were entertaining our guests."

21
———

COSMIC NOMADS

THAYA LOOKED AT THE MAN STANDING IN THE HIDDEN doorway they had entered through earlier. So, he had the power to open the secret door too, she thought. He wore robes like Theo—long, loose and light, with his arms bared for the warm climate, only his were midnight blue, and his hair was dark, slicked back like Theo's but free of any grey.

Theo turned from the window rapidly. "Mensar! How good of you to join us. Please meet Thaya Farseeker and Khy." Theo's easy, jovial manner had vanished, and his body had become stiff. The tone in his voice suggested he was anything but pleased to see this man.

Mensar stepped into the room with a grace that made him appear to glide. He smiled, and Thaya noticed a scar on his left cheek near his lip that made his smile lopsided. Thaya nodded but the man was no longer looking at her. He paused beside the silver box and rested the fingertips of his right hand upon it.

"Is this really what I think it is? Are the rumours true? Ahh, I can *feel* that it is." He closed his eyes and smiled in wonder. "So incredible! After all this time, it has been returned to us safely. You have my thanks." He bowed deeply to her. His tone of voice and mannerisms were mesmerising, and he reminded her of someone else she couldn't quite place.

She fidgeted uncomfortably. If only she'd had a choice in the matter—but it appeared the Rod's will had brought her here. "It's a long story, but it seems that the crystal, I mean the Rod, chose to come here, so here we are." She didn't know what else to say.

Khy stepped forward, his ears pricked and his eyes wide as he unabashedly stared at the man. Catching the unicorn's gaze, the man hastily looked away and smoothed his robes. Khy remained staring at him, unblinking.

Thaya found herself scrutinising Mensar as well, her suspicions rising. Was he an early version of an Illumined Acolyte? Could he be an Ordac? Was there a tail she might see poking out of his robes—there one minute and gone the next? Theo cast her an amused look as if he had read her thoughts. Mensar narrowed his eyes at her, then looked away.

"The council will want to know immediately that the Rod has been returned to us, Theo. We do not appreciate being kept waiting."

Theo tapped his fingertips together. "Manners and respect before rules and protocol, Mensar. Do you not remember Phasius' teachings? Our guest suffered portal sickness and disorientation, not to mention the fright of facing down a dragon, so we tended to those first."

"Phasius was a fool discredited by his own peers and students," Mensar sneered.

Theo raised an eyebrow. "The slander was never proven, Mensar, and the person behind it was never found, they were too cowardly to come forward."

"He was still struck off." Mensar made a chopping motion with his hand.

"After fifty years of faultless and immaculate dedication, numerous discoveries and an impeccable track record dealing with the Galactic Federation, Phasius was a genius. As well you know, the council was divided, and the decision swayed by only one vote. We do not need to cover old ground, Mensar, it is tiring."

"Indeed, Theo, I'm sure our guest is not interested in the troubles of the State. Portal travel is always exhausting, and they should rest in the guest quarters."

Mensar stood beside Thaya and reached down a welcoming hand. "Regardless, I'm pleased to meet you. No, please don't get up on my account."

She remained seated and took his hand tentatively, trying to formulate some semblance of a guard upon her palm to prevent any energy transfer. It was becoming clear to her that when dealing with people with power, too much could go wrong, too much could be read and known. She needn't have worried. It wasn't a proper shake, simply a momentary touch, however, her rudimentary efforts to create a guard appeared to work—she only felt a warm fuzziness on her palm, but she had trouble holding Mensar's intense, blue gaze. He took his hand away and nodded to Khy. Khy did not respond, yet he had not taken his gaze from the man. Mensar could not hold the Saphira-elaysa's gaze and stared at the plate of fruit instead.

As if losing interest or needing time to think, Khy suddenly turned and left. He walked under the large archway on the far side of the room and out onto the sunlit balcony. Had he been human, it would have been rude, but Saphira-elaysa did not play by human rules, *and probably scoffed at them,* Thaya mused.

"A quiet word if I may, Theo. Please excuse us." Mensar bowed slightly to her, then walked towards Theo who was still standing beside the window. He then spoke in a voice too quiet for Thaya to hear, but she noted his brief glance at her as he spoke.

Inigo Price! That's who he reminds me of.

Thaya suddenly placed the reptilian, shape-shifting vampire she'd had the misfortune of encountering in London with Arendor. They had got away from the whole evil nest of them, thankfully. While Mensar's gaze was on Theo, she scrutinised the man, but no matter how hard she looked, she could see no fault in his form, no flash of a long tail, clawed feet, or blunt snout. He was human, but she did not trust him like she trusted Theo.

She took a sip of wine, scooped up a handful of nuts, and went outside to join Khy. The sun was hot and bright, just like it would be in Siesta Key right now but all that time in the future. Was this really the same place she had been just moments before yet tens of thousands of years in the past? The trees were the same—lush, green palms swaying in the breeze—and a blue sea sparkling beyond. There was a beach, a thin line of pinkish sand, not the great expanse of quartz that was Siesta Key. She touched the quartz balcony which retained its coolness in the heat, *just like the sand on Siesta Key Beach. What a sad thing to transpire: the destruction of this beautiful place...*

Khy stood with his eyes closed, soaking up the sunshine that refuelled him as if it were a banquet, but clearly, he wasn't just resting and feeding, he was busy reading the energy flows. Why had he come out here so suddenly?

"What is it?" Thaya asked. They were alone-ish, so she felt it okay to speak out loud.

"I feel something...not right. It started a moment ago."

Now Thaya focused on it, she could feel it too, an under-flow of a low, disharmonious vibration.

"Grenshoa?"

"No." Khy shook his head. "Something far larger or more numerous, something darker. I'd like to be gone from here, I do not feel at ease."

"Is it him?" Thaya nodded behind her, meaning Mensar.

"That I can't determine, though I tried. Something is going on like he is deliberately distracting Theosos Rotoa while something darker brews. I do not trust him."

"What about Theosos?" Thaya trusted him, but she wondered what Khy thought.

"Intelligent. As intelligent as a Saphira-elaysa, but in a human way. Scheming, but not with an urge to do harm. He's a creator."

"You mean an architect? An inventor?" said Thaya.

"Yes, those words are also acceptable. I don't think he'll cause us trouble, quite the opposite. He wants to help us."

Thaya agreed. "Funny, but the people in the future and the past have so far been more welcoming than back home! The Leonites wanted me to return the Rod to them, but I feel it's safer with Theo, and much easier for us. How could I find them anyway? Surely if they want it, they can come here and get it themselves."

"You must do what you feel is right," said Khy. "I feel safer without it drawing attention to us. I don't think we could protect it for long."

"Indeed. All right, let's start trying to get home then." Thaya took a deep breath at the thought of returning to the dragon cavern. It was a cold and harsh environment, and the mere thought of portal travel made her feel queasy. What was the point of returning home if Theo could teach her things here, possibly more than the magi could?

Theo joined them, breaking her line of thought. He smoothed his robes and appeared flustered. "Forgive me for our abrupt departure. Mensar and the Council have called an urgent meeting, and I must leave you for a few hours, though there is still much we must discuss together, in private. Please rest, eat, drink and ask Ayalin for anything you need.

"To be honest, I could do with a rest and some quiet time alone, it's been a frantic morning," said Thaya.

Theo smiled. "Yes, it has. I shall return swiftly, so please, don't go anywhere."

Thaya nodded, and he disappeared back inside. She looked over the rooftops gleaming in the sunlight. They were not the same yellow and white buildings she'd seen in her dream before the tsunami came, so was that an ancient memory of a different place? Was it before or after this time now?

The strong urge to explore this fantastic city was overpowered by a wide yawn and a rumbling stomach. The sun at its zenith was very hot, too hot to stand in, so she left Khy, seemingly impervious to the heat, and went back inside to enjoy more fruit, nuts and wine. The white wine was exquisite, deliciously cool, and refreshing without being heavy and overpowering. She lay back on the chaise longue and let the chaotic events of the morning melt away.

"Miss Thaya?"

Thaya awoke with a start. Ayalin's pleasing face looked down at her and smiled. "Apologies for awakening you, you have been asleep a while. You might like to know that your personal room is ready if you want to freshen up before dinner. Theosos will be with us shortly."

Thaya blinked. How long had she been asleep? The sun had moved quite a bit in the sky. Khy lifted his head from behind the counter where he had been inspecting something.

"Right, sure," said Thaya, pushing herself up. "I guess I must have been more tired than I thought."

"It is quite all right," said Ayalin. "New visitors find the energy of the quartz tiring. They have healing properties too."

Not about to leave it lying around, Thaya scooped up the silver box containing the Rod and slung her pack over her shoulder. Her thoughts of exploring the city didn't look like they were going to come to fruition. Still, dinner with Theo, where she could absorb anything he could teach her, would be a great alternative.

"I'd prefer to explore the city," said Khy, sounding bored.

"He might teach us about Star Portals or something," replied Thaya.

"Being inside in these small, claustrophobic human dwellings gets to you after a while."

He snorted.

"I feel it too. For all the beauty and power of the crystals, I'd like to be in my own time. It won't be for long, and then once we ARE home, we'll wish we were back here and warm again."

Ayalin led them along a short hallway, up a narrow, winding staircase which Khy scowled at, then into a small room directly above where they had just been. Khy walked straight outside onto the balcony and Thaya stared at the huge crystal bed frame supporting a deep mattress, white pillows and soft linen.

"I'll return in half an hour when dinner will be ready, so

please, wear the clothes, wash, whatever you desire." Ayalin pointed to the simple, pale blue and white clothes laid out on the bed.

"Thank you," said Thaya, and the woman nodded and left.

On the opposite side of the room to the bed was a sink carved out of the wall and a spout above it. Beside it was a rail holding a stack of different sized towels. Thaya went over to it, and having experienced future Earth, quickly learned how to operate the taps. "Oh my, there's even hot water!" She trailed her hand through the stream.

How can civilisations be destroyed so that nothing remains?

She picked up the rose-scented bar of soap and washed her face and hands, instantly feeling fresher. The towel she held to her cheek was soft and thick, unlike the rough cloths she had back home.

Her clothes were still clean, but she fancied dressing like the locals and slipped into the looser and cooler linen robes they'd provided. This particular garment fitted more like a long, flowing dress than a robe.

Outside, the sun was still hot and turning a deep orange as it neared the horizon.

"Want a wash?" she asked, laying a hand on Khy's shoulder with a grin.

"Not likely," said Khy. "Ayalin arrives. I'll join you in a bit. I need a bit more time with the sunset."

Thaya nodded. "I don't think we'll be far."

"Take the Rod," said Khy.

———

Khy was right, Ayalin opened the door as Thaya went back inside. The Saphira-elaysa always knew when someone was coming. Thaya picked up the silver box and followed the woman back downstairs to the room in which she and Theo had spoken.

On one side of the balcony, a large table had been laid, and Theo sat drinking a glass of light red wine. There was a chair for her, which Ayalin gestured to.

"Where is our dear Khy?" asked Theo, standing up, a disappointed look on his face.

"He'll join us in a bit," said Thaya. She tentatively passed the silver box into his open hands. "I didn't want to leave this unattended."

"Wise," agreed Theo. He set the box down beside him. "After dinner, we'll take it to its proper location. I think you'll enjoy it immensely."

Thaya nodded when Ayalin offered to pour her wine.

Theo clasped his hands together. "Ayalin, my dear, we're ready to eat when you are. Excuse the rush; for all the lavishness we usually like to bestow on guests, we need to get the eating out of the way and move on to more pressing matters."

Thaya picked up a small bread roll from her side plate. It was soft and warm, and she tore a little piece off and popped it in her mouth. "Theo, I need you to teach me what you know, anything you can, about my abilities. Like, how can I properly operate portals? How can I locate the roaming ones and then use them? I fall through portals when I wish I had more control, and I want to stop the sickness. And how do you even read the star maps that appear when you find a portal stone?"

Theo raised his hands. "Whoa, easy now, one thing at a time. Those questions are all similar, but it's easier to show you than it is to explain with words, so let's save them for after dinner when I can take you to the gate itself."

Thaya wanted to know now, but she curbed her impatience and simply said, "I'd like that very much."

Was the gate here like a great stone circle? she wondered, finishing the last morsel of bread. *No, it'll be far more opulent than that—a crystal gate to the stars or something.*

"Tell me about the time and place which you have just left," said Theo as Ayalin set down bowls of warm, green soup in front of them.

Thaya described everything she had seen between mouthfuls of what could have been pea and mint soup but with a flavour she had not tasted before. "It's not my time, so it's hard for me to explain exactly what and why things are, but it is very different. It's not like here—opulent, advanced, powerful—it's more basic and functional. There's no magic. People don't know what it is, and if it *does* exist there, it's weak. It's like the people are preoccupied with other things; they're certainly not interested in the stars or the Invaders. Yet, the people are friendlier than they are in my time; they seem more relaxed, wealthier. My time by comparison is very basic, harsh, and people live close to the earth. The people of Earth seem cut off from the planet."

Thaya fell silent as Ayalin removed their empty bowls. Why did she want to return home to her time? She couldn't answer that question.

Khy stepped silently out onto the balcony, greeted them with a nod, then looked up at the emerging stars. His presence comforted Thaya, and Theo's face brightened.

"All things change," said the man. "Nothing stays the same. We rise and fall, not through our own hand but through the vile actions of those who are more powerful than we, those who use their powers to destroy."

"The off-worlders?" Thaya asked.

Theo nodded. "Oh, we aren't blameless. We let them in!"

"And then they destroyed us," said Thaya quietly. "But they haven't done it yet. We can still save Lonohassa." She suddenly wanted to plead and beg for the past to be changed—surely it was possible?

Theo pushed his chair back, got to his feet, and went to lean on the balustrade, staring out to the ocean beyond the trees. The night was calm, and the sea was very still. "I have tried to change the minds of my colleagues, but they refuse to see the peril of contracting with those coming from the stars—those with shadowy agendas and even more questionable machines. The technologies they offer are indeed incredible; on the surface of it, they *would* make our lives better, but at what cost? It is too late to stop them, for we are now in debt to these beings for what they have given us. We *willingly* work with them, but I see nefarious motives and darkness, and I fear the direction in which we have turned.

"Change is coming, especially now that the Rod has returned to us, but I will never leave my post; I am a Gatekeeper and I've sworn to do my duty to protect this place, whatever may happen."

Ayalin set down another dish. This one was a small bowl of leaves and thin slices of fruit interlaced with what looked like orange cheese.

Thaya's mind drifted back to her home. "In my time, the Nuakki enslave us. I was caught up in it, and for a long time, I worked as a mindless slave. They had driven all knowledge from my mind in a...in a *cleansing*. Look, see the pale mark on my hand? That's the shadow of the slave mark they chained me with."

Theo came over to inspect the faint swirl on her palm. "Tell me all about it."

She told him her story, as succinctly as she was able.

Sometimes her voice trembled with anger, sometimes with anguish, but it no longer broke like once it might have.

"Ena-shani." Theo laid a warm hand over hers and smiled at her as if she were his daughter. "Look for what has made you strong in your past. It's clear great strength has been given to you, and great things await you, for you have come here to *do* great things. Be not afraid of what might come, live fearlessly, and never compromise yourself or your soul—there is far more awaiting us than just this lifetime."

Thaya smiled. "It's easy to get lost down here."

"It is," Theo agreed and sat back down. "Now, tell me of your life back home. What were you doing or where were you going before all this happened? You must have had aspirations? I want to know the future through your eyes."

Thaya fiddled with her fork. "I've already spoken much about home, it's not as nice as here. I wish I could stay but I was on a journey with Khy, a long and hard one it turns out."

"Then that is a good journey." Theo nodded sagely. "Nobody ever learnt a thing on an easy journey."

That wasn't quite how Thaya felt, and she massaged her sore neck as she spoke. "I'm going to the magi, their *secret college,* if you will, in the mountains far from civilisation."

Theo snorted. "Yes, they would have to be far from civilisation, they are uncivilised themselves!"

Thaya raised her eyebrows. No one had ever said that about the magi before. "The esteemed wielders of the arcane? The wise masters of the elements, the ones who know all the Hidden Knowledge of the world and beyond? These same magi?"

Theo pursed his lips. "The knowledge is 'hidden' because they bloody well hid it! They took it from the people and taught it only to their own kind, forbidding the common man to know it. Over generations, the masses lost their precious 'knowledge' and became, well, a bit stupid." Theo sighed and sat back. "My apologies, don't be alarmed. I'm not here to attack them, for there *are* esteemed magi, and some very good sorts too, but their order, like so many others, has been infiltrated and corrupted. Why, Thaya, are you seeking them out?"

"I was hoping they could tell me about myself. Maybe they could understand my abilities, or what I'm supposed to do with my gifts. I don't know, it sounds foolish now since you've taught me far more about myself and these abilities we have than anyone else. Perhaps it's here I should stay where you can be my teacher and I your pupil."

"I would like that, teaching a willing and able student again," Theo said softly, staring at the crumbs on the white tablecloth. He muttered the next part seemingly to himself, "But we don't have that much time."

Thaya continued, "This soulfire, it's like magic or the closest I've seen. I met a magi called Solia. She could command the elements to do her bidding, a bit like my soul-fire. Maybe I could be a magi—maybe that's what I'm supposed to do."

"You are not a magi," Theo cut her off, and her balloon deflated.

She sunk back into her chair with a defeated sigh.

He looked at her and spread his hands. "Can you set fire to this table with a snap of your fingers? Can you cover the temple in hoar frost with a few words of power? Can you turn this knife into a toad?"

She stared at the butter knife he picked up and wielded. "I might be able to set the table on fire with soulfire, and maybe the other things I could learn how to do with train-

ing... I don't know, you see—that's why I was going." She
folded her arms and resisted pouting.

He shook his head. "No, you can't, Thaya. Maybe you
could with a hell of a lot of training; people like us have
more magical ability than most, but we are not magicians.
We are Gatewalkers, Gatekeepers, travellers through dimensions. We are cosmic nomads."

"And what the hell is the use of that?"

Theo blinked at her in surprise, then he broke into a
smile and laughed out loud. "I like that very much, my dear.
Indeed, what's the point of anything in this pointless,
painful and pressing life? Well, how about that we are
Ambassadors to other stars and to other races beyond
Urtha? How about that, Thaya?"

Thaya stared at him. "Ambassadors? I'm just trying to
stay alive on a planet that has been invaded by so-called
people from other stars. What do I know about meeting
dignitaries, or treaties, or matters of state?"

The thought was ludicrous, she'd just come from a
smallholding in Brightwater, hacking out potato fields, and
besides, did she even *want* to be an Ambassador?

Theo nodded. "I was the same but a long, long time ago.
My teacher prepared me for the life I would then lead, and
if yours is anything like mine, it will be the most interesting
and fulfilling one of them all. But only if you want it. It
seems to me that you are going to these magi for them to *tell
you* who you are. Why not go and *tell them* who you are?

"Discover who you are for yourself, that's the more interesting journey. For I believe that, despite all their powers
and wisdom, it will be you, in the end, who will be the wiser
one, who will be their teacher. We do not seek power,
Thaya, we are gifted with it in a lump sum. Magi forever

hunger for more. Greed is a terrible thing, greed for power is the worst. Ah look, they made my favourite pie!"

Ayalin carried over and set down two steaming bowls of something richly spiced and savoury-smelling. Thaya prodded the thick pastry crust with her fork and hot, brown gravy spilled out. She tucked in eagerly.

"Hmm, Ambassador Thayannon Farseeker," she said between mouthfuls. "I like the sound of that!"

Theo chuckled.

From then on, they spoke only of the food they ate, but Thaya's head was filled with thoughts about what Theo has just told her.

The next and final dish was a sweet desert of apples, pears and a tangy, white cream. Delicious though it was, Thaya was full to the brim and could only eat half.

As soon as they finished their last mouthful, Theo pushed his chair away from the table and stood. "No time to relax. Let's get us to the gate. We have one hour when the place will be ours alone."

22

A TRUE GATEWALKER

THEO PICKED UP THE SILVER BOX AND LED THE WAY BACK inside. The hallways were empty, and the palace, as Thaya now considered it since it had no religious aspects to call it a temple, was very quiet.

Khy grunted as they went down the spiralling stairwell. He hated it, finding the width far too narrow for his long body. She picked up on his keen desire to get outside but knew he was just as intrigued about the place as she was. Endless quartz floors and ceilings swept out ahead of them. Pale lights, showing them the way, lit up just ahead of their steps, along the edges of the corridor's floor as they walked, but she couldn't see any candles. Somehow, their presence activated lights within the quartz.

"The Council wants to meet you," said Theo, frowning. He had been silent and deep in thought for the whole journey. "They wanted to immediately, but I decided it was a bad idea, so I delayed them until tomorrow. Aside from your recent ordeal and need for food and rest, with the Rod returned to us, some of our members are...hungry for its power. I feel the need to protect it, and that worries me."

Thaya didn't quite know what to say, but she didn't fancy meeting a whole council. "I would meet with them, but what's in it for me? I need to return to my own time now the Rod is safe...or is it? The Leonites—"

Theo interrupted her. "Don't worry about delivering it to them, several are on the council as it is. No, don't look worried, they're not the power-hungry ones I mentioned. Indeed, many of them share the same worries I do."

"The Leonites are here?" Thaya's eyes lit up.

"Of course! There are many peoples here, not just humans. Hmm, I see that's a wondrous surprise to you. Don't others visit and commune with your councils?"

"No. The bad ones just come and take."

"Oh really? That saddens me. Hmm, I must think on this. I take it there are no good 'others' in your time?"

Thaya hesitated before she shook her head. "Not like this, not working with humans. Well, not that I know of. There are silent watchers over us, like the Agaroths, but they are hidden."

"Then the darkness really does come," Theo whispered to himself.

He paused before a long, blank wall at the end of the corridor. They had descended quite a long way and certainly down enough to be well underground by now, Thaya reckoned.

Theo placed both his hands on the walls, and beautiful script appeared above them: glowing letters of a language she didn't know. An arched door appeared and then vanished to reveal a stunning chamber beyond.

Thaya's mouth opened as she stared at the crystal-filled cavern they stepped into.

"Oh, wow!" She steadied herself on Khy's shoulder.

Crystals of every size filled the room; enormous shards,

taller than Theo, formed the walls, rising from the ground and reaching down from above. Smaller crystals clustered in the gaps between the giant pillars and covered the ceiling, and a flat floor had been smoothed out to form a sweeping walkway.

They stepped further into the grand cavern, and pink and blue floor lights came alive, lighting up the place and casting everything in a beautiful light. The crystals twinkled as if with their own light, and there was a peculiar crunching, tinkling sound coming from them, much like the sound an ice cave makes as the ice cracks and freezes. It was a wonder to behold.

She caught Theo grinning at her, the light of the cavern shining in his eyes. "Never mind the beauty, do you feel the power?" he asked.

She nodded, the hairs on her arms and neck rising with each step she took into the room. The air itself hummed with energy, and she truly felt as if the crystals were talking amongst themselves. Khy's horn shimmered and glowed when he bent his head down to sniff a particularly dense patch of crystals.

Deeper in, and in the centre of the room, rising directly out of the floor was a cylindrical pedestal—or perhaps the entire room was carved around it—about her chest high and two feet thick, perfectly round, and consisting of the same quartz as the rest of the chamber. Beyond, on the far side of the room, the chamber narrowed into a tunnel of crystals leading somewhere exceedingly interesting that Thaya itched to explore. She looked at Khy who paused his inspection of a sparkling cluster of crystals and looked at her. Any chance for a good nosey around this marvellous palace was definitely in her books, and she knew Khy felt the same.

Theo walked up to the crystal pillar. It had a slanted top, and into that smooth, straight surface, shapes had been carved out. He set the silver box down, intoned a series of sounds or musical notes, and waited for the box to click and unlock. Slowly, he opened it.

Drawing out the Rod, he stared at it between his finger and thumb. "We have not been able to engage the Rod since it was stolen. Those who still retain the original Angelic Human coding in their blood do not require such tools to open gates. However, the portals are out of alignment and thus unstable and unpredictable, so the tools were created to navigate these issues—a sort of manual override, if you will. I cannot thank you enough for returning this to our care."

"The Rod returned itself," Thaya reminded him.

"Yes, but it required someone to carry it, it doesn't have legs to walk." Theo smiled at her. "Remember, nothing occurs in isolation.

"First, we place the Rod which engages the Planetary Portals." He placed the Rod into the horizontal shape in the pedestal. It fit so perfectly Thaya realised it must have been made for it. A hum echoed harmoniously through the chamber, and the crystal pillar lit up with soft, pale light. The room glowed brighter as the entire chamber responded.

"Amazing," Thaya breathed. *The crystal has truly returned home.*

"You see this empty space here?" Theo pointed to the longer, vertical slot above the Rod. "The Staff sits here. The Staff engages the Star Portals. It opens above and below and is held in the hand vertically to power it, but sadly, it, too, is lost."

"Can't someone find it?" Thaya asked though the question was silly. Of course they'd be trying to find it, the most important object in existence upon Urtha.

"We know where it is, we simply can't reach it. The Fallen Ones have it—thankfully not the Ordacs but an Order of Nuakki who are their most hated enemy. If any of them were to have *both* tools, we will witness the destruction of the planet at their hands. As long as neither group of Invaders has both the tools, we are relatively safe. All of us are trying to get hold of them, and our history for the past one hundred and fifty thousand years has been about hunting and fighting to get the Rod, the Staff, and the box that rightfully contains them in one place.

"Now, come here before the Rod, for I feel time slipping away from us. Yes, step closer, good. Now, place your hands on the pedestal, either side of the Rod like this, and then get ready to resist that pull. Excellent! I can tell you will be a fantastic student."

Under Theo's direction, Thaya stood in front of him and gently placed her hands on the pedestal beside the Rod. The crystal surface was warm, and immediately in her mind's eye, a star map opened. She closed her eyes to see it clearly. Beautiful, bright stars scattered over a dark night sky, and she was amongst them as if she stood in the heavens.

"See the star map?" Theo asked beside her.

"Yes."

"Good. I'll place my hands beside yours and I'll see the same thing. Now then, find the closest point to you." He placed his hands on either side of hers, and she looked for the nearest star. There were several.

"This cluster of three?"

"Almost, but they're a little lower down than your focus. Bring your focus up and closer, and spot the faintest one. The lower cluster means it is south of your location, higher means north, and either side, west or east. The farther away they are, the further they are from you."

Thaya concentrated and spotted a small, faint point of light very close to her. "I see a faint one, really close."

"Yes, that's your nearest point. Do you want to know where it is? It's an island, about one hundred leagues directly west—we're currently facing west—and it's a minor vortex where two ley lines intersect. That's why it's so small and faint because it's a very small intersection. The closest portal to your current location is not the brightest star, so you'll have to get used to finding the faint ones. It gets easier with time. Now then, let's move around, so keep your focus and hands on the quartz."

She kept her eyes closed, and he placed his hands on her shoulders and guided her, step by step, clockwise. As he did so, the star map moved, and new stars were revealed.

"Another thing to know, the closest portal might be behind you, and so, not visible. The map is in three dimensions—well, more than that if you include time—but let's not get ahead of ourselves here and keep it simple. So, let's find the brightest star."

He let go of her shoulders, and she slowly paced around the pedestal keeping her focus and her eyes closed.

Again, there were several very large and bright stars. She chewed her lip, then randomly picked one. "That one, I think it's northeast? Hmm, I've lost my direction. How do I know if I'm looking east or west?"

"Almost. Remember this is three-dimensional, so look up as well as down."

"Ah, okay." Thaya looked up and spotted a very bright star just above them. "It has to be that one."

"Yes, it is, well done!" Theo clapped his hands.

She couldn't feel his hands next to hers, so how did he know which star she was looking at?

"That star you see is no ordinary star; it is Urtha, in the next dimension." He chuckled at the look on her face, and she closed her mouth. "Like I said, let's just focus on the easy things first. I just wanted you to know that you're not just looking at three dimensions. I'm training you to be a true Gatewalker, like those of times past, but I can't do it in an hour; years of hard training are required. I can give you the basics though.

"Right, so you wondered how I can see what you're looking at? Well, I can read your mind quite easily, but don't be alarmed, that's the power of this place, and especially when two similar minds are working together on the same task. And you saw how easy it was to become quite lost as to in which direction you were looking? So, let me show you something very useful. Close your eyes, keep your palms firmly on the quartz. Feel the heat in your palms? Excellent. Now, keeping a very clear and strong intention, imagine drawing the map towards you just as it draws you to it, and lift your palms and take one step back. Yes, gently, slowly. Well done. Now open your eyes."

Thaya opened her eyes and gasped at the star map before her; bright stars of all sizes surrounded and twinkled around them in her real vision. The crystal cavern was filled with stars. "Oh my! And you can see it too?"

"Yes, anyone near you can." Theo chuckled again. "It's a great way to get your bearing, but notice now, without the night background, how hard it is to see the fainter star? It's not always the best way to view the star map, just another way."

Khy sniffed a bright star and then prodded it with his horn. His horn shimmered, and the star shone brighter for a moment.

"Now then, see this star?" Theo picked one of the larger points of light a pace in front of him. "Focus on it."

She focused on the star, and a thin line of light shot out from her to the nearest faint star, then on to a brighter point, then to the star to which Theo was pointing, like joining up the dots.

"And that is the quickest path you would need to take to get to that portal," he said. "Now then, whilst we call this map a star map, apart from the brightest star, this is really just a map of Urtha's portals, and all these points are on the planet, so let's return to the pedestal and view the actual star portals. Close your eyes again. Good.

"Because we're at Star Portal Two of Urtha's seven star portals, we will be able to view the locations to the stars where we can go. Concentrate, and holding a firm intention, imagine you now are looking at a map of the star portals to other planets."

Thaya felt a strange sensation in her mind, a subtle shifting and raising of energy, and before her appeared a different star map that was incredible. Uncountable stars glimmered in front of her, brighter than before. There was so much she wanted to learn, she felt as if she had been starved of it, and her mind became a sponge to the information Theo was giving her.

"Well done," Theo commended her. "In a way, a star map is easier to read because it's brighter. Now, you see the nearest star just in front? That is Mericium. And you see this one to your right, the closest one but not as bright and much, much smaller? That is the moon. Very good. Let's have a break for the moment, this is quite tiring for beginners."

Thaya reluctantly lifted her palms off the quartz and stepped back, feeling disorientated and oddly fatigued. She had to blink several times to get her eyes to focus properly.

"That's partly why learning this stuff takes so long, it requires the body to adapt," said Theo. "You already know how to move through the portals from one place to the next, otherwise you wouldn't be standing here."

"But how do I know where the portals go or what's there?" asked Thaya.

"You don't. Captains of the sea didn't always have charts; they memorised the stars. I would suggest, in the very olden days, we could just recall the map of the portals in our minds with a simple thought. Only the Eternal Spirit knows what we were like in the first and second seedings. I still struggle to believe that nothing of us remains from those times." He shook his head sadly. "I know we looked quite different in the first seeding, that we did not need to eat and were more akin to etheric angels. In the second, we were more like we are now, this I have seen in the crystal discs. It's a complex yet intriguing history."

"I cannot believe it either," Thaya agreed, imagining all the people on the entire planet being wiped out. Once was bad enough, but twice? It was too much to bear. "But the coming cataclysms in your time...they don't destroy every-thing; we live on."

"That is what brings me hope." Theo nodded. "For I have seen dark times ahead indeed."

Thaya spoke quietly. "From what I know...the Age of Cataclysms lasts some time and is caused by the Fallen Ones invading. A great flood comes and covers the world...

Lonohassa and her greatness are destroyed, and everything is washed away. Those who manage to flee, and these are few, are hunted by the Fallen Ones because of their advanced knowledge and magical abilities, until none remain..."

Theo nodded. "This I have seen...infiltration, manipulation of our very genes—those things that make us—and forced interbreeding with aliens."

Thaya remembered Osuman, the Nuakki who had chained her and kept her as his pet, his concubine, and felt again the touch of his huge hand upon her naked skin... A shiver slithered down her spine. Arendor had also spoken of the interbreeding. "Lonohassa becomes a wasteland with pockets of people remaining. Some of these people still have the Lonohassan codes dormant in their blood. My friend Maggy had it, but we can use only a little of our powers—"

"I thought guests were not allowed down here, Theosos?"

Mensar's voice made them all jump a second time. He had the habit of arriving completely silently. They turned to face the man standing in the doorway, his hands clasped in front of his chest and an enigmatic half-smile on his face. He looked at Thaya. "You are privileged to witness our engagement of the portals, for these are under high security, especially in these times."

Theo replied, "I brought our highly esteemed guests for the power and purity they possess. Usually, a minimum of six people are required to run this gate. I assume you've noted we are but three?"

Mensar did not reply. He pursed his lips. "My students and I have booked this chamber for the rest of the evening; you have overrun by nearly half an hour."

"Then we're lucky that you are late," said Theo and

bowed respectfully. He turned to Thaya. "Mensar will be taking over from me when I...retire. He is adept but—"

"But Theosos refuses to relinquish his grip." Mensar's expression darkened.

Theo rolled his eyes and took a deep breath. "Well, now that you're here, it's time we were off to bed. Remember to protect the Rod at all costs, Mensar."

"Of course, Theosos, don't worry." The man nodded as they passed him and exited the room. Thaya noticed Khy glancing back at Mensar, but she couldn't read his thoughts.

They made their way back up the stairs, and between then and crawling into her fresh linen sheets, not much was said. Theo looked as weary as she felt and said his good-nights at her door. Only Khy still had a spring in his step.

Thaya left the curtains open, and as she relaxed in her bed, she watched Khy standing on the balcony. He looked pale, almost white in the moonlight, like all others of his kind. Only his mane and tail shone whiter than all else.

23

PROTECTORS OF THE FREE WORLDS

THAYA STOOD ONCE MORE UPON THE LONG STRETCH OF WHITE-quartz sand beach, the sea breeze gently lifting her hair. All was still—even the low waves rolling onto the shore were quiet.

It began as a knot in her stomach, a terrible feeling that grew and crawled through her body. A noise began, a constant high-pitched whirring that built into a screeching no human or animal could make. A shadow fell over her, cutting the warmth from the sun and chilling the wind. She stared up at the monstrosity hanging in the sky and slowly spinning on its vertical axis.

"No," she whispered.

The breeze dropped, the rolling waves lost their form and became flat, but the noise continued from the beast above her. It wasn't a monster made of flesh and blood but one of metal or some alien material she didn't recognise. It looked black in the shade, but it could be dark grey, and its texture was rough, not smooth, polished steel. Large and small angular protrusions and depressions covered it, and long, antennae-like radio receivers—similar to what many machines had on Earth—stuck out all over it, suggesting some function she could only ponder at. The beast was the size of a small village.

"Why don't you all just leave us alone!" Thaya screamed at it. "What have we ever done to you?"

Why did they have to come to Urtha and destroy her people? They had their own planets to live and prosper upon. Why couldn't they let Urtharians have their own?

A red beam burst down from the ship. It struck the ocean and went deep, creating a whirlpool ever-increasing in size. The sea began to froth and bubble, a grinding, low hum started, and the breeze became turbulent.

Thaya raised her hands, and soulfire burst alight in her palms. With a yell, she released it. Golden fire struck the underside of the enormous ship, scorching the side and breaking off an antenna before the fire fizzled out. She ground her teeth and poured more energy into her palms. The sea thrashed wildly, and on the horizon, a great wave rolled fast towards her. A mighty wind picked up, battering her backwards and forwards.

In a few heartbeats, the wave was barely a league from the shore. She screamed at the ship, hating it with all her being, but her soulfire was useless against it.

A sensation of cool calmness suddenly flowed through her, coming from somewhere else. It soothed her raging hatred, and the din of the wind and roaring ocean fell to silence. The ship and its red beam, the enormous wall of water, all faded until they were indistinct pastel shades, the blue sky a brush stroke of blue, the white sand a pale sweep beneath it, and the ship just a faint smudge.

A face formed before her: familiar furry features and rounded, lion-like ears. Golden eyes blinked back at her.

"Awaken, Thaya, from your prophetic dreams and come to us. Time is short."

The face faded, and Thaya looked up at a dark ceiling. A strong feeling that she should get up made her swing her legs out of bed rather than curl up and fall back to sleep. A soft ball of light appeared in the centre of the room, making her jump. It floated in midair and hung there. Khy entered and headed straight to the light, sniffing it with interest.

"Did you make that?" asked Thaya. He'd never made a ball of light before.

"Smells of Leonite," he said decidedly and looked at her with his head cocked.

"In my dream, a Leonite came and told me to come to them. Look, it's moving!"

The orb moved towards the door and then paused. Thaya hastily pulled on her leggings and tunic, grateful for the light, otherwise, she wouldn't have been able to see anything.

She went closer to the orb, and it moved away towards the door again.

"It's leading us," said Khy, swishing his tail.

"Then let's follow." Thaya giggled.

The faster they moved, the faster the orb moved, and they hurried after it down the stairs. She was hoping it would lead them somewhere exciting, through a secret passage to a secret room or something, but to her disappointment, it led them straight back to the large room she had first chatted with Theo in, and vanished. Parts of the floor glowed orange, giving a gentle and calming campfire-like light to everything.

Theo was there, seated on a chair with a weary and worried expression on his face. Thaya's stride slowed, for he was not alone but accompanied by three Leonites, each dressed in long, floor-length robes. Two were seated opposite Theo—a male and a female—and another male stood beside them, their cat-like faces immediately capturing her fascination. The males were larger in stature and had a thick, short mane of hair circling their angular faces. The female was smaller with a softer face and no mane of hair. The standing male had dark, tawny fur and the other was a lighter shade, but the female had white fur. All had golden eyes, but hers were much paler.

"Welcome, Thaya and Khy," said the female.

Thaya instantly recognised her voice as the one in her dream.

Khy lifted his head but did not speak. Instead, he watched the Leonites with intrigue. The Leonites and Saphira-elaysa looked at each other for a long moment, and Thaya sensed something passing between them but was not privy to their conversation. She knew Khy would tell her anything important, so she didn't feel left out.

"You came to me, in my dream," she said instead.

"I did. Thank you for gracing us with your presence, Thayannon Farseeker, we are indeed pleased to meet with you." The Leonite inclined her head.

"The pleasure is most surely mine," Thaya said, also inclining her head and resisting the sudden urge to bow. They looked so regal and powerful, she felt that she should. *Really, they just look different,* she told herself.

"I am Saroshi, and these are my brethren: Lim and Akesh," she said. Both males inclined their heads, one after the other.

Thaya wasn't sure if they were Saroshi's brothers or simply her friends or colleagues.

"Are you a Dreamwalker?" she asked, thinking of the elf by the fountain.

"I am," Saroshi replied.

"I knew one once, back home, or at least, back in my time," said Thaya. "I didn't actually know him well. He's an elf, and I was helping him retrieve a lost relic, much like I got roped into retrieving the Rod for your people. Hah! Funny how those two items entered my world at the same time. And here I am." She felt awkward after speaking and wondered if she should have said anything at all.

"By the grace of the Eternal Spirit, here you are indeed," Akesh said.

Thaya clasped her hands behind her back and stared at the floor. "Your kind...hmm, how to say it?" She thought for a few seconds and then continued, "I'm sorry about your kin who died trying to protect the shard, I mean, the Rod. There is a memorial to honour them. It rests where they died—their faces are imprinted on the mountainside forever, for what good it will do. The Rod may have been brought to safety for now, but it will be stolen again in the future, in my time."

The Leonites nodded sombrely, and Saroshi turned to her brethren. They spoke to each other in their own language, soft and fluid words interspersed with what sounded like purrs and many rolling Rs. They paused, and the darker male called Akesh looked at Thaya. He spoke in Lonohassan, and all eyes fell upon Thaya.

"It was actually from the past that the Rod was stolen, and to the future it was taken, and now it has returned. It matters not in which time the Rod is—time is inconsequential—but it must remain within Urtha's energy fields, and it must be protected."

"I don't quite understand its power, but I *am* relieved to be, relieved of it." Thaya took a deep breath, feeling that her task was finally done.

Akesh continued, "We knew that the Light Holder would come to us, thanks to your prophecy, Theosos, but we did not anticipate that she would be hunted. Indeed, given how things are, we should have expected that. Thaya, you have courageously taken on the burden of protecting the Rod that our fallen kin entrusted to you, and successfully delivered it to safety against all the odds; we're truly grateful.

"You and Khy are an enigma—two races paired in ways no one has ever borne witness to before. Yes, we have discussed your nature with Theosos, and we're in agreement that one day you'll become a member of the Protectors of the Free Worlds, as we all are, should you so wish. Don't worry about whether they exist in your time—they do—for at the highest realms, they are eternal, and time is but an illusion. The Protectors of the Free Worlds are an intergalactic alliance and a guardianship of like-minded, benevolent beings, in service to the Eternal Spirit, who wish to protect and keep free all the worlds. We are the opposite of what your race calls the Fallen Ones. Consider us Guardians.

"We, along with many other races, watch over humanity and each other, as other races also guard over Leonites on our journey back to the light. None of us are ever alone, though it might seem that way, but we do not watch your every move, we simply observe greater events from a distance.

"Guardians particularly look out for those holding greater power and abilities, for the Fallen Ones also watch these. Negative races seek to influence and control gifted beings in order to use those abilities to forward their own dark agendas. We try to make sure that doesn't happen unless, of course, the gifted being sadly chooses the dark road."

"Free will must be allowed?" Thaya had heard it said before that free will must be honoured, even if mistakes and poor choices will be made.

"Free will, always." The Leonite nodded.

"Like the Agaroths?" Thaya asked. Arendor, her Arothian friend, came to mind. Had he not been there with her, the Shades would have taken her.

"The Agaroths are not of our number," Akesh replied. "They are falling."

"But they protected me," said Thaya.

Akesh shook his head. "Falling races cannot be part of the Protectorate, for they risk bringing down the whole Guardianship. Do not be sad, your friend and his race understand this better even than we do. They have their own...Councils of Guardianship. They are hunters, warriors, seeking revenge upon the Fallen Ones who made them fall."

"Someone has to, don't they?" asked Thaya. There had to be *someone* fighting back!

"Revenge has no place in our councils, and it ultimately serves no one," said Akesh. "Reflect deeply upon this, and you'll feel the truth of these words."

Thaya nodded. These people knew much more than she did. Who was she to argue? But she longed for revenge for all the atrocities the Fallen Ones had committed against them. "I'm grateful there are those willing to protect us, and, yes, I did think that we were alone, but why don't you help us remove the Invaders?"

Why didn't they come and kick out the Nuakki? Where had these so-called 'guardians' been when she was a mind-less slave working in the Nuakki gold mines? What about all the people shackled or murdered?

The seated male, Lim, spoke for the first time. His voice sounded older than the others, his eyes wiser. "Many races feel as yours—alone, at the mercy of the dark wind. We can only assist humans insofar as it doesn't affect their free will. Humans have to ask for assistance; otherwise, it's a breach of free will to provide aid when such aid may not be wanted."

"But I'm asking for help." Thaya frowned.

He cast an amused look at Theo. "You have a willing student, Theosos Rotoa, but I see you have yet to really begin."

Theo nodded, smiled and said nothing. Something was bothering him, and now she thought about it, there was a pensive air in the room.

The Leonites conversed with each other quietly in their own language, and Thaya watched them silently. How had she travelled from the far distant future into the far distant past, yet these beings were *more* advanced and speaking of futuristic concepts she could barely fathom? She had already seen more incredible, unbelievable things here, now, than she had ever seen upon future Earth, for all its flying crafts and motor vehicles.

When they paused, she spoke. "And when I become a member of the Protectors of Free Worlds, what would I do?"

Akesh answered, "That has yet to be determined, but first, you must understand and master yourself. At the moment we have much need of...*travellers* amongst us— human Gatewalkers—for there are so few of you, and your race is in danger. With Khy at your side, and with training, you could be a valuable ambassador to other races, though it is a dangerous job at times."

"I could be an ambassador? Me?" Thaya tried to imagine

travelling to distant stars and speaking with alien races. *Yes, it would be dangerous! Imagine arriving on the Nuakki's planet Rubini or the Vormae's Geshol!* Neither she nor Khy would last long there.

"If you so wish, and it is your calling and where your skills lie, then yes," replied Saroshi. "Ponder upon it, Thaya, for now we must turn to our reason for meeting."

Theo, who had sat quietly all this time, suddenly got to his feet, deep worry creasing his brow. When he spoke it was as if he were continuing a conversation they had been having before her arrival. "As I said, I've wanted to talk but could not with Mensar watching everything. He is one of the Council and I feel I'm being...scrutinised. I saw that I would receive a student, and that I'd better receive her well because our time together would be short, extremely so. But her coming would inspire within me hope for the future."

That he thought she brought hope worried Thaya, and she spoke up. "I can't bring you hope. Where I'm from in the future, it's dark, and the later future I came from just now is darker still."

Theo looked at her and gave a half smile. "No, but there are others like us in the future; the Angelic Human lives on. Yes, we will move through the darkness for eons before we reach the light. But those like you, like us, wandering stars, are lights in that darkness, reminding others that all will be well, and we are not alone.

"But unfortunately, that's where we must leave that discussion, for I have bad news: a rumble has been felt in the ethers, and something terrible rolls towards us. There was a long and bitter argument at the Council meeting earlier, and a great split now divides us. Rumours are members have been working closely with councils of...of the other side, so to speak. Working too closely."

Saroshi nodded. "We believe an attack on this Star Portal is imminent. The argument earlier was the first outward expression of something that has been worked upon for a long time, perhaps even decades. A dark plan concerning a takeover, a coup, has been uncovered, and most likely the arrival of the Rod has expedited it.

"Ah, Thaya, don't look worried, this is not your fault. The plan was to be set in motion when the Rod arrived, they have simply been lying in wait for that time. I believe this creation of the divide amongst us was deliberate, just one small part of the plan, or one plan amongst many. But given what we know, the Rod is not safe here, it must be moved and hidden, and the portal gate closed immediately."

Theo pulled the silver box from under the table and lifted it onto his lap. He placed his hands on top of it. "I don't wish to let the Rod go, and the last thing I want is for our Star Portal to be closed, but the Leonites, in their wisdom, could be right...though I've been arguing against that decision all evening."

Thaya shook her head and took a step back. Khy looked at her, his ears swivelling back and forth. "I can't take it back again, there's no way I can protect it any longer," she said.

Theo and the Leonites chuckled, the genuine humour in their eyes making her frown.

"You won't need to take the Rod," said the eldest Leonite. "Your task is done, and you did it well. No, we'll take it with us as soon as our brethren arrive in the next hour or two. We cannot leave Urtha's surface, so we'll have to go quietly under the cover of night."

"Where are you taking it?" Thaya asked.

"That will remain a secret, even from you for your own protection," said Saroshi.

Thaya nodded. She didn't fancy being captured by the

Fallen Ones and tortured for what she knew; she'd already experienced the agony the Vormae and Nuakki could inflict without even raising a weapon.

"But this is where you two come in, Thaya and Khy," said Theo. He put the silver box aside and stood up. "All my life I have protected Elanta arn Bruah and this great portal to the stars, but in my heart, I know the Leonites are right: for the protection of all the souls here, we have to close it, although I *am* demanding it be temporary. I'm hoping to be able to keep the smaller surrounding portals and vortices open and under my protectorate, but I'm sorry to say, Thaya, with the main portal closed, there won't be enough power to get you back home."

"Then I'm happy to stay!" Thaya clapped her hands together. "I've been thinking about it, and you're right, the magi won't be able to teach me anything, not really. You're the only one who understands me and my gifts, and what this is all about."

Khy watched the pair as they spoke.

Theo smiled, but his face was sad. "And I would be your willing teacher. I've so longed to pass on what I know to someone else, but now is not that time. Your safety is in danger, and we must do what we can to get you back to your proper time."

"My life has been in danger ever since I was driven from Brightwater!" said Thaya. "What difference does it make now?"

"It matters a great deal to me, Thaya." Theo laid a fatherly hand on her shoulder, and she suddenly realised how much she missed Fi, her adoptive father back home. She swallowed a lump, but nothing could get rid of that dull, homesick ache deep in her gut. She placed a hand on Khy's shoulder, the feel of his soft fur calming.

Khy's voice was soft and low. "I go where you go, but I believe Theo is right: one day or another, we have to return to where we left off. We can't stay here."

Thaya clasped her hands together. "Every place I've travelled to via a portal I've wanted to leave...until now. And now that I want to stay, I can't! Ouch!" A sharp pain suddenly stabbed in her head, and she winced.

"What is it?" Theo asked. "Here, sit down." He steered her towards his chair and sat her down.

"I don't know," she said as the pain faded, and she rubbed her temples. She closed her eyes and immediately saw the white beach again, and the blue sea and sky, and the monstrous circular black ship above her, hanging suspended by some impossible technology.

"She sees them!" Saroshi stood up abruptly.

"What? The ship? Yes." Thaya gasped as another sharp, stabbing pain hit her.

A tremble, as if from an earthquake, suddenly shook the entire building, and the floor light flickered. All the lights went out, plunging them into darkness, and then they slowly came back on. A strange whirring noise grew, but Thaya didn't know if she heard it for real or if it was in her head.

"We must away!" said Lim. The older Leonite jumped up with surprising agility.

Theo grabbed the silver box, then Thaya's arm, and then they were all running to the hidden door.

24

LONOHASSA FALLING

"THE GROUND TREMBLES. THE CRYSTAL WALLS ARE AFRAID."

Thaya turned to look at Khy and nodded her agreement, then the pair of them, along with the Leonites, hurried after Theo who led them along hallways, up winding quartz staircases, and through doorways hidden in walls only he could open.

"I'm afraid, too," Thaya admitted.

"Stay close," said Khy.

They made their way along and up, and then up some more until Thaya thought they must surely be at the top, and then they passed through a wide archway into a large, circular room, the ceiling of which was a giant glass dome.

It kind of looks like an observatory, thought Thaya.

Through another archway to their left stretched a huge outdoor platform, softly lit by floor lights. To their right, all was glass window, and through it, Thaya could see the city lights stretching down to the dark sweep that was the ocean. She wondered what time it was because dawn felt far away.

Within the observatory, and around the edges of the

room, twelve human-sized crystals encircled them. The energy of the place was strong—the air hummed with it, and the hairs on her arms rose. That endless whirring noise was louder up here too, it really got into her head, but she couldn't see the source of it. Perhaps, out there somewhere in the darkness, an awful black ship hung.

A large, bright light appeared in the sky, and it quickly made a beeline for them. Her hand went to her throat, but the Leonites smiled and hurried outside onto the platform. She followed them, and her mouth fell open as a smooth, triangular-shaped craft with rounded edges slowly descended. Three spindly legs protruded from its under-side, and it settled silently on the platform. Its surface shone like metal that was whiter than steel and gleamed with a touch of pearlescence. Like all alien ships Thaya had ever seen, she could not see inside the craft, and there appeared to be no windows.

A small section on the lower side of the ship opened, and bright light spilled out from inside. Human-like shapes moved in the light as a thin ramp extended forwards to the platform, and then the figures emerged and walked down it: two Leonites in pastel blue tunics. Saroshi, Akesh and Lim clustered around them, and they all put their heads together in greeting.

"Thaya, there's no time for goodbyes. Come." Theo grabbed her hand, pulling her away.

She reluctantly left the cat-people, looking back over her shoulder at them and their beautiful craft. Khy followed, but he kept pausing and looking up into the sky. It was so black, this night, no stars or moon could be seen.

Back inside the observatory, Theo paused beside a giant quartz crystal. "Oh, and here, take this." From an inside pocket he drew out a polished, oval citrine that was smaller than her thumb. The crystal was a clear and yellowy-orange, like zesty amber.

He pressed the lozenge-shaped gem into her palm. "This is what we call a 'mind-opener.' Normally, I would give these to Gatewalkers in highly esteemed initiation ceremonies after years of training, but we no longer have such luxuries. It's not so much a drug as an extremely ancient elixir that will open your mind for portal travel. It's a gemstone with very special qualities."

Thaya looked at the gem and frowned; it was completely solid, not a liquid at all. "How does it work?"

"When you are before a portal, place this in your mouth," Theo explained. "After a moment, it will melt into a liquid. Keep this in your mouth for a short time before swallowing it. Then, hah! Hold on, for reality is going to get really wild!" His eyes blazed and he spread his hands wide.

Thaya eyed him critically. Was this for real? But the Gatekeeper continued, "Normally, we do this under strict supervision, but you have Khy with you, it will have to do.

"First, you'll feel wind, a cosmic wind that blows through your body and soul, cleansing it of accumulated debris. Then you will see lights, sometimes flashing, sometimes flowing, sometimes bright and sometimes dark. Quickly after comes the music, not music of bards or minstrels, no, this is the divine music of the cosmos, no words can describe its humbling beauty. When you hear the music, you'll feel like you are falling.

"All of what I described is much the same for everyone. How long it lasts varies according to the individual, but it is intense and all-consuming—the real world will be utterly lost to you, and there is no way out. You will see time and reality in ways you have never fathomed before. It is...it is... an incredible journey that will open up new pathways in your mind.

"What happens next is unique to you. I cannot say what it will be, but it will be life-changing, and it's irreversible. Don't be alarmed, I've witnessed no negative side effects in all my long years of Gatewalking. When all have passed, at the very end, you will understand, as if by magic, the functions of portals and the maps of the stars.

"Now, be ready, for you'll be exhausted, wild, exhilarated! You'll forever be able to see before you the star maps and portal maps as you did when you first popped the mind-opener into your mouth, only it will be different, unique to your understanding. How it will look and feel is different for each person, but the map will now have more information, and with each point of light you focus on, you'll get a reading, an image, an imprint about it, and...and this is why I have given you the mind-opener in the first place: if you know where it is you want to go, you'll see that point in the star map shining brighter than the rest or coming into your focus more than the others."

Thaya blinked. "So, you're saying this mind-opening crystal will allow me to navigate star and portal maps if I know where it is I want to go?"

Theo smiled and nodded once. "Indeed. I keep reiterating it, but it's different for each person, and you'll have to consume it to know fully what I've just tried to explain. Now again, afterwards, you'll feel exhausted for anything up to three days, so make sure wherever you exit there's somewhere where you can rest safely. Don't do what I did on my first try and exit into the middle of a battle, a battle at sea, for that matter. I lay in the bowels of a floundering ship that became a wreck all around me. I've no idea how I managed to escape that bloody mess. I've had seasickness ever since and never again set foot in a boat." Theo grimaced and shook himself like a dog. "But remember, its effect is immediate, violent, and unfortunately far too short."

Thaya nodded slowly, and dubiously slipped the strange gem into her pocket.

Theo set the silver box he'd been carrying down, spoke the codes to open it, and lifted out the Rod. It glowed merrily in his hands, but his chin was set, hinting at the strain he felt holding it. He walked to the centre of the room, squared his shoulders, and held the Rod straight out on his right side.

Something made her shiver. She looked at Khy and he at her, then he looked up at the glass dome and the black sky beyond it. *"We have to go, something bad is about to transpire here,"* Khy said.

"We should stay here with him and help fight whatever is coming," said Thaya. She winced as a sharp pain stabbed inside her head. The huge, round behemoth flashed through her mind, the black ship stark and imposing in a sunlit world. That incessant, ear-grating whirring noise thundered through her head, making her teeth chatter. The sharp pain intensified, driving her to her knees.

———

For a split second, Thaya was back fully in her dream of the tsunami with the magenta and saffron sunshades, the blue sky, and hot sun falling between them...and then the silence that swept through the city before the carnage. She once again stared up at the dark ship about to destroy her world.

Who were they? Why did she feel the pain in her mind? Why did she have these memories that were not of this lifetime?

She felt Khy nudging her and Theo pulling her to her feet by the arms. The pain receded, and she breathed deeply, supported by both of them.

"Who are they?" she gasped. "I saw them come! They destroyed everything...it was another life...another time..."

She blinked blearily up at Theo's worried face. "No," he said, shaking his head. "Not another time; you saw *this* time, just in another place. Perhaps that's why you're here now. Something ties you to this time, a lifetime lived thousands of years ago? Perhaps a part of you wished you could do something...but you cannot stop it."

A red sky broke above them as dawn rolled relentlessly forwards.

Now Thaya could stand by herself, Theo released his grip on her. His eyes looked far away, and there was pain in them. "As to who they are? I don't know for certain, but Mensar and many on the Council have been communing with an alliance—I call it a dark alliance, for they speak not of freedom but of control. They see these off-worlders as gods. I swear some even worship them! A section of defective Nuakki and Ordacs have formed an alliance and are now trying to make one with us, but—Eternal Spirit, forgive me—I can never trust them. Mensar and his lot disappeared after our meeting, and his bed was empty an hour ago."

He looked back at her. "Tell me what you saw."

"I saw a flying craft, huge, dark and round. There were many of them, and destruction follows. I keep seeing them in my dreams."

Theo rubbed his chin, his intelligent mind working so

hard she imagined she could hear it whirring. "But why are you seeing them now? Something connects you to them."

Thaya looked at the symbol on her palm where the swirling Nuakki slave symbol had once been. Its mark remained but it was pale, faint, only just visible, yet it tingled as she looked at it. Remembering her time as a slave to an alien race on her own planet left her feeling unsettled —it reminded her of how life could be and how bad things could get, of being a nothing and a nobody, worthless and forgotten by everyone.

Theo grabbed her hand. "Is this the mark?"

Thaya nodded. "But it's gone, just the scar remains."

Theo let go of her hand and spoke thoughtfully. "Your time with them, it has left you connected to them in some manner. Your connection with Khy, your connection with the Vormae that you told me about...it's all the same. I've been thinking on this, Thaya, and there's something more to you. You form connections—subliminal, subtle, covert—I doubt even the beings you meet know what is happening, and from the look on your face, neither do you. Empaths and Channellers have similar skills."

"Do you think they come because I'm here?" The thought made Thaya go cold. Were the Nuakki still hunting her?

Theo laughed. "No, my dear, I don't think you are *that* important, at least not to them, not at this time."

Thaya blushed. "Everywhere I go, trouble follows."

"On the contrary. I think you arrive where trouble is about to start. You bring change, Thaya, so be a vessel for the Eternal Spirit, and let the good change happen."

Sunlight broke through the red dawn clouds and illuminated the observatory in red and yellow. The giant crystals surrounding them suddenly hummed and glowed a stunning deep pink.

"Wow!" said Thaya.

Theo smiled. "I was hoping we'd make the dawn. The power of the sun's light assists in portal travel. Now then, come closer, both of you, into the centre of the room."

Thaya and Khy stepped into the concentric lines of quartz that marked the middle of the room. Theo went to stand by a crystal most illuminated by the sun and held the Rod out once more.

"Wait," said Thaya. "Why don't you come with us? Bring the Rod to my time, we can protect it together, and after a short while, you can return." That bad feeling lodged in her gut, the dull ache in her head...whatever was about to unfold, she couldn't just leave Theo and the Leonites, and all the people of Elanta to their fate.

"Impossible"—Theo shook his head—"for all the reasons I discussed before—"

A great tremor shook the palace.

"Theo, the Rod!" Saroshi shouted from the archway, her hand outstretched. She fell against the wall. Thaya staggered against Khy, and Theo grabbed hold of the giant crystal for balance.

Thunder that didn't end rolled around them, and the dull whirring that hadn't ceased all this time, reminded them it was there and crescendoed. A strong wind blew through the open door, tugging at their hair and clothes, and a shadow moved over them, cutting out the light.

Slowly, Thaya looked up.

The black ship, the nightmare in her visions and dreams, descended over the quartz city, a predator she had only ever seen in her mind now more real and stark and deadly than ever before.

A cold tremble swept through her and transfixed her to the spot.

"Thaya, don't look at it!" Theo grabbed her by the arms and shook her.

"Let's go," said Khy, simply, calmly, and out loud.

Thaya looked into his deep indigo eyes and saw no debate. He was not going to let her stay a moment longer.

Khy turned to Theo. "Prime Gatekeeper, do what you must do."

Theo, unused to hearing Khy speak, stared at him, nodded slowly, then stood straighter.

"Theo, hurry, we must away!" Saroshi shouted.

The other Leonites hovered at the door, staring up at the ship. To Thaya it already seemed too late. Any moment now, a thick, red beam would burst down from the underside of the beast and shatter the world. A terrible trembling shook everything, and she clung onto Khy for balance, for protection.

Theo grasped hold of the giant crystal with one hand, and it pulsed with light. He held the Rod directly out at his side and began chanting in his deep, melodious voice that was soon lost in the din of the rushing wind.

Beyond the domed observatory, the dawn chased away the clouds, and a clear, blue sky began to show. It was going to be a beautiful day in this doomed paradise. Thaya felt tears trickle down her cheeks, she hadn't even realised she'd begun crying.

The gut-trembling stopped, the wind dropped, and complete silence fell. During the din, Theo had been shouting. Now his voice rang out loudly, his words of power vibrating right through her.

He stopped chanting and shot the hand holding the Rod down to point at the floor. The twelve crystals flared into white light. He shouted another word and flung his hand up to point the Rod straight at the sky. The crystals released a sonic pulse that shuddered her eardrums. He shouted a third word and shot his hand out horizontally to point straight at her and Khy in the centre of the room.

Twelve rays of blinding light exploded from the crystals, straight towards them. The light engulfed her, and she was plunged into what felt like a waterfall—a rush of cold turbulent energy bubbled and tingled over her skin, so bright she couldn't see anything beyond the glowing crystals. Theo walked towards her, and light flared from the Rod, as bright as the giant crystals.

The energy condensed, and a strange noise started. It sounded like water running through underground tunnels, deep and resounding. Light began to refract, becoming angular waves that then softened and flowed into circles of light and dark. Sound distorted and deepened to such a low noise, she couldn't hear it so much as feel it vibrating through her.

An ear-piercing screeching cut through everything and made her heart race.

Behind Theo, a thick, red beam struck downwards. Thaya cried out, Khy tossed his head, but Theo did not look behind at it. He bowed over oddly, throwing both hands and the Rod in front of him as if he was hurling his energy forward with all his might. His intense white eyes never blinked but remained locked onto her and Khy as he controlled the immense energy.

The whole world trembled. The energy enveloped them, and then the ground was lost from beneath her feet. Sweat beaded on Theo's face and trickled down his cheeks from sheer concentration. Something told her it wasn't meant to be this difficult.

"He's struggling to form the connection, something prevents him, probably the alien craft," said Khy, over the din.

The sound of smashing glass echoed around them, and the whirring noise of the black behemoth could be heard again.

Khy tossed his head, and his horn burst into golden light. Thaya dared to trust the energy to hold her, let go of Khy's neck, and held her hands up, filling them with soulfire.

"Goodbye, Thaya," shouted Theo. The immense concentration had left his face, and tears filled his eyes.

"Theo, come with us! What's happening back there, we can't see!" Tears filled her eyes, she had to get back there and help him, she had to! She tried to move forwards to grab his hands, but the force of the maelstrom shoved her back.

Theo shook his head and shouted something, but his words were lost in the rushing vortex. Khy released his power, and it burst from his horn and into the Rod. Thaya released her soulfire, and for a moment, the three of them were joined together by golden light, just like they had been when facing Grenshoa.

The chaotic forces spun faster, but the noise lessened to hums and whispers. It was the strangest thing Thaya had witnessed. A tunnel of light and dark burst open in front of them and drew on her strongly.

Theo shouted a word and flung his arms down. Everything became pale light, and the noise vanished.

Theo was now below them, looking up at them as if they were floating in the sky. Through the haze and billow of black smoke, she saw that the glass dome of the observatory had shattered, and half of the crystal palace had gone!

Where once it had stood, black and green vitrified glass now smouldered. An explosion sounded below her, and smoke filled the air, turning it black. Thaya screamed but the vortex closed around her, and she could see nothing but spinning light and dark.

25

ITHUIN OF ORIVON

THAYA SCREAMED AND SPUN HELPLESSLY BEHIND KHY through the portal, her stomach churning in time with her cartwheeling. Was Theo alive? Was the Rod safe? She tried not to think, just to breathe, just to survive.

The chaotic energies of the portal dragged not just her body, but her mind and soul, pulling and pushing her forward so strongly, it felt as if she was being physically stretched. Perhaps it was unstable. Perhaps the off-worlders were trying to thwart their escape. Whatever, Thaya just wanted it to be over.

Light flashed ahead and hurt her eyes. Khy wasn't cartwheeling uncontrollably, but he held his head down, and rather than running, his legs were braced as if he were trying to slow himself down. Light flared from his horn, but she couldn't be sure what he was doing.

The bright light engulfed her, and a deafening thunderclap shook her senses. Consciousness left her for a moment.

She came round again. Dazed, she felt herself falling then floating, then falling again.

Voices echoed, and the light was so bright that she couldn't open her eyes against it.

"Theo? Khy?" she called, but her voice sounded odd: weak and disembodied.

"Catch her! And the Eye!" someone shouted.

She recognised the voice.

Strong arms engulfed her.

The light dimmed, and she blinked. Blurry figures moved all around her, some near, others far. Angry shouting came from farther away as well as the sound of metal clashing. Melodic voices spoke close—the accent was strange, the words too, and yet she recognised them.

"Where's Grenshoa?" asked a voice.

"She vanished!" replied another.

"Give her to me. Help the Saphira-elaysa stand, he's just dazed. The humans need help over there. Seal that entrance, the Ordacs are coming from there!"

Other arms took her.

"Thaya?"

The voice was so familiar, but she couldn't place it. Why did her body feel like jelly? Why were her eyes struggling to focus?

An image pushed into her mind, and she saw his face, the Dreamwalker, the elf-man by the fountain. *"Remember me, Ellasheem, gift-bringer,"* he said.

"I remember, but I do not know your name. Where am I?" It was much easier to speak telepathically. Her voice didn't want to work just yet, but her own words sounded strange as if she spoke another language.

"Your Elvish is perfect, ha-ha! I see Eir'andehari has given you the gift of Elvish. I am Ithuin of Orivon. You held Eir'andehari and the Pentolen together... Impressive or terribly foolish.

Then you and Grenshoa vanished for a dozen heartbeats. Now you have returned, but Grenshoa has not!"

Thaya struggled with reality for several long moments, then said, *"I am back in the dragon cave? But I've been gone days, maybe longer!"*

"It cannot be...not to our eyes. The light took us all for only moments. But Pentolen, the Rod, as humans call it, is no longer in your hands. Where is it? Did Grenshoa take it?"

Thaya smiled, suddenly relieved. *"No, it's safe. The Leonites took it. Why am I so exhausted? Theo?"* What had happened to him? What about Elanta?

"Calm, Thaya," Ithuin soothed. *"Look into Eir'andehari, find healing in the Eye of Ahro."*

He held up the elven relic, and the smooth surface swirled darkly. Her vision was drawn into the centre of it, and from it flowed calm and wellness. Her sight sharpened, and the thrumming in her ears faded. There was blood soaking through her leggings, a good amount of it, and she gasped at the pain in her calf. Ithuin was pressing a bandage onto it.

"You have glass in your leg, a shard," he spoke out loud in Familiar. "No, don't look at it. It needs to come out. But where did it come from? There's no glass here. No, don't speak, tell me later."

"Khy?" Thaya whispered.

"He's as dazed as you." Ithuin glanced up at her as he worked on her leg. "Grazed, but not injured. Look, he comes."

Thaya angled her head as much as her aching neck would allow and watched a blurry shape approach. A warm, soft nose pressed against her cheek, and under-standing passed between them. Khy was fine, just exhausted. The spaceship battling the power of the Rod and crystals had shattered the observatory, injuring her but not mortally.

"The Ordacs have fled, my Levenor." A breathless elf, wearing the thinnest and most ornate shining armour Thaya had ever seen, hurried up to Ithuin. His helmet was adorned with small, rising wings, and on his breastplate, endless swirls entwined through one another.

"Dragon-kin always flee when faced with elves," Ithuin said darkly. "Filth."

"Thaya!" a woman called out.

Thaya turned her head and saw a blurry female figure with a shock of blonde hair striding towards her.

"Engara?"

The warrior woman jumped to her side, her face covered in mud and blood—Thaya couldn't remember ever seeing her clean—and knelt on the ground beside her.

Thaya frowned. "How did you get here?"

"We tracked you," Engara explained, as two of her Shield Brothers came to stand beside her, breathing heavily from the fight and checking their swords over. "Something in me wouldn't let you go, not with that beast in the air, not after all that happened. I realised I couldn't start a new town, or ever settle down...that I must be forever free. So, I took whoever wanted to come to avenge our people."

Thaya struggled to sit upright, so Ithuin helped her. She fought the pain in her leg and strove to remember, to reconnect with all that had occurred here before she had left, but so much had happened, her head spun with it all. At one moment, she was with Theo and the Leonites, witnessing the destruction of the crystal palace, and now she was faced with elves and humans battling Ordacs. Had Engara and the elves not come, a far different, darker outcome for her and Khy would have occurred.

"I'm so glad you did," Thaya said, breathing through the pain. "Otherwise, we would not be—argh!" She screamed as Ithuin pulled three inches of glass from her calf in a burst of bright blood. He hastily worked, putting himself between her and the wound so she couldn't see what he was doing, but light flared from his hands, she was sure of it.

"My apologies, Ena-shani, the blood was clotting dangerously," he said, as she swooned. He placed a palm against her forehead and pushed her back down, waves of coolness flowing from his hands through her body and calf. She drifted away, just far enough that the agony was but a dull, distant ache, and their voices came from far away.

Khy, Engara and Ithuin spoke between themselves as she floated somewhere beyond.

"We must take her home through our portal for elven healing," said Ithuin. "It's too far a trek down the mountain, and darkness falls."

"Let us go now," said Khy.

"But we can't come..." began Engara.

"You and your warriors are welcome, Shield Brethren," said Ithuin, "but peace must be held, and you must disarm to us. Several of your kind require assistance too, some urgently."

After a long moment, Engara said. "So be it. We'd be honoured."

Theo's face was before her, tears in his blazing white eyes, a grimace of immense concentration ploughing deep furrows on his forehead. He held up a flaring Rod, and all around him a world of destruction rolled in slow motion: shards of glass sprayed everywhere, the quartz walls cracked and crumbled, and the giant crystal beside him shattered. Behind him, through it all, that hideous, thick, red beam thrummed violently.

A higher pitched but melodious and incredibly loud noise jolted right through her. She blinked in shock. Theo was gone, along with the cacophony of destruction. All was subdued light and calm.

Suddenly she was looking up into incredible, violet, almond-shaped eyes only inches above her own.

"Relax," Ithuin whispered, so close she could feel his breath gently on her cheek. She tried not to blush. Waves of calm flowed through her from his presence.

"Your eyes are gold and emerald. Are you sure you're not an elf?" he asked softly. "I was there in your dream. I saw what you saw. Theosos Rotoa?"

"Yes," whispered Thaya.

"You were fighting in your sleep again."

"Again? Asleep? I did not know I was asleep."

Ithuin smiled apologetically. "Forgive me, but I put you in one. It was easier to carry you that way and then to close the wound. I would have left you sleeping longer, but sometimes sleep takes away more than it gives...especially when one is tortured."

He stayed close as he spoke, keeping his face close to hers. "You've been through much, you have seen much, more even than most of my people see, Thaya."

"I don't know why; I did not choose it."

"Would you prefer a different path?"

The question caught her off guard. She thought about Khy, of never meeting him, and shivered. "No, I would not. I would die of boredom living an ordinary life. Where is Khy? Is he okay?"

She started to rise and their faces brushed before Ithuin

slowly moved back. "He is fine. Don't move too fast or you will faint."

He took her hand and helped her to sit up. The room danced and swam before her eyes and then finally settled.

The room was warm, cosy, and appeared to be completely carved out of golden-brown wood. Beyond her bed, a single, oval window was open. The wooden ceiling above and the room itself were also roughly oval—there wasn't a single hard edge in the room; everything flowed organically into each other from her bed frame to the adjoining chest of drawers, even the sage rug was rounded. It created a kind of peace and calm that was quite welcome after all that had happened.

"Wait one moment," Ithuin said as she started to get up. He bent to check her bandaged leg. "Good, no bleeding. It was a remarkably clean wound, and with any luck, it will heal without even a scar—but you must rest."

"Thank you, for all you've done, but where are my clothes?" Thaya asked, looking down at her new, thin shift of gossamer-soft material—which was actually quite sheer and enough to make her feel self-conscious.

Ithuin stood and tapped his lips. "Hmm, well, some were rather, shall we say, *worn?* And those not torn or tarnished are being cleaned."

"You took my clothes?" Thaya clasped her hands to her chest. Had he undressed her and put her in this shift?

"We'll replace them with something far finer?" Ithuin phrased it as a question.

"Huh? Oh, you would? Elven attire?" She imagined dressing in elven finery—who could say no to that? *I wonder how long I'll be able to keep them clean, though,* she thought and frowned. *Better have my old clothes back.* "But I'm on the road, pretty much permanently..."

"And you think elves don't travel? We ride through woods, and many of us live and vault amongst the trees—I'm sure you'll find our attire most comfortable, flattering, and manoeuvrable."

"Well, in that case—" Thaya blushed at his smile.

The door beyond him opened, and to her dismay, the most beautiful woman she had ever seen stepped through. Her skin was like a ripe peach, and her dark hair shimmered like silken cocoa. Thaya pursed her lips.

"She's awake," said the she-elf, and gave a stunning smile as she came further into the room.

Thaya forced herself to smile back.

"Welcome, Virasha. Your magic worked wonders, as you can see," said Ithuin.

The elf-woman nodded with satisfaction.

"Thank you." It was all Thaya could think to say, and it wasn't enough for all they had done. The presence of two tall and graceful elves made her feel quite small and, not quite ugly, but certainly not elegant or attractive. *And why should I care?* she thought. *Ithuin SHOULD have a wife, and what does it matter to me?*

"Khy Saphira-elaysa is asking for you," Virasha said. "If you like, we'll bring your food to you, so you can sit with him."

"Yes, that would be great," said Thaya. "And thanks again, for everything."

"It's our gratitude to you for returning to us Eir'ande-hari, that which is most precious, that which has been lost for a long time and will heal our kingdom," Virasha said, with an incline of her head, and then she left.

The relic was certainly important to these people, Thaya thought as she carefully slid off the mattress onto her feet. Ithuin stood at the ready to help her. Her left calf throbbed at first as she tested it, then the pain began to calm as she slowly walked towards the door.

Outside, a warm, sunlit world greeted her. Golden rays fell on carpets of green grass, upon which, sitting, laughing, drinking and eating, were Engara, her Shield Brothers, a handful of sturdy men and women from her clan, and Khy. Thaya stared at the Saphira-elaysa, for seated beside him and singing a song only angels could sing, were two elf-maidens, one combing his mane and the other his tail! Khy's eyes were half-closed, his lips pouting, and his nose twitching in obvious bliss.

"Thaya!" Engara shouted heartily, making her jump.

The warrior woman lifted her cup, and her other companions followed with a cheer. Thaya grinned and waved.

"Welcome, Thaya, to our world, Elva Shallas," Ithuin said. "Welcome to the Northern Realms." He took her arm and led her over to Khy. Other elves brought cushions for her to sit on, followed by a platter of fruit and a clear, pinkish juice to drink.

Thaya sat down, her eyes not leaving Khy the whole time. "Enjoying yourself?"

The elf-maids smiled but did not cease their beautiful song nor their combing. Khy opened his eyes ever so slightly. "Mmmmm-mmmm," was all he said, his lips trembling, clearly unable to speak through all the pampering.

She sighed and turned to her food, selecting a chunk of melon and then a strawberry. "Mmm, these are the sweetest I've ever tasted!"

"They're from the south," said Ithuin. He seated himself cross-legged on the grass opposite her.

As she ate the sweet, succulent fruit, she took in her lush surroundings, her eyes immediately drawn to the dwelling she had just emerged from. The doorway was carved out of the boles of the largest tree she had ever seen.

"Wow," she said in astonishment, her eyes travelling up the trunk to an enormous green canopy, reaching so high into the sky, she couldn't see the top. "How old is that?"

Ithuin looked to where she gawped. "Finngar? He's actually quite young, only four thousand years by elven standards."

Thaya choked. "Only four—young? Our trees, our veritable shrubs compared to that. And it has a name?"

Rather than mock her ignorance, Ithuin smiled at her. "It's funny how much I've come to learn about humans simply from studying your history and watching from afar. You know, a long time ago, humans also named their trees and were once very like elves. We were friends. A very, very long time ago, elves once sought the wise counsel of humans, but those times have long gone and have been forgotten from your collective memory, I'm afraid to say."

Thaya thought about what he said. It matched some of the ancient myths and legends. She had read about a tall, fairy-like race from across the oceans, who could do amazing things. She listened as he spoke.

"Our legends say humans were taller once, slender, cleverer even than elves—can you believe that? Some called you angels, for you were filled with the light of the heavens. All respected you for it was well known that you were created to help those fallen into dark places, those trapped in the denser time and matter of the Outer Worlds.

"I cannot speak for the past, but I do know why you have no ancient trees left, for I have seen this in the Waters of Layhara."

"Tell me." Thaya bent closer. She assumed the Waters of Layhara were a Looking Mirror of some sort.

"Urtha was attacked—"

"By whom?" Thaya cut in.

"I know not, but they came from the sky. They caused destruction, and the mighty trees were cut down where they stood. Those that survived could not withstand the shifting crust, the floods, the chaos, and neither could anything else on Urtha's surface. All was lost. It is said that the humans of then were no more, and the new humans created were different, as was Urtha different. Unfortunately, lesser."

"The destruction of the first seeding, could it be?" Thaya spoke to herself, staring unseeing at the grape she rolled around her palm. She felt it to be true.

Ithuin gave a sad sigh. "So, your massive wonders were destroyed, but if you look very carefully at your landscape, you'll see their remains, if you have eyes to see. The truth is all around you. Not all your mountains are rocks, but the remains of truly ancient forests." He tapped his temple knowingly.

"Some of your people remember the old world and the old trees, and they seek to preserve the knowledge of them —these you call druids."

Thaya mouthed the name. In the recesses of her mind, she recalled a child's picture book of legends: a man with long, white hair dressed in a robe girdled with golden rope. A sparrow danced on his fingers, and a ring of green leaves encircled his head.

"In the beginning, we all came out of the light, Thaya, so we are all brothers and sisters and not so different."

"Will we ever be again what once we were? Will we remember?" She so wanted that to happen.

Ithuin shrugged. "Who can know? All things are possible."

"I hope so." She nodded. "The man I left behind, the one

who helped me escape, his name was Theo, and he was a Keeper, a Gatekeeper, and a Record Keeper, but it happened a long time ago. Now he's gone, who will remember? What if all that we were will be forgotten?"

Ithuin shook his head. "It cannot be, for Urtha records all things as all planets do. Memory is in the air, in the water, in the trees. The Great Spirit sees all, remembers all. It is only us beings of flesh and blood who forget, who are *made* to forget."

Thaya realised she'd been holding her breath, and she let it out slowly. Her gaze wandered over the sunlit glade, which was surrounded by enormous trees, and she fixated upon a large, stone archway. It stood alone on the grass, several yards to the right of her dwelling within the tree. Behind it crowded dense foliage and a rocky cliff face, but the archway wasn't attached to a wall or any other structure, and it went nowhere. But that wasn't the strangest thing about it. Within the archway swirled a humming and shimmering pink and silver vortex.

She pointed at it. "Is that the portal we came through?"

Ithuin nodded. "Yes. It's open for now as our worlds pass close to each other; that much I *was* able to do alone. That portal is how I was able to reach you, and for the first time in our history, I had a chance at reclaiming the Eye of Ahro. Thank you, Thaya, I did not think I'd find one of your race willing to help."

Thaya looked at the grass, embarrassed. "Oh, I don't think I was *willing*...more just, er...caught up in it all. I'm glad we reclaimed it. Where is it now? What does it do, exactly?"

"Have you finished eating? Let me show you."

26

THE PLACE OF PASSAGE

ITHUIN HELPED HER UP. SHE NEEDED HIS SUPPORT, FOR HER leg suddenly felt weak.

"The pain will come and go in waves as it heals," he said. "Worry not, for we've put more than just bandages and poultices upon it."

She took a few unsteady steps, then paused. "Are you coming, Khy?" Her soul twin was still being pampered by the elf maidens who had moved on to brushing his body. Tiny, blue butterflies danced around them, and all the daisies had turned their dainty heads to face him as if he were the sun sending them rays of light. His half-closed eyes flickered, and his ears swivelled.

"Mmm-mmm." His lips trembled but no words came out. "Mmmm."

"Fine," Thaya huffed.

"I think your companion is taking some much-needed rest. If you like, we can comb your hair and massage you too?" Ithuin offered.

Thaya shot him a look but couldn't tell from his expression if he was serious or not. She sensed no mockery in his innocent gaze and cleared her throat.

"Ahem, well, maybe later?" She didn't want to offend him but she couldn't help but wonder if he would be the one giving the massage.

Placing her hand on his arm, he led her along a wide path, through a copse of more normal-sized sycamore trees —probably bushes to the elves—and slowly the voices of Engara and her companions, and the angelic singing of the elves faded away. Rich foliage greeted her wherever she looked. They walked through a veritable tunnel of emerald, so lush was the land. A rabbit hopped out of the bushes next to them and, quite unafraid, sat on its haunches and rubbed its whiskers, then bounded off into the tall grasses.

Ithuin took a left fork along a smaller path that led uphill. The path turned a corner and came to an abrupt halt before two guards dressed in scarlet and gold livery. They stood in front of a golden door leading into a tall but other-wise unremarkable stone building. So far, every dwelling she had seen had been in the bowels of trees, so the fact that this was out in the open seemed odd.

The guards' austere expressions took Thaya by surprise, even more so when they crossed their ornate spears tipped with deadly golden blades in front of the door. *Guards? Here in this beautiful, peaceful world?* Their hard faces were shaded by their tall helmets, and they eyed her suspiciously.

Ithuin spoke in a dialect of Elven and, despite having understood him earlier, she didn't know what he was saying now. The guards were impassive, and Ithuin gesticulated but kept his voice calm. It took some talking before the guards began to relax and respond. Eventually, they uncrossed their spears and stepped aside, their hard gazes transfixed upon them.

"They're the king's men, and they guard the returned Eye of Ahro," explained Ithuin, surprising her when he spoke fluently in Familiar, the tongue of Urtha. He placed a hand on the door and pushed gently. She wondered at his scowl. "As soon as we returned, we were surrounded by King Tekomin's men. Those loyal to me prevented a fight. Against my strongest desires, I was obliged to give them the Eye of Ahro, but my terms were that it should not leave here. Had I not done so, bloodshed would have ensued, and the imprisonment of our human friends. I could not let that happen, so I let them take it. They let us pass just now because I declared its erratic energy needed calming.

"They said the king has demanded its utmost protection, and for the king to know so soon that I had retrieved the other half of Eir'andehari, against all the odds, his magi must surely walk hidden amongst us. His spies are everywhere, watching me, reporting back... They did not think I would be able to open the portal after the damage it had sustained which caused it to lay dormant for a decade, but that was foolish of them." He shook his head, his brow furrowing deeper.

Thaya wondered at this king and Ithuin's relationship to him. Why would the king be spying on him? It sounded worrying. "Clearly you don't trust your king, I'd like to know more. Why would they imprison us? Wouldn't the king rejoice that something so powerful has been found? Shouldn't you have had the help of his most powerful magi?"

Ithuin smiled bitterly. "In a perfect world, yes. As soon as humans stepped through the portal, they leaped into action. Unfortunately, for many elves, humans are not trusted. There was a war a long time ago, not so much between elves and men in the beginning, but it became that way in the end, and it has not been forgotten. Elves do not forget."

"I'm sorry," said Thaya.

"Indeed, so am I. But we must not take on the guilt from the actions and decisions of our ancestors. They have nothing to do with us, or at least our choices, now."

A blast of cool wind greeted them as she followed him further inside.

"How could I not understand you then when you spoke to the guards, when I could before?" she asked. He'd said the elven relic had gifted her with the knowledge of Elvish. Passing through a star portal also removed the barrier of language within the mind of the Gatewalker—essentially having the same effect of gifting speech.

Ithuin smiled. "An inquisitive mind is a gift, my dear Thaya, especially amongst your superstitious kind, but there is so much occurring here that we would need weeks and barrels of the finest wine to discuss it all. The king and his employees speak the Royal Tongue, which they call the Language of the Pure."

He turned to face her, anger suddenly rising in his eyes. "But that's the lie right there, for it is *not* the pure tongue, it's not true Elvish as our language was meant to be but a corrupted version of it that entered our world when the Shadow Magi returned from Shen—the Fade, the Underworld, or Hell, as you might call it. Few elves know this for the history books have been removed and placed in the king's library, no less, for 'safe-keeping.'"

Ithuin took a deep breath and calmed himself. "I was once one of the king's magi, but I left when I saw the darkness inherent upon the throne. No magi ever leaves the king's service...but I positioned myself with...*leverage*. But anyway, you can see my position on royalty and why his guards watch me. I saw too much in the Waters of Layhara, and I know too much."

Thaya blinked in surprise and glanced down at her attire. Ithuin was once a king's magi? *A magi and a Dreamwalker...?* This man was powerful, had once been royal. She felt humbled and nervous. The things of which he spoke, she wanted to know more but feared it. She didn't want to become embroiled in another peoples' struggles, not when it was hard enough just trying to save her own skin.

Whatever he said next, he muttered so she couldn't quite hear, the frown remaining on his brow. She decided not to progress the topic of royalty, not when the king's guards were right outside; she'd wait until later when he was calmer and they were alone. "So, there's only one Elven language on the whole...planet? Eir'andehari gifted me your tongue, and apparently passing through a star portal to another world does the same...but is only one language imparted? Where I am from, Havendell, beyond the mountains that border us, there are two other tongues even I cannot speak."

Her question directed his thoughts away from the king, and his composure calmed as he considered her words. "In our myths of creation, all people have but one language they speak aloud. For who needs a language at all when the mode of communication is first and foremost telepathy?"

Thaya blinked. "Oh, I see! Well, that makes sense. I wonder what Urtha's first language was, perhaps Lono-hassan is a part of it." *Something to ponder upon,* she thought, *perhaps something Theo would know.*

Thaya swept her gaze from the stone tiled flooring to the ceiling, and to her surprise, found it reminded her very much of the temples back home: cold, stuffy, and dim. It was so unlike what she'd expected of fine elven architecture— her room in the tree had been stunning—it was out of place.

She shivered and stifled a cough. Sure, the finely chiselled stone walls, the incredibly high arched ceiling with its numerous crisscrossing beams, and those beautifully ornate stained-glass windows in purples and pinks were truly masterful pieces of work, but it was gloomy and unnatural, like a crypt, when compared to the vibrant living world outside. She realised Ithuin was looking at her with an odd expression.

"You don't like it?"

Thaya blushed. "Not so much. It reminds me of the temples back home. The Illumined Acolytes create oppressive places...they're not my favourite."

"I don't like it either, and I've told our elders as much." Ithuin clenched his jaw. "King Tekomin has...some strange tastes and ideas...and some strange acquaintances. Unrest rumbles in the kingdom, for the king is old. Many people hope that soon he will retire for the Silverillian Shores, though none dare utter their thoughts aloud."

Thaya imagined silken waves crashing upon a silver-lined shore, an Elven realm of peace and rest.

She inspected the rafters. "What is this place for?"

"We call this whole area Shingaron; it means 'the place of passage'. This building was intended to be a meeting place. There has always been a portal here, but where it leads to changes over the eons. There are other portals, larger ones, more popular, as it were—some contained within entire cities. This lies beyond a mountain range on one side and a turbulent sea on the other—hence its unpopularity. In actuality, this whole settlement has been in decline for a decade because the portal has been closed for that time. Only now have people begun to return."

"So, this isn't actually a city or a town, or whatever elves call such places?" asked Thaya. She'd imagined that beyond the trees there would be a stunning city to put all those on Lonohassa to shame.

"It was a small town once but no more. Halinshafar is the nearest city, and it lies a hundred leagues southwest. There are many dwellings here, and it could be a town again, for the trees keep them safe whilst we are absent. Until a few months ago, I resided here alone for a decade."

Thaya looked at him, her eyes wide. "Alone? For a decade?"

Ithuin smiled as if happy that was the case. He looked away. "It's part of my training, Ena-shani. Solitude. Away from the clamouring and chaotic minds and noise of people and cities. Here I can finally hear what is whispered in neighbouring dimensions."

"For Dreamwalking?"

"Yes, and also to reach other realms with my mind. I've been working to cleanse the portal from the damage that caused it to close. When I discovered it was opening, and to where it was opening, I couldn't believe it. The king, informed by the aforementioned spies—though they call themselves royal informants—immediately dispatched soldiers, suddenly finding he was interested in what lies beyond."

Ithuin's face darkened. "That's how kings think: invasion, plundering and war in the name of protection."

Thaya placed a hand on his arm and gave a half-smile. "It doesn't sound like elven kings and human kings are so different after all."

His face softened. "They are not like us, are they? Over the last few months, people from all over Elva Shallas who are loyal to the Northern Elves, and the Elven race as a whole, have been arriving. I'd done my best to spread the word that the hunt for Eir'andehari was occurring, but I've no powerful contacts anymore—what can I do? I know the king would have secretly raged about it.

"Turns out, some coming here are former soldiers loyal to the people, but most arriving are just ordinary folk seeking a return to the old ways, away from the king's policies. I did not ask them to come. I was left speechless at first and tried to turn them back. Somehow, they have turned to me; they think I can change things. They are loyal to my cause and that places me in an exceedingly dangerous position—the king will not allow an uprising, and I wish only to return to my studies."

Thaya raised her eyebrows. "They see you as their hero, their leader."

Ithuin looked uncomfortable and struggled to find the words as if he was holding something back. "I mentioned I was one of the king's magi many years ago. I stood at his side —the young fool I was believed in my king—can you believe that? Hah! How I loved the power, the prestige, the wealth—until it made me ill. So much happened, so much changed, too much to speak here now. But I saw the truth...I saw the truth, and I choked on it until I could deny it no longer, and so I left."

He dropped his voice to the barest whisper. "You see, Thaya, no magi has ever left a royal household, not ever. I should say, 'left' and lived. We hold power and knowledge, and this, royalty fears. Well, the lesser kings do, our mighty kings of old were different. So, I made a bargain, that leverage I touched upon earlier, a blackmail, if you will. I'm not proud of it, but it was the only way I could escape with my life. If the king didn't dispose of me, the magi would!

"I had gained knowledge of a dark secret, and I would spread it across the kingdom if they so much as threatened my life. They knew that even if they killed me, I could let the secret out and it would be known by all by morning—such is a Dreamwalker's power that even in death, we live. Suffice to say, our realm is in turmoil, Thaya."

His back was to her, his long, pale hair falling between his shoulders, straight as a waterfall. He sighed deeply and stared up at the rafters. "Ahh, Ena-shani, the problems of our land are legion, but they are not yours to bear. You bring a light, quite literally, to these troubled times. I knew all things would change when I first saw you in the Waters of Layhara."

He whispered to himself for a moment, then rested his hands on his hips and looked down at the floor. "And so here I am. With a handful of trained soldiers, hunters and archers—some of which are former kingsmen, now loyal to me—I was able to enter the portal to your world and help you fight against Grenshoa."

He turned and placed his hands on top of her shoulders, and his eyes blazed with excitement. "We retrieved the Eye of Ahro, Thaya. Do you know how incredible that is? Do you know what that means for our people? A new Age of Wonder dawns upon us. Come, come and look."

Glad to be doing something rather than learning this beautiful place had its own share of woes, Thaya followed him to another door that opened into a long hallway, then up a short flight of stone steps where they stopped before a thin, golden pedestal rising to about her head height. Above it, magically suspended in midair, hung Eir'andehari, glimmering darkly.

Ithuin spoke softly as he beheld the broken elven relic. "I wanted to take it to the Waters of Layhara where I could keep it safe, but the kingsmen were too fast, too crafty, and we were too weak from fighting Grenshoa and her minions."

Thaya stared into its polished surface, noticing nothing was reflected back by it. It shimmered under her gaze and gave a faint, tinkling sound as if it recognised her.

"Eir'andehari knows you," Ithuin whispered, his eyes transfixed upon the broken crystal and seeing far away. "It's grateful for your help in rescuing it from the dragon. For a long time, it was kept in darkness and abused."

"Oh, it's, um, welcome. I, er... Is it conscious?" Thaya whispered, looking at Ithuin.

He chuckled. "Of course, all crystals are but their consciousness is different to ours. I'm impressed with your ability to communicate with them when you've had no training. You have natural skills."

Thaya blushed. "Well, I didn't actually communicate anything." She inspected the crystal's jagged edge. "Where's the other half?"

"Kept chained and under lock and key by the king. If his guards are to be believed, the king brings it to us on fast riders as we speak. I'll do my utmost to protect Eir'andehari." Ithuin's violet eyes suddenly glowed with wonder. "This is the first time in millennia that the two will be together."

"Can it be mended?" She hoped to see it whole.

Ithuin shrugged. "Perhaps. I might be a magi, but that is beyond my powers."

"You really are a magi aren't you? Could you teach me?" The thought excited her but then, remembering the conversation she'd had with Theo, could a magician teach her anything?

"Yes, I was. A Magi of the Elven Arcane, but I have directed my studies away from magic now and into the Astral Realms. I could not teach you elven magic even had I wanted to, for you are not an elf, and I am no teacher. You are Ena-shani, Thaya, that's your strength and calling. I grew tired of the old lore and the Arcane Arts, for I believe the Astral Realms offer more power, but that's not why I chose this course: I believe something dark manipulates us from there. Actually, I know it. And I would understand that darkness better, so we can fight it before the Shen falls over our lands entirely."

Thaya wanted to know more but she also didn't want to move away from the previous topic. She brought the conversation back. "What is Eir'andehari exactly? Who made it and why?"

"Eir'andehari was created in the Third Age by the Arvenphim—creators and guardians of the Elvaphim, and of Elva Shallas—our world upon which you tread." He spread his hands. "The Arvenphim are our makers, and we are their children. Ultimately, they are ourselves in the higher realms."

Thaya frowned. "I've heard of Seraphim, angels with wings and stuff."

"Perhaps they're related," Ithuin suggested. "True eternal races are all angelic, and none are fallen.

"As for your second question, The Eye of Ahro is a protector of Elva Shallas and its people, and it is also a seer. It's a ward of extreme power, protecting us all from those who wish to harm Elva Shallas. In times long ago, it was used to look into the past, the present and the future, according to the viewer's current timeline. It is much, much more than I can explain with words but, as you can see, it isn't functioning as it should."

Thaya looked again at the shattered crystal. "It felt powerful enough when I held it, and that was just one half."

"Indeed." Ithuin nodded. "Think what it can do when it is whole."

"Who broke it?" Thaya paced around the relic, imagining it being shattered in a violent fight.

"There was a battle, like you imagine, only between the elf-magi Saelthin, and the dragon, Zindar." Ithuin shrugged. "Long ago, the Ordacs invaded Elva Shallas for the third time and tried to take the Eye. Mortally wounded, but refusing to allow Zindar to take it, Saelthin shattered it. No elf believed the Eye of Ahro could be broken. The war that followed was violent, costly on both sides. The shattering of Eir'andehari shook us to the core, weakened us immeasurably. However, that was a long time ago, and now...now it is here, and its sister-half approaches even as we speak." He glanced out of the window as if expecting it to arrive at any moment.

Thaya stepped closer to the Eye, and a faint noise emanated from it: the tinkling of music intermingled with whispering voices. She lifted a finger and touched its smooth surface. An image flashed through her mind of when she'd held Eir'andehari, as if it remembered.

"Elf-friend," a voice whispered.

The crystal clouded as she stared into it, and whatever Ithuin was saying faded into the background.

The clouds cleared to reveal a man. He was dressed in green and yellow silken finery, a golden band encircling his head, beneath which flowed long, copper locks. His face was hard, his lips turned down, and he rode a silvery-white horse so tall and dainty, she swore it had a touch of Saphira-elaysa within it. The Eye's focus moved to a velvet covered object tied to the back of his saddle.

"Make whole what was broken," the voice whispered.

"Ouch!" Thaya stepped back holding her bleeding finger. She'd been so intent upon the image within Eir'andehari that her finger had slid over the jagged broken edge.

Ithuin spun round. "No, don't touch the Eye! Oh." He looked at her finger then back at Eir'andehari.

A droplet of her blood ran over the edge and then dripped into Eir'andehari itself as if the surface had suddenly become porous. Thaya gasped. Her crimson droplet floated through the crystal and the clouds within, and then burst into a flash of golden soulfire. There it hung like sunlight bursting through storm clouds.

"I have never seen that!" Ithuin stared, his expression unreadable. Was he horrified or amazed? He pulled out a handkerchief and wrapped it around her bleeding finger. "Only the wisest Elven magi should touch Eir'andehari. It's dangerous, its energy chaotic."

"So why did you send me to get it then?" Thaya scowled and placed her other hand on her hip.

"Well, indeed." Ithuin checked himself and nodded guiltily. "I don't want you to hurt yourself, its power will be stronger now it's home."

"It spoke to me. It wants to be made whole," said Thaya. "I saw your king. He seems...unhappy."

Ithuin nodded. "Eir'andehari will show you much. Yes, he is ever thus. Come, let's get into the light and warmth. I find this place a tomb."

27

THE WATERS OF LAYHARA

THAYA GLADLY STEPPED OUTSIDE INTO THE SUNLIT WORLD where the sun's warmth enveloped her. She reached down and touched her throbbing calf.

"Let's return home so we can rest that leg," said Ithuin. He smiled and offered her his arm, both of them feeling lighter with each step they took away from the building and the watchful guards.

As they walked, Ithuin pointed out the plants and birds, keen to explain what each was called in Elven, and their peculiarities and tendencies.

"These are arven berries, edible, but only when the berry is pink. That bird there digging in the soil? That's a shuck. It has a yellow crest when raised." Ithuin spoke nothing of the king, and the earlier stiffness in his shoulders had now eased. "And now we're here. Look, your friends are satiated and sleepy, you should join them. I have things to which I must attend and make ready before the king arrives."

Engara's Shield Brethren were dozing in the dappled sunlight beneath the canopy of Finngar. They looked so languid, Thaya yawned and gladly sat beside them. She wanted to talk more with Ithuin about Eir'andehari, the king and the kingdom's unrest, and about a great deal more, but Ithuin was right, to learn more about these people and Elva Shallas would take weeks and plenty of wine, plus, she didn't want to bring that worried frown back onto his face.

Instead, she watched him gather a large group of elves who then left, walking the wide path between the trees and talking hurriedly amongst themselves.

Khy, now on his own, without his doting elf-maids, stood and stretched first his front, and then his hind legs. He flicked his tail and came over to nuzzle her. She noticed his hooves and horn had been polished so that they shone like silver and gold.

"Something bothers our new friend," he said.

"Yes, it's to do with the king coming. Great trouble rumbles in this seemingly peaceful, beautiful land. To be fair, I'd prefer to not be here when the king arrives, especially since I'm not keen on pomp and royal fanfare either."

In the early evening, after relaxing all afternoon, a handful of elves gathered Thaya, Khy and the other humans, and led them through the wide avenue of giant trees. Two of the elves were dressed in smart uniforms similar to that of the guards outside the building housing Eir'andehari, only these were oak green and silver, not scarlet and gold. They smiled at them rather than frowned, but there was an air of military about them, and she noticed long, thin swords attached to their belts. Were the soldiers loyal to Ithuin? She hoped so.

Thaya walked with the other humans, all of them staring up, agape at the enormous trees. The trunks were so huge, and many of them had more than one doorway leading to dwellings inside. The wood beyond the avenue was vast; there could be enough 'homes' here to fill an entire city, Thaya thought. The elves here lived like the dryads did back home, amongst the trees and ferns. She was enjoying being one of them for a short time, she thought with a smile.

"Oh, my goodness, just look at the size of that one," said Engara, pointing at an enormous, red-trunked tree that was the width of a village green. Thaya agreed and winced as she strained to see the top. Her neck was hurting from gawping up at their canopies the entire journey.

The elves led them to the base of a giant tree, larger even than Finngar, and in its boles rose two, grand, arched doorways, easily twice her height, painted ivy green and inlaid with beautiful silver leaves. Two more guards dressed in oak-green livery stood to attention outside, but rather than bar their way, they acted as if they had been expecting their human guests, and readily opened the doors.

Inside, stretching farther than the eye could see, flowed a large dining hall made entirely of wood. Many long tables, each surrounded by chairs, filled the floor space, but only three of the tables were set with plates, cutlery and a centre-piece of blooming orchids. Numerous elf servers filled the hall, busily setting the tables, hanging bunting or sweeping the floor. Thaya hunted amongst them for Ithuin, but to her disappointment, he was not to be seen.

The elves seated them one by one, and Engara took a chair opposite her.

"Thaya, I can't believe the things I've seen these past few days," she said, running a hand over her clean and freshly braided hair. "The horror and sorrow I've witnessed, and now the wonders of this...this Elven Land! I've seen a dryad, but I scoffed at elves. I've seen magic, but I scoffed at dragons. And Gryphons? Well, that I don't believe, not yet. But just look at this wondrous place!"

Thaya followed the warrior woman's gaze to the high, exquisitely carved ceiling—surely still part of the flesh of the living tree.

"And this food!" Engara wafted a hunk of soft, warm bread. "It's delicious! I feel alive inside. I don't ever want to go back home."

"Neither do I," Thaya agreed. "I really didn't think I'd make it out of that dragon's lair."

Engara chewed on a mouthful and shook her head. With her other hand, she ground her knife into her plate. "I realise now how stupid my idea was—attack the dragon? What was I thinking! We couldn't have done it without the elves. I had no idea the Ordacs would be there! But look..." She spread her arms wide and grinned. "*He who dares, wins,* right? We avenged our fallen, we took back what was stolen, and look at where we are now." She picked up her glass of wine and laughed heartily.

Everyone cheered and raised their glasses. With a grin, Thaya joined them and sipped the finest wine she had ever tasted.

Hors d'oeuvres were followed by fresh fruits, cool summer soups, crudités, and quiches. The food and wine never stopped flowing until they could eat and drink no more. When her leg started to throb, Thaya left the others to their merriment and joined Khy outside.

The cool air was wonderfully fresh on her face, and she looked up at a sky filled with constellations she did not recognise. She hugged her arms, feeling very small beneath them.

"You think Theo's okay?" Her thoughts never strayed far

from her brief friend and mentor. She shivered, praying he was all right, somehow.

Khy lowered his head and spoke quietly. "He did what he had to do."

"I'm sure he's fine. Did you see the amount of power he commanded? Incredible." Thaya swallowed a lump. She didn't—couldn't—think about him now so changed the subject. "So, is this how it will be? Portal Travellers? Like sailors never settling down, always on the move. I miss the idea of home, but what the hell would I do with myself if I sat alone back in Brightwater?"

"I think I prefer the term 'Gatewalkers' or perhaps 'Ena-shani'—Elvish is always better," mused Khy, also looking up at the stars.

"Yes, you're right. Maybe it's a term that can be applied only to humans?"

"Saphira-elaysa can be Gatewalkers, too." He flicked his tail.

Thaya rubbed her chin. "I guess, I dunno. Theo didn't say anything about that."

Khy looked at her, but she kept her gaze fixed on the stars. "Hmm," he snorted.

A firefly darted past, buzzing noisily. It paused near Khy's nose, circled once inquisitively, then darted off into the bushes.

"Have you seen Ithuin?" she asked. "I was hoping to see him."

"No, but I sense he's not far. An elf would be a nice match for you." He nodded to himself.

Thaya's mouth dropped open, but Khy's face was serious. "He's a friend, nothing more!" she said, her voice high-pitched. "An elf and a human? Come on... Are you trying to get rid of me?"

"You should have a mate. And so should I. It doesn't change *our* relationship."

"No, I guess not. I just—"

"You lack intimacy in your life, it would be good for you." Khy cocked his head as he looked at her. He was curious as to her indignant reaction.

Thaya coloured. "I'm not sure I want to talk about it."

"Hmm, I can see it's embarrassing you, is that a human thing? Peculiar. It's how things are, the nature of life."

"I know but...what about Arto? Am I just to forget him?"

She smiled, remembering him. Arto—Artorren Eversea, an honourable captain, and once a knight—he'd become more than just a friend to her. He had been there when the Vormae Invaders attacked Havendell Harbour and destroyed his ship and crew. She'd saved his life, and then he hers. He'd been there again leading the assault against the Nuakki, and freeing the slaves alongside Thaya and Khy. Their time together had been far too brief for after both events their paths diverged.

Khy shrugged. "He's not here. What's wrong with both?"

Thaya blushed even harder. "I can't believe what I'm hearing!" Thinking of Ithuin in that way...and then remembering Arto...Khy had no shame! But looking at him, there was only innocence in his eyes, and a care for her well-being. Clearly, he saw the world very differently from humans. She scratched the bandages around her leg, grateful when he didn't press the matter.

They ambled along a path lit by fireflies and starlight, with the hooting of owls in the distance. A fox barked, then darted across the path in front of them. They found themselves back in the glade, and ahead loomed the darkly glowing pink portal.

"Why does it glow? I've never seen a glowing one," Thaya asked as they headed straight towards it.

The elves had created an ornate stone archway around it, and the portal somehow filled the space within perfectly.

"Elven technology. Perhaps it helps to concentrate the energy?" said Khy, sniffing the base of the portal. "I smell strong elven magic. I suggest the magic controls the portal's energies, stabilising them perhaps."

"Reckon we could just walk through, have a quick look, then come back?" Thaya giggled and looked at Khy mischievously.

"Great, you can vomit twice." He tossed his horn.

Thaya lost her mirth. "Yeah, let's just go to bed then. No more adventures tonight." She yawned; the idea of bed was a welcome one.

Khy looked back at the dark forest. "Unfortunately, I'm not that tired, so I might explore a little. We're quite safe here, safer than I've ever felt outside of the Ellarian Fields. Elves and Saphira-elaysa have a long and positive history with each other. I'm glad we are here."

Thaya snorted. "It's no surprise you're not tired, you've been dozing all day!"

Khy blinked and looked the picture of innocence.

For all the softness of her sheets and the calm and peace of her home, safe in the trunk of the tree, Thaya slept badly. She tossed and turned, unable to get comfortable, but unable to awaken from the dreams that would not let her go.

Theo was beside her, the Rod glowing brightly in his outstretched hand, the ring of twelve, giant crystals blazing around them. Wind rushed in from all directions, and the whining of the monstrous, black sky ship made her teeth chatter. Chaotic, turbulent forces shoved her back and forth, and the red beam throbbed and hummed behind Theo.

"I can't hold the portal open, Thaya, you must go!" he screamed.

"Come with us. Please don't stay!" She grabbed his arm, but the portal had hold of her and pulled strongly.

His face became slack, and his eyes became unfocussed as he envisioned something far away. "They're coming, Thaya. Run." He gripped her hand, squeezed, and released it.

She screamed as the vortex sucked her in. She spun through light and dark, strange metallic noises grating, the sound of distorted voices echoing, then she landed, hard. Her hands moved through something soft, and she blinked at the blades of grass in front of her face. She pushed herself onto her knees.

"Ugh. Theo?"

The elven portal stood to her left, bruised pink and purple energies swirling within a stone archway. The energies began to boil and bubble, suddenly bulging grotesquely outwards from the portal, then violent flares shot out from it. Voices echoed within the vortex, too distorted to make out. Another voice came from behind her, and she turned around, but a dense mist blanketed everything.

"Khy?" she called, her eyes hunting through the fog.

A red light flared, and the fog began to clear. A few yards away, the broken Eye of Ahro hung above its pedestal on the grass. It bulged and flickered with the same energy as the portal, mirroring it. Standing between the two, Thaya looked back at the portal. It darkened to a deep red, and the Eye's energy darkened in response. Their red rays spilled over the grass towards each other, becoming thick and viscous, flowing and clotting like blood.

"Urgh!" She tried to step away, but the liquid pooled too fast, splashing onto her feet, spraying crimson droplets on her dress.

Screams echoed around her, the sound of swords clashing, the boom of magic deafening. She hurried back into the mist, her heart pounding.

"Thaya!" Ithuin's voice made her jump.

Hidden in the mist, a tall figure moved. She ran towards it. The sound of fighting dimmed, and a paved path appeared beneath her feet. Ahead, she saw warm light and trees, their leaves moving gently in the breeze. The mist cleared as she walked, and a familiar fountain took shape with a figure standing beside it.

"Ithuin!"

The elf-man smiled as she approached. Relieved, she embraced him.

"It's just a bad dream, Thaya." He stepped back to look at her, his violet eyes holding hers for a moment to check she was all right. "You found your way here, good. Find solace beside the Waters of Layhara, drink of them. Nothing can touch us here. Tell me what you saw."

She told him about Theo and the portal, and the blood-red rays of Eir'andehari.

"A premonition," he said. "I feel it too, Eir'andehari is troubled." His voice was deep and calm. It echoed in this place.

"Is this a dream?" Thaya pinched her arm. "Ouch!" It seemed real enough.

"It was until now," he replied. "I sensed you struggling just as I and Eir'andehari were struggling."

"What's wrong?" she asked.

Ithuin frowned, his smooth forehead forming a tight wrinkle. "I know not. Only that darkness walks close."

"I saw blood, lots of it." Thaya glanced down at her feet, seeing only tendrils of mist clinging to the green grass.

"Where?" Ithuin studied her.

"Back there, everywhere between the portal and the Eye of Ahro. Their red light turned to blood on the grass."

"Trouble comes." He rubbed his temples with both hands.

"Is it the king?" Thaya asked.

"I cannot know. But we must get you away from here and to safety; you and Khy and your warrior friends must return at first light."

Thaya had hoped to see the king from a distance despite all the royal pomp she hated. After all, it wasn't every day one got to see an Elven King. But Ithuin's words were truly ominous.

"If I can help, I will," she said.

Ithuin's worried face broke into a smile. "Brave Thaya, you've already done more than anyone could have by returning Eir'andehari. Honestly, I did not think it would be possible. The worries of elves and this troubled Northern Kingdom are not of your concern, I'll not let you get harmed by them. However, now this half has returned to us, I fear the unsettled undercurrents of this kingdom will boil over.

"To put it simply, King Tekomin laments the return of the second half of Eir'andehari, and I believe, within it, we'll find the truth of his negotiations with the Ordacs."

Thaya inhaled sharply. Could it be true? If it was, then the king had betrayed his own people. To even utter such treasonous words out loud placed Ithuin in grave danger. She looked at him and saw his face was pale, expressionless.

"Yes, Thaya, I would only dare utter such treasonous

words here, beside the Waters of Layhara, where I am safe. I dare not say this out there in the material realm."

"This place isn't real? I mean, is it a dream place?" Thaya looked at the tree. There were birds tweeting amongst its branches, how could it not be real?

"This is not the physical world, nor is it the astral world where we dream, but somewhere between them," said Ithuin. His eyes became troubled again. "I know the king hates his Shadow Mages, though they've made him strong. He seeks to be rid of them, for he trusts no one—he is almost mad with suspicion. He must, at whatever cost, prevent them from taking the Eye of Ahro—and it's my belief, knowing how they think, that this is indeed what they are going to do. The king is correct in his paranoia, but to make deals with the Ordacs, which I cannot yet prove, is unforgivable. We must protect Eir'andehari, Thaya, and I will do so with my life."

"Please don't let it come to that." Thaya touched his arm, a lump in her throat. This was all too much for her, but the thought of losing her new friend...

Ithuin continued, "When whole, Eir'andehari is a truth teller, and it remembers all that it's seen, thus the half you returned remembers all it witnessed in the hands of the Ordacs. This, the Ordacs know, and they will not let it go easily. Imagine if their invasion plans are known? Imagine their deepest desires being disclosed to others? They're a warrior race—they think in terms of domination and survival, and they are exceptional at war.

"But look around you, do you see our soldiers preparing at the gate in case of an invasion? No, you do not. We are unprepared for an attack. I can't help but wonder if the king wants it... No, sorry, these are not concerns of yours. Through the other half of Eir'andehari, I saw many things...

things that happened in our past that should not be forgotten. Things the king would prefer to forget. I dared to challenge the king and his council and...never mind. We should not trouble the still Waters of Layhara any further. Look at you, you're becoming quite the Dreamwalker yourself." He smoothed his frown away with a hand and smiled in that way that made her blush.

She lowered her gaze. "Oh, I... This is surely all your doing, bringing me here. I'm just glad the nightmare has gone."

"My pleasure, but you found your way here yourself this time." He took her hand and kissed it as if she were a lady. "Rest now, Thaya, and worry not about tomorrow, we'll get you to safety. You'll have nice dreams, I promise."

Everything began to fade into a soft, pale mist, and Ithuin stepped back.

"Wait." Thaya tried to follow. "I want to remember what we spoke about." Dreams had a way of making you forget them in the morning light, and she didn't want to forget anything.

"You will remember." His disembodied voice floated back.

28

THE ARVENPHIM

GOLDEN SUNLIGHT SPILLED THROUGH THE GAP IN THE shutters, awakening Thaya. She yawned and stretched, feeling more well-rested than she could remember. Her leg tingled, but there was no pain, not even any throbbing. Slowly, she unwrapped the bandages and gasped. The ugly wound had healed—there wasn't even a faint scar.

A knock came at the door, then an elf-maid with long, flaxen hair and pale green eyes peeked through. "Miss Thaya, your clothes are ready. May I bring them in?"

"Yes, please do." Thaya beckoned her inside and got out of bed.

The elf-maid passed her a bundle. "Your shirt is intact, so we washed it for you, but some of your old clothes were quite torn and bloody, beyond repair, I'm afraid, so we replaced them."

"Oh my, you really didn't have to," said Thaya, inspecting the new clothes.

"We're honoured to provide for our guests, particularly one who returned to us our sacred Eir'andehari. It's the least we could do." The elf-maid smiled at her, a hint of awe in her eyes that Thaya felt she didn't quite deserve.

Thaya picked up a sage green overcoat. It was fitted, made of an interesting strong fabric material but not thick and bulky. It matched her form perfectly, coming to just above mid-thigh level. The tails at the back were shaped into leaves, and she could zip up the neck if it were cold. Small leaves, stitched in silver thread, worked their way over the garment, and buttons and zips marked the many pockets. A pair of dark brown leggings were woven of a cotton-like material, but again, strong and yet flexible so as not to hinder.

"This material and style are best for running and riding," explained the she-elf.

"I don't doubt it," said Thaya. "I like the green and brown mix, like a tree, and good camouflage."

"Here's your underwear." The elf pulled out a camisole and some knickers in a white, stretchy, satin-like material. Thaya blushed as the woman held them up. These weren't plain or simple at all. "The top can be tightened or loosened and has excellent support without being inflexible. They're not the most practical but...this style is most preferred amongst us elf-women." The elf smiled and her eyebrows twitched.

Thaya giggled.

"Lastly, the boots...again, best for riding. They're simple but comfortable and will mould themselves to your feet."

Thaya inspected the near-black, knee-length boots that had been polished to a high shine. She couldn't wait to try everything on. "I guess I'll need to look good if the king is visiting."

The elf-maid clasped her hands in front of her and looked out of the window. "We're loyal to Ithuin. When he was exiled, many followed... All of us here no longer feel the king is working in the best interests of the people. As such, not everyone is looking forward to his arrival."

Thaya paused her inspections. "Exiled? He did not mention it, well, not specifically."

She was under the impression he had left the king's service a long time ago to pursue his studies of Dreamwalking, so why hadn't he been completely open? Was Ithuin keeping something from her? *Why wouldn't he be? It's not like he owes me an explanation of anything at all.*

The elf-maid shrugged. "Our troubles are not an outsider's concern. King Tekomin exiled him for trying to convince the High Councils to retrieve Eir'andehari, which the magi also wanted. He was accused of disturbing the peace, stirring up unrest, and even rallying an army—none of which Ithuin had intended to do. Ultimately, the king exiled him because he knew too much.

"Ithuin had managed to gain access into the other half of Eir'andehari—the first person ever to do so—but what he saw was not what the king wanted to hear. Rather than listen to Ithuin, he banished him. Initially, Tekomin ordered him to be executed! But that was a mistake—many people were loyal to Ithuin—he had helped many with his gifts. A division was created by Ithuin simply telling the truth."

Thaya shook her head. "I'm so sorry, I didn't know."

The elf-maid shrugged. "Whatever happens today, I shall be glad when it's over."

Thaya inhaled sharply, seeing again the blood-soaked grass, red splashing her ankles.... She rubbed her eyes and looked at the elf-maid. "Ithuin saved our lives when the dragon would have taken them. We're all loyal to him too. You can trust us."

"Thank you, Lady Thaya. Elf-friend." She inclined her

head. "Would you like breakfast with your companions outside? The morning is warm and dry."

"I would like that very much, thank you."

A horn sounded, loud and clear, echoing even through closed doors. The elf-maid's rosy cheeks turned pallid.

"What is it?" asked Thaya.

"That's impossible," hissed the elf, looking panicked. "It's far too soon... The king is already here!"

"Here? Now? Are you sure?" Thaya pressed, wondering what was going on.

The she-elf nodded, stricken, then turned and ran out the door.

Thaya hastily dressed in her new clothes. There was no time to admire them in the mirror, and she doubted there'd be time for any breakfast now either. She wanted to put kohl on her eyes and rouge to redden her lips—the dressing table was all laid out for her—so she rushed the brush through her hair and darted the pencil and paste over her eyes and lips. It would do, she'd made the effort, or at least it looked like it from a distance.

Now, where was Khy?

She ran to the door, but her hand froze on the handle as Theo's face entered her inner vision.

"They're coming," he whispered.

Was she imagining it? Was he warning her now or was she remembering her stupid dream? Who was coming? Could he mean the king? It was the most likely, yet why should she fear the king? If anything turned sour, the portal was only paces away. Could it be something else? She took a deep breath and opened the door.

Khy was right outside, waiting for her. The grassy plain was filled with elven guards, dressed in their smart, oak green livery, running this way and that. There were far more of them than she had seen before.

Engara was watching the spectacle on the far side of the grassy plain with her Shield Brothers. She left her clan and came over to Thaya, a frown creasing her forehead. The bloodied cuts that had scarred her face only yesterday were now mostly gone, only faint, red lines on her jaw, cheek, and temple remained, but they would probably vanish in a day or two, thanks to the work of elven expertise.

"What's going on around here?" Engara asked, looking at the panicked elves.

Now that Thaya had time to watch, she noticed the non-uniformed folk were rushing to construct a stage by erecting long, wooden beams. Others were pruning bushes and planting flowers. Directing them were the king's guards, dressed in scarlet and gold.

Thaya watched their speedy work. "Apparently the king has arrived...and far too early."

"That was what the horn meant?"

"I guess so. I was hoping to be gone before he arrived, but seeing an Elven King..."

"Same," agreed Engara. She looked at Thaya and reached over to straighten her collar. "Well, you scrub up all right!"

Thaya grinned. "Likewise. I don't think I've seen your face fully until now—no blood or dirt, incredible."

Engara chuckled and fist-bumped Thaya's shoulder. "The elves worked wonders, hey? I might rediscover my beauty. Look, they fixed our clothes, gave us some new ones, and gave me this dagger in thanks for saving one of their warriors from an Ordac blade."

Engara pulled a beautiful leaf-shaped blade out of her belt. A single groove swirled gracefully down from the haft to the tip, and elven writing encircled the pommel. Its sheath was dark green leather and decorated with ivy leaves. "Its name is Windsheer, and apparently it says, 'My Cut is True' but I can't read Elven."

"It's beautiful," said Thaya, appreciating the light that gleamed off it. "They've been very giving hosts; I hope we've been good guests."

"Best behaviour." Engara nodded curtly and grinned.

Thaya watched as flows of people began to arrive—people from neighbouring villages had come to see the king, no doubt. Beyond them marched scarlet-clad soldiers, and amongst them, she glimpsed elves dressed in dark purple robes, their eyes surveying everything and missing nothing. *The Shadow Magi?* she wondered. She stroked her throat as an unsettled feeling lodged into her stomach, and instinctively placed a hand on Khy's shoulder, his silent presence always comforting.

She glanced at the elven portal. It was calm and serene, unlike in her dream, so perhaps there was nothing to worry about. The unrest in the kingdom was none of her business. Once she'd seen the king, she'd gather everyone and leave quietly. What if they simply left now through the portal? Did it go back to the dragon cave? She didn't fancy returning there, plus, it would be rude if they left just like that. Besides, she wanted to see Ithuin again.

"He's coming," said Khy, reading her mind. *"Look, there by the other dwellings."*

Ithuin's long, pale hair shone brightly in the sunlight. His slender form moved powerfully, proudly, through the rushing elves. He held his head high, almost too high, and squared his shoulders firmly, almost too firmly. She caught his eye, and he immediately strode over, his handsome face's hard expression softening with each step. He opened his mouth to speak but was cut off by a loud and long blast of a horn.

Ithuin shut his mouth and scowled as everyone turned to look at the approaching entourage.

———

Thaya had seen a similar affair occur once before when a prince from a neighbouring realm had visited Havendell Harbour—she'd long since forgotten the prince's name, the name of his realm, and even his face. She clearly remembered the streets decked with red ribbons, bunting, garish bouquets, and the bright flags of many nations. As the prince rode past on his black stallion, people threw rose petals at his feet. It seemed like a lot of fuss for someone no one knew. She couldn't help but feel the same now as she watched the king's procession.

At first, mounted royal guards approached, dressed in scarlet and gold livery, shiny, golden helmets topping the uniform. Their steeds were magnificent mahogany horses with heads more elegant than the working horses she'd seen back home. They didn't trot, they danced over the grass. There were lots of guards, more guards than people, and no one threw rose petals at their feet.

The king rode behind them on that marvellous, pure white mare, and behind him rode another legion of what could be guards or were, perhaps, soldiers. The king was dressed in green and yellow silks, just as she had seen in the Eye of Ahro. A band of gold crowned him, and his long, copper locks flowed beneath it. He looked young, but then, all elves looked young, and he was handsome, like any elf, but he held his head so high it was almost tilted backwards and his lips were downturned. She wondered if this was meant to make him look strong. If so, it failed because he merely looked like he had a bad smell beneath his nose. He looked snobbish.

She expected no less from a king.

An odd, indistinct whispering began in her head as the king swept his gaze over the crowds. At first, she thought his eyes lingered on her but then realised he stared at Ithuin, beside her. She felt her friend tense, saw his chin clench just as the fist by his side did. For a moment she thought he might speak, but instead, he lowered his gaze respectfully, as befitted one staring at a king, and the king nodded his satisfaction.

When King Tekomin halted his horse, his entourage also stopped. His guards rushed to help him dismount.

"You didn't tell me you were exiled," Thaya hissed under her breath.

Ithuin gave her a pained look. "I did not want you to think less of me before I had a chance to explain myself."

Thaya blinked in surprise. Did her opinion matter so much to him? She didn't know what to say. "I'm flattered you care what I think."

"I trust you slept well? No more bad dreams?" he asked quietly.

"Yes, wonderfully, in the end, thank you. And you?"

"I did not sleep. I could not." He looked away, and Thaya noticed the shadows under his eyes.

"I'm sorry. Maybe when this is over and the king has gone, you can relax."

He nodded but said nothing. Two royal guards strode towards them, their eyes hidden beneath their helmets. Ithuin took a deep breath and clasped his hands behind his back.

"Master Ithuin of Orivon, King Tekomin requests your immediate presence."

Ithuin bowed. "Then he shall have it. Does he also request the presence of our esteemed human guests?"

"No." The guard was curt and did not even look at Thaya.

Ithuin turned to her. "My apologies, my lady, common courtesy has been forgotten in this kingdom."

"Enough talk," the guard commanded, and though they did not touch him, they came threateningly close and urged him to move.

He dutifully did as they asked, and Thaya watched him go.

"Will he be all right?" she asked Khy.

"I don't know, but I'm reluctant to get involved in Elven affairs," Khy replied. "They tend to have long-lasting consequences. Elves live a long time. Look, see that velvet-wrapped object on the king's horse? There's something about it."

Thaya stared at it. "The other half of Eir'andehari! The half we rescued showed it to me yesterday. It looked just like that, tied onto his horse. It wants to be rejoined."

The crowds of elves deepened—Thaya hadn't realised there were so many in this settlement she'd barely explored —and she quickly lost sight of both Ithuin and the king. Now that she looked, she saw most of the townsfolk gathered were also soldiers, or guards dressed smartly in different livery, and nearly all of them carried swords or daggers or bows. Should fighting break out with the king's guards, and she hoped she was just fantasising, both sides were evenly matched.

"In my dream, Theo said 'they' were coming," she said.

Khy thought about it then nodded. "What he meant is unclear."

"Maybe we should stay by the portal..." She spoke her thoughts aloud.

Khy agreed.

Thaya looked back over her shoulder and glimpsed the king and Ithuin surrounded by guards and walking swiftly away. Crowds of people followed them, all trying to get a look at the king. The whispering in Thaya's head remained, and her eyes were drawn back to the object on the king's horse.

"Whilst everyone's watching the king, do you think we can get close to the relic? Maybe to touch it?" Thaya asked.

"Impossible," Khy snorted.

Thaya watched as the king's horse was led away by his guards. Damn, she'd have to leave the portal if she wanted to reach the relic. She started to follow them, keeping her distance, and trying to look nonchalant.

Khy rolled his eyes, then followed her. "Why do you need to get close?"

"What if I can touch it and see what it knows?" Thaya asked.

"Why would that help?"

Thaya paused. "I don't know, but don't you want to know the truth?"

Khy cocked his head. "Hmm, which truth? Maybe not in this instance, or at least, not this very moment."

Thaya tutted. The burning desire to see the other half of the Eye of Ahro, to touch it, and to maybe know what it knew, would not go away.

"All right." Khy sighed. "Do you want to do it quietly or cause a scene?"

She considered this. "Quieter is better, no?"

"Better—but harder. Look at all the king's soldiers guarding it; they're not simply going to leave a powerful elven relic unattended."

Thaya couldn't fault Khy's reasoning. "You're right." Thaya tapped her chin, thinking. "There must be a way."

As she considered her options, Khy looked intently at the mare and his horn shimmered brightly for a heartbeat. The king's horse suddenly neighed and reared up, yanking the reins out of its unsuspecting handler's grip. The horse lashed out her hooves and bucked, forcing the guards back, then she rammed through them, sending two rolling along the ground, and cantered straight for Thaya and Khy.

"Oh!" Thaya took a step back, but Khy stood calmly.

The mare stopped abruptly before them, tossing her head and flaring her nostrils. She sniffed Khy excitedly, and her ears swivelled backward and forward.

"Quickly now," said Khy.

The guards were already recovering and running their way. Thaya reached up and pulled back the plush velvet. The broken Eye of Ahro gleamed darkly in the folds. She licked her lips and thrust her hand upon the smooth surface.

The Eye of Ahro was at first frigid, then it burned as an explosion of images entered Thaya's mind. Time melted away. She had no control over what she saw—her intention had been blank, perhaps an oversight—so Eir'andehari showed her what it wanted to.

The to-and-fro of people, elves pushing against other elves, struggling, fighting, shouting, swords clashing and the whoosh of arrows. Chaotic white magic flashed against a backdrop of purple darkness...

An elf-man came into view, tall and robed in darkly shimmering robes that reminded her of a beetle's back. He held a staff tipped with crystals above him, his face contorted in fury. A magi, an Elven High Magi, and around him, shadows swirled and coalesced.

Beyond him, a great beast moved, circling. Inky-green scales shone as the elf's magical lightning flared off them, singeing and scorching where they touched. A great golden eye, split down the middle by a long, black pupil, narrowed. Teeth larger than her arm gleamed, and then orange fire filled the world.

The fire raged and flowed like water over the magi, but it could not penetrate the pale magic flowing from the man's hands and staff.

On the ground, between the elf and the dragon, she glimpsed the Eye of Ahro—egg-shaped, whole and unbroken.

She looked at the elf again. His ears were pointed, his hair long and pure white, and the veins in his neck bulged as he fought unseen forces. The magic he wielded! It was more than she had thought possible. It raised every hair on her body, felt as heavy as lead, and then light as a feather— but it was not enough.

The dragon lunged; the magi's shield shattered. Eir'andehari was within the dragon's reach.

"You shall not have it!" the elf screamed.

He brought his staff down hard over Eir'andehari. Crystal cracked against crystal. Two magical powers smashed against each other. A great explosion shook the world. The staff vibrated in the elf's hands and then shattered. Chaotic light and wind burst from the destroyed staff.

The dragon roared.

Pain, deafness, blindness...Thaya groaned and tried to take her hand off Eir'andehari, but could not.

Eir'andehari shattered, white fire flaring around it, terrible screams of pain. The sound of the elf-man crying out and the dragon roaring was lost in the magical storm that engulfed all.

The chaos faded into calm, pale light.

"He broke it—the elf-man did, not the dragon," said Thaya telepathically. *"The dragon was trying to take it, but the elf-man broke it."*

She didn't know if Khy could hear her, she didn't even know if he was there or not. The Eye of Ahro had her.

Tall beings of light approached. She counted three close to her, but beyond them there were more.

She tried to see their faces, but they shone too brightly. The closest one spoke in a soft, incredibly airy voice that sounded like the wind. "Eir'andehari was created by the Ahrophim—the oldest and greatest of the Arvenphim—to protect our children from the worlds of Shadow they saw sweeping towards them."

The unbroken Eye of Ahro appeared between them, filled with golden light.

"Its very name means The Light, the eyes of the Ahrophim, and through its power, Shen, the Shade, the Fade, the Shadows, could never penetrate Elva Shallas.

"Created to watch over and guard the Elvaphim, it was placed at the heart of Elva Shallas, and from there, its light spread across the land. Millennia after millennia passed of days lived in peace and plenty, until the Ordacs came. It was by peace and not by invasion at first, for a small band of them sought refuge."

As the beings spoke, Thaya saw reptilian folk of gentler

disposition than Ordacs, disembarking from a landed space-craft. They held their clawed hands palms up in supplication, their demeanour humble and beseeching.

"These refugees fled the harshness of their own kind, having themselves been attacked and infiltrated by Fallen Ones a long, long time ago. They were the last free and pure Reptifarions of their kind. Our caring and giving children naturally helped them, but sadly these refugees were followed. Their own kind would not let them be free, and they wanted back the ancient relics of power that the refugees guarded.

"War came, and many Elvaphim died, for they had never experienced aggression; they had never learned to fight. With the power and grace of Eir'andehari, they were saved from extinction, but their numbers were now few.

"Some of the Elvaphim, those steeped in magic, and in their desperation, sought help from the Shen, and the Shadow Realm moved closer, ever eager to assist. Darkness entered their hearts as they strayed from the light and turned to blood magic. With this newfound power and their Shadow Magi, the Elvaphim were able to fight the Ordacs, and they won—but now they were in debt to Those of the Shadow."

Shadows clustered around Thaya, moving like the Shades sent from the Vormae. These were much larger, more ghost-like, and hissed in whispers. White eyes flashed; the intelligence within them was so unlike the mindless Shades, it made her blood run cold.

The beings of light spoke. "King Tekomin's ancestors were magi and the first to reach out to the Shen, and so the shadows flow in his blood and darkness sits in his line, and always it desires more power—an insatiable lust, a thirst that can never be quenched, for it feeds upon itself. Many a

Shadow Magi has gone insane and wrought terrible destruction in that madness. Seeking to be free of Shen, they destroy others and themselves. King Tekomin suffers this same madness. He both fears and loathes the Shadow Magi even as he is part of them."

Still in the Eye, Thaya saw the king seated alone in a room. He paced from corner to corner, muttering to himself, his hands clasped behind his back, jumping at voices only he could hear, staring at shadows only he could see.

The being of light spoke as she watched the king. "He sees enemies in his own people when there are none. He sees plots and scheming where none such exist. He let the darkness consume him, and the voices he hears are the voices of the Shadows, for they seek to take more power. The Eye of Ahro sees all, knows all, it cannot lie. In its light, all shadows are banished, all pretenders exposed."

Thaya frowned. "Then that is good. Let them make the Eye whole, and we can all go home and rest easy." It was a great idea, but somehow something didn't sit right, and she remembered what Ithuin had told her. "Don't tell me, somehow this twisted king doesn't want that to happen."

The beings of light quieted, and Thaya looked at the image in the Eye. She inhaled sharply. There stood the king, and before him, three Ordacs in a dingy room lit by sparse candles. They were discussing something, not fighting— they were making a deal.

"Give us the remaining half of the Eye of Ahro, and we'll deal with Those of the Shadow. They plague us also." An Ordac spoke in a garbled voice, showing he was not used to their tongue. "Your afflicted magi will be wiped off the map, and we'll also give you our weapons, our knowledge."

The king nodded, yet a scowl twisted his features. "You'll

have all that you need, but see that it is done and done discreetly."

"The king sought to trick the Ordacs." The light being's airy voice floated down to her over the image. "He thought the broken Eye of Ahro could never be mended and so could never serve them. But he was wrong. The Ordacs are masters of the elements and would, in time, make Eir'ande-hari whole again and use it for dominion.

"The Ordacs are exceedingly clever; they knew the king was trying to trick them, and they also sought to trick the king. They would fight Those of the Shadow, and they would destroy the magi—but all of them across the land, not just the Shadow Magi, for they stood in their way. And then they would take Elva Shallas.

"That is how the fallen work, through deception and trickery. Whether the king *will* give them the broken half of Ahro or not remains to be seen, but Eir'andehari is not his to give; it belongs *to* the Elven people *for* the Elven people, and its intended purpose cannot be misused for long.

"We made Eir'andehari, Thaya, but within *you* lies the power to make whole that which was broken."

"Me?" Thaya shook her head. The last thing she wanted to do was to get involved in this.

"You are involved already, by will or by not," said the Arvenphim.

The beings of light were not wrong.

"But I've no idea how!"

"Through you, we, the Arvenphim, can make Eir'ande-hari whole. It requires a conduit for its power. It requires a powerful Ena-Shani, a Gatewalker, one who walks between worlds and dimensions. You are that conduit, but you must act fast, for time is running out."

Thaya had hoped to be rid of the Elven artefact, that just

delivering it would be enough, but now even more was asked of her.

"I have no choice, do I?" she groaned. "Okay."

Rough hands grabbed her shoulders and pulled her back, wrenching her hand off Eir'andehari.

"Aaargh!" Intense pain stabbed in her mind. The sudden dislocation made her swoon, and the world wobbled before her.

29

EYE OF THE DRAGON

Khy barged forwards, knocking the king's soldier who had grabbed Thaya to the ground. The stunned soldier lay blinking up at Khy's powerful chest. Thaya had assumed all elves would be able to see Khy as he was, but apparently not all could, or not all cared.

A pointed spear was suddenly under Thaya's chin, the blade almost as shiny as Khy's horn that thrust itself close to the spear-holder's face.

"The horse ran at us!" Thaya gasped.

"Release her!" Engara's booming voice caught everyone's attention.

Thaya glimpsed her running over, hand about to draw her Elven knife and, bizarrely, at her side, were Elven guards, dressed in oak green and silver livery. The opposing guards looked not at Thaya, Khy, or Engara, but at each other, their eyes hardening, the air charged. Thaya did not like her predicament.

"Eir'andehari is unharmed," proclaimed a royal soldier. "Stand down."

The royal guards lowered their weapons and the blade

at her throat. Thaya exhaled loudly and then stiffened at his next words.

"Do not dirty your blades with human blood; the non-elves are not supposed to be here. Withdraw."

Engara's face reddened, and Khy stamped his hoof.

"Let's all just relax." Thaya motioned for calm.

Heads held high, the royal guards about-turned and marched away, leading the horse and the broken Eye of Ahro. The king's mare turned her head to look back at Khy and whinnied as if sad to leave.

"Phew," said Thaya, her hand resting on her chest.

A green-clothed guard glared at the red-clothed guards' backs and spat on the ground. "We should not dirty *our* blades with *their* blood," he hissed.

These guards were loyal to Ithuin. It would be too much to say they were Ithuin's soldiers. *Green good, scarlet bad,* Thaya said to herself, memorising who to run to if things turned ugly.

She smoothed her tunic. "I'm sorry for causing this unrest. They are right, we should not be here."

"On the contrary..." A welcome and well-recognised voice warmed her thudding heart. "I brought you here, and you could not have come at a better time with such a precious relic."

Thaya turned around and smiled at Ithuin.

"You deserve a royal welcome, a hero's welcome, not racial slander. Please forgive us, we're not all...feral." He bowed slightly, making her blush.

"My Levenor?" A guard dressed in friendly oak green and silver livery approached Ithuin, and they moved away and lowered their voices.

She'd heard Ithuin called 'Levenor' a few times and

decided it must be an Elven term of address, maybe like a captain or leader.

"I guess that was our chance," Khy said, staring at the disappearing relic. He sounded disappointed.

"What do you mean?" Thaya asked.

"We need more time with it," said Khy.

"No, I saw enough."

"How? You barely touched it for a second!"

"What? A second? No, it was far longer than that! I saw beings of light called the Arvenphim—the creators of Eir'andehari—the makers of the elves, I think. They told me what I needed to know. It lasted ages."

"Really? Incredible." Khy cocked his head, considering her words.

Engara approached and checked Thaya's neck for nicks. She nodded, satisfied there were none.

"Engara, there might be trouble, so be ready."

"You don't say." The warrior woman rolled her eyes.

Thaya remained serious. "There's something I have to do; I don't know how it will be done. But after, we leave. Okay?"

"I'm ready." Engara straightened her shoulders. "I'll make the others ready."

"Ithuin," Thaya said to the elf when he'd finished speaking to the guard. "You've shown us nothing but courtesy and generosity, and we're honoured. As much as I'd like to stay here, probably forever, I feel our presence only exacerbates the unrest already brewing here, and we should return to our own realm."

Ithuin bowed formally. "Indeed, brave lady Thaya and

Khy, the honour is ours. What you have done may very well, in time, heal the rifts amongst us today. There is to be a ceremony, and a banquet, apparently. We...*I*, would love for you to stay."

There was a pained look in his eyes, as if he knew she should go, that it was his idea they should leave soon—but he also wanted her to stay. A cold wind touched Thaya's neck. She did indeed want to stay with Ithuin a little longer, and the warriors would certainly want to eat and enjoy an Elven banquet, so she nodded.

Under his breath, so others couldn't hear, he whispered, "I haven't been able to ready the portal. Its energies are chaotic at the best of times. The king and his guards have not turned their gaze from me since they got here." He coughed and straightened as a royal guard passed closely by, the man's hard stare not leaving Ithuin.

The Dreamwalker spoke louder. "Before dusk, I'll accompany you and your companions home. With your assistance, we'll be able to direct the portal to somewhere more amenable than a dragon's lair." He winked, making her smile.

A plain-clothed elf approached him, and he was called away on another duty. Thaya hugged herself against an internal chill and turned to watch the elves' frantic work. The wooden stage was nearly finished and was being decorated with white and pink flowers, along with the kingdom's various flags, insignias and emblems. More elves were arriving—people from all around hearing of the king's travels had rushed to join the festivities. But rather than feel the excitement of the place, the sense of dread in her stomach only deepened.

"Come get some breakfast, I'm famished," Engara said.

Thaya nodded, but though her stomach rumbled, the

thought of eating left a bad taste in her mouth. She followed the warrior woman anyway, towards a table set back in a quiet clearing and laid out with fruit, jam and various breads.

As they passed by the portal, she paused, caught by its mesmerising, swirling, dark pink depths. She saw Theo's face in her mind's eye and heard his warning again, but what did it mean? She tried to reason through all the things she'd heard and seen. Eir'andehari wanted to be made whole, its creators and guardians of the elves wanted that too, and unfortunately, they had asked her to do it. That aside, there were things that didn't add up.

How had the king arrived here so soon? She'd literally only just turned up with Eir'andehari; how had he even known to come? If he didn't want the Eye to be made whole, why didn't he just banish one or both parts? Why not just bury them at opposite ends of the world? Perhaps he hadn't known to come, perhaps he was already on his way. But why? Ithuin said his spies were everywhere, but even the Elven magi could not have known she had the orb—only Grenshoa knew.

"Busy minds need busy stomachs." Engara ginned and passed her an enormous chunk of juicy, pink melon.

"Thanks," she said. After a few bites, her stomach stopped groaning, and she returned to the food-laden table for some bread and jam. The laughter, the talking, the rushing of people and now the playing of music—she needed somewhere quiet to think. When Engara walked off to join her clan, Thaya hung back with Khy, and they found themselves wandering over to the swirling portal again.

It was the king's voice that jerked her out of deep reverie as it boomed over the people. A wave of silence settled on the place, and people jostled closer to the stage. Guards, both oak green and scarlet liveried, hung back on opposite sides of the grounds, with those in red keeping close to the king. It looked like they were positioning themselves for battle, and Thaya really hoped that wasn't true.

"Behold, Eir'andehari!" the king shouted, holding up the two broken halves of the crystal.

A wave of awe and wonder flowed over the crowd, followed by excited chattering. The two halves glimmered darkly, very different to the bright, whole Eye of Ahro the Arvenphim had shown her. As she looked at them, she heard whispering, but when she looked away, the whispering ceased. Was it trying to speak to her?

In the corner of her eye, behind the king, a shadow moved. She stared at the space behind him, but there was nothing there. *I'm seeing things now!* She wiped her sweaty forehead. It was warm today, too warm.

There it was again, a shadow! It moved behind the king and vanished. She looked around, analysing first the guards' faces, then the people, but all watched the king intently, even Ithuin, and no one appeared to be seeing anything out of the ordinary.

She looked at Khy a few yards away, but rather than gawp at the king he, somewhat disrespectfully, had his back to him and was inspecting the portal. Thaya turned back to the king's speech and tried to scrutinise the shaded area behind him. Still nothing, even when she looked away and then back again quickly.

"They are close, Thaya." Theo's disembodied voice echoed in her mind, making her jump. Could he really be talking to her? She rubbed her eyes, feeling even more unsettled.

"...And it is with deep sadness that we must detain Ithuin of Orivon for the safety of the realm." The king pointed at the Dreamwalker.

Thaya smarted. What had the king been saying before? Had she heard that right?

"You've been meddling in affairs of state that are far beyond your remit for too long, Ithuin," King Tekomin said loudly, his eyes glowering at the Dreamwalker. He pointed at a group of angry-faced, green-uniformed guards. "You've even gathered an army to undermine the peace of the realm. No king will stand for it. Arrest him!"

Thaya gulped. This was a public humiliation to win the minds and hearts of the people against Ithuin, she thought. It was a gamble, a bloody one on the king's part, for if the people chose Ithuin over the king, *royal* blood would be spilled.

Royal guards pushed through the crowds towards Ithuin. He did not move, he did not run, yet he scowled as pinpoints of colour appeared on his cheeks, and his fists clenched. The crowd murmured in displeasure, and the scarlet guards dropped their hands to their swords.

"Soon, Thaya." Theo's voice again distracted her. She held her breath as the brink of civil war moved closer. Engara and her clan stood to attention, their eyes darting from the king to the soldiers, to Ithuin and back again. Khy came to her side. No! She could not let them take him and throw him in jail.

"Stop!" Thaya cried out before she could stop herself.

A thousand pairs of Elven eyes looked at her. She swallowed. Khy looked at her, his ears pricked forward.

She tried to speak loudly without trembling. "*I* found the other half of Eir'andehari. *I* returned it to your people, nearly at the cost of my own life, but I did not know it would cause *this!* Ithuin had nothing to do with it." She didn't like lying, but everything was happening so quickly. How else could she save him?

She glanced at the Dreamwalker, but he shook his head and mouthed, 'Stop!'

The king narrowed his eyes at her. "Trust humans to meddle in our affairs. *We* remember our history. It's a trap to deceive us and foment unrest so that we are weak when they invade!"

The king moved the narrative too fast for her to keep up.

Ithuin glared at her, then at the king. "That's not true. How can the mighty Northern Kingdom be fearful of a she-human and a few warriors? From afar, I discovered the missing half of Eir'andehari, and I sought to bring it back home where it belongs. Humans might be liars, but they have never invaded Elva Shallas."

The king struck the air. "If she lies, she lies to protect *you,* disruptor of the realm, which makes her no better than you. Lock her up too!"

Royal guards now started towards her, and Khy stepped in front of her.

"Maybe we should go, like, now?" she said. The portal was just behind her, she could step away any moment.

Green-clothed guards stepped in front of Khy and crossed their spears, barring the royal soldiers from getting closer.

One oak green clad guard hissed. "Guests are under the protection of the realm. Let me remind you of our ancient custom."

"Not if they threaten the peace of the realm, then they are criminals," retorted a royal soldier.

The guards began to push against each other, and the crowd grew nervous, muttering and whispering.

"Leave her alone, and I shall come quietly," said Ithuin. "I've caused no dishonour to the realm but sought to find that which was lost." He walked towards the royal guards, holding his arms up, his shoulders slumped in defeat.

What price the truth? Thaya thought. He would imprison himself to protect her and the people. It was all so wrong, yet what choice was there? Thaya hung her head and rubbed her eyes.

She turned around so as not to see her friend shackled and did a double-take. Something was *moving* in the portal, a darker patch that undulated like a fish swimming just beneath the surface of a pond. It had to be a trick of light. She stared and took a step closer, feeling the pull of the portal upon her, and there, right in the centre, came movement that wasn't the normal swirling energy. She looked at Khy, but he was engrossed in the king's speech.

Cries of, "That's not fair!" and "He's innocent!" came from the crowd, and they jostled against the royal guards escorting Ithuin away. The guards shoved them back roughly.

A creeping feeling moved down Thaya's neck, and she turned back to the portal, peering as close as she could. A black spot appeared in the centre and expanded rapidly into a long, dark slit, making her jump back. The swirling energies trembled and turned green. Enormous, scaled eyelids that filled the entire portal, blinked, and a reptilian nictitating membrane slid back. The black pupil widened like a cat's eye and then narrowed as it looked at Thaya.

"Run, Thaya!" Theo's voice rang out clearly.

Thaya couldn't breathe. She shook her head, stepped backwards, and tripped over Khy's hoof. A tremendous roar tore out of the portal. The crowd fell silent and cowered. Even the guards froze.

"It's a trap!" Thaya screamed as the great eye of the dragon blinked.

She didn't know what it was, other than a dragon, but some deception was being wrought this day. One thing was for certain, she wasn't leaving via the portal just yet, it was clearly occupied.

Everyone looked her way. She glimpsed the king's face. At first he appeared shocked, and then a strange smile curled the corners of his lips.

Ithuin turned ashen and struggled against the royal guards holding him. "Captain Themarin, get the magi! Curse the dark, let me go!"

That terrible roar came again. The portal boiled and bulged, and then a torrent of fire exploded out of it. Thaya was still on the ground after falling over Khy's hoof. Light blazed from Khy's horn and spread over them. The flames flowed harmlessly over his shield. People to their left and right tried to flee but were hampered by their numbers.

Screams of agony tore at Thaya's ears, screams that turned into garbled sizzles. The flames flowed over them all, an endless wave of red and orange, burning and torching everything.

The fire from the portal ceased abruptly, leaving a hundred smaller fires and great billows of smoke in its wake. In the horror, silence. The dragon fire had torched nearly everything. People who had been talking in front of her a heartbeat ago were now smoking, black corpses. The wounded rolled on the ground holding blackened limbs and crying out.

Just like the destruction of Taomar, she thought, seeing the same horror before her. *Thank the Creator for Khy's shield!*

"Let's go." Khy thrust his horn under her arm, and Engara grabbed her other, helping her to her feet. The shock on the warrior woman's face was stark, the memories of Taomar also vivid in her eyes. Thaya saw Derry's face again, the smoke rising from his charred body.

"We can't let it happen again!" Engara rasped, then her eyes widened as she stared at the portal.

From it leapt warriors; warriors wearing scales, not armour, and with sharp teeth, deadly weapons, and flaring staves of power.

Guards, Ithuin's and the king's, pressed towards the Ordacs, whilst ordinary, unarmed elves tried to flee from them. Thaya, Engara and Khy were caught between them all, the howling Ordacs now breathing down their necks.

Shoved and shunted, Thaya found herself beside the breakfast table still laden with tasty melon. The fruit suddenly exploded and splattered over her as the clawed feet of a huge Ordac smashed on top of it. The table shuddered, groaned, then collapsed under its weight. Its long, red tongue darted out as it raised what looked like a scythe but shorter, its tip glimmering with magic.

Thaya dropped to her knees and rolled, finding her fireshot in her hand. She didn't hesitate. A fire bolt exploded forward and struck her target. The flaming ball incinerated the reptilian without a sound. Rather than leave a bloodied, blackened husk of a body like dragon fire did, only a pile of ash sprinkled to the ground.

To her right, Khy leapt to impale an Ordac with his horn, tossing it like a toy into the air. The reptilian spun, flailing, and smashed into his comrades. More Ordacs poured out of the portal, an army of them flowing into the Elven soldiers who struggled to push them back.

Thaya did not know what to do. She looked for Ithuin, but he was being washed away in a tide of fleeing people, and then her eyes settled on the king. He was screaming madly as his guards tried to drag him away to safety. "I knew you bastards would betray me in the end!" he screamed at the Ordacs.

So, he *had* done deals with them and betrayed his own kind, Thaya thought as his tirade continued. "But you won't have it, you won't. I'll destroy it utterly!" He shoved away the guards and held up the two halves of Eir'andehari.

Thaya went cold.

A blow struck her across the face, and she saw stars as the world slid to the right. Her palms flared with soulfire, and she held them up, blindly blasting it into whoever had attacked her. An Ordac screamed and jumped back, clawing at its bleeding eyes. An arrow struck it in the chest with such force it was lifted bodily from the ground and impaled on a tree two yards away, the golden haft shivering under the impact. The reptilian struggled and then went limp.

Ithuin dropped to her side, a beautifully carved longbow in his hand as he helped her up. She couldn't see Khy, somehow they had become separated. Suddenly she glimpsed his shining horn in a sea of elves and Ordacs several yards away.

Thaya touched her smarting cheek, and her hand came away bloody.

"It's not deep," Ithuin assured her. He had a cut across his forehead, and bright red drops rolled down his fair skin, but otherwise he looked unharmed.

Thaya grabbed his arms. "The king, look! He's going to destroy the Eye!"

The king was again being carried away, the two halves of Eir'andehari still in his grip.

Ithuin paled.

Thaya wanted to be with Khy, but she had to stop the king. Ithuin looked at her, and they both nodded in mutual agreement. Together, they ran after the king.

The Ordacs pushed in one direction, towards the king and the orbs he clutched. Thaya and Ithuin found themselves beside a tight cluster of reptilians. One raised its scaly hand and pointed at Thaya. Ithuin pulled her behind him and drew a long, golden dagger.

The Ordacs lunged forwards, and rather than fall back, Ithuin leapt to meet the closest, surprising it. His blade slid cleanly, terribly easily, through the Ordac's throat. Then the second was upon him and thrusting its own blade. Thaya stared as the elf moved in a blur, rolling over the back of the falling Ordac as it clutched at its own throat, kicking his feet out at another approaching, then slicing down the face of the Ordac lunging for him.

The one he kicked recovered fast.

Thaya fired her fireshot, the ball of fire smashing the reptilian and disintegrating it. Ithuin struggled with the Ordac he had sliced across the face, but the one who had initially pointed at her, lingered.

Thaya narrowed her eyes as she noticed the gold chain and strange jewel hanging around its neck. The Ordac also wore a short cape on its shoulders—did these adornments mean it was a magi? It placed its clawed fingertips together. Thaya had seen them do that before. *The reptilian acolytes back in the village!* She braced for magic.

The space between the reptilian's claws flared blue. There was not so much light as there was sound, a sudden complete lack of it as the crashing and screaming of the battle was suddenly sucked away.

The silence was broken by a boom that battered her eardrums and shook her bones. Everyone in a three-yard

radius was thrown to the ground: human, elf and reptilian—
all apart from the one who had cast it.

The Ordac placed his claws together again, and Ithuin
grabbed her collar and started dragging her away. "Where
are my magi?" Ithuin gasped.

Thaya raised her fireshot and pulled the trigger. The
flaming ball sped towards the Ordac. The space between the
reptilian's palms flashed, and the firebolt exploded harmlessly over an invisible shield.

Thaya peered through the smoke, but the Ordac was
gone; elves battling reptilians filled the space where it had
been.

Ithuin helped her to her feet, and they began hunting
for the king.

"There!" Ithuin pointed.

Strangely, rather than being taken far away and hidden,
King Tekomin was on the makeshift stage, surrounded by
royal guards. Beyond them stood a semicircle of three
people dressed regally in gold-trimmed, dark purple robes.
They looked like magi to Thaya, or perhaps she could sense
their magic. Neither the guards on the stage nor the magi
were involved in the battle, although the guards had their
weapons drawn and struck any Ordac that attempted to
scale the stage.

The king was shouting and gesticulating madly, but no
one could hear what he was saying over the crash of metal
and the screams of the dying, and no one appeared to care.
One half of Eir'andehari lay carelessly at the king's feet, the
other half he gripped tightly.

30

FIGHT FOR EIR'ANDEHARI

Ithuin and Thaya inched towards the stage. The Dreamwalker grappled with an Ordac, twisting to pull it off-balance, then stabbing forwards with his blade. Thaya shoved between them, slammed into a scaly back, then ducked to crawl between their legs.

A gap in the fighting opened up by a wall of rock, and she crawled through it to avoid attracting attention. She sensed Khy was not far behind her, and to her right, beyond a horde of Ordacs, Engara and her Shield howled their battle cries, fighting in their element.

Three Ordacs not far ahead of Ithuin, grabbed a guard on the stage and dragged him off. A cudgel smashed down, crushing his helmet to a bloody inch, his body twitching. Thaya's stomach turned. The defence partially breached, the Ordacs forced themselves forwards and leapt onto the stage. Two more guards fell, but others pressed in to close the gap.

The royal magi behind them held their hands up, and dark blue light flickered on their fingertips. They threw their hands down, and blue lightning flared and snaked around them, but then the magi furthest to the right turned to face his colleagues. He raised his hands and struck them down fast, sending his snaking, electric magic whipping towards the other two magi. They were lifted into the air and hurled off the stage.

Thaya looked back at the remaining magi and saw not a man in royal robes, but an Ordac. She caught her breath. Its thick tail swung out from beneath its robes, and for a moment she caught its eye. She blinked once, and the Ordac was gone, leaving again the man and his true being concealed. Thaya breathed hard. *What the hell is going on?*

A scythe-like weapon cut the air in front of her, and she barely made it out of the way. She didn't have time to think. She fired. The Ordac was incinerated. She ran through the falling ash.

Shadows swirled over the stage, and they didn't go away when she blinked. The royal magi who had been hurled off it were gathering themselves, their faces blackened and oozing blood. Thaya stared as they rose bodily off the ground and levitated amongst the swirling shadows, blackness seeping from their hands. One of them raised its palm, and the shadows raced towards their fellow magi who had attacked them. The other cast shadows towards the king.

Shadow Magi.

Thaya rubbed her eyes and watched total chaos: elves fighting elves; Ordacs hidden as Elven Shadow Magi; Elven Shadow Magi turning upon their own king; and now the Shadows rising from Shen that Ithuin had spoken about. Humans were caught in the middle of a fight that was not their own. She took a deep breath. *Protect Eir'andehari, that's all that matters.* Stumbling over the bloodied body of a royal guard, she pressed forwards towards the stage.

The royal guards struggled desperately to get the Ordacs

off the stage, their spears with their long lengths proving more useful as prodding sticks than swords. Somehow the crude, makeshift platform had become the frontline, but they were losing it inch by inch.

Shadows darkened the air.

"The Shen!" Ithuin gasped.

Thaya grabbed his arm. "That other magi, he's not a man, he's an Ordac!"

"We're being attacked on all sides!" Ithuin's violet eyes were wild.

Blackness engulfed them.

Thaya could see nothing. It was as if the darkest night had become substance and descended upon her. The sound of the battle became muffled and muted like being underwater, and each breath was sucked in with increasing difficulty. Eyes flashed in the dark, and the thick, woozy feeling of evil magic made her giddy.

"Khy!" she cried out in the dark. "Ithuin!"

A light sparked ahead—it had to be Khy's horn.

Khy!

She ran towards it. The darkness vanished, and she slammed into an Ordac, its amulet smacking into her face. The light wasn't Khy's horn at all, it came from the jewel hanging on its chest. The Ordac grabbed her upper arms in a crushing grip. She couldn't raise them to lift her fireshot or cast her soulfire.

She strained to look over her shoulder and saw Khy, several yards behind, rear up in a panic. Ithuin screamed her name. The elf lifted his hands, his blade cupped between them, then opened them. The golden dagger shot forwards, but the Ordac was fast. It caught the knife in a movement too fast for her to see and held the thrumming dagger an inch from its face.

With her arm now free, Thaya slammed her soulfire-filled fist into its eye. The Ordac howled and fell back but did not let go; it dragged her along. It fought courageously through the pain and grabbed her throat.

"You see us!" it hissed, its voice deep and masculine. "How?"

Thaya couldn't answer the question since he was crushing her throat. "I..." she rasped.

Khy landed beside her as if dropping out of midair. He raised his hooves and smashed them down, but the Ordac vanished. Khy's hooves hit only dirt. Thaya staggered against his flanks, breathing raggedly.

A terrible howl cut through everything. It was Ithuin. The elf was running towards the stage. Bladeless, he used his longbow to smack Ordacs out of the way, leaping over them where he could. He raised his fingers, and pale magic flared, blasting one aside.

Thaya followed his direction and saw the king. Her hand flew to her mouth. The king hefted a broadaxe over his head, glaring at the two halves of Eir'andehari at his feet. The black cloud over the stage coalesced and shivered, gaining strength.

The king roared and swung the blade down.

Ithuin was not going to make it.

The shadows above the stage doubled in size and flared with dark magic. Ordac magic moved. It felt different to elven magic: harsher, alien, distasteful. Khy's horn pulsed brightly. Thaya's palms tingled with soulfire.

All powers surged towards Eir'andehari, and the king's axe descended.

The broken Eye of Ahro, as if sensing its demise, flared with angry light.

"No!" Thaya cried and threw up her hands. She couldn't

let the king destroy the Eye, not after the Arvenphim had beseeched her. Soulfire surged from her palms.

Unseen energy took hold of her, lifted her, and dragged her bodily across the battlefield.

The two flaring halves of Eir'andehari also lifted into the air and flew straight towards her. Everything in their way was shunted aside by an unseen force—elves, humans, Ordacs and the bodies of the fallen were flung aside.

The broken Eye of Ahro smacked into her palms, one half in each, and a strange power bolted through her, not unpleasant, but not human. Powerful, natural energies surged into her, extremely concentrated with a kind of purity she had not felt before, along with a feeling of a deep connection to this world and the elves.

Elven magic, elven power, she thought.

Eir'andehari whispered in a score of voices—ancient Elven words of power she did not know but her subconscious understood. Myriad pale-yellow lights darted over her hands and the broken relic she held, each tiny light leaving a glowing trail of shimmering magic that tingled. She knew what she had to do. Slowly, she brought the two halves closer together, the magic flaring brighter and brighter as they neared each other.

Through the magic, Thaya glimpsed the king's horrified face.

"Stop her!" He shouted the words slowly as if time had slowed down through some power of the Eye combining with her own. She focussed on the whispering voices of Eir'andehari.

Below the king stood Ithuin, staring in wonder at Eir'andehari in her hands. The Ordac gripping his bloodied arm also stared at her but with an unreadable expression, his long tongue flicking slowly out. Khy reared in the corner of her eye, and the portal flared and bulged violently.

An ear-breaking roar shook the land, and a long, green snout the size of the portal itself, emerged through it. Enormous green eyes opened and blinked, then pitch-black pupils narrowed and focussed on her.

Grenshoa!

Great claws reached through, gripped the stone archway, and crushed the stone surrounding the portal to dust. The portal bulged and doubled, then tripled in size. The dragon roared as it struggled through into Elva Shallas.

Everything in the dragon's path fled, even Ordacs. The dragon fear could not touch Thaya, Eir'andehari had her completely, and the two halves in her hands moved inexorably closer together, only inches remaining between them. The whirling lights around it buzzed faster and faster, and the two halves started to spark between each other. The whispering voices intensified, and elven power surged through Thaya. She gasped and gritted her teeth, unable to contain it.

The dragon heaved through the last of her bulk, her long tail snaking behind her as she stalked towards Thaya. The black cloud bulged and darted towards Eir'andehari. The king shouted and pointed, and fearful royal guards pushed to get to her.

The shadows reached her first, engulfing her and blanketing out the world. The air turned thick, smothering, and black tendrils wrapped and tightened around her neck, torso, and hands. Its shadowy finger touched Eir'andehari, screamed and disintegrated.

The dragon roared again, and Thaya heard the rumble of dragon fire through the blackness rather than saw it. Beaten back by the dragon, the Shadows of Shen weakened and began to thin, revealing daylight beyond. The monster that was Grenshoa loomed over her.

White fire flared as the two halves of Eir'andehari connected. Power surged from the elven relic in a silent boom that shuddered through all matter, shattered all thoughts, and scattered light and sound. The light broke into a thousand pieces, the whispers crescendoed and then faded, and a great sigh breathed out.

Immense gratitude flowed from Eir'andehari and into Thaya. The world wobbled and returned, light and sound recollecting itself. Thaya looked over a sea of fallen people and Ordacs. They moaned, clutched their heads, and tried to get back onto their feet.

The stage was gone, wooden beams smashed and splintered, the royal flags and emblems smoking and blackened. Amongst the rubble, the king and his royal soldiers groaned and staggered. Even the great Grenshoa had been thrown aside and lay quivering, her sides heaving.

Thaya stared at Eir'andehari in her palms. It was whole, bright and beautiful like she had seen it long ago. Within its bright depths, beings of light stood. The deep gratitude she felt was emanating from them, and she sensed them smiling. The Arvenphim nodded and bowed gracefully, and she saw they had wings on their backs. The Eye of Ahro flared with a stunning, golden-silver light that grew and spread all around it. It flowed over the destruction, over the great trees, farther and farther until she could no longer see where it went.

The light had an effect on the elves. They suddenly stood up, all injuries and confusion gone, and they began to glow with the same light of Eir'andehari. They stared at their hands and then at each other.

The light reached the Ordacs and had the opposite

effect. The reptilians bent back their heads and howled and thrashed. Unable to get onto their feet, they clawed across the ground, away from Thaya and Eir'andehari's light.

Grenshoa raised her snout and roared, a sound of pain and defeat. The great dragon heaved herself up and dragged her quivering bulk towards the portal. With a powerful shove, she forced herself into the vortex, her tail sliding through and disappearing with a defiant flick.

One by one, the Ordacs crawled after her.

The Shadows of Shen were gone.

"Seize them!" The king, his crown now missing, and his hair dishevelled, pointed at Thaya. "That *human* has captured Eir'andehari!"

Royal soldiers looked left and right, frowning at what had just occurred. A few struggled over the bodies of the dead to obey their king's command, then others began to follow. Ithuin got to her first. He picked her up and ran as easily as if she weighed nothing.

She squirmed as he leapt over the fallen towards the portal. "Wait, I can run!" she gasped. "What are you doing? We can't go after the dragon!"

He stopped before the portal and set her down. Khy came to her side, and several yards away, Engara shouted to her Shield and pointed towards Thaya. Beyond them, the king's guards ran forwards.

Thaya hugged Eir'andehari to her chest, looking left and right and finding nowhere to go. "What will they do to us?"

Ithuin forced a grim smile. "Imprison us forever at the very best. Spread lies and deceit about us so the people hate us. We'll be outcasts forever."

Thaya licked her lips and stared at the portal. "I'd prefer to be killed by the dragon than imprisoned—I'll never be enslaved again!"

Ithuin's intense eyes beheld hers, and he smiled at her. "Brave Thaya, that will not be your fate, I'm sure of it."

Out of the ethers, shadows sprayed towards them from midair—long, tendril-like fingers seeking as Shen tried once more to engulf them. Eir'andehari flared, and the shadow fingers fell back, screeching. Khy tossed his horn, his magic shimmering in protective waves around them. The guards were only yards away, but Engara and her Shield leapt between them.

Words whispered in Elven echoed in Thaya's mind.

"Use Eir'andehari, the orb has the power to control portals."

Thaya shook her head.

"What is it?" Ithuin asked.

Thaya frowned. "Eir'andehari, it speaks to me, or maybe it's the Arvenphim? It has the power to control portals."

Ithuin looked down at the Eye of Ahro flaring in her hands, his face filling with wonder. He raised his hand and closed his eyes and touched the surface. There came no movement or sound, just light. It surrounded them, and with it, sudden silence.

She and Ithuin stood alone in a space filled with very pale pink luminescence. The light had substance as if it were made of tiny, shimmering particles.

Thaya gasped and stared at the world that no longer was. "You did this?"

Ithuin nodded. "We're in a space within Eir'andehari. We should not remain long, the energies are too powerful even for elf magi like myself, let alone elf friends. Were you not beloved of Eir'andehari and have the powers that you do, you would not be able to come here. I've learned much about it; it has been my life's work."

"You should take it." Thaya pushed the Eye towards him.

Ithuin waved his hands. "No, do not let go, it will break the spell. What you heard was correct; Eir'andehari has the power to control portals, even create them now that it's whole. Together we can return you all to your world, safe where the dragon does not walk. You hold the intention, and I'll direct Eir'andehari's power. Let us go, now, before your friends can no longer withstand the guards."

Ithuin clapped his hands together, and a strange rumble sounded. The light darkened, and the world partly materialised around them, yet the pale pink luminescence remained, and all appeared hazy and surreal in the magical light. Engara and her Shield fought against the royal guards, but there were too many to keep back, and they were fast losing ground.

"Get into the portal," Ithuin cried. He grasped her arm firmly and pushed her towards the swirling vortex.

"Come with us!" Thaya gasped, the whooshing sound of the portal filling her ears. The thought of Ithuin being imprisoned filled her with dread.

He shook his head. "I cannot. Eir'andehari is under my protection. I can't let it leave Elva Shallas. I must stay with my people and fight the king. Events this day have set in motion civil war; can you see that? I must be here."

Her heart lurched. "Will I see you again?"

Ithuin smiled at her. "You are not of one world, Thaya, but of many worlds, Child of the Cosmos." He leaned forwards and kissed her ever so gently on the lips. He remained there for several long seconds that she did not want to end. Then he pushed her away, and she let go of Eir'andehari.

"Hold the place you wish to go to firmly in your mind," Ithuin said, telepathically.

She swallowed back the sudden tears and focused. *No, don't think of the dragon lair! There's another portal beneath it.* She saw the portal stone clearly in her mind and stepped back, staring at Ithuin. Khy was beside him, and the unicorn and the elf exchanged silent words. Then she lost sight of them as the vortex grabbed her.

She screamed and spun down as if through the centre of a tornado. She glimpsed Khy galloping towards her, and beyond him, the other humans tumbled helplessly.

The rushing wind, the flaring light, the overwhelming forces were too great. Just as she felt her consciousness slipping, she hit the ground with a jarring thud.

Khy thudded beside her, only just managing to stay on his feet rather than collapsing on his rump. Thaya's stomach lurched. She barely had time to get out of the way of Engara's flailing body before her insides emptied themselves. There was no dignity, no control, nothing she could do, she just heaved.

As Thaya vomited in the bushes, Shield Brethren thudded and rolled on the ground with gasps and groans. So, it wasn't just she who suffered spinning out of control. Her smirk vanished as she heaved again. Khy stood there blinking, and the Shield sat either holding their heads in the hands or between their knees, groaning. One by one, they began to vomit until the bushes were filled with bent-over humans. Khy lifted his nose high away from the smell and silently left the area.

The minutes passed. The vomiting calmed for Thaya

when nothing remained in her stomach. Eyes glazed, body shaking, she looked at the unremarkable portal stone surrounded by four smaller ones. She laid her head on one of them, enjoying the cold, hard rock pressing on her cheek. Her stomach churned but, thank the Creator, the retching had ceased.

"Dear Gods, that is unnatural," a Shield Brother moaned.

Thaya was glad she wasn't alone in feeling that. She looked up at the great mountain rising before her to the cavernous hole of the dragon's lair. She shivered in the frigid wind and hugged herself, immediately missing the gentle climate of Elva Shallas.

No dragons here, I hope.

Khy picked up on her thoughts. *"I sense none."*

One of Engara's Shield Brothers approached—Ethren— at least Thaya thought that was his name, his eyes also glued to the cave in the mountain. "Reckon it's still here?"

"No," Thaya replied. "Not yet, at least."

"'Yet...'" repeated Engara. "Some comfort that is."

Thaya remembered the talisman she had found amongst the bodies. She pulled it out and gave it to Engara. "I found this up there. Before you came, there were more bodies, half-eaten. I'm sorry." She swallowed a lump.

Engara stared at the blackened talisman, kissed it, then put it around her neck next to the other one.

"We should go back up there." Ethren nodded grimly. "Complete the ceremony for our people and return their belongings to our clan. I, too, saw silver rings in the rubble, a clan medallion...these things should not be left for dragons *or* thieves."

Thaya grimaced at the thought of returning to the lair and hugged her chest. As she did so, she felt a lump dig into her ribs and, with a frown, reached into one of her pockets. She found the offending object and pulled out the citrine gem Theo had given her. Sunlight managed to break through the thick layer of clouds illuminating the land briefly, and the gemstone gleamed like honeyed lemon between her fingers.

"You're not coming with us, are you," Engara stated as she adjusted her numerous buckles and sword belts. "And I don't blame you."

Thaya sighed. "I'm done with this place. I wish I could have stayed with the elves, but it turns out even paradise has its woes."

"Me too," Engara said. "I never thought I'd see the fabled Elder Folk, least of all their lands or, indeed, a dragon. Wherever you go, Thayannon Farseeker, change happens, at first for the worse, and then for the better. We just walked out of a civil war, so I'm glad we left. Now my future lies with my Shield and, I guess, our paths diverge once more."

They grasped each other's forearms. Thaya nodded, her chin set with emotion as the warrior woman squeezed her shoulder.

"I've already said goodbye once, I'll not say it again, Shield Sister." Engara pulled her into a hearty embrace that forced the air out of her lungs.

"See you soon." Thaya grinned as they parted.

Engara nodded. "I hope you find what you seek amongst the magi, though my gut tells me you won't. It will be you teaching them of the world and beyond, and not the other way round. But please, take this; you should have more than one or two weapons. No, don't worry about me, I have another from a fallen Sister."

She unbuckled the shorter of her swords and thrust it into Thaya's hands, refusing to listen when Thaya protested.

"Well met, Thaya, and good journey." A Shield Brother the size of a horse slapped her on the back as he passed, heading towards the mountain. Ethren hugged her roughly but spoke no words. The others followed suit, eight in all, saying their goodbyes and slapping her on the back. They nodded respectfully at Khy who watched silently from between the portal stones.

Engara was the last to leave, a sad smile on her face that mirrored Thaya's feelings. The warrior woman had become a good friend, a true friend, one she had not had since she'd left home. One she needed. They embraced and parted without words.

Then Engara followed the others along the path leading up the mountain. She paused once and said over her shoulder, "I hope you meet your elf friend again. The way he looks at you...you two are cute together."

Thaya laughed nervously, struggling and failing to find any clever retort. Engara waved and grinned impishly.

Thaya watched them until they were lost behind a craggy precipice. She looked at the stone in her palm and took a deep breath. *A Mind Opener, Theo called it.* She saw his face again, and tears welled up. He had been a good friend, too.

"Are you going to use it now?" Khy asked.

Thaya shrugged. "No point in hanging around. This place gives me the creeps. I've nothing left to vomit either."

The thought of portal travel again so soon made her feel weak but hanging around here made her feel worse.

"Theo said, 'When you are before a portal, place this in your mouth. After a moment, it will melt into a liquid. Keep this in your mouth for a short time before swallowing it. Then, hah! Hold on, for reality is going to get really wild!'"

She made her way to the main portal stone and stared at

the crystal between her finger and thumb for many long moments. Khy came close, his ears pricked forwards and his tail flicking constantly with excitement. Nothing ever seemed to worry him, and his desire for adventure was insatiable.

Thaya felt none of his intrigue this time, just a deep dread as if she were about to jump off a cliff. She took one long breath and lifted the crystal slowly to her mouth.

"Oh boy!" She sighed and popped it in.

31

A WILD RIDE

THE STRANGE GEM *BUZZED* IN HER MOUTH. THAYA COULDN'T describe it any other way: cold at first, then it grew warm and began doing something *strange*, spreading through her being as if it was interacting with not just her body but her mind and soul. Solid at first, it suddenly melted into a thick, tasteless gel that she involuntarily swallowed.

She could see Khy peering at her closely, and then he began to waver in her vision, his whole form turning into ripples like the surface of a pond. Yonder evergreens looked a deeper, richer green than before, and the portal stones became starkly outlined, glowing faintly with a life of their own. Everything pulsed with life, even the dirt beneath her feet had its own heartbeat.

A gentle, warm breeze started blowing from the south. Thaya frowned. No, it wasn't coming from the south but from somewhere else entirely, and it blew right through her, body and spirit. All worries melted away; all disturbances calmed.

Brilliant, golden-white light exploded through everything, blinding her. Khy was there, but he was no longer a solid form. Instead, he glowed as a pure white light. She held up her hands; they were made of the same light as he. The trees were a mass of swaying green, the ground below was a throbbing mass of brown earth, and the stones were no longer grey but golden. They beckoned to her, and she couldn't resist. She planted her hands on the central stone, and electrical energy flared and crackled from it to all the portal stones.

Ecstasy flooded through her—not wild and chaotic but subtle, controlled and ordered as if she was undergoing a sequential process. Her mind opened like a flower blooming —and then she was falling.

An expanse of purple skies unfurled around her as she was transported to another dimension entirely. She looked upon solar systems where a thousand stars spun, upon universes, multiverses, and sprinkled through the sky were twinkling, silver stars that hung alone or in great cosmic clusters. In the brighter areas, enormous pillars of pink and orange cosmic clouds rose, dwarfing everything. She felt like God, like the Eternal Spirit beholding the entire cosmos that she had brought into being.

Her ears became attuned to an incredible orchestra of tones, melding and moving—the sound of angels singing, their celestial instruments creating stunning acoustics the likes of which she'd not thought possible. It was the song of the seraphs the Mystics spoke about, the sound of the eternal cosmos.

It was overwhelming. Thaya could not think or analyse, she could only be, witness, and endure.

Stillness fell as she floated deeper through the cosmic wonders. She felt she'd reached a tipping point and, with a great whoosh, she found herself shooting forwards.

The cosmos darkened, the purple expanse becoming

indigo and then swirling in a vortex around her. She did not spin helplessly, she did not feel sick, but she had no control over anything; the tunnel of light had her, and what was more peculiar, she found she wasn't afraid.

The tunnel twisted and turned, the cosmic music intensifying, filling her ears, rumbling through her being. The cosmic wind blasted around her, shaking out and transmuting anything within her that was not of the pure and true cosmic order. Everything became waves of undulating energy—light and sound that flowed through her. Time did not exist. There was only this pure space beyond the crude realms of matter. Her thoughts sharpened, her desires pinpointed, her innate knowledge expanded.

She focussed her mind on the stone portal, and immediately it appeared—four stones surrounding a central one and glowing brightly. She abruptly stopped beside it, her hands resting upon its hard surface as if she had never left. Khy stood beside her as before, but now it was night and the clear sky was filled with stars. Those same stars were reflected in Khy's eyes. He said nothing but she knew something profound was taking place, something was being unlocked inside her.

She focussed again on the portal stone and pushed her awareness into it. The star map unfolded before her physically, more brilliant and clearer than it had ever been. The pinpoints of light glowed brightly, and the thin lines connecting them pulsed with life.

She looked at the nearest point, a small, pale light, and it moved towards her. She smelled clean air and a cold wind blowing, heard a river flowing nearby, and saw a deep, dark night engulfing a forest. A tall, stone pillar commanded her view, but there was no civilisation here, no evidence of the magi, and there had not been for millennia. She withdrew, and the sensory image faded.

"Show me the Magi of Loji," she said, knowing intrinsically that if she asked, she would be shown.

The map responded, and three bright points of light lifted from the rest: one near, the second far away, and the third further still, over to the east in distant lands.

She focussed on the nearest. It had to be the place she had for so long tried to reach: the Magi of Loji. Was Loji the name of the place or the creed? Or perhaps even the school of magic? The star map could not tell her that. She smelled incense—cinnamon and musk, and a blazing sunrise turned the clouds into ribbons of fire.

A temple made of great blocks of stone and smaller, pyramid-like domes dominated a high plateau. Around them stood several smaller dwellings covering an area less than the pyramids. A thick, deciduous forest, filled with ancient trees, hugged the settlement, and swathes of flowers decorated any area between dwellings that was not a path or a road. A warmer wind blew, but beyond this oasis of knowledge and power, snow-covered mountains encircled it, providing protection and warding off all travellers, suggesting winter was held firmly beyond the bounds of this place.

Magic holds the cold at bay. Here it is always spring, full of life and promise... This is where I have to get to, this is where I have to be.

A gong sounded from somewhere, the deep, sonorous waves echoing over the awakening settlement and serenading the dawn.

Before the great temple, a stone circle stood, unlike any she had seen before. This stone circle was *new* and unweathered, or it was ancient and had been expertly preserved, for the twelve stones stood perfectly angular and erect, and on each, writing and pictures were carved.

In Theo's palace, the Observatory had twelve stones also, like the months in the year, the hours of the clock, the standard units of measurement. The people of this place know what the portal stones do. She smiled. *Finally, I have found people on Urtha who know! If I travelled there now, I would arrive here, in the centre of those stones.*

As soon as the thought arrived, she sensed a deep foreboding.

Perhaps I should not arrive there, perhaps there is a protocol or danger or suspicion.

She licked her lips. It would be wise to be cautious, she did not know the magi, she'd only ever met Solia.

Thaya reluctantly withdrew from the intriguing place, and the image faded back to the three pinpoints of light. She focused on a fainter point of light immediately before the Magi of Loji portal and it moved towards her.

An early dawn sky opened up where the sun had not quite risen, and a dense forest of evergreens spread in all directions before her. Beside an overgrown track there was a clearing, and in that clearing, a tumble of rounded stones. No erect stone or stone circle remained of the portal—something had destroyed it a long time ago—yet the point of interconnecting energies remained here. After all, she reminded herself, portal stones only helped anchor the energies and made them visible and more accessible for humans to use. Ultimately a portal required no stone to exist. The place was unremarkable, and perhaps that was a good thing.

Thaya took a deep breath, reached a hand out to touch Khy, and willed herself forwards.

The vortex opened, responding eagerly to her desire,

and a tunnel of both dark and light formed and pulled her into it. She let out her customary scream.

She fell forwards, rolling, flailing and kicking. All the calm and serenity of before—the expanded knowledge, the comprehension of infinity—was gone, shredded by the sound of her screaming. She closed her eyes and tried to breathe.

Her tumbling slowed.

She tried to move herself upright and facing forwards, or what she felt was upright, and ever so slowly, she found herself turning.

Praise the light, hah! It's working!

As soon as she thought she had it, she lost it and began to spin again.

A heartbeat later, she hit the ground, face down, with a mighty thud. Spiky grasses pushed into her eyes and up her nostrils. She sneezed and rolled over, gasping for breath, her head still spinning in the vortex.

Khy nuzzled her, and she groaned.

"Oh, I feel bad. Oooh." She managed to sit up, and with Khy's help, got onto her feet. Leaning heavily on him, she made her way out of the shrubs to a patch of gentler grasses down the bank and behind the stones. Birds chirped their morning chorus in the trees, and patches of mist rose from the ground as the world warmed up with the rising sun.

She collapsed onto her haunches, swallowed some water from her canister, then flopped onto her back, clenching her eyes shut to try and stop her mind and stomach from rolling. Theo was not wrong about the after-affects: exhaustion hit her like a brick. With a moan, she curled up and drifted in her mind until she fell into a deep sleep.

It was almost dawn again when she next roused. The sun hadn't fully risen, and Khy wasn't there. A significant time appeared to have passed, but she still felt exhausted and woozy, her body aching in many strange ways.

Theo said the exhaustion would last up to three days. Great.

At least she was somewhere quiet and hopefully safe enough. She wiped the dew from her face, feeling cold and damp all over. Thankfully, it looked to be a clear day, the sun would help dry her out, but still, making a fire would be nice. She set about gathering kindling and foraged for food along the way.

An hour later, she had a small pile of kindling, some of it just about dry enough to light, a length of keyen root, a handful of morels, wild garlic and another handful of some tough-looking blackberries. She didn't fancy eating any of it raw, but if she had enough water in her canister, she could use the steel bowl in her pack that Engara had given her to boil it all up.

She had some provisions left that would see her through until she reached the Magi of Loji, or at least she hoped she had. How far was it from here to there? There was no distance hinted at in the star maps. Perhaps Khy would return with more information.

It took her nearly half an hour to light the fire. The damp kindling resisted her sparks, and the twigs and logs were damper still, but she persevered—she wanted that fire! —and eventually it smoked into life. She smirked and held her hands up to the flames, then dug around in her pack for Arto's knife to cut up the food. She was surprised to find two: Arto's knife, and in her belt, a golden-gilded, leaf-shaped knife just like one Ithuin had carried. How had the elven knife found its way there? *Elven deftness or magic.* She smiled, he must have somehow put it there.

She studied the leaf-shaped knife. For all its beauty, it was wickedly sharp and sliced through the tough keyen root as if it were cheese. She added water to the pot, balanced it on stones in the fire, then sat back and watched it boil while she chewed on the hard and sour blackberries.

As she took her first sip of soup, Khy returned. With a swish of his horn, four apples rolled on the grass at her feet.

She grinned. "Thanks. Find anything else? Is Loji far?"

Khy sniffed her soup with interest. "You've been busy. You slept a whole day. West, about twenty miles, a civilisation rises from the wilderness. It must be Loji. I spied it from a cliff edge but the terrain is hard: a long and deep ravine cuts across the path, and I smelled no trace of a traveller on these roads for many years."

"I'm kind of relieved," said Thaya. "I'd prefer to pass through no more villages or deal with superstitious town folk, but it might take more than a day to get there."

"You're weak still," said Khy. "We'll travel slowly, there's no rush... Only..." He turned and looked west, flicking his tail once.

"What is it?" asked Thaya. What was he not saying?

"There's strangeness in the woods between here and civilisation. I did not go as far as I would have liked, for I didn't want to stray from your side. It felt foreign to this land, alien, yet also familiar—we've encountered it before— and I turned back, not wanting you to be alone with just a magical shield. I circled around, and there is nothing but wilderness north, west and south. A river runs south to east, half a mile from here. The terrain is difficult but not impossible.

"We'll head there once I've finished breakfast; I need to fill up my canister."

The river was large, four yards wide of frothing, white rapids. The hardest part was finding a bank between the sheer-sided, slick, grey rocks. They came to a fallen tree that had slowed down the flow of the river, and clear water burst over the top of it. Carefully, she reached across one of the branches and caught the spewing water in her canister.

They made their way slowly back to the path if that's what it had once been. It was mostly overgrown and confused by criss-crossing animal tracks. Thaya kept as alert as she could through the tiredness, feeling for the 'strangeness' that Khy had mentioned.

The roaring river faded into the background, and after two hours hiking, they reached the ravine Khy had come across earlier: a great, craggy drop of several hundred feet, about as wide, and stretching left and right as far as the eye could see.

She felt it then or heard it—a strange metallic ring that sounded once then faded away. It was just at the border of her audible perception, so she couldn't be sure if she'd heard it in her head or in reality. It was accompanied by an unsettling feeling as if reality distorted in this area.

"It's almost like there's a magical barrier or some concealing magic that's been placed here," she mused.

Khy nodded. "It's familiar. It feels like Ordac."

Thaya imagined Grenshoa's great bulk languishing in the ravine and shivered.

"Don't worry, she's not here, but *something* is," Khy said.

"Maybe it clears the other side," said Thaya. "Perhaps there's a path around?"

"I tried to find one," Khy replied, "but the track goes straight over the edge."

Thaya followed it to the rocky drop-off. Squinting, she could just make out the track continuing on the other side, hundreds of feet away. Perhaps there had once been a bridge, destroyed by time and weather, causing the ground to collapse. She looked left, then right. All the way along the sheer drop, thick forest bustled.

Thaya sighed, her energy sapping.

"I can make it across, possibly carrying you, but that strange magic...anything that might be here will notice us," said Khy.

Thaya licked her lips, considering the risk. "Detouring around could take days. If there's trouble, perhaps we could flee to the magi?"

"Hoping they're friendly," Khy replied.

"So, you're just gonna fly across?" Thaya asked.

"On this planet, I can glide, for a time. I can fly in the Ellarian Fields but not here—the magic is too weak."

"You can glide that far?" She pointed across the ravine.

"I think so."

"'*Think*' so? Not '*know*' so?" Thaya licked her lips some more. "What happens if you don't make it?"

Khy shrugged. "I glide down to the bottom."

"Then we're stuck in the ravine."

"It's a possibility."

"I see." Thaya squinted at the other side for a long time. Khy stood patiently.

"I can probably help you a little, but I'm rather weak in all areas," she said finally.

Khy motioned for her to mount, and she did so dubiously. He trotted to the edge of the forest, a few yards away from the edge. She gripped him tightly and sucked in deep breaths as he turned and faced the ravine.

"A little run-up always helps," he said, quite unperturbed.

Despite the chill wind, Thaya started sweating. She pooled soulfire into her palms, but her efforts were ragged, and exhaustion tugged on her. Khy's muscles bunched beneath her, and he leapt into a run.

Thaya's continuous groan turned into a scream as he launched into the air. The path disappeared beneath them, and the ravine opened its maw. She only just remembered to open her soulfire to him, the energy flowing from her hands and into him, feeding his own in small, stuttering waves. On Khy's sides, shimmering, translucent, white wings emerged and spread wide, making her gasp in awe.

Gracefully, they glided with speed across the ravine.

A sharp pain struck deep in her head, and she winced. Below them, the ravine wavered and suddenly became a mass of tangled hunks of metal, large creatures clambering over it all. Blinking through the pain in her head, Thaya stared at the mess of debris littering the entire area. A craft had been destroyed here, reminding her of the Leonites' sky ship that Grenshoa had crashed, only this craft must have been much larger given the great pile of smoking metal. The pain vanished as soon as it had arrived, and so did the image of the downed craft. Below, there was now nothing but brown rock and earth and trees as before.

The other side of the ravine neared. Thaya forgot about the ship and clung to Khy. They were going to make it! Khy flapped his etheric wings and lurched forwards with a kick of his hind legs to give them more momentum, but they were beginning to dip. They were only just going to make it.

Thaya held her breath, offering up the last of her meagre energy. Khy lunged to make it. His golden hooves struck the ground, his back hooves clipping the very edge of the cliff, sending dirt and rock tumbling below. Thaya released her breath and slid off his back, shaking.

"You saw it?" he asked, somewhat breathless.

"Yes." Thaya nodded and bent over to rest on her knees.

Khy shook himself. "They saw us too."

Her blood ran cold.

"Get back on, let's keep moving. I'm getting off the path."

She hesitated then sighed, too tired to think things through and certainly too weak to fight should it come to that. She did as he told her. Khy galloped down the path until he came to a gap between some trees and pushed through the thick knot of bushes. He was breathing harder than before, traversing the ravine had cost him, and now he needed rest as much as she.

He didn't stop. After half an hour of leaping over thorn bushes and struggling through the undergrowth, he paused, his ears pricked forwards. Thaya remained silent, listening for the faintest sound. She heard and sensed nothing apart from a woodpecker hammering a tree trunk. The moments passed. Neither of them moved, and then she detected the very faint splashing of running water.

"Let's find that stream," Khy suggested. "I can feed and create a stronger field around us there."

"Good idea." Thaya nodded.

The stream was just deep enough for Khy to stand in and drink from. He cast a shield around them as Thaya tried to relax.

"I feel something watching us, but from afar," said Khy. "As if someone scries from a distance."

Thaya took his word for it and imagined an Ordac looking into its medallion or pool of water and seeing her and Khy. "If it is an Ordac, then they're strong in magic and mind control."

She set her pack down and sat, pulling out an apple and munching on it.

"The feeling passes," said Khy, and his withers relaxed.

"Rest here?" Thaya swore she could sleep on her feet right now.

"Okay," agreed Khy.

Thaya at first didn't know she was dreaming; everything was so real. She had flopped down onto the grass, put her head on her pack, and closed her eyes whilst Khy cast wards about them. A rustling noise made her open her eyes and sit up. Khy was sleeping beside her with his head on his forelegs, and a thick mist hung over them. Khy often cast mist to hide them, so that was nothing to worry about.

"Must have been a bird," Thaya muttered, but just as she laid back again, she glimpsed a strange orange glow coming from deep within the mist. It faded away. Silently, she got up and padded towards where it had been, careful to keep Khy in view—the last thing she wanted was to get lost in the thick fog.

The orange light shone again, glowing thickly and then fading away. She gasped. A tall figure stood in the mist ahead, a cloak and hood concealing it, if indeed it was a 'he.' The orange ball of light glowed again. It came from between the figure's hands and illuminated its reptilian face and protruding snout. Thaya stifled a cry.

It reached a clawed hand towards her and beckoned. She found herself suddenly walking forwards against her will. She fought to turn around, but her legs would not obey —something in that orange light compelled her body forwards.

"Run, Thaya!" Ithuin's voice cut through the spell.

She paused, blinking, then ran.

Khy awoke her with a nudge, making her jump. She gasped and looked above him at the great ball of magical fire sailing high over his head. It crashed through the treetops, setting light to branches and boughs as it passed. Familiar animalistic howls of Ordacs cut through the forest, followed by the shouting of men.

Thaya jumped to her feet. "Ordacs fighting humans?" What on Urtha was going on?

"Let's go," Khy said.

"We must help them!" said Thaya. She started running towards the noise, checking her fireshot was tucked in her belt and adjusting Engara's short sword that slapped uncomfortably against her thigh.

"Something's not right," Khy said, but he followed her anyway.

She ran past a trail of scorched bushes and paused, breathing hard.

On thick, scaled legs, Ordacs leapt over scrub, wielding their strange, bladed weapons, red tongues flickering, long fangs bared. Behind the Ordac warriors, and casting huge, searing balls of red fire, stood Ordac Magi in their orange acolyte-like robes—an odd sight, akin to seeing animals wearing clothes.

But the Ordacs were not what froze her to the ground and made the blood drain from her face. They weren't fighting against humans, but beings that were human-*like*. This race was a foot or more taller than humans and heavyset with powerful muscles and bronzed skin. Their heads were elongated, twice the height of a humans', their thick skulls encasing an enormous brain no human intellect could match. They were handsome and hardy and mostly male, although there were some equally powerfully built and handsome female warriors amongst them.

They wore armour that looked like polished gold plate, and they fought with curved swords and batons that flickered with powerful energy. Half of them wore garish red, white and black war masks covering their faces, making them look both fearless and fearsome. They also had their own magi fighting behind them. These wore white robes and held aloft silver and gold staves that crackled with vivid electrical magic.

Nuakki!

Thaya froze at the sight of her former slavers, the sudden fear driving all courage from her heart and rooting her to the spot. She thought her legs would collapse beneath her and nearly lost control of her bladder. On opposite sides of the battlefield, the two nearest magi spotted her.

One was an Ordac, the other, Nuakki.

32

THE BLUE ORDER

THE OPPOSING MAGI FORGOT ABOUT EACH OTHER AND FOCUSED on Thaya. The Ordac cupped his claws together, and light flared between his palms. His robed silhouette and the heavy medallion hanging on his chest reminded her of the reptilian from her dream. The Nuakki raised his silver baton, an arrogant smirk twisting his features.

Khy stamped his hooves, and his horn flared. Thaya lifted her left palm, feeling it fill with soulfire, and with her right, she held up her fireshot.

Thinking the Ordac would attack faster, she fired and released her attack at him. Her aim was correct, but the Ordac vanished, and her flaming shot careened harmlessly into the bushes, incinerating everything it touched. The Ordac had managed to cast in that split second, and his flaring magical fire shot not towards her but to the Nuakki. Blue lightning burst from the Nuakki's baton and intercepted the reptilian's magic in an explosion of chaotic forces.

Bushes were flattened, Khy staggered, and Thaya was

lifted off her feet and thrown to the ground. She sucked air into her winded lungs and crawled back up.

The Nuakki grabbed her neck, one hand engulfing her throat in a choking grip. Her bladder protested as she looked into his cruel, sneering eyes.

The Ordac materialised beside her, clasping her shoulders with his powerful claws and wrenching her from the Nuakki's grasp. Khy slammed into both, sending them rolling. He skidded to a stop and reared to turn while Thaya jumped to her feet. Again, the two magi fought each other, and beyond them, more ran to their aid as the battle between the Invaders turned in their direction.

They had a slim chance to get away, so she and Khy ran, aiming to back out through the forest, but behind them gaped another ravine, half the size of the first but still hemming them in. An Ordac warrior ran at them, but it was no match for Khy. The Saphira-Elaysa leapt over it and bucked it powerfully over the cliff. Then there were more Ordacs, many more.

Thaya pushed to the right, but the Nuakki were more numerous there and the battle raged dangerously close to the cliff edge.

She shoved her way through the bushes, ignoring the thorns, and crawled through a knot of ferns, hoping Khy followed—there was so much shouting, explosions and clashing of weapons, she was deafened. She kept low, then peeked over the foliage. A thick knot of warriors fought, blocking Khy's path to her left.

A magical explosion ripped through everything. It tore apart trees and sent dirt and debris flying everywhere. A thick, billowing smoke followed the explosion, smoke that choked. Sudden light blinded her, and heat singed her skin.

"Argh!" She tried to blink the light away and shielded

her head with her arms from the falling dirt. When the showering earth stopped, she rubbed her eyes, then looked behind her. Khy, unharmed, battled his way through the trails of smoke rising from the ground. Thank the pure light he was unharmed. She turned and belly-crawled frantically through the flora and mud.

Ahead, she spied a clearing where sunlight streamed through the canopy and no smoke billowed. Soon she'd be out of it, and they'd run to the safety of the Magi of Loji. It wasn't far now. She scrambled forward.

A wave of thick fog rolled over her, dampening out the sun and drowning out the din of the battle. An eerie silence fell.

Thaya held her breath. What magic was this? Had Khy cast a ward over them?

This isn't Khy's magic!

Her heart lurched, and she screamed as a robed figure appeared in front of her, a medallion glowing orange on his chest. She rolled into the ferns, hauled herself to her feet, and ran, but the robed figure materialised again, this time in front of her, and she slammed into a thickly muscled torso that was covered in scales. The medallion flashed, and she couldn't move. The soulfire that had kindled in her solar plexus went cold. All her power left her. The reptilian's mind aggressively grabbed hold of hers and forced its way in. A dull ache started in her brain.

"You see us," he said telepathically. *"You're different to the others; we must know how."*

"Why? So, you can work out how to trick me, too?" she threw back. She felt the truth, that they wanted to trick humans, all humans, but why?

The Ordac paused its shuffling through her mind. She

sensed his surprise that she could answer back tele-pathically.

So, they can walk amongst us undetected and do whatever they please... Manipulate us with their superior mental abilities to do what they want? Why? So, they can use us to fight each other? Or maybe the Nuakki?

Or perhaps it was all those things. Each question she thought she sensed the Ordac picking up on and trying to evade. *Hmm, interesting.* Whilst he was affecting, *infecting*, her mind, the connection appeared to work both ways—she was also affecting his mind, his thoughts, and finding answers to her questions there.

Her head throbbed, and her vision blurred as the dull pain increased.

She closed her eyes and tried to force him out, but the pain intensified. To her horror, she knew when he read the memory of the bonding between her and Khy, the touching of her hand to his horn and the twinning of their souls. He saw the Vormae who'd taken her and imprisoned Khy. He saw the Nuakki and the slave mines, her stomach twisting as she gazed again on Osuman's face.

How dare the Ordac force himself into her private memories! She pushed back through the pain, and blood burst from her nostril as the pressure increased unbearably. She forced her eyes open and stared straight into those unblinking, green, reptilian ones, barely inches from her face. She felt a resistance that suddenly gave, and then, with a shock, she found herself inside his mind in a dark, quiet place.

He tried to push her out, but she shoved forwards aggressively. Images came.

Legions of Ordacs stood in neat, ordered rows, all facing one way, an army standing to attention. She looked to where they gazed and stared at the enormous dragons facing them, one red and one white, and each larger than three galleons combined, larger even than a Nuakki spacecraft. Black horns like crowns encircled their heads, and their huge eyes flared red.

In front of these dragons were smaller, green ones, the size of Grenshoa, and before *them* were black creatures with wings: gargoyle, demon-like things, twice the size of a human. Some hovered off the ground, and all were very ugly. The minions—the legions of Ordacs before them— suddenly all bowed down and pressed their snouts to the ground in subservience.

The image turned into a sky ablaze. Fire and beams of light blasted from great spacecrafts; some had long, fat shapes like cigars, *Nuakki ships!* Others were black and of all shapes, irregular and ugly.

The image changed again and became dark and enclosed. Beings moved in the gloom, and then a candle sparked alight, pushing back the darkness. Another candle was lit from the first, and then another, until there were six, and in the dull orange glow, she glimpsed the round snouts of hooded Ordacs standing in a circle, their heads bowed in reverence. In the shadows behind the six illuminated by the candles, more hooded figures moved. The atmosphere was dark and laden; a craven hunger hung in the air, laced with excitement and expectation.

She strained to see what they stood around, what was in the centre, and wished she hadn't.

The terrified face of a young human boy looked her in

the eye, his blue eyes wide with terror yet unfocused from some drug he'd been given. For a moment, he reminded her of Derry—he had that same lost and confused look in his eyes—but this was a different kid. His skinny arms and legs were tied down, and he was naked. He groaned, and his chest heaved with quickening breaths. In the candlelight, a knife flashed.

Thaya screamed and jerked backwards, exiting the reptilian fully. The Ordac howled from the tearing apart of their minds.

Thaya fell to the ground, quivering as the Ordac writhed and groaned. He grabbed her leg with a clawed hand, but from somewhere else a bronze blade flickered, spinning. Suddenly, the scaled arm was gone, and instead, bright red blood spurted from a stump of bone and viscera.

A Nuakki warrior leapt upon the thrashing Ordac, slicing it from belly to throat with his curved blade, his eyes blazing with hatred. The Ordac jerked, blood gushing towards Thaya and pooling near her.

The warrior turned to her, raised to slash his blade, and then paused. Young human women were prizes to them. His hesitation was costly. Thaya's fireshot exploded into him. She looked away to avoid seeing him falling to the ground as nothing but black dust. A pang of human guilt knotted her stomach.

He didn't save me; he was just fighting Ordacs. Nuakki save no one.

She looked around for Khy but could see nothing other than smoke, fire, forest and chaos. Bodies and blood littered the ground. Thaya pondered how strange it was that none of them belonged on Urtha, none of them came from Urtha, and yet here, on a planet far from their home, they made their graves.

Maybe I should go back and find Khy...

No, he'd want her to push ahead; it may be that he was ahead already.

A deafening roar made her cower. It shook the trees, the ground, and her insides. The sun vanished, and she looked up at the underbelly of a huge green dragon. It swept so low above her that its wings brushed the treetops. It was so large, its passage was slow.

Thaya sucked in a breath, failing to control the tremble that shivered through her.

Another noise superseded the dragon's roar—a strange, mechanical whine that sent deeper chills through her. Her dream, her memory of another life, flashed before her: the round, black ship above them, the fearful people on rooftops looking up at it, a devastating red beam, then a wall of water destroying entire civilisations.

A red beam blasted into the dragon. It was so thick and so close, she could see substance in the beam; it wasn't just light, it was almost liquid, viscous. *Plasma.* The word came to her. She didn't quite know what it was, but it reminded her of the clear albumen of eggs, or the consistency of frogspawn. The dragon gave an ear-splitting roar, and the ground rocked from an explosion.

Dazed by dragon fear and staggering on the quaking earth, Thaya never saw the Nuakki behind her. He grabbed her by the hair and hauled her over brambles and stones. She grabbed his wrist, clawed uselessly at his tough skin, trying to hurt him enough to release her. Beside him she glimpsed his comrades, two males and two females, and all hope of fighting or escaping vanished.

The Nuakki growled, dragged her in front of him, and smacked her across the face. The world shuddered, and she saw stars dancing. Something hot trickled from her lip.

There was so much noise, it all blended into one: Ordacs roaring, Nuakki shouting, the strange sound of a great beast groaning, and the mechanical drone of a spaceship.

Where was Khy? Was he dead?

She squeezed her eyes shut against the tears, ashamed of herself for being unable to fight. One or two, maybe, but who can fight a whole army?

The din became a roar of flames as the whole world turned to fire. Blazing orange flames tore through the trees and bushes, setting light to everything and singeing the hair on her arms. The Nuakki paused and shielded their faces from the immense heat. Those with staves raised them and began to cast.

Suddenly, the bank they stood on collapsed, and they were falling. Thaya rolled with them alongside tree trunks, roots, dirt and stones.

The Nuakki male rolled over her once and then twice, crushing the breath from her lungs and retaining his grip on her hair. She gasped in a breath, and her mouth filled with dirt. They tumbled to a stop, and she found herself sprawled on top of him. She screamed and punched him in the face, in the neck, anywhere she could. The fury stoked her soul-fire and her palms began to fill with it.

The Nuakki grabbed a wrist, his hand smothering it and crushing it until her metatarsals creaked. He slammed his other palm against her forehead. An explosion of agony made her go limp. Waves of pain tore through her body, her teeth snapped against each other and ground hard, and her eyes felt as if they were bulging out of her head.

She panicked. *The Cleansing! He's trying to wipe my mind...or kill me—but this feels different from before.*

With all her willpower, tears streaming down her face from the strain, she channelled her soulfire up to her forehead, right to where his palm pressed, and released it. The Nuakki screamed and snatched back his hand. The pain vanished, and she flopped, breathing raggedly. His hand was now red and swollen.

Dazed and weak, she couldn't fight. The Nuakki roared and threw her to the ground. He wrapped his good hand over her throat and choked her so hard her neck creaked, the world turned dim, and all sound faded.

A glint of light flashed through the dimness mere inches from her nose. She heard a gargled grunt of surprise, followed by the feeling of something heavy lifting off her. Suddenly, she was rushing back into her body, all sounds and smells and vision returning.

The Nuakki was staggering backwards. A thick, silver dart, half the length of an arrow was sticking out of his neck, and his eyes were wide with shock. He tried to talk but blood spilled from his lips. Then he toppled over.

Thaya pushed herself up, rubbing her painfully bruised throat and sucking in great lungs full of air. Two more Nuakki, a male and a female, lay sprawled, the same thick, metal darts sticking out of the chest of the male and the back of the female. The remaining two Nuakki were further down the bank, their crushed and bloodied bodies just visible beneath the tree trunks and rocks that had fallen on them in the landslide. Thaya's eyes followed the direction of the darts and froze.

Where the ground had collapsed under opposing magical forces, dragon fire and spaceship beams, a high, ragged bank of loose earth and trailing tree roots now rose.

At its base, partially hidden under the dirt, stones and dangling stems, slumped an Ordac. His bloodied chest rose and fell rapidly, and in his claws he held a device, and in that rested another silver dart. He had it pointed directly at her.

She stared at him. Blood smeared his jaw and trickled freely from his side. It was clear to Thaya, even from this distance, that he was not going to make it. But he could still kill her now with barely a twitch.

Slowly, she stood and held her palms out to show she held no weapon.

Slowly, he lowered his but kept it ready at his side. Step by careful step, she walked towards him.

"You saved my life." The sudden impact of what had just happened hit her.

An Ordac has saved my life... Why? He could have killed me, too; he could have...

The Ordac nodded once, his head hanging lower as if he had not the strength to raise it back up.

She paused beside him. She was a fool to even get this close! His claws lashed out, and he grabbed her arm with surprising speed despite his condition. She yelped and pulled away, but he was too strong, even now, and he dragged her down next to him. He did nothing but hold her there, his gaze looking ahead of them, his elongated pupils widening and contracting erratically. When she became still, he relaxed his grip but did not let go.

"You just want me to sit with you?" Thaya whispered, cold sweat trickling down her back.

The Ordac was huge, his jaws could easily engulf her head, and his claws were long and sharp, they could rip her to shreds. Dark reptilian blood pooled on the ground beneath him.

"Yes," the Ordac hissed. Speaking cost him greatly, and blood trickled from his lips if you could call the scaly skin around his mouth 'lips.'

"I can try to help, I can—" Thaya began, wondering if her soulfire would work.

"No." He shook his head. "See."

His grip on her arm slid down until his palm rested upon hers. Warmth spread from him there, and he pressed upon her mind with his own.

At first she resisted. What if she saw horrific images like she had witnessed within the mind of the Ordac Magi? But this Ordac was breathing his last, she could at least acquiesce to his final request. She closed her eyes and relented.

Emotions and sensations, mixed with abstract images, flowed through her swiftly, too fast to think about or label. She glimpsed a beautiful green planet, an endless jungle, body-hugging warmth and humidity. It was the past, a long time ago—she didn't know how she knew, she just knew—a *long* time ago before even Urtha had been born.

A great creature, larger than the trees, lifted itself. It wasn't a bird or a reptile but something in-between—a plumed serpent, a feathered dragon, a scaled bird. Stunning teal and lapis lazuli feathers rose to create a crown upon its elegant head, and sky-blue feathers covered the length of its back. Azure scales shimmered on its undercarriage.

Thaya sensed the serene beast was female, god-like in some manner.

Its gentle, golden eyes looked down upon a vast number of creatures, many reptilian, fewer birds, but they were all manner of shapes and sizes. Some had feathered wings, others golden scales that shone. Some walked upright, looking part human and part bird or part human and part reptile.

These were the children of the blue-feathered dragon— she had created them all.

"Some of us remember, whilst most of us want to forget." The Ordac's voice was broken and rasping—she couldn't be sure whether he spoke aloud or in her head—but she didn't open her eyes in case it caused the images to fade.

"Our memories are passed on in the blood, though many try to suppress them," he rasped. "Humans also have this memory of their origins, but it lies dormant. The Nuakki caused that, not us, but it was we who instilled violence in your hearts, and our wars destroyed the first civilisation."

Thaya felt anger spread through her body. She wanted to express it, to hurl obscenities at the Ordacs who had invaded her planet, but more images came, and her anger was dampened.

Fire spread over the sky, and the images turned dark as the Ordac rasped, "We were pure once too, before we were attacked, almost destroyed, and revenge entered our hearts... So much happened, too much to show you how we became what we are... but some of us still remember..."

Thaya was in an enclosed space, a chamber or a cave, somewhere secret. Floating, blue orbs cast everything in soft light. At least ten Ordacs were there, each wearing blue plumes of feathers on their heads, a crown or hat or something, the feathers were not their own. She sensed the Ordac that gripped her palm was there, that this was his memory and not a race memory.

She looked down and saw they were surrounding a pool of perfectly still liquid held in an enormous stone bowl or chalice about two yards in diameter. The Ordacs chanted peculiar words that did not sound like the Ordacian language she'd heard. The same incredible, blue serpent-bird appeared upon the surface in response to their calls.

"Some of us long to be...free." The reptilian's voice broke, and his grip on her palm weakened. The image wavered.

"No." Thaya wanted to see more, she *had* to know more. She placed her other hand over his, pressing it firmly against her palm.

It appeared to give him strength, and he mustered enough to speak some more. "It's hard to want one thing when most of your race are choosing another. But we of the Blue Order remember."

Thaya gazed upon fields of blood: slain and dismembered Ordacs everywhere, every one of them wearing a blue-feathered crown. And over them walked other Ordacs, triumphant.

"For all that we might do, remember what we were." His green eyes beheld hers, suddenly glowing with an inner fire.

"I will," Thaya said. She blinked, and tears rolled down her face.

The fire in the Ordac's eyes began to fade, and his head slowly lowered to his chest. His scales began to lose their green lustre and became tinged with a greyish sheen.

In a hissing voice, so quiet she could barely hear, he said, "You see through the disguise, something is awake in you, in your blood. They will want it."

"Why are they here? Why are you here?" Thaya gripped his hand harder, willing strength into him. She wanted, she *needed,* to know more.

"To take."

The reptilian's hand lost its grip on hers, and his eyes flickered.

"Wait," Thaya rasped. "Please stay. Tell me more."

A howl tore through the air, making her jump. It was replied to by another howl, then another very close. On the bank above her, reptilians jumped down, scores of them leaping away fast—too fast to notice her crouched beneath the overhang. Thaya hunkered down beside the dying Ordac and held her breath. The last few stragglers followed the main horde into the foliage, and then there was nothing but the cries of Nuakki in the distance.

She let go of her breath and turned back to the Ordac. "They've gone."

He was gone, too.

She stared at his closed eyes, his snout resting on his now-still chest, the warmth in the palms rapidly cooling. It was strange to see a reptile turn grey in death. She'd assumed only humans did that. Only moments ago, she'd been fighting and killing his kind, now tears fell unhindered down her cheeks for him. His claws slipped out of her hands, and in her palm remained a beautiful lapis lazuli feather, the end tipped in gold.

33

MAGI OF LOJI

"Thaya!"

Khy leapt down the bank, his horn lowered to attack the Ordac. Seeing it was dead, he stopped charging, his ears swivelling forwards as his intelligent mind tried to piece everything together.

Thaya stared at him. The Saphira-elaysa looked a complete mess—his white mane and tail were stuck through with twigs and leaves, every inch of his body was covered in mud, and dirt was smeared across his face. "What the hell happened to you?"

Khy tossed his head indignantly. "I fell."

"You fell?" Thaya raised an eyebrow.

"Yes. Off a cliff." He rolled his eyes. "Never mind. The Ordacs are fleeing, ; they'll threaten us no more."

Thaya stood, twiddling the Ordac's blue feather between her finger and thumb. "And the Nuakki?"

"Quite. Let's get out of here." Khy nudged her to climb on his back.

"Wait, we must set his spirit free." Thaya pointed at the Ordac.

Khy frowned. "Help *him?* What for?"

"He saved my life. I'll tell you what happened, but let's do this first and go."

After a moment, Khy nodded. "Let's be quick."

Thaya drew upon the soulfire in her solar plexus and pooled it into her palms. Khy's horn glowed, and they joined their energy together. Their combined golden fire spread rapidly over the Ordac's body, and rather than burn and singe flesh, the body turned into light, flared brightly, then faded. All that remained of the Blue Order warrior was a greenish-blue ash so fine that the wind picked it up and carried it away.

Thaya took a deep breath and climbed onto Khy's back. Without a word, he leapt up the bank, and then they were zipping through the forest at breakneck speed.

"How far?" she shouted over the wind. She meant to Loji and hoped he picked up on that.

"Close," he shouted back.

She settled into his stride and told him about the Ordac telepathically.

He remained silent, even after she'd finished, thinking upon it. She was about to probe him about his fall when they burst into a clearing, and the stone temples of Loji speared above the treetops. He reared up, and Thaya had to cling to his neck to stay on. Her eyes fell upon what had caused his abrupt stop.

In front of them sprawled the great bloody mass of a green dragon.

Grenshoa!

Thaya inhaled sharply and slid off Khy's back. The dragon was covered in blood and a thousand gashes. Blackened flesh seared up the entire left side of her body. Her lower jaw was smashed into a bony, bloody pulp, and her huge, gore-encrusted tongue lolled out.

Khy turned and looked at his thigh where Grenshoa had left a lasting wound. "I thought I felt something. The scar, it's vanished."

Thaya touched where he had been injured, and found the raised welt had gone. There was no trace of it.

"How the..." Thaya began.

"A magical creature wounded by another magical creature will only fully heal when that creature dies," replied Khy, matter-of-factly. "True magical creatures cannot kill each other. Now she's gone, killed by another, my wound heals."

Thaya shrugged. He had said similar before, but the concept was alien to her. "She caused us a lot of trouble."

She sighed heavily. The dragon that had hunted them and caused them so much trouble lay dead before her. She hadn't needed to face her again, so why did she feel so disturbed? Was it because of everything the Ordac of the Blue Feather had shown her?

They'd been good once; they weren't all evil.

Did he have a name like Grenshoa? Did any ordinary Ordac have a name?

I shall call him Blue Feather; he should have a name.

"So, the Ordacs lost. I'd never thought it possible." Thaya rubbed her forehead.

"Only the battle. They fight on forever, like the warrior race they are," said Khy. "The Nuakki were more numerous this time, that's all. Ordacs are actually able to breed faster."

The sight of such a huge, stinking, dead thing was too much to take for long, and she sidled past it to the path leading to the stone gates of Loji, then loped into a run. The magi and their powerful magic would protect them from the

Nuakki. She just had to warn them if they didn't know already.

A hundred yards ahead, on the wide expanse of green grass to the west of the stone-paved road, a Nuakki craft sat neatly on four spindly legs, a row of steps leading down from the open oval door.

She slowed to a walk, her elation subsiding. A terrible knot formed in her belly.

This was one of their smaller ships. She'd seen them docked next to the huge ones at the slave mines. It was covered in matte metal, one side completely blackened from fire, the metal buckled and ripped in large sections.

Dragon fire did that, she thought. *But the smaller craft can't have taken down Grenshoa alone, there had to be other Nuakki ships, probably the mothership somewhere close by.*

Between the craft and the dead dragon lay scores of slain Ordacs, left like trash where they had fallen, and a neat row of Nuakki warriors, a piece of cloth or clothing respectfully covering the faces of the dead. Her eyes settled on a fallen human male in the open space between the Nuakki and Ordac bodies. She stared at the man's uncovered grey face, his blank eyes open wide as he stared unseeing to the heavens. Was he a magi? She thought from his plush, blue robes trimmed with orange, that he might be. Solia, the only other human magi she had ever met, had worn similar robes.

She forced her eyes from the fallen and walked in halting steps along the well-kept, paved road. Beyond the Nuakki craft stood two, great, stone pillars marking the gateway into Loji, and between them, hung brightly coloured flags in blue and orange.

At last, after all this time, I've finally reached the gateway into the secret and incredibly mysterious Loji.

But the wonder and awe she should have felt, and

wanted to feel, was lost in the dread that bloomed within her. Her faltering feet finally stopped, and she stared, disbelieving. It took Khy nudging her to get her off the path and into the ferns and bushes before they were seen. There he knelt and she crouched, her mouth hanging open.

Six Nuakki stood facing a growing number of human magi, who were rushing out of the gates to meet them, their blue velvet, orange-trimmed gowns swishing around their ankles. Behind them, followed other people, ordinary folk not dressed as magi and probably the maids, cooks, cleaners, and so forth, she supposed. All had worrying looks of joy and awe on their faces as they hurried to greet the Invaders. Thaya looked from the humans to the Nuakki, desperately trying to work out what was going on. Why weren't they attacking the Nuakki? Why weren't the Nuakki attacking the humans?

Four of the Nuakki were warriors: two wearing their garish red, black and white war masks were cleaning Ordacian blood off their weapons; the other two were magi dressed in white. One of them was of the highest priest cast, marked by the thin, white hood covering his head. Her blood ran cold at the sight of him. They were the cleverest, the cruellest, the most powerful, and the most revered of all the Nuakki.

Thaya swallowed and shivered as the high priest stepped forwards to meet the humans. He towered over the most-esteemed Magi of Loji who looked insignificant, weak and diminutive by comparison.

"Praise the Divine," said one of the elder Magi of Loji, clasping his hands together and nodding his head in joy. "You, our beloved brethren from the stars, saved us from certain death and ruin."

Ignoring Khy's protests, Thaya rose and walked in slow,

stuttering steps, forcing herself forwards until she was behind a tree and could hear better what they said.

The Nuakki high priest smiled—it always looked like a smirk—opened his arms magnanimously and straightened to appear even taller. "It was nothing," he said.

Thaya looked at the devastation, the blood-covered bodies, and the virtually melted ship. It certainly didn't *look* like nothing, and it certainly hadn't been easy for the Nuakki.

The Magi of Loji pressed his hands together in praying supplication. "Please, Great Ones from the stars, come into our humble homes. What's ours is yours and more."

Thaya glared at the grovelling Magi of Loji.

No, this can't happen, not like this.

She stumbled forwards, raising her hand to speak, to scream, to stop this horror of supplication, of begging, and inevitable despicable infiltration from unfolding. It was like a bad dream where you cannot scream, where you cannot run, where your voice fails and your legs buckle.

They're not your friends! She wanted to scream. *They'll take all that you have and enslave you!*

The great Magi of Loji began dropping to their knees in reverence, in submission.

The words died in her throat, and her breath came in loud, choking rasps. Thaya couldn't breathe as they raised their hands to the sky and then lowered themselves to plant their faces in the dirt before the Nuakki Invaders.

The Nuakki's smiles deepened, their gloating intensified.

Thaya dropped her outstretched hand, her fingers curling into a fist as she staggered. Khy was suddenly at her side, and together they sank down into the ferns.

"So, this is how it's done, this is how we fall," she whispered. "No fighting, no resisting, no alleging, just ignorance and willing supplication, pure and simple."

Khy nuzzled her neck, trying to impart some comfort. "These are not your people. You are free. These are slaves, slaves to an idea, slaves to the false thinking that someone is better, more worthy, more deserving than they are."

Thaya blinked back the tears. How could these people, whom she had spent months trying to reach, the most learned and powerful people upon Urtha, fall down and worship those who had enslaved, tortured and killed thousands of people? "My heart wants me to turn and run into the forest, to get away from here and never come back. But my soul will not let me. At least the Ordacs never bowed down to the Nuakki, not ever."

"Great beings fall always through trickery and deception. Always," said Khy.

From the tops of the ferns, they both watched as the humans rose to their feet, and then, with the Nuakki at their side, they laughed joyously like brothers and welcomed them through the gates and into the fabled city of Loji.

Thaya buried her head in Khy's mane, beyond tears, beyond fury, just hollow, empty, despairing.

Khy rose, pushed his nose under her arm to help her to stand before steering her towards a path that led left of the city gates and into the forest. Once they were surrounded by old oaks and giant sycamores, he motioned her down onto the grass where she sank willingly.

"All this time trying to get here...all this time," Thaya whispered, seeing nothing.

"It's better we learn the truth of these people now," said

Khy, looking back the way they had come and towards the secret city.

"But they must know," said Thaya. "They must know who the Nuakki are and what they have done. Our most learned men and women can't be ignorant of the fall of Lonohassa, and if they're not ignorant, then they must be complicit." Her voice trembled. The scale of the betrayal was unimaginable.

"We cannot know what has transpired," Khy said.

Thaya sucked in her lip and chewed on it. So, what was she supposed to do now? She didn't know, and so she just sat.

Khy walked a few paces to stand in a beam of sunlight falling through the trees, and there he stayed, thinking. He was so deep in thought, even his superior senses did not pick up on the threat. Perhaps it was the exhaustion, perhaps it was the sorrow and anger, or perhaps a spell had been cast to conceal it, but they reacted too late.

The hairs on Thaya's neck suddenly rose, and her stomach tensed. She tried to rise but was jerked up by an invisible, incredibly cold rope that appeared around her neck. The invisible noose radiated waves of pain through her, holding her rigid and paralysed so she couldn't even speak.

In the same instance, Khy's horn sparked, and he whirled towards her. She couldn't see her captors but she recognised the deep, almost silky tone of the Nuakki male's voice.

"I'd make no move if I were you," he said to Khy.

The noose around her neck tightened, and suddenly she struggled to breathe, her face growing hot and sweaty as she laboured for each breath. A forearm, knotted with muscle, tanned and adorned with a golden bracer, wrapped around her waist, lifted her up, and crushed her against a solid chest. Khy's horn dimmed, but his indigo eyes never blinked, not even a quiver rippled his flanks.

The noose loosened, and Thaya sagged, gasping for air.

A man was thrown forwards by other Nuakki hands into her field of vision—a young human male wearing the clothes of a novice Illumined Acolyte. He stumbled and fell upon the ground, his hood falling forwards over his face, which he shoved back over his shaven head. A sheen of sweat covered his face, and his eyes darted nervously over Thaya and the Nuakki.

Thaya gave a start, recognising the acolyte she had let go after the destruction of Taomar. The action had nearly lost her her friend; Engara had wanted to kill him, but she had to let him go. *An act of mercy that was perhaps foolish in the end.*

"Is this the one?" the Nuakki gripping her asked.

"You said she was alone," another Nuakki spoke, a female outside of Thaya's vision. "Go get the others immediately—they're not far."

Footsteps of a third Nuakki sounded—snapping twigs and crunching leaves that faded away into the forest. Thaya felt that now there were only two Nuakki and the human man. She tried to reach the fireshot in her belt, but the slightest movement sent waves of agony throbbing through her.

"Any movement you make will cause pain," her captor hissed into her ear. She hung limp, a crushing headache descending. "If your friend does anything, we'll snap your neck in an instant."

There were only two Nuakki now, so why wasn't Khy attacking? He'd taken on far more before. Instead, he stood watching, still as a statue.

"She *was* alone when the flaxen-haired village whore left her," the acolyte spat. "You promised me safety for my information."

"He works for the Ordacs, your enemy," Thaya rasped through clenched teeth.

"He works for us now." The Nuakki female chuckled.

Thaya glared at the snivelling acolyte. "Traitor. I saved your life!"

"Hardly." He sneered at her.

The noose tightened, and she struggled to breathe again. *Engara was right, I should have killed the traitorous runt.*

"And look at this—what do we have here—one of our own?" The Nuakki gripped Thaya's left palm, splaying it out to reveal the faint, white swirling scar of the slave mark that she could never quite get rid of.

"They said she was one of yours, and now I've led you to her," said the acolyte, brushing the dirt off his robes. "I've kept my word."

Through the blinding headache, Thaya's mind whirred. So, the Ordacs had seen her slave-mark too; they knew of the Nuakki and their human slaves. The acolyte had switched sides, probably to save his skin.

"Shut it, human," barked the female Nuakki. She stepped into view, brandishing a copper-coloured, curved blade, her mass of luxurious, black hair tumbling down her back and held back from her face by a stylised, golden helmet.

The acolyte stepped back and swallowed, dropping his gaze to the ground.

A sharp, whistling noise came from somewhere, crescendoed rapidly, then stopped on a hard thud. The Nuakki's grip around her suddenly tightened, making her yelp. Her captor made a ragged, gasping sound, his grip slackened, and then they fell sideways. Hot blood spilled over Thaya's shoulders, and she stared at the arrow embedded in the Nuakki's chest just above his heart. The invisible noose vanished, and she lay gasping on the ground. Another arrow whistled through the air and struck the ground a foot from her face. There came a scuffling noise, the Nuakki woman growling, and then silence.

"Thaya!" Arto leapt in front of her and dragged her up.

She stared at her friend in shock. Had the lack of air affected her vision? Was he really here? "How did you...?"

Khy was busy cleaning his blood-covered horn on the tall grasses, the Nuakki female lay bloodied and unmoving at his feet. Beside her lay the acolyte, several arrows sticking out of his side.

"No time to talk, more are coming." Arto half carried, half dragged her away.

Khy came to her side and spoke in her mind. *"I didn't act because I saw them coming, hidden in the trees. It was safer to wait."*

Still weak from the noose, Arto had to lift her onto Khy's back. In a daze, she looked at his company. There were five humans—three armed with bows, and all wearing clothing in hues of browns and greens—the camouflaged shades of the forest. Two were women who looked like twins with identical, long, black braids hanging over their shoulders, tanned skin, and hard expressions. One of the men was in his teens, the second looked to be forty and the third in his fifties. All were rugged and scarred.

Thaya focused on breathing and hanging on to Khy, the throbbing headache slowly receding. "We should fight, drive them out."

"An entire college of magi and a legion of Nuakki?" Arto said and laughed.

They hurried into the forest and through a natural archway made of rock. Hidden in the bushes behind it stood a man holding the reins of six horses. Silently, the humans mounted, the twins sharing a steed, and then they were whipping through the forest with Arto following the guide who had been guarding their mounts.

Nothing was said, not even after they passed over a hill, crossed three meadows, and traversed a wide, shallow river. Dusk began to fall, and at the edges of the trees, where the oaks and sycamores gave way to evergreens and a trickle of a stream ran, Arto called for a halt. They all sat in their saddles for a long time, listening for danger, but only the faint sound of the river and the chirping of birds in the bushes could be heard.

The headache gone, Thaya gave in to fatigue. She slid off Khy's back and leant against him.

"Thaya, meet my crew," said Arto and dismounted. He threw his reins to the horseman with a nod. "Crew, meet Thaya and Khy. There'll be plenty of time to get acquainted later, but for now, keep silent."

Arto's crew looked at Thaya and nodded in silent acceptance, their keen eyes taking in everything.

"Hi," said Thaya, nervous under their scrutiny, but their gaze swiftly switched to Khy. Thaya sighed, her soul twin was far more interesting than she was.

As the others dismounted, Arto came over. He cupped her chin gently and tilted her head back to inspect the bruises on her neck. She groaned from the pain, and he let go. Instead, he pulled her into an embrace until the pain subsided.

"I can help with this," he said, ever so gently stroking the back of her neck. "Relax."

Before she could reply, he'd grasped the base of her head and gave a firm jerk.

She stifled a yelp, not from pain but surprise as her neck made a quiet click and the pain lessened. He let go of her, and she frowned, finding she could turn her head without searing pain.

"Wow, that feels...better," she said.

He smiled. "Happened to me too, once. Or maybe twice."

He'd grown a short beard, it was a shade darker than his chestnut hair, and his green eyes were as clear and penetrating as always. He let go of her chin.

"I like the beard," she said and smiled.

He rubbed it self-consciously and said quietly, "That happened more through lack of a razor. Bandits on the road stole a pack, thankfully only my wash bag." He looked back the way they had come and shook his head. "We would have attacked those Nuakki sooner, but then one of them ran off. We got lucky, especially since the big one could use magic."

"You said you'd be here, but I didn't think our paths would cross so soon." Thaya remembered their parting: Arto had said he had business here with the Magi of Loji, a delivery to make. It wasn't all she remembered, and she blushed at the memory of their parting kiss. Nothing else had happened—just a kiss, she reminded herself—he may even have found someone else.

Arto nodded. "Our business was short. Just a delivery of base materials for the magi from the coast. I don't know the details—sometimes it's better that way. We couldn't have come a moment too soon, and now it's a shame we didn't leave sooner. The Ordac and Nuakki attacked each other whilst we were here, and we couldn't get out. Those arrows...they'll know they're human, and it won't take them too long to put two and two together and point the finger at us."

"The magi know about Lonohassa? They know about the slave mines?" Thaya tried to keep the pleading out of her voice but failed. She had to know her fellow humans cared.

"They know, Thaya." Arto gave a sad smile. "But they don't care. I even told them about our war with the Invaders, the numbers we lost at the slave mines, but they weren't interested. I don't know why, maybe it's a magi thing—curse the lot of them. They said, 'Nothing comes before knowledge; mastery of the elements is mastery of the self.' I wasn't there long, but it's clear to me the Nuakki have been here before. I even think they were already here!"

Thaya swallowed, remembering Theo and Mensar and their conflict. There was trouble long ago, now it seemed they were doomed to repeat it. Seduced by the power of these Invaders, humans had no hope. She held back the tears. "What if we went back? What if I tried to tell them everything?"

"No, Thaya, I tried." Arto sighed. "We were leaving as the Ordacs came, then we got caught up in it all. The Nuakki wanted us to fight with them, but I couldn't, not after fighting them in Lonohassa. If I'd have known those bastards were here, I would never have come! When the battle really got going, we planned to escape. We nearly did, and then I saw you come out of the forest. I couldn't believe it, and so I made us wait. We can't stay here long, I'll not put my crew in any more danger."

"Why did the Ordacs attack?" Thaya asked.

"They didn't, not really." Arto shook his head. "I'm not sure exactly what happened, but that dragon flew past—"

"She was hunting for me," Thaya whispered.

But Arto continued, "...And the Nuakki attacked it. Their ships appeared out of nowhere as if they were already here, hanging around but hidden. We should get ourselves far away and somewhere safe."

Khy spoke to Thaya telepathically. *"I can place a ward upon us this night. You need rest, and I see some of his people have injuries."* He started to inspect the area, sniffing the ground.

Thaya nodded, the thought of lying down very seductive, especially with her myriad minor injuries and weariness. She also wanted time to think through her options. She'd just arrived here, and the goal of her entire existence for the past few months—just to leave like that, with nothing... She also had thoughts of storming the place, of burning it to the ground, of doing *something!* What if she could get close to the portal stones inside the gates? What if she could touch them? She might learn something, she might... *Too many thoughts,* she mentally shook herself. "We can protect this place for the night. It will be dark soon, and I'm exhausted."

Arto rubbed his chin, frowning. After a time, he said, "I don't like it one bit, but two of my men are injured. Trampling through the forest at night, even without Nuakki and giant, upright lizards stalking the lands, would have me questioning the wisdom of continuing now." He ran a hand through his hair and took a deep breath. "All right. But we leave before dawn."

34

A LAST GOODBYE

THAYA STOOD UPON THE LONG STRETCH OF WHITE SAND THAT was so familiar to her now, watching the white horses racing atop the deep blue sea.

"Thaya."

She turned around and blinked. *I must be dreaming.* The world behind her was nothing but dense fog, and through it walked Ithuin, the mist billowing around him.

"Ithuin!"

He smiled and they embraced.

When they parted, he said, "Walk with me to the Waters of Layhara. There, someone awaits you."

Thaya frowned, but he said no more and simply took her hand. Together, they left the beach and walked into the mist.

After a time, it began to clear. Ahead of them appeared rich green trees surrounding a dappled, sunlit glade. A fountain stood in the centre, its crystal-clear waters, that Ithuin called the Waters of Layhara, tinkling merrily as they filled each stone bowl and collected in the wide basin at the bottom. A person stepped from behind the fountain, and Thaya stared at his white hair and pale eyes.

"Theo!"

"Thaya," her friend and mentor replied, a deep smile wrinkling his face as he held his hands open in greeting.

She ran to him, not believing he was real, and yet when she hugged him, he felt solid, warm and alive in her arms. "But you're..." Thaya frowned. He must have escaped the destruction.

He let her go. "Dead?" He chuckled, that same bright intelligence sparkling in his eyes. "Yes, I suppose you could call it that. My physical body is gone, but the *master* lives on." He clasped his hand to his chest magnanimously, then laughed again.

Thaya shook her head, trying not to cry, trying not to laugh. "But how are you here? What happened?" She couldn't work it out, there were too many pieces missing.

"Thrice the sun rises after the body dies and then must the soul depart," he said mysteriously. "My time has come, Thaya, and having done all I could in these three days as they passed in my time, I—my true spirit self—must soon depart. I wanted, I hoped, to say a proper goodbye without all the stress and chaos—my last goodbye was rather rushed, don't you think? I had not thought it possible, but this marvellous Dreamwalker arranged it so we could meet one last time." He patted Ithuin's shoulder, and the elf smiled.

Thaya swallowed, once again remembering Theo's pained face wrought with concentration as utter destruction rained down. She nodded. "I'm so pleased to see you again, truly."

Ithuin spoke. "When I saw Theo in your dreams, I had to meet him—a fabled Gatekeeper, an Ena-kalesh, as we say in

Elven, and I wondered fervently if he had seen the Eye of Ahro. But alas, he had not. And now, it seems, both our worlds lie in ruins."

Theo spread his hands. "Ah, my friend, such is the way in the external worlds of matter. I look forward to my next journey elsewhere, and hopefully, it will be a more peaceful one."

"Wait," said Thaya, putting two and two together. "You *were* there. When I heard your voice in my head warning me, it really was you."

Theo grinned. "Indeed, it was quite the blast. At first, I didn't know if you could hear me, but every time you stopped and fretted, I knew you could. It was so much fun being a Spirit Guide for a short time."

"Thank you," said Thaya, shaking her head in wonder. "What happened after I left? No, maybe I don't want to know. But I *must* know." She had to know how her homeland had been destroyed.

Theo placed a hand on her shoulder. "They took down Lonohassa, Thaya," he whispered softly. "Elanta arn Bruah...shattered it to dust."

Theo looked at Ithuin, and the elf nodded at the fountain. "Look into the waters, Thaya, and together with Theo, dip your hands therein once. It will show you what you wish to see."

Thaya and Theo did as he asked. The cool water sparkled and tingled on her hands, and as the surface stilled, images took shape.

In the still waters, the stunning temple carved out of quartz gleamed majestically against a blue sky still tinged pink with the dawn. Above it, an enormous, black, sky ship rolled into view. A red pulse burst down from its underside and flared across the Waters of Layhara. The temple trembled, and a moment later, shattered in an awesome display of shimmering crystal. Thaya flinched and shielded her eyes, then slowly lowered her arm as the image turned dark.

Theo sighed, his voice heavy. "I fell into darkness for a time just as my beloved home Elanta arn Bruah fell into darkness. It was over for us. The star portal was destroyed."

The image changed, and from a bird's eye view, Thaya looked down upon mile after mile of dirty, debris-filled ocean. She couldn't make anything out, but it stretched on a long way.

"The waters rose and as we speak are still ravaging the land," said Theo. "All because of the destruction wrought by those plasma-ray ships."

"The Nuakki?" Thaya asked. The ships were different though, not of the Nuakki design she knew.

"Yes, but not just them," Theo replied. "Much has become known to me now I'm outside the mortal realms. Some of the Nuakki formed an alliance with some of the Ordacs, some of the Vormae and some of the Boruga—the United Intruders, they will come to be known as. Usually, they are hell-bent on fighting and killing each other, but now this unholy alliance is a terrible thing to occur—they're stronger united. We can blame the fallen ones all we want, but it is our own people who struck a deal with them."

Thaya stared at nothing and whispered, "Everyone is gone?"

"Everyone good, apart from those who remained in high mountainous places. Many, many people died...many are still dying, back there in my time."

"I died too, myself, back then, so long ago." Thaya swallowed and pushed back the memories. "But what about Mensar? The Leonites?"

"Mensar escaped. He was evacuated by the United

Intruders, taken up with the other traitors into one of the Invaders' plasma ray ships. More than anything, I cannot come to terms with the betrayal of our race by our own kind."

"No." Thaya wanted to say more, but the physical pain she felt would not let her. She placed her hand back in the water. "What happened after?" She directed her thought into the surface, wanting to see what became of Lonohassa. And it appeared that she looked down upon a world where time sped up.

Storms raged across the surface for a long while before they began to clear. At first, an endless mass of dirty ocean swirled, and then, slowly, the waters receded, and a rocky land, devoid of the lush foliage that had once covered it, was revealed.

Nothing remained of the great civilisation that had been there, not even the foundation stones of palaces and temples. The land itself was fragmented into islands spread over a vast ocean. The largest island lay in the centre, but as they watched, the image moved to the southern mass of islands, and there, she saw a long seep of white sand form along the coast as the ocean pushed back the remains of the shattered crystal city.

"All that remains of Elanta arn Bruah," whispered Theo.

The sorrow in his voice brought tears to her eyes. "I'm sorry." She swallowed against a painful lump, again recalling her recent time upon all that remained of Lono-hassa. "I was a slave on the remains of Lonohassa in this life-time. I guess it was the central land mass the Nuakki were mining for gold, stealing it from Urtha."

"They mine it everywhere they can, for they use it to keep their race from ageing," said Theo. "I have seen in the future a time when even these lands masses are gone—

another flood, another event caused by our despicable, cosmic, criminal brothers. And thereafter, only small islands remain, in the north, in the centre, and in the south. At this time, people will no longer remember Lonohassa the Beautiful, and they will doubt it ever existed, consigning it to the realms of fanciful myth and legend."

Thaya dared to think about that lifetime lived so long ago, but all she could remember was what her dream had shown her. "I wonder where I was in the lifetime I had when it happened. I wish I'd met you then."

In response to her question, the waters shimmered, and a new image revealed: a sunny, hot city whose familiarity warmed her heart.

Theo smiled and nodded, recognising the place in the waters. "You were to the east, a little way inland where the mountains peter into foothills. If I'm not mistaken, the name of that city is...let me think...Jenora, yes, that's it."

"Jenora," Thaya mouthed, the word familiar on her lips. She blinked back tears.

Theo touched her arm. "Thaya, don't let past lives, not even past events in your current life, destroy who you are. You are spirit, true and pure, and these are simply experiences. Look, look at the good news." Theo pointed into the waters where several figures now appeared.

Thaya leant close and saw they had whiskered faces and round, furry ears. "The Leonites! Is that Saroshi? She's holding something bright."

Theo grinned. "Yes, they took the Rod to safety. We won that part."

Thaya laughed and hugged him. He patted her on the back.

She took a deep breath and wiped her eyes. "And what

happens now? The Nuakki have infiltrated the Magi of Loji. I had hoped to 'find myself' there."

Theo looked at her and placed both hands on her shoulders. "You will only find yourself within."

"But where do I go? What do I do?" Thaya asked, feeling utterly lost.

"Only you can decide that. Sit and be still, and once you're there, in the centre of your being, find the guidance you seek."

He was right, but it didn't help. She wanted someone to tell her what to do—she *needed* that right now—so she simply nodded.

An idea came to her, and she said, "The waters show us what we want to see, don't they? Like a scrying mirror. Can they show me my friends? I want to know if they're okay. Engara and...what happened to Mystic Mary? Is she safe?" Did the Men in Black take her...

The waters did indeed change, and she looked upon a huge, rugged amethyst lying upon a familiar wooden table —the same table Mystic Mary had read her palms upon. One side of the purple crystal was sheer and polished to a high, glassy shine, and Mary's face appeared upon the surface, her glasses making her eyes large and owlish. The mystic blew upon the amethyst and rubbed it with a cloth whilst humming a tuneful song. Just visible behind the mystic was her veritable forest of plants, bookshelves and crystals. Mary looked remarkably happy and well.

"There we are, all mucky dust gone!" She sounded so close it was as if she was right beside Thaya.

"Mary?" said Thaya.

The mystic jumped and looked around. Thaya jumped too, the woman could actually hear her!

"Mary, it's me!"

Mary turned back to the crystal and peered into the polished surface. "Thaya? Oh, my dear Goddess, what on Earth? I'm seeing things! I knew I should never have smoked it, not at my age."

"Mary, it's okay, I just wanted to say 'hi,' and that everything is okay."

But Mary leapt up, shaking her head. She smoothed back her hair and disappeared from view.

Thaya chuckled; it was enough to know the mystic was well. "And Engara, how fares my Shield Sister?"

The image changed, and this time a wall of flames filled the waters. Thaya stepped back. Dragon flames? But Engara's face appeared the other side of the flames, her eyes alight with the fire that she stared lucidly into. Thaya realised she was looking at the warrior woman looking into a campfire, and above it, hung a large pot with something cooking. The darkness of night was all around her, and it was pitch-black beyond the flames. The warrior woman smiled and whispered, "Thaya."

Thaya grinned. The warrior woman, her mind calm, could see her or sense her.

The image faded, and a leaden weariness dragged on Thaya. The Waters of Layhara clouded over as if mirroring them.

"Enough for now, Thaya," said Ithuin, gently taking her hand. "The Dreamwalk is hard to stabilise with more than one, and I feel it weakening as I also grow tired."

"And I am well overdue and must away," said Theo. "Thank you for these last moments, my good friend." Theo clasped the elf's hand between his. They looked at each other, a telepathic communion passed between them, and then they parted. Theo turned to Thaya, many unspoken words in his pale eyes, and then he hugged her tight.

There was so much she wanted to say, but the weariness increased with the rising mist, and as soon as they parted she lost the two men from view.

"Don't go," she said, but her voice sounded airy and far away. Slowly, she felt herself sinking and drifting.

Thaya awoke and shivered. It was dark, and the ground was hard and cold.

"Goodbye, Theo," she whispered, finding tears already on her cheeks. At least she'd got to say goodbye.

One of Arto's men stood watch by the horses, and the rest slept around a smouldering campfire. Khy wasn't there, but she could see his sigils shimmering on the ground. She stretched out her aching neck and back, then went to find a bush to relieve herself behind.

On her return, she glimpsed Arto standing away from the others. He was on a ridge and looking up at the stars and turned as she approached.

"Couldn't sleep?" she asked.

"Never after a fight." He sighed and took hold of her hand.

For a moment, she felt as if she held back an ocean of emotions: saying goodbye to Theo forever; the destruction of Lonohassa; the death of Derry after she tried so hard to help him; the loss of Loji; and the deception of the invading off-worlders. The list was endless, and with one small movement, the entire dam could break. Arto pulled her close, and she closed her eyes, feeling the tears fall against his chest. He stroked her hair and kissed her on the top of her head, letting her cry it all out.

When she was done, he said, "Let's sit over there by the tree and watch the stars."

He led her over to a huge oak tree, a little farther along the ridge from the camp, and tugged her down to sit beside him, pulling her against him as he leant back against the trunk.

For a long time, they stayed there. She found comfort and solace in the strong beat of his heart, and the rise and fall of his chest. She glimpsed white and a flash of silver in the trees down below and smiled. Khy was scouting the area, he wasn't far.

The night was clear and cold because of it. Bright stars sprayed across the sky with the Dark Road splitting them apart clearly visible. A half-moon just tipped the treetops to her right.

She turned her face up to his, and he kissed her on the lips. The softness, the moist heat, the hunger in his green eyes made butterflies dance in her belly, and if she hadn't felt so exhausted, she would have sought for more. She didn't want to part, sensed he didn't want to either, but shyness made her pull back. She hadn't known Arto long, didn't actually know him well at all, but then, why should she care when people passed into and out of her life so quickly these days? Hopefully, they would have enough time together for it to develop into something more.

"I knew you'd be here," he said when they drew apart.

"How?" she asked.

"I'm a Truth Seer like you, remember?"

"How could I forget?" She grinned. "Well, I'd forgotten all about you."

"Is that so?" His mirroring grin said he didn't believe her.

She twiddled a button on his shirt between her fingers.

"Well, it's partly true, but you simply won't believe what happened to me after we parted." She let out a long sigh.

"Well, my dear Thaya, I doubt you'd believe what happened to me, either. That I even made it here—"

"—Was a miracle." She finished his sentence for him and laughed. "Likewise." She wanted to tell him everything that had happened, and learn what had happened to him, but she was too tired. In the end, all she asked was, "So, what now?"

"Well, one thing's for sure, I'm not letting you go. You're coming with me this time." He grinned down at her.

"Oh, I am, am I?" She stroked his beard. "I like this even though it tickles."

"Don't worry, it's temporary. My ship, if that floating wreck can be called that, lies on the Ebben Flow five leagues south and west of here. I have a final shipment to make in the Western Bank, then nothing after. Come with me. How about sailing the Southern Seas? Maybe we can even make it to Roa."

Thaya considered it. She loved sailing, loved the endless blue, but, "Khy's gonna hate it."

"Hmm, maybe we can convince him?"

"I'll try," said Thaya doubtfully, "but I'm definitely up for it. I need an adventure somewhere totally different, totally new."

She hugged his arms tighter around her. A quiet life sailing with Arto, with her soul twin, Khy, at her side, could it be so bad? No, it actually sounded like fun. If she could let herself enjoy something just a little bit, she might just look forward to it. She relaxed deeper into Arto's arms and watched the beautiful stars. How wonderful it would be to visit each of them, she thought, and imagined floating amongst them as she fell asleep under their light.

Memories mixed with imaginings entered her dreams, and she heard Theo speaking.

"What are you, Thaya?" his voice echoed around her.

"I'm Thaya, Thaya Farseeker, you know that." Her voice sounded strange, echoey, as if she were in a cave, and it was dark.

"No, Thaya, that's your name, it's what you are called, it is not who you are," Theo replied.

She squinted into the darkness but couldn't see him.

"Who are you, Thaya?" he whispered again.

Crystals glowed, filling the chamber with soft, pink light. They shone all around, from the ceiling where they clustered, to the smooth quartz floor beneath her feet, to the giant crystal shards that were the walls. She was in the beautiful crystal chamber again, and Theo was somewhere nearby. How she'd wanted to return here, to see him again and continue under his tutelage.

"Who are you, Thaya?" Theo shouted, making her jump. Was he angry? He sounded more commanding as if trying to make her understand something.

The crystal chamber shivered, a crushing pressure filled it, and a great boom shook the room. An immense headache made her cry out, and blood burst from her nose and trickled down her lip. The answer came to her in barely heard whispers that echoed around her, and she finally understood what Theo was asking her.

"I'm a Gatewalker!" she cried through the pain.

"Very good," Theo whispered.

The metallic, groaning drone of the red beam from that deadly ship suddenly filled her ears once more. It came from all around, shaking her, the crystals, and the entire room. The crystal chamber shattered. Thaya screamed and fell, and all sound and light vanished.

"Then be one," Theo said, right in her ear.

"I'm a Gatewalker." Thaya opened her eyes.

She lay, curled up beside Arto, who stirred as her dream faded. The arm he had draped over her shoulder gave her much-needed warmth as the dark forest slowly took shape around her, and the faintest pink touched the sky.

Thaya carefully slipped out of his embrace and stood. She walked a few paces down the hill, rubbing her pounding temples, then sank down onto her haunches, breathing hard.

"I'm a Gatewalker," she whispered, the words in her dream still echoing in her ears.

She smoothed back her hair and chewed her knuckles. She became very still as an idea, a thought that had been trying to make itself known, finally came to the forefront of her mind.

She leapt up with an overwhelming sense of purpose. "It's not an idea—it's what I must do!"

"Arto wants to go," said Khy.

She spun around to see her soul twin trotting towards her. How long had she been musing? The sky was brighter now.

"I sense unrest in the woods," Khy said, looking back over his shoulder. "The birds are wary; they say non-Urtharians are coming."

Thaya nodded. "We're not running."

Khy looked at her, then back at the camp where the others were getting up. "Right. And them?"

"They may come or leave as they wish," she said. "If I

can get to the portal, I can get us all to their ship in a fraction of the time it will take them to ride there. We can get there in moments, otherwise, it will take days, maybe more."

Khy flicked his tail. "I think I see your plan. I don't like the danger, not to myself, but to you."

"I know, I don't either, and I don't want to endanger anyone else, but..." Thaya narrowed her eyes in the direction of Loji.

"But?" Khy pressed.

"But I am a *Gatewalker*." Thaya strode towards the camp, checking her fireshot was in her belt and feeling the soulfire spark in her palms.

35

GATEWALKER

"No, Thaya, I'll not let you kill yourself in this way!" Arto chopped his hand to the right, points of red appearing on his cheeks.

His crew shifted uncomfortably as she and Arto argued about her plan. Everything he said to stop her only showed her how much he cared, and she was touched but would not be moved.

Thaya spoke softly but firmly. "This is how it is, this is the plan. We go in there and take control of the portal. You cannot stop me, I need this, it needs to be done. I'll make my teacher proud of me. *I am a Gatewalker!* With Khy at my side, we can do anything."

Arto scowled, battling within himself, knowing he couldn't stop her as he clenched and unclenched his fist around his sword hilt. He kicked a stone, watched it bounce into the bushes, then sighed. "All right, all right, I'll do what I can to protect you. But they *will* be looking for us; our arrows in those Nuakki aren't that hard to identify. I suspect they're even scouting the area as we speak."

"That's true, Khy has seen them," said Thaya. "But them

out here is better for us than more in Loji when we storm in."

Arto shook his head and turned to gaze upon Loji, the tips of the temples just visible above the trees in the far distance. "Let's get on with it."

Thaya, with Arto beside her, led the way back to Loji. Khy took the rear and began his task of protecting them. A shimmering shield fell over them, only visible to him and Thaya, and possibly anyone in their party able to use magic or skilled in sensory perception.

Under Thaya's direction—and to Arto's annoyance—they set the horses free. They made them too visible and they made too much noise, and now Thaya and her party had to move silently like ghosts through the forest. She glanced at Arto and whispered. "I'm sorry about the horses. I daren't take them through a portal either, and, well, Khy's different."

The scowl Arto had been wearing the entire journey now softened a little and he gave a slight shrug. "It's all right, they weren't ours anyway. The magi had loaned them to us to speed up the delivery of their goods. Fine steeds like that? They'd be recognised anywhere. I'd probably have done the same thing under the circumstances, but still..."

They turned their attention back to the forest. No one spoke. No one paused to break. They ate as they walked and kept the pace fast. All the time, Thaya sensed danger in the forest beyond Khy's shield, but her eyes and ears never picked up anything.

·   ·   ·

Only when the gates of Loji came into view did they pause. Arto held his hand up, and everyone halted. They hustled into the trees and stared ahead. The towering stone gate now looked ominous, not impressive, the trees on either side and the falling dusk making the entrance dark and foreboding.

Nothing had changed. The rotting corpse of Grenshoa and the Nuakki ship remained, even the bodies of the fallen still lay there. The only thing that had changed was that there was not a soul to be seen, except for clouds of flies over the dead, and a deepening stench.

"Remember the plan," Thaya said, under her breath.

"Thaya," Arto began. "Please reconsider. We can still round up the horses and ride, they won't have gone far in those meadows. It doesn't matter how long it takes and we can all live that way."

"The more we give, the more they take," Thaya said firmly. "We must stand."

Arto rubbed his eyes. "I know, I know. I want to fight, I have fought, but we're so few, and I...I would like to see more of you."

Thaya smiled, her eyes misting over. She didn't want to risk losing another friend. "I know it seems we might die this day, but you haven't seen what we can do. Like I said when we discussed my plan. Inside that gate lies a portal, a big one. All I need to do is touch it and open it. All you need to do is hide, wait for Khy's signal, and run to us, run to the stones. You'll see."

Arto licked his lips, hating every minute. "But what if it goes wrong?"

Thaya looked back at the dark entrance. "I know you don't know what a Gatewalker is, neither do I fully, but do you doubt the power of a Saphira-elaysa? Do you doubt the power of the ancient portals?"

"I doubt the power of so few against so many," said Arto. "You're going to take on a legion of Nuakki—God knows how many there are—and an entire college of the most powerful magi in the world."

Thaya laughed. It sounded crazy when he said it like that. It was true, partially. "We only have to be there for a moment, we won't have to fight them."

"Just survive them long enough..." he said.

"Yes."

He took her hand and held it to his lips.

She stroked his cheek and then turned to face the gates. *What the hell am I doing?*

"A crazy, half-concocted plan of a very human design," replied Khy to her thoughts. *"It's going to be exceedingly interesting."*

She looked at her soul twin and laughed. His ears were pricked forward, and he was keen to get inside the gate. She smoothed her Elven tunic, adjusted Engara's sword, checked her Arothian fireshot, Arto's blade, then Ithuin's dagger, and took a moment to admire her collection of weaponry. But rather than arm herself, she reached into her sack and withdrew an ancient scroll sealed in a golden tube—a scroll she had found in the Old Temple near her home in Brightwater, the finding of which had changed her life forever.

"The truth of Lonohassa," she whispered, touching the gold tube.

She tapped the scroll and strode towards the gate, straightening her shoulders as Khy held his proud head high. Her heart pounded, the blood rushed through her veins, but she refused to let the fear overwhelm her. The Nuakki were her weakness, they had a hold over her that nothing seemed to erase, but she would face them now as she had done in the past, and she would not let the fear get her.

A huge, dark cloud suddenly spread over the land, which was odd, since this sunny day was windless. Thaya looked up, and her heart missed a beat. The enormous, cigar-shaped, Nuakki mothership hung between the land and the clouds, watching, waiting.

Terror gripped Thaya's heart. *But I can't stop, not now! I won't! We cannot run from that.*

"Thaya!" Arto shouted behind her.

She turned and looked back at him. He and his crew were only half-hidden in the trees, and now they stood still, their weapons drawn, their faces pale as they stared from her and Khy to the sky.

"Stick to the plan!" Thaya cried.

She whirled away and ran toward the gates.

Thaya's hunch was lucky, or maybe it was just the 'knowing' that often accompanied Truth Seers, but the excellent stone circle and its central majestic pillar, marking a major portal, stood within reach, only a hundred paces inside the gate. It was the first structure to greet and impress any visitor, and behind it, nestled the fabled city of the Magi of Loji, rising proudly between the cliffs and ancient oaks and sycamores.

Beyond the stone circle, and before the city's grand pyramidal domes and towers, stretched a wide paved area, probably the main square where stalls were set up on market day. A fountain spurted close to where the buildings began.

In this open area, walking towards the gate through which she now strode, were Nuakki—maybe ten that she could see—and countless human magi of all ages and races, both male and female. Every one of them halted mid-stride, and stared at her. Thaya's pace did not falter, her shoulders did not tremble, her purpose did not waiver, but her heart pounded, and her mouth was dry as a desert.

The elite magi's eyes opened wide in shock as their gaze fell upon Khy. The users of magic knew what they saw: a Saphira-elaysa stood in their midst.

The Nuakki's hands fell to their weapons, either blades or batons of power, and their eyes narrowed into slits. Two priests wearing white lowered their chins, and power gathered around them. Did they know her? Had rumours spread of the human with a Saphira-elaysa who had evaded them and destroyed their gold mines? She hoped so. Such thoughts emboldened her.

She spoke loudly. "Who's in charge here? I bear a message, an extremely important message."

The elder magi, whom she had seen greeting the Nuakki at the gates, stepped forward, opened his mouth to speak, and then paused. He looked at the Nuakki priest at his side as if asking for his permission to talk, as if the Nuakki was the one in charge.

The priest softened his scowl and motioned impatiently for the magi to proceed. The magi coughed and walked forwards uncertainly. "I am High Magi Rethren of Loji, and whom might you be?"

"Thayannon Farseeker," said Thaya, her voice ringing out loud and clear in the stillness of the square. "Thaya of Lonohassa."

In-drawn breaths echoed amongst the magi, and their hushed whispers filled the air. The Nuakki glowered, their gazes darkening further. Latent power charged the air. She felt Khy amassing his energy though his horn barely glowed at all. A slight glance at him, and she saw his coat had darkened considerably to a deep purple that in places looked black. A strange emotion came from him, it felt almost like anger but not quite, maybe a Saphira-elaysa equivalent.

The elder magi cleared his throat and tried to stride more confidently and purposefully just like she. They neared one another, and Thaya halted, careful to keep the stone circle just a few paces to her right. The Nuakki and other humans stepped to within earshot but kept their distance. She noticed some of the magi had separated from the main gaggle and hung back. Their expressions were different to the majority; rather than anguish and, perhaps, anger, their faces were thoughtful, expectant. They spoke to each other under their breaths, and Thaya wondered what they said.

She glanced at the Nuakki ship above. Its shadow fell both over the gate and Grenshoa's body several yards behind her. Were more Nuakki coming? This wouldn't take long—it couldn't.

"What is this?" Magi Rethren asked as she thrust the golden tube into his hands.

"Open it and read it, loud enough so all can hear," she said loudly.

With a frown, he unscrewed the lid and tipped out the scroll.

"This is a message from our ancestors," said Thaya, addressing the crowd. "They witnessed the Age of Cataclysms. You have traitors and deceivers in your midst, and well you know it! Do not betray your own people, your own planet and home, Urtha. Make a stand and stand now! These Invaders are not your gods!"

Some of the Nuakki growled and pressed forwards, but

their priests held up hands to keep them back. Unrest rolled through the crowd, Invader and Urtharian alike.

Wherever I go, I bring trouble. Thaya sighed inwardly.

"This is great!" Khy replied, flicking his nose in the air with a snuffle.

Thaya rolled her eyes and tried to ignore her pounding heart and sweaty palms.

Magi Rethren read part of the scroll under his breath, his face going pale. He looked at her, shaking his head.

Memory of the hot and dusty slave mines raced through Thaya's mind: Amwa's kind face, the old man they took away and she never saw again; Maggy shaking the wired fence that was her prison as she screamed out Thaya's name; Osuman's powerful form above her and his chain around her wrist...

"Read it!" Thaya screamed.

The magi all began talking loudly now. In her mind's eye, she saw and felt the huge Nuakki ship turn in the sky and begin to lower.

Rethren turned to face the crowd. "Calm, good people, and our blessed cosmic brothers and great teachers." His voice was clear and strong, a man accustomed to addressing large gatherings of people. Yet still, he swallowed and rubbed his throat many times before reading the words on the scroll. A sheen of sweat made his face shiny as he began, his words stumbling before he found his pace. The crowd fell into silence.

"We are not the First Peoples of Urtha, we are the Third. The First and the Second were destroyed by the Fallen. And now they have returned..."

The magi read the next paragraph from the scroll then

paused, wiped the sudden sheen on his brow, and loosened his collar before carrying on.

"With their powers from the darkness, they unleashed the Age of Cataclysms. The seas rose, great storms ravaged, disease spread as fast as the wildfires torching the land. Our history they destroyed..."

Thaya glanced over the Nuakki as he spoke. She'd expected them to intervene, to stop this in some manner, but they did not. They took it with glowering gazes that never left her. She could almost hear their minds whirring, no doubt thinking up more lies and deception to get them out of this, she thought, and tuned back into what the magi was saying.

"Let this be a warning, for we have foreseen a future when beloved Urtha and her people are no more. Before the End, the Hidden Darkness will move amongst us, pretending to be as us, infiltrating in silence, dominating from the shadows, twisting and destroying all things holy and human to an agenda that is evil utterly. We will be their slaves, and all humanity will fall as they have fallen."

The magi paused for a short coughing fit, and Thaya fidgeted. *For God's sake, get on with it, man.*

"They came and conquered, destroyed, burned, raped, and killed, but the blame is ours. For it is we who let them...we let the gods in, and they destroyed us."

"Yes, Magi of Loji," shouted Thaya as soon as he had finished. "Hear the words of your ancestors and the mistakes they made, for you are about to commit the same. You have let these imposters in. These despicable deceivers are not your friends or your gods, they have come to plunder and enslave. Cast them out now, or prepare for your fall!"

The audacity of her words in the face of her enemy shook her to the core. She struggled to breathe.

"Destroy her!" A Nuakki priest pointed at her with his stave of power, that same Pain Stick that had beaten her into submission so many times, and his face was a brilliant, furious red. A heartbeat later, white light burst from that stave, and a brilliant spray of magic arced towards her.

It never reached her. Khy was faster.

Golden light burst from his horn, blasted through the white magic and slammed into the Nuakki, lifting him up and hurling him over the crowd.

The square erupted into chaos.

———

Human magi began casting. Energy gathered and sparked over the square. The still standing Nuakki priest raised his staff and a legion of Nuakki warriors charged towards her and Khy. The small group of human magi who stood apart from the others, ran at the casting humans, and an internal battle began. Some Nuakki tried to hold back the charging Nuakki, but she couldn't hear what they were shouting. Why were some humans and Nuakki turning against their own?

Thaya had no time to ponder, the vast majority were attacking. She pelted towards the stones with Khy barely a pace behind her. She hit a force field, an invisible sponge in the air that tingled over her skin and held her back. Then it abated as if the stone circle agreed to let her pass. Khy then passed through beside her.

"You cannot enter!" Rethren screamed.

And yet she had.

The stones began flaring with light, suddenly coming alive as if her presence had stoked them. Soulfire bloomed in her solar plexus, and she let it fill her and flow into her palms. She slammed her hands against the central portal stone, and a great mass of cool energy filled her. Light flared all around. The force field the magi had placed upon the portal began to shimmer in waves of cascading silver light. It trembled, bulged, and in a great spray of light, exploded. The force hurled the nearest Nuakki and magi rolling to the ground.

Thaya filled herself fully with the power of the portal, understanding it in ways she never could have had Theo not taught her, had he not given her the Mind Opener. And the stones knew her, the stones wanted her presence. She let her soulfire flow through her hands unhindered into the central stone. Their combined energy branched out to the twelve stones surrounding it, and there amplified into a brilliant light display of flaring blue, violet, white and gold.

"Signal now, Khy!" she shouted, wondering if he could hear her over the rushing energy.

Khy reared up tall and struck his silver hooves together, creating a spray of sparks. Light burst from his horn, a beacon to the others.

Somewhere behind her, Thaya heard the cries of Arto and his party as they charged.

The Nuakki raged against the new force field surrounding the stones, but the stones would not let them pass, they could not get to her or Khy. The human magi behind the Nuakki held their hands out to cast flares of blue light at the stones, but it flickered and bounced off harmlessly. Nothing they did had any effect; they could not break her connection to the portal stones.

At her intention, a brilliant star map filled her vision, blotting everything else out. She counted at least ten lines leading out from her position. There were more, but they criss-crossed over each other. She formed her will into words. "Show me the Western Bank on the Ebben Flow."

The star map rolled and rushed towards her. Suddenly, images, feelings and sensory perceptions impressed upon her.

Murk.

Cold.

Wet.

The image of a tall, slender monolith, at an angle, subsided by time and the elements, submerged in a swirling, green current. Was this the right place? She couldn't know, and right now she didn't care where it was as long as it was away from here.

She blinked and pulled away from the star map. The circle of stones, the flaring force of her soulfire and the portal's power, and the braying Nuakki rushed back into her reality, and overlaying it all was the star map: thousands of pinpoints of light glimmered over everything. She had her destination in focus, and the portal awaited her bidding.

Blue magic from a Nuakki Magi flared over their heads and the stone circle. The ground trembled and shook. She saw Arto and his people stumble; the captain and his crew were locked in a battle just yards from the circle.

Khy turned and ran towards them, leaving the safety of the stones to blaze a path of light through the magical maelstrom.

Thaya reached for more soulfire and forced it through

her hands into the stones. They amplified her power tenfold, and an enormous burst of energy exploded from the pillars. Everyone was thrown to the ground. The ancient temples of Loji trembled. A great crack snaked up the walls of the city. Masonry crumbled and fell, smashing onto the pavestones below.

More power flowed both within her and within the stones; it didn't stop, it was endless. With her will and a word, she realised she could flatten the entire city. The thought was awesome, terrible, seductive. She forced her mind from it and focused on rescuing Arto and his crew, allowing them passage into the stone circle.

Khy shoved them forwards as they struggled through the force field of the stones, their hands outstretched as magical winds tore at them. Shielding their eyes, one by one, they inched through the boundaries of the stones.

Thaya focused on the point of light marking their destination. She drew upon her soulfire, feeling it flaring in her solar plexus, and released it again. Light exploded. The world trembled. Nuakki and humans rolled away from the stones. The world disappeared into magic and light which folded over each other and began to spin. A tumbling circle of light and dark formed, bulged and burst outwards, becoming a mesmerising swirling tunnel.

With a deep breath, Thaya closed her eyes, lifted her palms, and let the vortex take them.

They rushed forwards, and everyone screamed. She kept her eyes closed, barely able to withstand the cosmic forces that raged through her. This time, she did not spin. Instead, the vortex spun around her, magical wind tearing at her clothes and hair. Her right hand gripped Khy's mane—she hadn't realised she'd reached for it—and her left hand Arto clasped tightly. Squinting, she saw his eyes were shut and his face scrunched up.

Energy flowed through her in an incredible rush, and she started laughing.

The vortex ended, and she plunged into cold, green, murky water, the shock bursting all the air out of her lungs, and her laugh becoming gargles. She gulped in pond scum and thrashed, unable to determine which way was up. The surface appeared above her, and she burst through it, choking.

One by one, others emerged from the depths, red-faced, choking and spluttering.

Dazed and blinking the water out of her eyes, Thaya looked around.

It wasn't a pond. They were in a wide but calm and slow-moving, greenish river with tall bullrushes on either side, banked by mud and thick bushes. She grasped at the reeds, and a frog clinging to one of them croaked in her face, then leapt, disgruntled, into the water.

Thaya hit the water with her hands and laughed loudly. "It worked!" she shouted and started coughing, then laughing some more. "Oh my God, it worked..."

Arto splashed beside her, choking out river water. "Really, Thaya? Here? Why here?"

The others were either coughing or floating on their backs, gasping. Khy, his ears flat against his head and scowling, was already kicking towards the bank a few yards away.

Thaya stopped laughing and frowned. "Indeed, why here?" She looked around but couldn't see the portal stone. She ducked under the water, and there, three feet or more below the surface and leaning at an angle, stood the slender and majestic portal stone, reaching for the light from the dark depths.

She swam back to the surface. "This is the closest portal exit to the Western Bank. Unfortunately, it appears to be underwater. Hey, don't blame me, you chose the destination."

Arto looked at her. She nodded innocently, and he started chuckling.

"Did you see *their* faces?" one of the female twins said and began laughing.

The oldest man of the crew grinned. "The Nuakki scum...at first so confident, then that look of horror!"

Everyone started laughing as they drifted downriver. They laughed hard, utterly grateful for escaping death, and didn't stop until they had clambered up the muddy bank. Even then, dripping muddy water and still coughing, they chuckled.

"It could be worse. It could be night," Thaya offered apologetically.

Arto grinned, grabbed her arms and dragged her into a wet and muddy embrace. His beard wet and dripping, he kissed her on the cheek and nuzzled her neck as she squirmed and grimaced.

"Ew!" she cried. "Urgh!"

Then everyone screamed as Khy bent his head down and shook himself madly like a dog, spraying everyone with muddy water and reeds as he cleaned his splendid coat.

"Let's go find that heap of junk we call my ship." Arto sighed, wiping the mud off his face.

He placed an arm around Thaya's shoulders, and they walked along the path beside the river, towards a town whose rooftops were just visible in the distance. The morning sun was warm and welcome, and a world of possibilities and journeys began to open up to her.

"So, that's what a Gatewalker is," said Arto.

Thaya nodded. "Well, that's what a Gatewalker *does.*"

She grinned and looked at her palms which were still tingling with the power that had flowed through them from the stones. This moment, between Arto on her left and Khy on her right, there was nowhere else she'd rather be.

ALSO BY JOANNA STARR

Joanna Starr also writes classic High Epic Fantasy under her pen-name, Araya Evermore, author of the award-winning, bestselling series, *The Goddess Prophecies*.

THE GODDESS PROPHECIES

by Araya Evermore

Goddess Awakening ~ A Prequel

When darkness falls, a heroine will rise.

The Dread Dragons came with the dawn. On dark wings of death they slaughtered every seer and turned their sacred lands to ruin...

Night Goddess ~ Book 1

A world plunging into darkness. An exiled Dragon Lord struggling with his destiny. A young woman terrified of an ancient prophecy she has set in motion.

He came through the Dark Rift hunting for those who had escaped his wrath. Unchecked, his evil spread. Now, the world hangs on a knife-edge and all seems destined to fall. But when the dark moon rises, a goddess awakens, and nothing can stop the prophecy unfolding...

The Fall of Celene ~ Book 2

Impossible Odds, Terrifying Powers

"My name is Issa and I am hunted. I hold a power that I neither understand nor can barely control..."

The battle for Maioria has begun. Issa faces a deadly enemy as the Immortal Lord's attention turns fully in her direction. Nothing will stand in Baelthrom's way—he must destroy this new power that grows with the rising dark moon...

Storm Holt ~ Book 3

Would you sell your soul to save the world?

The Storm Holt... The ultimate Wizard's Reckoning, where all who enter must face their greatest demons. No woman has entered and survived since the Ancients split the magic apart eons ago. Plagued by demons and visions of a strange white spear, Issa must take the Reckoning to find her answers and fight for her soul to prove her worth to the most powerful magic wielders upon Maioria...

Demon Spear ~ Book 4

Demons. Death. Deliverance.

All these Issa must face as darkness strikes into the heart of their last stronghold. Greater demons are rising from the Pit, Carvon is brutally attacked, and a horrifying murder forces Issa and her companions to flee. But despite the devastating loss, she must keep her oath to the Shadow Demons and alone reclaim the spear that can save them all...

Dragons of the Dawn Bringer ~ Book 5

An Exiled King. A Broken Dream. A Sword Forged for Forever.

Issa can trust no one. Her closest allies betray her and nobody is as they seem. When a Dromoorai captures her and a black vortex to another dimension rips into her room, she realises the attacks will never stop and there is far worse than Baelthrom reaching for her out of the Dark Rift...

War of the Raven Queen ~ Book 6

"Be the light unto the darkness...Be the last light in a falling world."

They had both been chosen: he to save another race; she to save her own from what he had become. Now, both must enter Oblivion and therein decide the fate of all...

BOOKS BY JOANNA STARR

Farseeker

Enlightened. Enslaved. Erased.

Earth, 50,000 years ago before the magic vanished. Invaded by aliens posing as gods, advanced civilisations crumbled. Now, these powerful off-worlders war for control of the planet, and the people who remain no longer remember what they once were. Seduced then enslaved, humanity has fallen...

Gatewalker (A Farseeker Novel)

Haunted by the past... Hunted in the present... Trapped in the future...

Caught in a battle between a dragon, a horde of reptilian aliens, and a spaceship, Thaya and Khy are forced to run for their lives. When she's contacted by a mysterious elf, Thaya must risk everything to enter the dragon's lair and take back what was stolen.

STARTER LIBRARY

If you would like to read more about Thaya and the worlds of *Farseeker*, I've gathered together exciting extra and deleted scenes not included in the main story. I'm also giving away my award-winning, best-selling Epic Fantasy novel, *Night Goddess,* and the prequel, *Goddess Awakening,* written by my pen, Araya Evermore, exclusively to subscribers.

To receive this epic free starter library, please go to my website and join my mailing list. As a subscriber, you'll also be the first to hear about my latest novels and receive exclusive content.

FACEBOOK GROUP

JOIN A FRIENDLY GROUP OF FANTASY BOOK LOVERS.

Starr & Evermore's Raven Guild has been created for fans of the books to chat, share fantasy art, debate storylines, and meet other fantasy readers. You can also ask me anything about the novels.

The Guild is where you'll *first* hear about giveaways, discounts, new books and previews. It's a friendly, fun place to be and you're most welcome to join:

facebook.com/groups/starrandevermore

ABOUT THE AUTHOR

Joanna Starr is an award-winning author, a half-elf, and creator of two best-selling, epic fantasy series, *Farseeker,* and *The Goddess Prophecies,* written by her pen, Araya Evermore. She has been exploring other worlds and writing fantasy stories ever since she came to Planet Earth. Finding herself in a world in which she didn't quite fit, escaping into fantasy novels gave her the magic and wonder she craved. She left her successful career in The City to return to her first love; writing Epic Fantasy & Sci-Fi.

Originally from the West Country, she's been travelling the world since 2011, and has been on the road so long she no longer comes from any place in particular. Originally from the West Country, she's been travelling the world since 2011, and has been on the road so long she no longer comes from any place in particular. Despite loving forests and mountains, she's actually a sea-based creature and you'll find her residing somewhere by the ocean.

Aside from writing, she spends time working, talking to trees, swimming with fish, gaming, and playing with swords.

Connect with Joanna online:
www.joannastarr.com
author@joannastarr.com

LEAVE A REVIEW

ENJOYED THIS BOOK? YOU CAN MAKE A HUGE
DIFFERENCE...

If you enjoyed this book, I'd be honoured if you could leave a quick review for other fantasy and sci-fi lovers (it can be as long or as short as you like) on the book's Amazon page.

Thank You!